# FINDERS SEEKERS

*To Fiona,
who continues to
find whatever
she seeks — and
then conquers it.
Love & blessings,*

INNER SIGHT PRESS

# FINDERS SEEKERS

Gail Harris

INNER SIGHT PRESS

© Gail Harris 2013

All rights reserved. No part of this book may be reproduced by any mechanical, photographic, or electronic process, or in the form of a phonographic recording; nor may it be stored in a retrieval system, transmitted, or otherwise be copied for public or private use—other than for "fair use" as brief quotations embodied in articles and reviews without prior written of the publisher.

ISBN 978-0-9885760-3-2

Cover and interior design by Damian Keenan
Printed and bound in the USA

1 2 3 4 5 6 7 8 9 17 16 15 14 13

Published by Inner Sight Press

7021 E. Earll Dr. # 103,
Scottsdale, AZ 85251

# *Dedication*

FOR JOHN: my beloved, my husband,
my wise and witty companion every step of the way.
Who knows (and who cares?)
how many lifetimes it's taken us to get together.
I am happy and grateful that
I saved the best for last.

# ADVANCE PRAISE FOR *FINDERS SEEKERS*

"*Finders Seekers* is a great read, with something for everyone who loved *Eat Pray Love* and *Under the Tuscan Sun*. When I thought I knew where the story was going, it careened off in a totally surprising direction. By the end, when all the threads had been woven together into a beautiful metaphysical tapestry, I had tears in my eyes and a big smile on my face."
   *JESSIE PEDIGO*, author, *Views From the Pew*

"Every now and then one comes across a book that lays the foundation for a whole new genre—Spiritual Romance. In *Finders Seekers* Gail Harris has crafted a fascinating tale that seamlessly weaves subtle lessons about synchronicity, karma, past life connections, and valuable tools for spiritual growth with a riveting behind-the-scenes-look at a woman's struggle to find her voice in the competitive world of network television. Part mystical romance, part free course in how to create the life you want to live, *Finders Seekers* does double duty as a spiritual guidebook wrapped up in a heartwarming tale of love across time."
   *SANDIE SEDGBEER*, author and host of *Conversation at the Cutting Edge* on Awakening Zone Radio

"Warning: you won't be able to put this book down and you'll still be thinking about it long after you're done. We've all read the avalanche of non-fiction books prescribing steps to how we can improve ourselves or find true love and happiness. But through the power of great storytelling, *Finders Seekers* gives us a front row seat on love, heartbreak, intrigue and suspense—all in service to learning the art of creating a happy life. This is an accessible book that is easy to love."
   *GARY MALKIN*, Emmy Award-winning composer, public speaker and author, *Graceful Passages;* founder, WisdomoftheWorld.com

"*Finders Seekers* is a joy. It's an important book with a great message, as it reveals the secrets of happiness in a very intriguing and inviting way. While the story may have been aimed at women more than men, I loved reading it too—especially since I think a key part of happiness for men is respecting, valuing and enjoying the feminine part of ourselves (and vice versa for women)."

>*DOUG SMITH*, former CEO, Kraft Canada and Borden Foods; lecturer for DePauw University and Canyon Ranch on Finding Happiness, and author of *Happiness: Living with Peace, Confidence and Joy*

"Empowering. Inspiring. And a really good read. *Finders Seekers* weaves a compelling personal story around guidance on how to find your voice and claim your power in life. In the Age of Empowerment this is more than a story of awakening. What you hold in your hands is a road map to an empowered lifestyle. Are you ready to awaken from the dream?"

>*STEVE & BARBARA ROTHER*, authors of 6 books in 15 languages, hosts of the monthly VirtualLight Internet TV Broadcast and the E Channel, and five-time presenters at the United Nations on two continents. Lightworker.com and Paths2Empowerment.com.

"*Finders Seekers* is riveting, an entertaining and insightful road map to how all of us can live life to the fullest by following our hearts and a few timeless rules."

>*ELLEN BONEPARTH*, blogger at juno.com and author, *Positive Women*

"From the moment you begin *Finders Seekers,* you are drawn in with an irresistible desire to absorb page after page. This beautifully written and eloquently woven story takes you on a journey through intrigue, romance and spirituality, inviting you to discover and claim your own power, to discover who you are at your core and what you really want in life."

>*LIZ BRUNNER*, news anchor/reporter, WCVB-TV, Boston

"A soul-stirring work of fiction that nevertheless feels resonantly true, complete with a heroine to root for, a life philosophy to aspire to, and a conundrum for our times: how do you become mindful when so many around you appear to have lost their minds? From the bustle of the network TV newsroom to the English countryside as Jane Austen would have it, Gail Harris manages a very neat trick indeed, wrapping a meditation on living with purpose inside an epic love story that has all the elements of a good mystery. *Finders Seekers* is a clarion call to the alive at heart to have the courage to seek it and the wisdom to recognize it when you find it. I didn't want this novel to end."

*KELLY HORAN,* **award-winning public radio producer and co-author,** *Devotion & Defiance*

"By combining the struggles of an all-too-human heroine with a touching romance and a behind-the-scenes look at network television, *Finders Seekers* offers an important reminder of how to seek—and find–what you really want in life."

*MERYL BRALOWER,* **Psychotherapist, Career Management and Social Enterprise Consultant**

# Past/Prologue

Alexandra's pale blue eyes steeled with determination as she gathered her skirts in one hand and lifted the latch. She would not, *could* not, remain inside the stuffy cabin for one more moment; she had to know what was happening on the deck. Her nerves were too on edge to remain below, where the ship's captain had shooed all the passengers following a hasty mid-day meal. For the past hour or more she had been bracing herself against the narrow bunk as the vessel lurched from side to side, its timbers creaking ominously with each new onslaught of waves from the storm.

The door slammed behind her with a loud bang of wood against wood, but she was so intent on her destination that the noise barely registered. The passageway was narrow here, the footing treacherous, especially in seas as rough as these. Still, it was the quickest way to the foredeck at the far end of the ship.

The burgundy velvet was not the traveling costume she would have preferred for a journey this early in the fall, but it had had to do. As soon as Lord Geoffrey's carriage had disappeared down the driveway to London these two days past, she had snatched it from the mahogany armoire, her hands shaking with nervousness as she fastened the intricate passementerie frogs of the jacket across her breasts. Weeks ago, while planning her escape, she had carefully wrapped a few pieces of jewelry in linen strips and sewn them into the hem of its tulip-shaped skirt. Her betrothal ring—her real betrothal ring, not the diamond-and-emerald monstrosity Lord Geoffrey had given her—she had pressed into her maid's hands for safekeeping.

At the moment, however, the suitability of her outfit was the least of her concerns.

Balancing herself against the swaying passageway, she stopped for a moment to take as deep a breath as she could manage against the constraints of her corset. Beneath the close-fitting jacket she could feel a trickle of moisture between her breasts from the oppressiveness of the air and the weight of the velvet. She closed her eyes for a moment against the motion of the ship, hoping the few bites of food she had forced down earlier would remain where they belonged.

Thank goodness, she thought, gulping back her nausea, the young man waiting for her in America would not care what she was wearing or even how she looked once she appeared. A few weeks more and they would laugh about her dramatic escape, as they built a new life together far from here. The thought brought a tender smile to her face, softening the stubborn set of her jaw line.

*If* she appeared.

Alexandra clung to the banister as the ship listed violently to the right, pounded on its port side by another gigantic wave. Her courage wavering, she paused, wondering if she should return to the safety of her cabin.

"Steady, now," she chided herself, as she pushed open the trap door leading to the deck. Stifling a shriek as gallons of seawater doused her upturned face and cascaded down her neck, she flung the icy water from her eyes with a violent shake of her head, turned her gaze upward and gasped. The flesh on her arms rose into goose bumps as she took in the ominous greenish-orange of the sky. Instinct took over that she didn't know she possessed, instinct that pushed panic into the far corners of her mind. She dropped to her hands and knees and scrambled for the closest balustrade before another wave could hit.

"Captain!" The wind tore the words from her mouth as she rose to a half-crouch, ignoring the ache in her arms and chest as she clung to the railing. She could barely make out his bulky form in the downpour that separated them as she began a slow, hand-over-hand journey toward the ship's wheel where he stood, glaring at the sky.

In another moment Captain Reilly saw her struggling toward him and made a furious gesture for her to go back. "Get below, milady! Are ye mad?" he bellowed. "We're caught in a nor'easter. Get below!" Scowling, he motioned again in dismissal before turning his attention back to the sails flapping wildly overhead.

*No*, Alexandra thought, setting her chin in rebellion. *If I am going to die on this ship, it will be up here, in the fresh air. I cannot bear it down below.*

Just then, another towering wave slammed into the ship and took the decision out of her hands. The water's force loosened the grip of fingers gone stiff with cold, pitching her slight form over the railing and headlong into the raging sea.

*My baby.* Only those words flashed through her head as the waves closed over her startled face. Her eyes wide with panic, she surfaced long enough to catch one last blurry glimpse of the ship. Her pale pink lips formed an "O" of surprise, as the sour tang of seawater flooded her mouth and nose. Then there was no more time to think as the weight of her velvet skirts pulled her under. The indifferent waves churned on, bearing her down, down, down into suffocating darkness and the cessation of thought, down to a place where there was no more anguish or heartache. Only peace, and the end of pain.

# 1

## London, 1981

"Whatever the reason for that pleading look you're giving me, Jeremy, the answer is no," Shannon Tyler said with a scowl, tipping the phone from her mouth. "You didn't see me, I'm not here, and I can't do whatever it is you're about to try and talk me into. I'm on assignment to follow around the Congressional delegation—remember? I just came in to check the wires and use the phone, and I am *not* available. Now. What can't I do for you?"

The London assignment editor for WorldWide Broadcasting flashed his most winning smile. "C'mon, Shannon," Jeremy Wharton coaxed. "You know you're my favorite correspondent. Besides, you can't say no until you hear what it is."

"Sure I can," she said, then relented as his face fell. "Oh, all right. What is it?"

"Our favorite Prime Minister has decided to answer a few questions from the foreign press this morning and New York wants us to be there. All my other correspondents are elsewhere today, so—you're it."

"Uh-huh. You want me to be a walking mike stand."

"Not me," he protested. "New York wants it. Y'know, show the flag. Show your legs. Whatever's required. We just need to be there in case Miss Maggie says anything interesting."

Shannon sighed. At the other end of the line, her producer in Washington was chuckling at the exchange. "Janie, I've got to go. Jeremy the slave driver is sending me out the door—can you believe it? And I'm not even supposed to be here."

Pause.

"God knows. New York wants it. I'll call you later. And listen—keep that little weasel Theo Tanner from snooping around my desk, will you? Last time I was away, half my interview files were missing when I got back..."

Jeremy turned to hide a triumphant smirk as she hung up. As much as she liked to play tough, Shannon was a pushover. There was no way she'd turn down an assignment, no matter how petty—especially not one from New York. He knew very well, as did she, that the major goal in life for every network correspondent was to please and placate the mysterious powers on the New York desk. They were the unseen someones who dictated what got on the network's precious 22 minutes of news each night, wedged between eight minutes of commercials. With dozens of correspondents all over the world engaged in a daily struggle for air time, a pair of sharp elbows and a willingness to please were prerequisites for success.

Shannon rose with a show of reluctance, just to let Jeremy know he owed her one. Truth be told, she didn't mind forgoing a few tourist attractions for a chance to meet the Prime Minister—a woman, yet. The Protestant work ethic was deeply ingrained enough not to complain too much, and even after ten years in television she found it more exciting than she was willing to let on.

"Oh, shoot, Jeremy, wait a second." Shannon looked at her feet in dismay. "I can't go like this. And my other shoes are back at the hotel."

Jeremy followed her glance to the ubiquitous pair of sneakers. Her crisp white cotton shirt and navy blazer were fine; the jeans she could probably get away with, but the sneakers? He sighed, trying to hold back a disapproving frown. A proper Brit from his scalp to his socks, Jeremy would never understand why Americans couldn't seem to put on real shoes and look like the grownups they were, instead of overgrown six-year-olds heading for the playground.

"Hey, I wasn't supposed to be working today," she reminded him. "The plan was to play tourist, and darned if I'm going to be uncomfortable. Do you have any idea how many stairs there are to climb around the Tower of London?"

"Well, at least the P.M. isn't doing a sit-down. She's just going to come outside Number 10 Downing for a few minutes and take questions. No one will even notice your feet," he assured her, crossing his fingers behind his back.

"If they do, I'm telling them it's *your* fault." She gave him a pointed look, but a slight twitch at one corner of her mouth gave her away. "The very idea, sending me flying out the door like this. My face isn't on, my hair isn't straight—"

"Right. As if any of that would ever stop you."

Shannon shook her head in mock resignation. "And my crew for this adventure is...?"

"You'll have to meet them there. I had to grab a couple of freelancers—all our guys are out. I told them to look for a brunette with great legs," Jeremy said, deadpan.

"How would they know? I've got jeans on," retorted Shannon, mollified by the compliment but unwilling to acknowledge it outright. Jeremy grinned and shrugged as she scooped up her raincoat and headed for the elevator.

"Thank God for the LM-HO's," he muttered as she disappeared.

"What's an LM-HO?" The bureau's college intern, on leave from Harvard for a semester of study abroad, had been taking in the conversation from one desk away.

"Low-maintenance, high-output," Jeremy said, unable to keep a certain loftiness out of his voice. He had only been with the network for two years himself, and still enjoyed using insider's lingo whenever possible.

The intern looked confused.

"It's a ranking system for correspondents," Jeremy explained. "Someone who works hard and gets the job done without having to have their hand held all the time is a LM-HO. At the other end of the spectrum there's the HM-LO: high-maintenance, low-output. Most people fall somewhere in between. She," Jeremy nodded toward the doorway, "is pretty low-maintenance, and less of a pain than most of them."

The assignment editor reached for the stack of newspapers he dismembered every day for stories to be pitched to the desk in New York. "Good thing she was here today, actually," he added. "Otherwise it might have been you holding the mike."

"Oh," said the intern, disappointed.

Downstairs, Shannon flagged a cab, rummaging through her bag to make sure she had her press credentials as she climbed inside. The British seemed less strict about security than the Secret Service she'd grown accustomed to during her years in Washington. Still, she could hardly muscle her way into a briefing with the Prime Minister without proper identification. Ah, there they were: her old White House credentials, her newer Capitol Hill ID and network press card, all strung together on a metallic silver cord that dangled just below her chest.

She rubbed her thumb over the perfectly coiffed image on her ID with a rueful smile. Who *was* this glamorous stranger? Not that little oddball misfit from Georgia—Shannon Grace Taylor—for sure. "Shannon Tyler" sounded much more sophisticated, which was why she opted for her first name and a more stylish version of her last, when she made the switch from newspaper reporting into television. Her family might persist in calling her Grace Taylor, but to the inhabitants of her new world, she was someone else entirely.

And now, here she was in London—on her way to meet the Prime Minister, no less. Who would ever have imagined such a thing?

*Not bad, lady,* she grinned. *Now just don't mess it up.*

Settling into the black leather cushions, she surveyed the passing scene with the pleasure she always felt when she was here. The afternoon was unusually mild for early December, with only a few puffy clouds scattered across a brilliant blue sky. She might not even need the Burberry trench coat that had been one of her first acquisitions as a network correspondent.

Turning from the window, Shannon ran an appreciative hand over the immaculate seats, noticing as she did how the dark leather set off her new ruby ring.

She wasn't usually given to impulse purchases, especially something as expensive as this. But the antique store's display of Victorian inkwells—her new collecting passion—had stopped her in mid-stride on the way into the London bureau. Upon closer examination the inkwells had been a disappointment, but the ring nestled on a nearby velvet tray was irresistible.

*Anyone watching must have thought I was a complete fruitcake,* she smiled, remembering how she had turned around at least three times out on the sidewalk in a fierce argument with her more practical self. 'Yes, I want it,' 'No, I don't need it,'—until finally she went back inside to ask if the proprietor if she could try it on one more time. He was still polishing the ring with a velvet cloth, calm as you please. "I knew you'd be back," he nodded. "It's meant for you, isn't it?" She had laughed and agreed, pulling out a wad of traveler's checks to make the purchase.

As the taxi scuttled through the crowded streets, Shannon's smile widened. As many times as she'd been here before—several times with the president and now with a congressional delegation—something about the place felt like coming home. London was so calm, so civilized, with a cheery politeness that her Southern soul responded to right away.

"I guess when you grow up saying 'yes sir' and 'yes ma'am' to everybody, this seems like the way life ought to be," she murmured, her head swiveling at the outdoor museum of architecture that made up the city: Georgian mansions bumping up against sprawling Victorians next to sleek towers of steel and glass that jutted their way into the sky along the Thames. As beautiful as it was, though, there wasn't nearly enough work to do. Not for someone as driven as she was, anyway.

Her eyes closed in contentment at the thought of her return home tomorrow, back to Capitol Hill and her frenetic life. Visiting London was a kick, but she'd go crazy if she were here all the time: sitting around with her tongue hanging out, pestering Jeremy for juicy assignments that never came. Europe and the rest of the world were increasingly an afterthought on the network news agenda, unless someone royal was either getting married or assassinated...

"Close enough, Miss?," the cabbie inquired as he pulled up to the street corner opposite Number 10 Downing. Shannon jerked back to full consciousness, with the oddest sensation that she had been clop-clopping along the London streets in a carriage instead of a cab.

"Oh, ah, yes, thanks," she replied, trying to overcome the fog in her head long enough to convert pounds into dollars and calculate the proper tip. Even when her math didn't come out quite right, she had noticed that London cab drivers didn't snarl the way New York ones did when they got less than what they considered their due. Some even refused to take what they thought was too much.

"Here you are," she said, finally, aware as she handed over several pound notes that she had probably over-tipped again. Oh well. Better over than under, any day. She didn't mind over-tipping, really; she could afford to be generous. It helped alleviate the guilt she felt about how much money she made, for work she would have happily done for free.

"Do what you love," her dad had always told her, "and then it won't feel like work." It had been one of his better pieces of advice.

Outside the shiny black door at Downing Street, a small crowd of reporters and photographers were waiting, most with their coats peeled off in acknowledgement of the mild weather. No one was on deadline, so there was no real hurry, no overt jockeying for position among the crews from Italian, German, Japanese, and American television. Unless the prime minister was planning to declare war on somebody, it was unlikely her comments would ever see air, at least not in the States. Mrs. Thatcher was making herself available largely as a courtesy. The TV crews were there for much the same reason, although there was always a remote chance she would say something deemed newsworthy. You never knew what would happen in this business, or when, so the only reasonable response was to keep the network's backside covered as much as possible—especially when dealing with foreign heads of state.

One duo didn't appear to have a reporter with them but, Shannon noticed, did have a WorldWide Broadcasting logo on their bulky canvas equipment bag. Inside were yards of mysterious electrical wires, extra microphones and cables, blank videocassettes, duct tape, extension cords and assorted other paraphernalia whose purpose Shannon could only guess.

"Hi guys," she said, sliding smoothly into professional mode. "Shannon Tyler, from WorldWide Broadcasting. Are you my crew?"

"Indeed we are. I'm Julian," the closest one nodded. "Carl will be running sound for you." The second man gave her a shy smile as he handed over a microphone topped with a foam windscreen, in case she wanted to ask a question.

"What time is she supposed to come out?"

"Two, they said." Julian responded. It was three minutes until the hour.

Shannon eased into the front row of reporters with a slight smile of apology as the correspondent from NHK made room. She thought he had been in Japanese television's Washington bureau for a while but wasn't sure. Observing how impeccably he was dressed, she tried to find a place to stand where her sneakered feet might be a little less noticeable.

A sudden clatter at curbside and all heads turned to a brown Rover across the street. In a scene that looked like clowns in a circus act, half a dozen people crawled out of the little car, one by one, pulling with them an astonishing array of equipment: a tripod and camera, a long boom microphone with a furry cover, four gigantic lights and light stands, and bag after bag of additional gear.

"Bloody Yanks," growled Julian, his competitive instincts bristling at the sight of so much expensive camera equipment. "Wot d' they think they're doing, making a bloody movie?"

Shannon raised her eyebrows in agreement but chose not to comment. As the first member of the entourage grew closer, she did a double take. "Steve! What are you doing here?" she blurted. "I thought you went to work in Boston. Little out of your zip code, aren't you?"

"Hi, Shannon." The slightly built blonde man acknowledged her teasing with a sheepish smile. "Guess you could say that. I'm working on a documentary for 'The World at Large.' WGBH produces it for PBS, out of Boston."

"No kidding," replied Shannon, impressed. A documentary for PBS? That *was* big. Steve Mapping had been a senior producer for WWB's morning show in Washington when she knew him. He must have talents she wasn't aware of. But then, many people at the network did. The problem was, the task of delivering a 90-second snippet of news a few times a week seldom demanded them. Even for those who did want to do something different, something more substantive, the network paid so well that few were willing to abandon it.

"Why are you wasting your time with this?" she asked. "We're just here to cover New York's ass. I doubt there's any news to be made, especially for a documentary."

"I know," Mapping shrugged. "At the moment we're just following the P.M. around for a while. Day-in-the-life kind of stuff."

"When's it going to be on? I'll look for it."

"We don't have a definite air date yet. Probably sometime in May."

Her eyes widened. May? Six *months* to do one project? It was hard to imagine such a luxury.

"Wow," Shannon said at last. "Lucky you. I wouldn't mind having that kind of time to work on one thing. All this run-and-gun stuff gets a little tiresome after a while."

"I know. That's why I left."

"Aw, c'mon," she couldn't resist a teasing smile as the heavy door to Downing Street began to open. "You don't miss the bright lights of the big network? All the money and all the fame?"

"Not for a second," Mapping answered in an emphatic whisper. He pulled a notebook from his back pocket and began to scribble as Mrs. Thatcher appeared in the doorway.

The Prime Minister walked to the waiting circle of microphones taped to a sturdy metal tripod, pausing for a moment until she was certain the cameras were rolling. Britain still wasn't quite used to the grocer's daughter who had risen in her party's ranks until she was chosen to carry the Tory standard in Parliament, a short time before the Americans chose another conservative, Ronald Reagan, as their leader. Margaret Thatcher bore herself well, however, and seemed to be growing rapidly into the job. Regardless of what others might think, she seemed to have no doubt that she could handle it.

Madam Prime Minister has beautiful skin, Shannon noticed, hoping she might age as gracefully. It was a constant fight to keep her complexion clear, especially under the layers of heavy makeup that were required for television. Even the most rugged face looked pale and sickly without it, so men and women alike submitted to the thick pancake as part of the price for being on the air.

Shannon had to stifle a giggle. If she were still back in Atlanta doing her talk show, the producer would probably want her to ask for the prime minister's skin-care secrets—or something equally ridiculous. *Thank God I got out of there*, she thought. In fact, it had been her incredible good luck that just as she had walked away from the Atlanta job in disgust, the Washington bureau chief for WWB called to offer her a job.

"Thank you all, ladies and gentlemen of the press," the Prime Minister began in her precise, clipped tone. "I have a brief statement I should like to read regarding the coal strike and then I shall be happy to take any other questions you may have."

*Oh, great, the coal strike*, Shannon groaned inwardly, but was careful to keep her face expressionless. Nobody in New York—or anywhere else in America, for that matter—would give two hoots in hell about another coal strike in Yorkshire.

She leaned against the iron railing, propping a wrist against her elbow for support as blood drained out of the hand holding the microphone. This might take a while. She kept her face alert but her mind was elsewhere as the NHK correspondent followed up with two long and complicated questions on the strike and German television asked two more.

Thoroughly bored, she stretched her neck slightly and glanced around. As she did, her scalp tightened around the back of her head, the same kind of feeling she'd had before when someone was staring at her. Shannon tilted her head to see if she could tell—without being obvious about it—exactly who was giving her the eye.

Sure enough, a delegation of some sort was waiting for the news conference to end so they could enter Number 10 Downing. At the front of the group a man stood transfixed, his piercing blue eyes intent on her face.

She flushed and looked away. Accustomed as she was by now to being stared at, this man's scrutiny seemed different. He appeared to be puzzled more than admiring, as if he knew her and was trying to figure out from where. She glanced over again, a little taken aback by the stab of longing that had accompanied her first glimpse of him.

Handsome devil, whoever he is, she noted, by far the most attractive man she had seen since she came here. Too handsome, in fact. Black hair streaked with silver... and those eyes. Probably thought he was God's gift to women. She knew the type: there had certainly been enough of those in her life over the years, men who wanted to take her out so they could brag to all their friends about dating someone who was on TV. Men who turned out to be far more trouble than they were worth.

She frowned as she lowered the microphone, clenching and unclenching her fist to get the circulation going, as Mrs. Thatcher ended the briefing and hurried over to the waiting delegation.

"Lord Michael," she could hear the prime minister say, her stern face creasing into a welcoming smile. "I do apologize for the delay. We so much appreciate your joining us this morning."

Shannon turned away with a scowl. Her striking stranger was a Lord, yet. Probably as stuffy as they come, even if he didn't have one foot in the grave the way the rest of them seemed to in Parliament's upper chamber.

"Ah, well. The vultures must be fed, I suppose," the man replied, as the Prime Minister took his arm.

Shannon's cheeks flamed. Vultures, eh? She should have known he'd be a jerk. Just another arrogant, press-bashing politician…

All the same, her eyes followed him until he disappeared through the doorway, his head bent attentively over the prime minister.

She sighed and turned back to the crew.

"If you guys are heading back to the bureau, can I grab a ride?" she asked Julian.

"Nothing," Shannon reported to Jeremy, dropping the videocassette on his desk with a thud. "Twenty-five minutes of blah-blah. Boy, do you owe me."

"Quite the contrary." Jeremy folded his arms across his chest and gave her a complacent smile. "You owe me. David Moore just called, and when I told him what a good sport you had been he said to call him right away."

Her eyebrows shot up, telegraphing her skepticism. "You're sure those events are related."

"No," he had to concede. "But no harm in claiming the credit."

"Yeah, that's what I thought," replied Shannon, but she was smiling as she dialed the executive producer's direct line in New York.

Ten seconds later, she turned to the wall to hide an excited grin.

"Really? Christmas Eve? Sure. Okay. Thanks," Jeremy overheard as he strolled up behind her. Shannon carefully placed the receiver in its cradle, her face bland.

"Yes?" Jeremy prompted. "What's happening Christmas Eve?"

"Oh … nothing," she said, savoring the moment for as long as possible.

"Shannon," he warned, "It's a very bad idea to keep secrets from Uncle Jeremy."

"Oh, all right," she replied, beaming. "They want me to anchor in a couple of weeks. On Christmas Eve."

"Really," he exclaimed, impressed in spite of himself. "Congratulations. That's lovely. They've never had a woman news reader before."

"Tell me about it. I was starting to think they never would. And by the way, we call them 'anchors' across the pond."

"Well, whatever you call them, it had to happen sooner or later. You ladies seem to be taking over everywhere else," Jeremy teased, then had the good sense to duck as she crumpled a sheet of paper and threw it at his head.

Now all she had to do was get herself safely back home. For some reason, she didn't mind flying as long as it was over land, but flights over the ocean gave her the willies.

*Ah well*, she told herself, setting her mouth in a firm line of resolve, *a couple of vodkas on the plane and you won't even notice.*

# 2

"Stand by!" The floor manager was new, and nervous, so what should have sounded like an authoritative command came out instead somewhere between a shout and a squeak.

Behind the blue and gray anchor desk, Shannon took a deep breath and glanced down at her script. Straightening a slight pucker where the microphone had been clipped to the lapel of her navy suit, she made a mental note to take him aside later for a few pointers on giving time cues. She remembered all too well when she was the rookie, thrown into the deep end of the network pool with no instructions and no expectations beyond "sink or swim." Still one of the very few women at the network, she tried to help other newcomers when she could.

Not that she wasn't at least as nervous as the new floor manager tonight. Her dream for the past decade had been to fill in on WorldWide Broadcasting's nightly newscast one day. Now that it had arrived, a little more than a month after her thirty-first birthday, she was determined to show that she belonged up there with the heavy hitters. Even if it was Christmas Eve and none of the network's big guns wanted to be there.

Peering toward the camera to make sure she could see the white letters of the teleprompter, Shannon ran her tongue across her teeth, hoping to generate some moisture in a mouth that was parched with nervousness. The last thing she needed was to have her voice crack while she was on the air, something that had occurred with some regularity in the early days of her career. Over the years, she had learned to control her nervousness, but with all the pressure she felt right now, all the millions of eyes that would be upon her in a moment, she was petrified—although she would have died before admitting it. On live TV, almost anything could happen at any time, as hundreds of blooper reels around the country could attest. There would be no do-overs of this moment.

"60 seconds," announced the floor manager. Good. At least he seemed to have his voice under control now.

"Mike check at the desk," commanded a voice from the speaker on the wall to her right.

"One, two, three, four... four three two one... got it?" Shannon responded, her voice automatic as she scrawled a final note to herself about when to pause on the first page, her pen clutched in fingers that felt more like icicles than flesh in the chilly studio. The cameras functioned better at sixty degrees; apparently nobody cared very much whether people did. Hearing no response from the audio engineer, she continued in an exaggerated Southern drawl, "This-here's a mike check? We fixin' to do a little tee-vee here. So ya'll come see us, now, y'heah?"

Her usual speech was so anchor-crisp that the contrast never failed to get a laugh from her camera crew whenever she lapsed into it, most of whom were astonished to discover that she was from the South. But this time her attempt at humor got no reaction from the shadowy figures behind the cameras. Only the floor manager gave her a weak smile before turning back to his stopwatch as the seconds ticked away. Oh, well. What the hell. It made her feel better, anyway.

"In five, four, three..."

He gave Shannon the customary countdown on one hand, pointed his finger and fell silent for the last two beats as the five-note trumpet blast sounded, heralding the WWB news theme.

Shannon took another deep breath, faced the camera and smoothed her face into the pleasant but serious expression that had become her trademark. As she began to speak, she relaxed and regained her confidence. These were, after all, words she had written herself just 15 minutes before. It was a downer of a story—especially for Christmas Eve—but the pictures that accompanied it were a vivid reminder of the power of this medium.

Tonight, the newscast beamed into living rooms across America opened with a touching memorial service for victims of a fiery midair collision two days ago off the coast of Florida. This was her story, now, that she was reading. Her own words, written to reflect how she spoke. Suddenly her nervousness gave way to the importance of what she had to say.

"Good evening," she began. "Friends and family members of the 153 people who boarded Flight 687 for a holiday trip to Disney World were in Jacksonville today... to say a final goodbye. Federal investigators, meantime, still don't know why the jetliner and a small plane didn't see each other... until it was too late. Janis Arnold has our report."

Shannon shifted her gaze slightly from the camera to the studio monitor six feet to her left, careful not to move so far that she appeared to be turning away from the audience at home. It was a studied gesture, but done properly it seemed natural instead of rehearsed.

Inside the control room upstairs, the executive producer let out a tense breath as the screen switched to the Florida video. It had been David Moore's idea to let Shannon have a shot at the coveted anchor slot tonight. Christmas Eve or no Christmas Eve, this was still the network's signature newscast, and it would have been his job on the line if she hadn't been able to handle it. He had believed all along that she could do it, and had been quietly fuming as Shannon was passed over time and again as a substitute anchor by other correspondents who weren't as bright, who didn't work as hard as she did, but who did happen to be male. As the father of three daughters, David felt a personal stake in whether she could compete with the big boys or not.

Shannon propped an elbow on the anchor desk, resting her chin on her knuckles as she watched the correspondent's report. Plane crashes were always horrifying; the idea of sudden death at thirty thousand feet played into the secret fears of everyone who flew regularly.

This one felt especially heartbreaking. In addition to the usual businessmen, families and holiday travelers, the passenger list aboard Flight 687 had included a school group. Thirty inner-city kids from Chicago, whose churches and community organizations had raised money for a year, were headed south to experience for themselves the wonders of Disney World. But the jet had gone off course, for reasons no one could explain, and collided with a private aircraft two miles off the coast of Jacksonville.

Relatives who arrived for the memorial service were, understandably, almost crazed with grief. With no bodies to identify, with only bits and pieces of wreckage brought up so far, there was nothing tangible for them to gather around, nothing to confirm that something this awful could happen so unexpectedly. Nothing physical to hold onto and help make their loss real.

The report began as a series of pictures over a voice track from the funeral services, a montage of images that made the ministers' words and the songs of faith and hope even more powerful. The stricken face of an elderly woman clutching a Teddy bear to her chest dissolved into a man in a business suit who waded into the surf to fling a dozen roses onto the blue-green waves. A barefoot couple, their toes gripping the sand at the water's edge, buried their faces in each other's necks as they tried to comprehend their loss.

"Good girl, Janis," Shannon said under her breath. Her reaction to the story was superseded for the moment by admiration for how the reporter had chosen to put the piece together. Sometimes the most powerful thing you could do on television was to shut up and get out of the way. Let the pictures tell the story—as long as they were strong enough to carry it.

Shannon swallowed hard as the series of images began to penetrate her heart. No matter how much of it you saw, you could never get used to this; not really.

Even now, nearly nine years later, the pictures of the first plane crash she had covered as a cub reporter were still etched vividly in her head. For weeks afterward, she had awakened uncovered and shivering in the middle of the night, feeling an urgent need to fold blankets for the survivors—only to find, next morning, her sheets stacked in a neat pile at the foot of her bed, with no conscious memory of how they had gotten that way. Now, as she watched the tragedy unfolding on the screen in front of her, it struck her again how brief and capricious life could be. How quickly it could be snuffed out, for no apparent reason. Who knew why we were here? Who knew if there was any real purpose for anyone's life? Especially when that life could be snatched away so easily.

As the music swelled in the background, tears rose to her eyes and threatened to spill over. Life was so unfair, so damned unfair. The kids, especially, never had much of a chance to begin with, and now, just when they were finally about to have some fun, it had been taken from them.

Although—it occurred to her, still riveted to the pictures, one hand twisting the ring that suddenly felt too tight on her finger—at least they had someone to love them. Mothers to mourn them when they were gone. *That's more than you had, Shannon,* a voice deep inside reminded her quietly. *You never had one to begin with, not* since two days after you were born, anyway. Never had a mother to hold you in her arms, to smooth your hair and comfort you. She bowed her head as her heart contracted with a pain so fierce it made her gasp.

*JULY. The scarlet heads of her grandmother's favorite geraniums were wilting and turning brown in the searing heat of the Georgia sun. Elizabeth Birmingham Taylor—Grammie Lib to all who knew her—tucked back a tendril of gray hair from the bun at the back of her neck and leaned over to drizzle a stream of water around the parched plants.*

"Drink up, children," *she crooned,* "I know you're thirsty in this heat. Drink up, my darlings. I don't want you to go dying on me now, you hear?"

*A sudden crash and thump drew her face sharply upward to the picture window. Oh no. Not again.*

"Grace?" *she called to the little girl playing tea party on the shady terrace, too absorbed in her game to hear her grandmother.*

"Shannon Grace," *Grammie Lib called again, a little louder this time. Poor motherless child, how she loved those dolls of hers. No wonder she preferred living in her own world of fantasy and imagination. No wonder she was so often oblivious to what was happening around her.*

"SHANNON GRACE TAYLOR!"

"Yes'm?" *Thick ringlets bounced in an arc around the little girl's head as she turned a pair of startled green eyes to where her grandmother stood, one hand rubbing the small of her back, a tin watering can in the other.*

"Fetch me the shovel from the garden shed, will you, darlin'?" *she called.* "There's another bird that's gone splat right into the picture window."

*"Splat!" Shannon said, her eyes sparkling, trying out the sound of the new word as she ran to obey.*

*"I'm afraid it's nothing to smile about, honey," her grandmother sighed as she took the shovel. "This little bird will never sing for us again, or fly away home with the wind in its wings. I'm afraid this one's dead."*

*She bent down to examine the bird more closely.*

*"Oh, honey, I think this is the momma redbird that made her nest outside the kitchen window. Remember? We saw those blue speckled eggs she laid just a few weeks ago."*

*Shannon's somber expression turned to one of horror as she squatted beside her grandmother. She reached over to pick up the still-warm body, a chubby finger smoothing the silky feathers across its head.*

*"Babies need their mommies," she said with the conviction of someone who knew what she was talking about. "D'is bird can't be dead, G'ammie Lib." Shannon's speech was clear for a four-year-old, but she still had some trouble with "th's" and "r's."*

*"I'm afraid she is, sweetheart," her grandmother said gently. Shannon rose, her eyes round and trusting as she gestured with the bird.*

*"Here, G'ammie Lib. You can fix her. I know you can."*

*The old woman paused. The air around them was heavy with humidity, so thick it could almost be felt. Silent, all at once. Timeless and still.*

*"Here," Shannon insisted, extending her hands to her grandmother.*

*Grammie Lib took a deep breath and closed her eyes in silent prayer. "Please, Lord, don't let me disappoint this little girl," she pleaded. "She's had so many disappointments already."*

*Shannon watched as the old woman briskly rubbed her hands together a dozen times, then opened them to receive the robin. Cupping her fingers around the little body, her lips moving in words too low to hear, she began to blow on her hands, as if trying to warm herself on a chilly day. Shannon's eyes widened as they moved from her grandmother's intent face down to the gnarled fingers that trembled slightly as they held the bird.*

*Was that a movement she saw, a faint flutter of wings inside her hands, wrinkled and spotted with age? Shannon held her breath as Grammie Lib continued to stroke the fragile little body, then with infinite care opened her hands to the sky.*

*"Fly away, momma bird," Shannon whispered, "fly away home."*

*The old woman and the little girl stood spellbound, almost afraid to breathe as the robin ruffled its feathers, looking around groggily before launching itself into an oak tree directly overhead. As they watched, motionless, the bird took three careful steps sideways on the swaying branch, like a drunk trying to steady himself after a bad night. The robin paused for another moment, then suddenly flapped its wings as if it had made up its mind about something and soared out of sight.*

*"Thank you," her grandmother whispered, her eyes moist as she turned her face to the skies. "Thank you so much."*

*"I knew you could do it, G'ammie Lib," Shannon crowed.*

*Grammie Lib shook her head. "I didn't do it, darlin'," she said softly. "That was heaven's miracle, not mine. But death isn't anything you need to worry about, anyway. We come, we go; sometimes we're in physical bodies, sometimes we aren't. Either way we're just fine..."*

From his chair next to the executive producer in the control room, the correspondent whose narrowed eyes had been observing her every move nodded toward the monitors showing Shannon's lowered head.

"Think she's okay?" Theo Tanner whispered in exaggerated concern, his fingers tightening on the pages of his script as he rose to a half-crouch. "Maybe I should go out there, just in case..."

David gestured at him to stay put and reached for the private line connecting him to the anchor desk. "Shannon on the phone," he barked to the director, who relayed the instruction to the studio floor.

"We're back in thirty," the floor manager announced, as the light next to the phone under the anchor desk began blinking. "David on the hot line."

Startled out of her reverie and a little flustered, wondering what she must have looked like just now, Shannon reached over and picked up the receiver. Whatever David wanted, he obviously intended it to be private; otherwise he could have just talked into the earpiece that linked everyone together.

"Yes?" she managed, trying not to gulp.

"Shannon. Everything okay out there?"

She stiffened her spine and looked straight into the camera, her expression cool and controlled. "Of course, David, everything's fine," she lied. "The lights are just so bright they made my eyes water."

"Fifteen," said the floor manager. Shannon replaced the telephone in its cradle, then dabbed carefully at the corner of each eye with a fingertip and examined it for black marks, to see if any of her mascara had run. It hadn't.

When the red light blinked on again, she was ready. "In a moment, the crisis that's keeping the lights burning late at the United Nations this weekend," she said, her voice crisp and professional.

In his corner office on the 38th floor of the WWB headquarters building, Rusty Parmalee glanced up from a pile of paperwork when he heard the opening theme music. Normally, he would have been home in Connecticut by now, but with the kids grown and gone, the holidays seemed much less important, somehow. And what network news president would miss the debut of the first woman to anchor its prime broadcast? A lot was riding on this, for everyone concerned. He had even taken Theo Tanner aside several days ago and asked him to stick around tonight as a backup, just in case she developed a last-minute case of nerves.

"Oh, you know," he had told Theo, careful to keep his voice non-committal as he slapped the correspondent's back. "Just stand by 'til the show's over. You know what it's like when we put somebody new on the air."

Despite his fury that Shannon was getting a shot at the anchor desk ahead of him, Theo had assured his boss that he'd be glad to, forcing a smile that vanished the instant Rusty disappeared around the corner.

As he glanced at the screen now, Rusty liked what he saw. Shannon looked beautiful tonight: calm and poised, with shiny chestnut hair that just skimmed her shoulders, wide green eyes, high cheekbones and a generous mouth curving slightly upward at the ends. Her navy suit and pearls were appropriately conservative, but the fuchsia blouse kept the combination from looking too boring.

He already knew she was capable, hard-working and smart. Hadn't she been covering Congress for them? And the White House before that, when her fellow Georgians were running the place?

Decision made, Rusty scribbled a note to call Shannon's agent after the first of the year. An anchor slot would be opening up soon on the weekends; it would be a shame to waste talent like this, especially with the FCC's growing complaints about the scarcity of women on all three networks. NBC had promoted one as a weekend anchor already. If that was the way things were going, he'd rather have WWB in second place instead of last.

## 3

"... and that's our news. Thank you for joining us. Good night," Shannon concluded with a brief, controlled smile. People who smiled too much on the air—especially women—could easily get written off as airheads by colleagues as well as the TV critics. Shannon preferred to err on the side of seriousness.

As the shot changed from a close-up of the anchor desk to a panoramic view of the newsroom and then dissolved to the WWB logo, the floor manager let his stopwatch drop from his hand to dangle from the cord hanging around his neck. Wiping sweaty palms on his corduroy trousers, he approached the anchor desk with an eager grin.

"Wow, Shannon, that was great," he enthused. "It was really a pleasure working with you."

"Thanks—Chris, right?" Shannon smiled at him and finished gathering up the pages of her script. His time cues had improved throughout the broadcast so she decided against saying anything about his somewhat shaky start. Probably just nerves, anyway. The only difference between them was that she was forced to hide hers.

"I hope we can work together again," she told Chris, as the audio engineer walked over, unhooked her mike and stalked away. Her eyebrows lifted as she looked after him in amusement. Clearly, not everybody was as impressed as Chris by people on TV. Or maybe just women on TV. Oh, well. On this night, there was no one and nothing that could get her down.

As she stepped off the set she called out a general "Thanks, guys," to the production crew still remaining. It had always seemed a little unfair to her that dozens of people worked as long and hard as she did, behind the scenes, but never received the credit, glory, or money that went to those whose faces appeared on camera.

Shannon rolled the pages of her script into a hollow baton to be kept as a souvenir of her big night and headed for the stairs to her office on "Correspondent's Row." Whew. She'd done it. She had made it through her first network anchor assignment without stumbling, mispronouncing anything or throwing up. Even more, she had managed to recover from whatever had blindsided her during the plane crash story. She let out a relieved sigh, then decided on a quick detour into the third-floor newsroom.

This was where the network's regular anchor had his office, where all the real decision makers labored around a horseshoe-shaped desk. The cavernous room seen on television was mostly window dressing, a place where the current crop of interns could stroll casually across the room whenever a wide shot was coming up, so the folks back home could see them in the background. *This* room was where everything important happened.

Empty. Only a few of the most loyal interns remained, to answer the phones and keep an eye on the wires in case the world decided to blow up while reporters everywhere weren't paying attention.

Wait: not entirely empty, after all. Stu Siegel caught a glimpse of Shannon through the glass doors of his office and hurried out to intercept her. Balding, in his early forties, his blue button-down oxford shirt and rep tie carefully in place as always, Stu was one of the few people she had liked from her first day at WWB. Something about him always made Shannon think of the smartest kid in school, who at best might be tolerated but never fully accepted. Knowing well how hard it was to be an outsider, Shannon made it a point to stop for a few words with Stu whenever she could.

"Ah, there's our new star now," he greeted her.

She smiled, then made a face to let him know she wasn't taking her new status too seriously. "I was just looking for David."

"Our illustrious executive producer went tearing out as soon as the show was over. Didn't even wait to see his name on the credits. Said something about his daughter and a Christmas pageant at church."

Stu leaned against a filing cabinet and took note of the disappointment that flashed across her face. "He said to tell you 'nice job,'" he added, reasoning that if David hadn't been in such a rush to leave, that's probably what he would have said. Maybe.

With no idea the compliment wasn't genuine, Shannon was happy to soak up the praise. "So, what are you still doing here? Big senior producer like you—no reason for you to stick around."

"It's Christmas Eve, remember? Not my holiday," he said, with a dramatic flourish of the wire copy he was holding. "Welcome to Jews for Jesus night."

"What?" she laughed.

"Absolutely," he assured her. His face was so solemn she wasn't sure at first if he was teasing. "My tribesmen and I spring forward each year at this time so the rest of you folks can go home and light candles and open presents and whatever else you do the night before Christmas."

"I see," she replied, a little embarrassed. She should have known that without asking, she supposed, but there hadn't been any Jewish people around when she was growing up. In her suburban Atlanta neighborhood, anyone more exotic than a Presbyterian would have been suspect. "Well, please accept the thanks of WorldWide WASPs."

He brushed her discomfort aside. "So. Want to keep me company on this cold Christmas Eve? It's just me, the college kids, and the wires. I'll even bring out the champagne I stashed away for later."

"Thanks, pal," she said, trying to soften the refusal by sounding more regretful than she actually was. "I'm out of here in about five seconds myself."

"Hot date, huh? And on a holiday, too," he smirked. "Must be something if you're in that big a rush..."

Her face froze as she turned to walk past him. "Now, Stu," she cautioned over her shoulder, careful to keep her voice even, "mind your manners."

"Hmmph," she heard him grump behind her. "Well, whoever he is, I sure hope that boy appreciates you."

Instead of answering, Shannon gave him an enigmatic smile and a wave of her fingertips as she disappeared through the doorway. It wasn't the kind of observation she liked thinking about, and she certainly had no intention of responding to it. Let him think whatever he wanted. He should only know the truth...

Shannon rounded the corner to her office, wincing as a click of the switch flooded the room with glaring fluorescent light. She sank into the chair, feeling normal for the first time in hours as she dialed home to Atlanta, eager to get the first reviews of her performance from her dad. Instead, she was greeted with the insistent buzz of a busy signal. *Damn*, Shannon groaned. Now she'd never get through. Everybody he had ever known must be calling to congratulate him. Lord knows he must have alerted the entire county to her appearance. As impatient as she was to speak with him, the thought of how proud he must be made her smile.

After a thirty-second pause, she dialed again. Bzzt, bzzt, bzzt. The phone company really ought to come up with a better sound than that, she scowled; it was so annoying. She shifted in her chair, letting her eyes roam over the tiny office that was shared by visiting correspondents, mentally redecorating her surroundings as she waited another minute before trying again.

The plain beige walls would look a lot better with some of her antique sailing prints, she decided. She loved to look at boats, even though actually being on the water made her uneasy. And a few plants in brass pots would warm up the place considerably, although they would have to be fake; there wasn't enough daylight in here to allow anything real to survive.

Bzzt, bzzt, bzzt. Damn and double-damn. Forget Dekalb County: everybody in the whole state of Georgia must be calling. Didn't they know *she* wanted to get through, too?

She drummed her fingers on the desk. Was there anyone else she could call? There was always Aunt DeeCee, of course, but matters between them had always been cool at best. Getting her own place after all these years of helping brother Ben keep house and raise his daughter hadn't seemed to improve her disposition any. Besides, if she phoned now it would be obvious she was fishing for praise and Aunt DeeCee was just contrary enough not to say anything, for fear she'd get the big head.

*I know who I'd really like to call,* she thought, as a mischievous, almost gloating grin spread across her face. Regina Lancaster. Wouldn't it be fun to interrupt the dinner hour of Miss Perfect Cheerleader. Just to inquire, oh, ever so casually of course, how life was going, back home in Atlanta. How are things at the garden club, and the Junior League?

*Oh, and me?,* she would reply. *Why, nothing much. Well, I did just anchor the network news tonight, in front of millions of people ... and oh yes, did I mention that I was the first woman to ever do that here?*

Not that Regina would give a damn, of course. Regina never had thought she was worth the time of day, which was probably why her opinion mattered so much. No doubt Regina's life was every bit as perfect as a grownup as it had been through the long years they had shared in school, from first grade right on through the day they had been liberated from high school. Except that Shannon had paid far more attention to Regina's existence than Regina ever had to hers. What she wore, how she fixed her hair, which boy she went out with: everything Regina did was deemed perfect in their closed world. Oh, yes. Blonde, pretty, and popular—Regina's life had always been charmed. No wonder Shannon had yearned to step into her life, wanted desperately to *be* Regina. So had all the other girls.

*EIGHTH GRADE. West DeKalb Junior High School. Each morning the long line of yellow buses disgorged their sleepy-eyed passengers at the bottom of wide concrete steps. Every inch of the steps and sidewalks—like everything else in junior high school—had a strict hierarchy, unspoken but acknowledged by all. The popular girls claimed the right side of the stairs. The jocks took up their position on the left. Each group looked over everyone else as they passed by, cracking jokes and making fun of anyone who didn't pass their flinty-eyed inspection, until the bell rang. Every morning, those deemed as the scum of the school—the pockmarked, the unpopular, the geeks and nerds—scurried through the gauntlet of their peers with downcast eyes, hoping to remain invisible long enough to cover an escape to their lockers.*

*For Shannon Grace Taylor, just getting into the building each morning was agony, especially walking past Regina Lancaster on the top step. As befit her position as the undisputed queen of the school, Regina held court there, her scornful sapphire eyes homing in on each unfortunate who passed. Her running commentary—shared in a giggled whisper behind her hand—covered how everyone looked and what they were wearing. It seemed to Grace that she was often singled out for special attention. At least once a week someone muttered "crazy Grace" loud enough for her to hear, or a burst of laughter broke out behind her as she hurried inside.*

*On this particular morning, it was Georgie Moran who took up the chant, for the third day in a row. Georgie, who had been pulling her hair and stealing her pencils since first grade. Georgie, who made her a special target after the teacher caught him flipping up her skirt, hoping for a glimpse of her panties, and stood him in the corner for the rest of the afternoon. Georgie, who shoved her head underwater at the church picnic by the lake, claiming he was doing a baptism.*

*For the past week Georgie had been trying to get Regina's attention long enough to ask her to the sock hop that Friday. After three straight mornings of taunts, Grace had finally had enough. This time, she whirled on him when she heard the singsong chant of "cra-azy Gra-ace, cra-azy Gra-ace" in a voice loud enough to carry across the steps into Regina's ears.*

*"How dare you make fun of me, Georgie Moran, with your sister knocked up and not married and your mother a drunk," she hissed, making no effort to keep her voice down.*

*"Wh—wha—," he stuttered, backing away in confusion. How did she know about his sister? He had only found out about it last night, when he overheard his parents fighting after they thought he was asleep. And his mother—was that why she was so grouchy all the time, why she was often still in her bathrobe, her hair uncombed, when he arrived home after football practice? Georgie's mouth opened and closed but no sounds came out for a few seconds as he stared at her.*

*"Wha—what'd you say?" he finally croaked.*

*"You heard me," Grace snapped.*

*On the steps to their right, Regina's eyes had widened. She glanced around, observing the shocked silence that had fallen over the crowd.*

*"Well," she sniffed, patting her blonde pageboy. "Guess she told you," she murmured to Georgie, who hadn't moved, his face frozen in terror and embarrassment. Giving Grace an odd look, Regina stepped delicately around him and through the double doors.*

*By noon that day, everyone in school had heard the story about what Grace had said, and how frightened Georgie had been. From then on, Grace found that her classmates--Regina included--left her strictly alone.*

Bzzt, bzzt, bzzt. Oh, all right, she decided crossly. Guess it'll just have to wait until I get home.

Shannon stood up and stretched her aching shoulders where the tension of the day always seemed to accumulate, then began to stuff piles of paperwork into her tote bag: clip files and research for her interview with the chairman of the Senate Foreign Relations Committee, a book she'd been meaning to get to for weeks to see if the author was worth interviewing, a dog-eared copy of *The Economist* she had dragged home from London and had yet to finish.

Some news anchors were content to let the writers and producers do the heavy lifting, to rewrite without much thought the wire service copy that clicked relentlessly into newsrooms around the world. Shannon always wanted to devour everything possible on a subject before sitting down to write a news story or interview someone. Deep in her heart, she still felt as if she didn't belong there. Her secret fear was that any day now she would be found out, dismissed as inadequate and told to go home. Luckily, she had discovered that being thoroughly prepared helped keep those feelings at bay.

"If you write it, you own it," Shannon believed, and so she told journalism students when she was invited to guest lecture and her network schedule was able to accommodate it. "If you've read all about a particular story, then you truly know what you're talking about... and somehow, the audience senses that about you as well. That means they will believe you, whether you're male, female or Martian. But you can't be lazy. There is no substitute for knowledge, and preparation. You have to do your homework," she would emphasize to the rows of rapt faces, most of whom wanted to know how they could get *her* job, preferably starting tomorrow.

With her hands on a lectern, her voice booming out on loudspeakers around the room, she sounded powerful, all-knowing. She was a role model for a whole wave of women making their way into the previously all-male domain of television—wasn't that what all the newspaper articles about her said? Reason enough, surely, not to need anything else.

Outside, she stood in the swirling snow for what felt like forever before managing to flag down a cabbie looking to make a few extra bucks on Christmas Eve, one who didn't mind a long trip in bad weather. A few minutes were all it took, though, for the muffler she had pulled over her head to get soaked, matting her heavily sprayed hair into a sodden mess. As she clambered into the back seat, the thick makeup that had looked so perfect just an hour ago on national television was dripping down her face. Snowflakes landing on her long eyelashes had melted her mascara into raccoon-like smears around her eyes. Pulling out a compact to check the damage, she had to choke back a laugh that bordered on the hysterical. *Good thing they can't see you now. They'd send you back home so fast your head would spin...*

Shannon shook her head as the cab crept through slippery streets to the FDR parkway. What was she doing here, indeed. She certainly hadn't planned it this way. Women weren't on television news when she was growing up; how could she ever have imagined that's what she would be doing one day? Her, of all people. The outcast. The weird kid. The one girl, far as she knew, who had made it all the way through high school without a single date, with not one boy who had ever gotten up the courage to ask her out. And yet... here she was, with a glamorous job that half the country would have killed for. Here she was, rich... successful. Alone...

She stared out the window, her eyes as bleak as the wintry landscape.

"They lied, Grammie Lib. It isn't enough. Not nearly enough," she said aloud, then jumped as the cab driver said, "Excuse me, Miss?"

"Nothing," she muttered, resolving to keep her thoughts to herself. She leaned back and closed her weary eyes, trying to lessen the sting of the smudged mascara. She must be a sight. But it was too dark to try and fix it now. She'd have to wipe away the mess later on with soap and water, once she got on the plane—if the planes were even flying tonight.

Her mind drifted back to her triumph at the anchor desk.

She had done it, all right. But where was the "happiness" part that was supposed to come with success? Why did she feel so lost and empty inside, when by all rights she should be turning cartwheels? If this didn't make her happy, deep-down happy—if this didn't bring the kind of joy and satisfaction that would linger for more than a minute or two—what could?

*Look inside, darlin',* a familiar voice said quietly in her head. Grammie Lib's voice. *You can always find out what you need to know, if you'll take the time to listen...*

Her lower lip began to quiver. "I miss you, Grammie. I wish you were still here," she whispered, her eyes filling for a second time that day.

*But I am here, darlin' girl.*

Then tell me what to do, she pleaded.

*I did tell you. Look inside.*

But where? How?

*Espavo, dear one,* came the voice, soft as a butterfly wing against her cheek. *It's time.*

Es—what? Shannon shook her head at the unfamiliar word and frowned. What do you mean, it's time? Time for what?

The voice fell silent.

*Fat lot of help you are*, Shannon grumped, a shiver crawling up her spine as she gazed at clumps of snowflakes that seemed to be coming down faster than before. Despite the heater going full blast in the front seat, it was cold back where she was sitting. Cold, and quiet, and alone.

# 4

The announcement came two weeks into January, summoning WWB's Washington staffers into Studio A for a closed-circuit statement from New York. Nothing had been disclosed in advance what it was about. As reporters, videographers, editors, producers, and all the support personnel dutifully filed into the crowded basement where most of the Washington-based shows were taped, each examined the face of his neighbor, hoping for some scrap of knowledge that might let them know how worried they should be about this unusual event.

Whatever it was, it had to be big. No one could remember the last time everyone had been assembled like this. Shannon slipped into the crowded studio at two minutes before ten o'clock, counting herself lucky to find a folding chair in the next to last row. Catching her favorite producer's eye from across the room, she telegraphed a question with her eyebrows, but Janie looked as mystified as everyone else.

Still hugging her own exciting news to herself, Shannon assumed that the network announcement, whatever it might be, would have little impact on her. Just after New Year's, the network news president had called her agent, Sol Hurwitz, to open discussions about her anchoring WWB's new Sunday night newscast. It was still too early to tell anyone—Rusty was a tough negotiator, and resolving terms for a more lucrative contract could take weeks—but the news had put a sparkle back into Shannon's eyes. She could hardly wait until it became public knowledge. Maybe that was it. Maybe the network was announcing the new show. She considered that for a moment and then shook her head. No. It might be a huge event in her life but it was hardly that big a deal to everyone else.

Heads turned as a live picture suddenly popped up on the monitors from New York. The president of the news division was standing at a podium, flanked by a man Shannon had never seen before. The buzz of speculation racing through the room quieted as Rusty Parmalee began to speak.

"Ladies and gentlemen, I'm sure you're wondering why you've all been called together like this. I'm pleased to announce some very exciting news for WorldWide Broadcasting this morning, news that will affect all of us in the months and years to come. First, though, a few words about the competitive situation in which we find ourselves in broadcasting these days. I'm sure you know that there are those who believe the networks will soon be dinosaurs. In fact there's a fellow down in Atlanta who seems to think that cable television is the wave of the future, and he claims he's going to see to it personally that the 'Big Three' will cease to rule the airwaves. We don't believe him, of course," Rusty paused to chuckle at the very idea, "but we do plan to head him off at the pass.

"One of the ways we will do that is by continuing to offer the American viewing public the very best news and entertainment possible. And good television—*outstanding* television—is expensive, as I'm sure you folks already know. I'm happy to tell you that we've formed a partnership in this new endeavor, with General Dynamo—"

"Dynamo?! The defense contractor? The guys who make airplanes—and, and washing machines?" An incredulous stage whisper went up from two rows ahead of where Shannon was sitting.

She was too stunned to react. General Dynamo had deep pockets, all right, but what could an international conglomerate possibly know about news?

"... now, I'm sure you're all wondering what this will mean to each of you, personally," Rusty was continuing. His face was somber as he leaned over the podium to address the camera. "I can assure you that while we will continue to be ferociously competitive in the new and more challenging broadcasting climate of the eighties, while we will need to work harder, leaner, smarter, every day, we do not plan layoffs at this time. Your jobs are secure."

Shannon glanced over at Janie, whose face had gone white. Her scurrilous ex-husband was more than six months behind on alimony and child support, and she needed this job more than most.

"Bull," her producer mouthed. A quick survey of the eye-rolls across the room confirmed how much WWB staffers were buying that one.

Shannon turned back to the screen for Rusty's concluding remarks.

"Now, I know you all will have a lot of questions in the coming days about this, all of which we will do our best to answer. We will be sending out a packet with more complete information about this later today, but we wanted all of you, our valuable employees, to hear the news first. *Before* you read about it in the Wall Street Journal."

Rusty's smile appeared forced as he stepped back from the podium. Then, prompted by the man to his right, he lifted his hands to quiet the worried hum of conversation. Rusty adjusted the microphone and waited for silence.

"Forgive me, ladies and gentlemen, there's one more important point I neglected to make. Any of you who might be wondering about what this means for top management at WWB, let me assure you that I'm not going anywhere. I will remain at the network as chairman of the board, while Jim DiMonzo, here, who has been running things at General Dynamo for the past ten years, will become chief executive officer of the new broadcast division of the company. I'd also like to introduce to you the new president of the network news division, someone who General Dynamo believes—and I believe—will be instrumental in helping us attract new audiences during this decade. I'm sure you've heard of his success down South, a record we are confident he will be able to duplicate for WWB. Jack, will you step up to the podium, please? Ladies and gentlemen, Jack Reardon."

As a smattering of applause came over the speakers from New York, a loud gasp went up from the room in Washington. It took Shannon a moment to realize that it had come from her.

Jack Reardon? The man who had been news director, then general manager of her old station in Atlanta? The one whose "let it bleed" news philosophy had led to WSYA's huge jump in the ratings—followed by the loss, one by one, of its most able and experienced reporters and anchors? The man whose contempt for his employees as well as the audience had become so intolerable that she, too, had finally left without another job to go to? Since then, he had acquired quite a reputation for himself as a man who stopped at nothing for a ratings point, someone unwilling to let the facts stand in the way of a good story. Still, there was no denying he had made a ton of money for the station. No wonder General Dynamo loved him.

"Reardon? That jerk?" she heard from behind her and turned to confirm the source. Ah. Andy Calhoun, one of the tape editors who had been among the first to go but was too good to remain unemployed for long. WWB had scooped him up for the Washington bureau more than a year before she came to the network. Andy was slouched in his chair, arms folded across his chest, his head shaking slowly from side to side as if to say that now, truly, he had heard it all.

Their eyes met and she nodded in sympathy with his comment, as around them the room exploded into speculation about what all this meant. Turning for a final look at the monitors, Shannon saw the camera pull back for a wide shot from New York. At the front of the room, his hand pumping in an enthusiastic handshake with the network's new president, she could see a broad back and blonde head she knew all too well. For a moment there, Shannon had forgotten that Theo Tanner knew Reardon too.

"You can both rot in hell, far as I'm concerned," muttered Shannon as she rose unsteadily from her chair. She winced at the sudden pain in her stomach, a pain so sharp it felt as if someone had stuck a knife in her belly and twisted, hard. She squeezed her eyes shut for a second and then looked around, hoping no one had noticed her ashen face. She'd better get out of here before anyone could ask what *she* made of all this.

Shannon fumbled for the phone, her voice still blurred with sleep as she answered.

"H'lo?" she croaked. "Oh, hi, Sol. Sorry to sound so groggy. I was editing an interview last night into the wee hours. I was thinking we could put it on the new weekend show—"

Sol Hurwitz's twenty years as an agent had left him short on patience, especially given the nature of his call this morning.

"I have some news you aren't going to like," he interrupted. "Rusty called this morning to say the network has decided to give the weekend anchor slot to someone else. They're assigning you to London."

"L-London?" she sputtered, too shocked at first to mourn the loss of the anchor job. "London's a graveyard. Are you kidding me? I'll never get on the air from London!"

"Maybe. Maybe not. To be honest, Shannon, I don't think you have much choice. Rusty promised me they won't forget you—maybe you could do a documentary or something. Who knows. Maybe Reardon will forget he doesn't like you if you're not on the air every night."

Still clutching the telephone in dismay, Shannon flashed back on her last trip to London, to an empty assignment board she had seen at the bureau—weeks ago? No, a lifetime ago. Back when her path was certain, her star on a straight trajectory, ever upward. Back when she was sure that hard work was the answer, that fame and fortune were not only her certain reward but everything she needed to be happy.

London? London was death by boredom. Buried alive, never to be seen again. Never to have the adrenaline rush of too much to do and not enough time to do it. Exiled to a place where someday, if she was very lucky indeed, she might have a chance to do real work again. Maybe.

"Oh, yeah, Sol, I'm sure life has all kinds of wonderful things in store for me." Her voice was etched in acid as she slammed down the receiver.

# 5

Damned airplanes. It was almost impossible trying to find a position comfortable enough to fall asleep.

Shannon shifted sideways in her business-class seat, but it was no use. Even with the wider seats at the front of the aircraft, even with two of the little white rectangles that passed for pillows these days and a blanket over her knees for warmth, her body was still cramped into a shape that made sleep impossible and even rest unlikely. She squirmed again, turning toward the window, and sighed. She was tired. Her head hurt. And she was almost positive the two women seated across the aisle to her left were talking about her. They had been staring at her and whispering, heads together, since they had come on board.

"... Sharon, or Susan, or something—isn't that her name? You know, the one who used to be at the White House—"

The voice was just loud enough to carry across the aisle.

Oh great. That was all she needed, some adoring fans to remind her what a success she was. No, she corrected herself, what a success she had been.

*But that's exactly what your life would be if you were anchoring,* came a voice inside her head. *You'd be more exposed than ever. Sure you want that?*

*Of course I do,* she argued back. *It's all I've ever wanted. All my dad's ever wanted for me. And,* she had to admit, *my career is all I've ever had.*

Shannon leaned back and closed her eyes as a wave of sorrow washed over her, as deep and endless as the ocean, drowning her in despair. For once, she didn't care if the moisture welling beneath her eyelids might smear her mascara.

"Hmpf," Shannon sniffed as she plopped her tote bag onto the nearest desk, glancing around the London newsroom with a frown. "The place sure looks bigger on TV. A lot nicer, too."

"Ah, yes, the grand illusion of television," Jeremy agreed, treading carefully in the face of her displeasure. "You should know that better than anyone."

"Sorry, Jeremy," she replied after another sweep of her new surroundings. "This has nothing to do with you. Give me three more minutes to feel sorry for myself and then I promise I'll try to be a good soldier again."

"We can talk whenever you're ready. I even have a story or two for you to think about."

"Oh, good. I was catching up on the London papers this weekend and I thought perhaps a piece on immigration might be interesting. Especially the influx from India and Algeria. That seems to be becoming more and more of an issue, especially in the city..."

"Tell me about it. I've been pitching New York on that one for weeks to no avail," Jeremy said with a sigh. "What *they* want is a piece on a woman here who claims to talk to the dead. She's written a best-selling book about it and the new people running the show want us to go after her. I know," he added hurriedly, catching her impatient expression. "Not your usual sort of piece, to be sure..."

Shannon stopped in the middle of an exaggerated eye-roll, suddenly remembering what Grammie Lib might have to say about such a thing. About how, even now, she could sometimes hear her grandmother's voice in her ear... could even, at times, sense her presence, when she had been dead and gone for more than twenty years. Or that weird thing that she herself had come out with when she was six, that led to her awful nickname. Better not, she decided. Jeremy would think she had become completely unglued.

Besides, it might be interesting after all.

"Who's the producer?"

"Actually, Stu Siegel is coming over for a few days. He's chasing some kind of hush-hush interview but he said he wanted to stay a little longer and didn't mind doing another piece or two. Not everyone thinks London is purgatory, you know."

*No*, she sighed to herself, *just those of us who'd rather be somewhere else.*

Shannon rose to her tiptoes, craning her neck to see if she could locate a balding head towering above the crowd. At least sixty people stood pressed together on narrow steps outside the small brick church, waiting to go inside. At six-feet, four inches, Stu was usually easy to spot. But not tonight. Despite her survey, extending to the streets surrounding the church, he was nowhere to be seen.

The spiritualist author's speech was scheduled to begin at 8. When the heavy wooden doors swung open at 7:45, Shannon decided to wait for him inside.

"You made it," Stu said, as he materialized around a back pillar. "Good. I got here early and talked my way in so we could get a good seat—but hurry up," he added, propelling them through the gloom. "I want to sit up close so we can see what's going on."

"Sure you do," she teased. "You want to see if she's wearing a hearing aid, right?" WWB had uncovered a scam at a Texas revival meeting last year in which the faithful had filled out cards as they came inside the tent, describing their various afflictions. Someone offstage then fed the information to the preacher on the podium through a small earpiece, so that he could make a "miraculous" diagnosis of the petitioner's ailments before pretending to cure them.

Shannon looked around curiously. By now the dozens of people had dispersed into rows of folding chairs, some chattering excitedly to each other, others lost in contemplation. They seemed the sort of average, mostly middle-aged people who might be in any church, anywhere, on a Wednesday night. A few younger faces were scattered throughout the crowd, but the majority appeared to be at least in their mid-forties.

After everyone had been seated, a lanky man with gray-flecked hair and a face washed with calm stepped behind the pulpit.

"Thank you for coming, my friends. We begin tonight with music," and at that he began to sing in a deep, sonorous voice.

Shannon and Stu looked at each other as a few people in the congregation began to chime in.

"Don't know this one. Wasn't in my prayer book at temple," Stu confided in a stage whisper.

"Didn't make it to the Sandy Plains Baptist Church, either," she murmured in return.

When the last notes had faded away, the man paused, slowly scanning the faces in front of him.

"My name is Nick McAllister," he began. "I first started working as a healer twenty years ago. Some of you may be familiar with the process. Others may be encountering it for the first time. It's simple, really. What we do is known as the laying on of hands, much as Christ did. We place our hands upon a person's shoulders and offer up a silent prayer for healing, a prayer to God and the universe, so that anyone in search of healing might discover the inner peace that will help them deal with any physical or mental challenge. It has been my observation that only when the spirit self has been calmed and quieted can healing in the physical body take place. If any of you have been in the practice of meditation you already know how calm you feel afterward..."

Shannon leaned over to Stu. "I used to meditate to help me get to sleep when I was doing a morning show in Atlanta and had to get out of bed at 3 a.m. He's right. It does make you feel calmer."

Stu shot her a quizzical look, then turned back to the speaker.

"This is the time we have set aside for healing," Nick continued. "Anyone who feels the need for it, whether it's physical, emotional, or spiritual, we invite to step forward..."

One person rose, then two and three and finally half a dozen moved into the aisle toward the front of the church. Shannon felt Stu's elbow in her ribs.

"Get up there," he whispered.

"I don't want to. *You* go up."

"You're the reporter."

"Yeah, and you're the producer. Besides, I don't need healing."

*Oh, really*, he thought. "Aw, c'mon. You already said you used to meditate..."

She gave him a long-suffering look and got to her feet. Actually, it might be interesting to find out what this was all about. Grammie Lib certainly did far more eccentric things than this; maybe it was time to learn more. All in the spirit of scientific inquiry, of course.

Nick greeted her with a smile, his gaze traveling from face to face in the circle. Moving from one person to the other, he gently placed his hands on their head or shoulders.

"Mother Father God," he began in a quiet voice, "All-That-Is... we ask you and the universe for a healing..."

Shannon lowered her head with the rest but couldn't resist peeking through her lashes to observe. Even with their eyes closed, each person being prayed over had the rapt expression of a five-year-old first encountering the tickle of a caterpillar's feet. As Nick finished and moved on, one by one they opened their eyes and smiled.

Finally he paused in front of her, compelling her to lock onto two of the kindest eyes she had ever seen. A longing she couldn't identify suddenly rose so strongly from her chest that her eyes swam with tears. Nick cupped his hands around her head, his thumbs touching in the center. She blinked to clear her vision, hardly daring to breathe. As with the others, there was no mumbo-jumbo, just a simple prayer, and a warm and peaceful feeling when he had finished. Startled by the rush of emotion, she opened her eyes again to find him smiling at her.

"May all be well with you, and with all beings, everywhere," he said, nodding to each member of the group. He extended a hand to the people on either side of him and indicated that they should do the same. Shannon felt a little foolish but obliged. For a brief moment as they stood silently in a circle of clasped hands, she understood for the first time what the church of her childhood had tried to tell her about faith and love and the warmth of human connection. As her gaze traveled around the circle, she didn't feel like an outsider, a reporter mentally taking notes, but a seeker, just as they were, trying to find something larger than herself or her job to believe in. Here they were, total strangers, people she had never seen before and was unlikely ever to see again, yet suddenly they were people she felt connected to, in a way she might have scoffed at a few moments before.

How bizarre, she thought. I believed it when I read years ago that hell is other people. I was always glad—proud—to be a loner. I preferred to think that I didn't want anybody. Didn't need anybody. But what if Sartre had it all wrong?

She returned to her seat, still lost in reflection, as Stu grinned and whispered, "Well?"

"Tell you later," she mouthed back.

"And now there's someone I know you're all waiting to meet," Nick said, gesturing to a woman with soulful brown eyes who rose to join him. "This young woman has been given a powerful gift—the ability to communicate with loved ones who have passed on. Her name is Clare, and I will let her tell her story."

Clare appeared to be in her early 30s. Shannon leaned forward as the medium gripped the podium in both hands, swallowed hard and began to speak, her voice quavering with nervousness.

"Actually, my personal story will have to wait for a moment. As Nick has been talking, I have been getting a message from someone on the other side, someone who's very eager to let his wife and babies know that he is all right."

She stepped away from the podium and moved into the crowd, stopping in front of a young woman in the second row.

"There's a young man standing behind you. His name is William, and he died in a car accident two years ago—"

Before Clare could say any more, the woman let out a startled shriek and burst into tears. Clare looked stunned and began to move away, then returned to the woman after taking a few steps toward the other side of the room.

"I'm sorry," she said. Her voice was very gentle. "I know this is upsetting to you. But I've been asked to try again. Would you like me to continue?"

"Yes, oh yes," the woman gasped. "I need to know... Billy was married to my sister...."

Clare leaned over and took her hands. "He wants you to know how sorry he is for what happened. I guess you and your sister used to complain about how fast he drove? Yes. And then one day he lost control and slammed into a tree. His body was thrown from the car; he died immediately, but he wants you to know that his spirit survived, and he's helping your sister and the children any way he can."

Shannon rose a few inches in her chair to get a better look at the woman's face gaping at the medium in astonishment. The room was still; the rest of the audience seemed as mesmerized as she was.

"A little boy and girl, is it?"

The stupefied woman could only nod.

"He's saying... tell them Daddy loves them. I take it the baby was born after Billy passed over?"

"Yes," the woman whispered. "My sister hasn't been the same ever since. She was just two months pregnant when he died."

"Well, tell her what you've heard tonight. Her path will become easier as time goes on."

"I will," she said, wiping her eyes. "Thank you—thank you so much."

"This is amazing," Shannon whispered.

Stu shook his head. "Lucky guess."

Clare continued to move around the room.

"Oh," she said after a moment. "I see there are some friends from across the pond with us tonight. Lovely. I do so enjoy Americans."

Stu placed a cautionary hand on Shannon's arm, sensing that she was about ready to dive under the chair in front of her. To her relief, Clare had stopped two rows behind where they were sitting, on the right side of the room. Both twisted around to get a better look, Stu wishing for a third time tonight that he had brought a camera.

"Now then," she said to a heavy-set woman with blue-green eyes and blonde hair that fell to her shoulders. "As I stand here, I'm aware of a man who died of cancer connected with you..."

"Actually, the person I want to make contact with is my mother, who died last year?" the woman said, in a distinctive Southern drawl that ended each sentence as a question.

Shannon's eyes widened. She leaned over to Stu with an excited whisper. "I could swear that's Regina Lancaster!"

"Who's Regina Lancaster?"

"A girl I went to school with, back in Atlanta..."

"Ssh," he said. "Tell me later. I want to hear this."

"If we could make contact with your mother," Clare was continuing, "what would you like to know?"

"Are she and Mimi together?"

"Goodness. Let me see. I'm aware of a lady who had problems with her chest and her breathing. She tells me she died rather suddenly, that her heart just gave out. She says to tell you her head is fine..."

The woman's mouth formed an "O" of astonishment. "She had heart trouble all her life but the doctors thought it was a stroke that finally killed her..." she agreed.

Clare closed her eyes and continued.

"I'm safe, she's saying, tell her I'm safe. There's some connection also I think to a locket. Yes. With your grandfather's hair? She's saying tell her to keep it safe, to wear it sometimes. She's smiling and waving and saying she loves you. I'm asking are you with Mimi and she's just laughing. And I'm seeing some sort of animal—she's mentioning a dog and says tell her we're all safe and all together."

Shannon stared. She was almost positive that the woman behind her, now smiling through the tears streaming down her cheeks, was Regina. But her face was so chubby! She must be at least thirty pounds overweight. What had happened to the superstar head cheerleader, the prom queen whose voluptuous figure had been legendary at West DeKalb High? If there was anyone in the world who would marry royalty or become a movie star—at the very least, wind up rich and famous, Shannon was sure it would have been Regina. But not this Regina. This woman looked...

Shannon shook her head, trying to take it all in.

And then it hit her. Regina looked tired. Ordinary, even. Hardly someone to be afraid of, intimidated by. After all these years of looking up to her, envying her, wanting on some level to prove something to her—

It was an incredible thought.

She looked again to see if she could recognize the woman sitting next to Regina who was alternately laughing and sobbing, their hands clasped together.

"She's talking about the life beyond, now...," Clare continued in a low voice. "It's so different than we would imagine, she says, but more beautiful. She's very emotional. Tell her I'm in the light, she says. She keeps saying tell them I'm sorry I had to leave, but it was my time to go. I could hear everything while I was in the hospital, and I know you all love me because I could hear you saying it. Peter will protect you now, she says."

The room was silent, everyone in it straining as hard as Shannon was to hear Clare.

"And now I'm aware of a lady who had problems with her head, I'm not sure if it was some sort of hemorrhage," Clare said, turning to the small, dark-haired woman at Regina's side. "She tells me she's been waiting patiently to talk to you ever since you were a small girl..."

"Oh my God—it's my mother." The woman began to sob and rock in her chair, covering her mouth with both hands.

"She talks about, there must have been some sort of a head-on collision, she's talking about her head again, it was one brief moment of discomfort but no more than that. Just before it happened, she says, she knew she was going on a journey. Tell my daughter I'm safe, and please don't cry. We have never been apart, even though time and space may keep us separate. There are so many of us in the spirit world who want to talk to loved ones, there's so much to teach all of you. Be my voice for one more moment, she's saying to me, tell my child I stand close by her. Tell her to trust me and I will guide her..."

Regina put a comforting arm around her friend as she continued to shake with sobs. "May I ask you one more question..." she finally said in a gasp. "Was she watching us... Regina and me... that April morning..."

"Mmn," Clare said, closing her eyes once again. "This sounds a little confusing. 'Bury me softly,' she's saying, 'I see that your hearts are breaking. But know that my eyes are open, that I am not in that grave and when I see you all and know that you are thinking of me, think not to bury me softly, for I am alive and see your every move.'"

"That's beautiful," the woman gulped as she pulled out a handkerchief and wiped her streaming eyes.

"She says these words are from my heart," Clare continued, with a gentle smile. "She is my child, your mother is saying, and I love her. Lift your face to the sun and smile, knowing that I can see you and let us rejoice together. God is with you and I am with God. Your tragedy was my journey and my journey continues. Never forget that I am with you. And when it is time for you to make the journey, know that I will be there to lead you home."

Clare stopped speaking. She smiled first at the two women who sat in front of her wiping their eyes, then at the entire group waiting goggle-eyed to hear what else she had to say.

The dark-haired woman was still crying so hard that her "Thank you," was barely audible.

Almost against her will, Shannon could feel her own eyes filling for the second time in an hour—she, the tough reporter, who tried hard to deny herself the luxury of tears—afraid that if she truly let down her guard, she might never stop bawling. She looked around and noticed handkerchiefs being touched to overflowing eyes all across the room.

Clare smiled at the two American women and walked back to the front of the church.

"I'm hearing now from someone named Diana," she said. "But I'm not certain who this message is for. She won't tell me, because she isn't sure you want to hear it..."

Her eyes scanned the crowd. Shannon sank in her chair, her face flaming, her heart hammering with fear. Clare was right—she did not want to hear any more, from anybody. And definitely not in public. Besides, what could her mother possibly have to say to her now? If it even were Diana....*her* Diana.

Clare hesitated a moment, seeming to wait for direction. When no one spoke up, she smiled a little and shrugged.

"Ah, well," she said. "Perhaps it's too soon. Whoever you are, she wants to tell you she's sorry. There was...something...she couldn't face. She was too afraid. But she didn't mean to hurt you and she's asking for your forgiveness."

The crowd remained silent, with several people swiveling around to see if they could figure out the recipient of this mysterious new message. Shannon's eyes were riveted to the hands she kept tightly clasped in her lap. Her face felt so hot she was sure she must be scarlet all the way up to her hairline as she waited for the awful moment to pass.

"She's saying she has a gift for you, something precious from thousands of years ago. An ancient word, that will help you along your path. S—something? No." Clare paused and cocked her head, as if straining to hear through a faulty telephone line. "E-s, she's telling me. E-S..." She waited a moment more, then smiled regretfully. "I'm so sorry, she's trying to spell something out for me. She's quite insistent but I'm having trouble getting it..."

Stu studied Shannon as she scrunched in her chair. Curious almost beyond endurance, he could feel the radiant heat of her embarrassment but was unwilling to give her away.

"Well," Clare concluded after another scan of the room, "perhaps we should leave it at that."

She returned to the front and addressed the audience, relaxed now, her eyes moving from face to face in the expectant crowd.

"Despite what you've seen and heard here tonight, if you came here this evening hoping for absolute evidence of life after death, you're likely to go away disappointed. All I can do, really, is give you something to think about. Some new way to consider your life, to understand there is more to God's plan for us than what we can see or feel or touch. If we can lose our fear of dying, we can get on with the business of living, and loving each other. We can know that there is nothing to be afraid of. We have been here before, we will be here again. Our mission on earth is quite simple, really: to discover who we truly are, to love ourselves, and to love one another. Perhaps that is the greatest lesson here—one that should give us hope, and strength."

She smiled and sat down to a smattering of applause.

Shannon rose from her seat and stretched, refusing to meet Stu's inquiring eyes.

"Well? What did you think?"

"I'll tell you after I catch up with Regina. Give me a minute, okay?"

"Minute, nothing. I want to hear this."

They elbowed their way through the crowd to Regina, who by now had been swarmed by audience members eager to get confirmation of what they'd just heard.

"Was that true—"

"Do you think it was really your mother—"

"What about the locket—"

"And the accident—"

Shannon stood to one side with Stu at her elbow, wanting to listen in without identifying herself yet.

After ten minutes of animated conversation the crowd around Regina had thinned out enough so that she could catch her eye.

"Why, Grace Taylor—oh my God, is that you?" Regina shrieked as she enfolded her in an enthusiastic hug. Shannon couldn't have been more astonished if Regina had pulled out a gun and shot her. Anyone watching would have thought they were lifetime friends, brought together by fate for a joyous reunion.

"Good God A'mighty! I heard you were off doin' TV, up north somewhere—changed your name, and everything—what in the world are you doing here?"

"You first," Shannon said, finally managing to release herself from Regina's grasp.

"Why, I came to London with my church group—we're on our way to the Holy Land?—and when I heard about this woman that could talk to the spirit world, Miranda and I just had to find out what she had to say."

"And...?" Shannon prompted.

"Well, my Lord, didn't you hear her?" Regina dabbed at her eyes and face with a delicate lace hankie, trying to erase the streaks of mascara that traced a line from her plump cheeks all the way down to her chin.

"Yeah, it was amazing. I just wanted to confirm some of the details. Like the locket—do you have one, really?"

Regina gave a vigorous nod. "I sure do. My Momma gave it to me for graduation, years ago. It has my grandfather's hair in it. And the message about Peter? Why, that's my husband. Third time's the charm, I thought, although we're split up now. But he was with me in the hospital when she was in a coma, and we sat by her bed, holding her hand for hours and telling her how much we loved her."

Shannon watched as Regina's eyes widened and one hand went to her mouth to cover a gasp. "Oh. I wonder what she meant about Peter takin' care of me. Maybe we are supposed to be together after all..."

"What was the thing about 'bury me softly?'" Stu jumped in.

"I better let Miranda tell that part. Miranda, turn around here for a minute and say hello to my friends—"

Miranda took a final swipe at the mascara smearing her eyes and greeted them with a wobbly smile.

"This is Grace Taylor from home, and—I'm sorry, what was your name again?"

"Stu Siegel."

After a flurry of handshakes, Stu returned to his original question. "What was the 'bury me softly' speech about?"

"Well, Regina's mother and my mother grew up together and were closer than any sisters, until my mom was killed in a car accident thirty years ago. She hit her head on the windshield and bled to death. I was just a toddler at the time—I barely knew her except what I heard about her from Regina's mom. And so when Regina lost her mother last March we had a little private ceremony a few weeks later, just the two of us, you know, because they were buried together. I want to tell you, we just sobbed our eyes out, we were so sad, laying flowers on those two graves...," Miranda's voice broke and she began to wipe her eyes again.

"Really," Shannon said. "But didn't Clare just say that your mom could see you the whole time..."

"She did, didn't she?" Regina bubbled. "And I didn't even tell her what we were doing that day. She came up with that 'bury me softly' part all on her own. There's no way she could have known that's why we were there."

Regina put an arm around Miranda's shoulder and as they beamed at each other, Shannon began to think she could actually come to like the woman one day. Somehow she didn't seem nearly so scornful and distant now that they were both grown up.

"How long are you in town?" Shannon asked.

"We leave first thing tomorrow, but here," she said, fishing in her bag for a pen and paper, "here's my address in Atlanta. Write and let me know how you're getting on, now, y'hear?"

"Sure. It was great to see you," Shannon said, backing away before Regina could remember to inquire what she was doing there.

As they made their way down the steps, Stu said, "How about a nightcap at Annabel's? I could use a drink, myself."

"You and me both."

Buttoning their coats against the crisp night air, neither noticed a silver Jaguar pulling out from across the street. Lord Michael Willoughby-Jones had hurried from the lecture before anyone could see him. After all, a spiritualist church was hardly the place where a distinguished member of Parliament would want to be spotted, no matter how good his reason for being there.

# 6

"I don't get it," Stu snorted in exasperation the following week. He tossed a folder overflowing with yellowing newspaper clips and interview notes onto the rug. "If the administration really was trading arms for hostages, why would the president keep denying it? We've got him on the record half a dozen times. He had to know that the truth would come out sooner or later."

Shannon shrugged. "Who knows. Maybe the guys who work for him didn't tell him what they were up to. Or maybe he didn't want to know, exactly. You know, plausible deniability. Easier to cover your tracks that way. He probably figured that once the hostages came home, nobody would care very much about how they got there. Besides—people in politics are capable of infinite self-delusion."

*Pretty much like the rest of us,* she added to herself.

Shannon eyed her surroundings appreciatively as she gestured for a refill of her champagne glass. The story about Clare having been passed on to the morning show, they were doing final prep work for the interview with Stu's Middle Eastern whistle-blower. The champagne may have been premature, but they couldn't resist celebrating what was sure to be a major scoop.

"Now why can't I find a place like this?" she said. "I've been looking and looking for someplace Victorian—you know me, I love the architecture—but every place either has something major wrong with it or it's just way too expensive..."

The network's rental flat in Knightsbridge had once been the library of a nineteenth-century townhouse, with carved mahogany bookshelves lining the walls and a bay window overlooking a tidy garden. A compact kitchen opened off one side of the foyer with a bathroom opposite. Fifteen-foot ceilings framed with elaborate plaster molding made the room seem larger than it actually was.

"Oh. Sorry. What were you saying?"

"The eternal question. What did the president know and when did he know it. And—even more to the point—how can we prove it," replied Stu.

"Right. Not a good time to get distracted by the décor, huh?"

She flipped through several pages of the yellow legal pads stacked up on her lap.

"Well, I don't know if we'll be able to nail them on that one until we get your guy on tape, so I'm not going to worry about it just yet." Her voice was breezy, but he noticed her eyes were troubled.

"What's the matter? You seem a little out of it tonight."

Shannon shook her head and tucked an escaping strand of curly hair behind one ear. "I don't know. Worried about the interview, I guess. It just means so much to me to do some solid reporting again. Most of the time I keep pitching things to New York and I keep getting turned down, so I really want to get this one right before I turn into the invisible woman."

She let out a frustrated sigh. "The way my stomach keeps jumping around, you'd think this was the first story I ever covered."

"I know what you need to relax you," Stu replied, with a predatory smirk.

"Yeah, yeah," she laughed in response. When he didn't join in, her expression turned severe. "Stu Siegel, that is the oldest line in the world. You can't think I'm going to fall for it."

"Oh, all right. I'll shut up. On one condition."

Shannon stiffened, instantly on guard. "What?"

Stu looked away, a little abashed. "Actually—never mind. I guess it's really none of my business."

"C'mon, Stu. If something's on your mind you'll never be able to keep it in for long, anyway, so go ahead. What did you want to know?"

"You're probably right. But feel free to tell me to shut up at any time."

She studied his expression, wondering why he seemed so uncomfortable all of a sudden. It wasn't like Stu to be so circumspect. In the past few weeks they had become good enough friends they could talk about almost anything.

Still, he avoided her eyes as he asked the question. "When we went to that lecture at the spiritualist church... why were you so uptight when Clare asked about somebody named Diana at the end?"

"Is that all," she scoffed. "I thought you were going to ask something really impertinent, like my bra size."

That got him to grin, which was what she wanted. After all her years as a loner, this friendship business still took a little getting used to. She wasn't used to confiding in anybody—especially a man. Particularly one who sometimes acted as if he might want more than friendship from her.

"I guess if I acted a little funny it's because my mother's name was Diana. She died a couple of days after I was born, so—classic story—I've gone through life thinking it was my fault. But I can't imagine what she'd have to say to me. I didn't know her in life, so why would I want to hear from her now that she's gone? And that's assuming it's even possible."

Shannon grabbed the poker to rearrange the logs, sending a shower of sparks up the chimney as her voice turned somber. "Who knows, Stu. Who the heck knows. I sure don't. I keep thinking about what happened that night and I still don't know what to make of it. It's pretty amazing to think that she might want to apologize to *me*, though."

They sat in silence, watching the dancing shadows cast on the wall by the newly awakened flames.

"It's getting late," Stu observed, with a glance at his watch. His voice sounded casual but his eyes were hopeful as they searched her profile. "I don't suppose you'd have any interest in staying over. And, no, I'm not kidding."

The color surged into her cheeks as Shannon's heart began to thump. She had guessed that this moment might come up one day and had been dreading it, with no idea how to respond when it did. She cared about Stu very much, enjoyed the time they had shared and admired his abilities as a producer. At least he wasn't like the men she had experienced early in her career: guys who wanted to take her out just so they could brag about sleeping with a TV star, even if all they had shared was dinner. Still...

An awkward pause ensued as she wondered what to say, and how to say it.

"They tell me sex has ruined more great friendships," she offered at last. "I'd sure hate to jeopardize this one."

"Yeah, and they tell *me* the best relationships start with friendship," he countered. "Maybe you shouldn't be so quick to say no."

"Aw, Stu," replied Shannon, only half kidding, "look at me. I'm the last person you'd want to start up with. I'm already committed—to my job. Go find yourself a nice girl who wants to settle down with a terrific guy. Besides, news people shouldn't wind up together anyway. Bad for the gene pool."

To her relief, he clinked his champagne glass against hers in resignation.

"Okay—for now," Stu said. "I'll just have to catch you in a weaker moment, I suppose."

"Good luck with that one," she replied, smiling to take the sting from her words. Her antique ruby ring glinted in the firelight as she tapped his glass in return. Dear Stu. Wasn't it obvious she was no good at romance? She couldn't even keep her professional life under control, never mind her personal life. No, she would be much happier growing old on her own, with her work to keep her occupied. Love was too hard. Too complicated. And clearly, not worth the trouble.

"Where did you get this little bauble?" he said, grabbing her hand to examine the ring more closely.

"Oh, it's just a little something I picked up the last time I was here. Pretty, don't you think? But it's the weirdest thing. Every time I put it on I feel like I should be in an old movie or something. I'll be crossing the street and reach down to pick up my long skirts—and then I realize I'm actually wearing jeans."

She laughed as Stu rolled his eyes.

"I know, I know, it's totally ridiculous. But I do like bringing it out sometimes, especially when I'm feeling festive."

She turned it proudly for his inspection. Happy for an excuse to touch her even for a moment, he took his time observing the delicate old-fashioned gold filigree clasping a square cut ruby, finally having to agree that it was indeed beautiful, perfectly suited to her coloring, perfectly suited to her style.

"It really does suit you. You must have worn it in a previous life."

"Yeah, right," laughed Shannon. "Back when I was Queen Victoria."

Stu reluctantly dropped her hand and forced himself to look away from her glowing face, her cheeks flushed from the fire, the mass of curls tumbling over her shoulders. He wished that he dared tilt her back over the pillows and kiss her until she was flushed and panting for him, kiss her until she was moaning and incoherent, as crazy about him as he was about her.

Instead he rose and offered a hand to help her up. "If you want to get out of here untouched, lady, you'd better go. Now." His voice was deep with resignation.

And so she did.

"Anything for me?" Shannon called to Jeremy the next morning as she wound through the newsroom to her desk.

Jeremy looked up from the stack of paperwork he was sorting from the bureau's overnight mail bag from New York. "Not a thing. Why? Were you expecting something?"

"Yeah. Like, a response to the sheet of story ideas I sent to David last week. Like some explanation for why I keep sending in great ideas and never get an assignment. Like—"

"Temper, temper," Stu cautioned as he came up behind her from the kitchen. He swung a brimming cup of coffee out of her way as Shannon pitched her bag to one side of the desk and flopped into her chair.

"Damn them..." she muttered. "Why are they keeping me around if they're not going to let me do anything?"

Across the room, Jeremy held up an assignment sheet and called out her name. "Here's something from the morning show for you. A five-minute segment for tomorrow. Live, no less. One-fifteen, our time, but you're young. A late lunch shouldn't cause you any harm."

Shannon's head swiveled toward him, her face changing in seconds from fury to delight. "The morning show? Great! I told David if he couldn't use the Falklands idea in prime time he should at least pass it on to the morning show folks. I've been begging him to do something on that for weeks now..."

Jeremy shook his head as he ambled across the room. "It's, uh, not the Falklands."

She looked at him in disbelief. "You're kidding. They want something on how Thatcher's going after the trade unions? I pitched that one too but I never dreamed they'd go for it..."

Another shake of the head from an increasingly uncomfortable Jeremy. He held out the sheet to her as if it had suddenly caught fire between his fingertips.

She grabbed it and began to read as Jeremy hastily retreated.

"Oh my God. Jeremy! You can't be serious." She turned to Stu, color draining from her face, and passed the sheet on to a second pair of incredulous eyes.

"Why Shannon, whatever are you complaining about?" Stu responded in a high-society falsetto, struggling to keep a straight face. "I think an interview with the Royal Family's milliner would be just lovely. You've been wanting some air time, haven't you? And here's a whole five minutes..."

Too upset to form words into sentences, Shannon stood and fumed for a minute. Then, seized by a sudden thought, she turned to Stu in triumph.

"Wait a second," she said, as a smug grin replaced the disgust on her face. "They'll have to get somebody else to do it. I won't be available. We've got our informant interview tomorrow."

"Ah—," Jeremy began to shake his head.

A noise at the door swiveled all three heads to attention. "Hi, gang," said Theo Tanner, wrestling a brown leather suit bag off his shoulder and onto the nearest desk. "Miss me?"

Shannon turned to Stu, her eyes widening in horror. "You don't think—" she began, clutching his arm.

"I don't know. Let me go talk to him," he said, his face suddenly grim.

"Theo! You look like a man who needs a cup of coffee. There's a great place downstairs..." Stu called as he made his way across the newsroom. He turned to give Shannon a reassuring wink, then clapped Theo across the shoulders and steered him out the door.

"Holy moly," Shannon said, as she ran a trembling hand through her hair. She collapsed into the closest chair, trying to breathe past the fear clogging her chest.

"Holy moly, indeed," Jeremy echoed.

# 7

"Stu! Where the hell are you? Where's Theo? And where have you been?" Shannon's voice was frantic, her fingers clenching and unclenching around the telephone. For the past two hours she had sat at her desk, afraid to move, her brain whirling with a thousand impossible thoughts.

No. They wouldn't. They wouldn't take this story away from her. Not even the new regime in New York would pull something this big from the person who had been working on it for weeks now. Not after depriving her of the anchor slot.

Oh, sure they would, another voice argued inside her head. Rusty may have wanted you but he's not the big dog any more. Theo is the network's chief correspondent now. Reardon's golden boy. He's the one getting the glamour shots these days. Not you. Not you, probably ever again. You had your chance, at the White House and Capitol Hill. Even got to anchor the big show. Once. But there's a new day dawning, Shannon girl, and you're not part of the grand plan any more. Remember? Your star rises and your star falls in television, and right now you don't have enough star power to lift a lightening bug off the ground.

"I'm at the airport," growled Stu. "If he's not at the bureau, I imagine Theo's checking in to his hotel." Even over the phone, she could guess his expression. Shannon had never seen Stu ruffled about anything, never even heard him raise his voice before. But the way he was spitting out his words now, she was just as glad not to be having this conversation in person.

"The airport," she repeated, uncomprehending.

"I'm going back to New York and talk to those bastards myself. It's unconscionable what they're doing and I'm going to have it out with everybody from Reardon to Rusty if I have to."

Shannon's body sagged lower into her chair. *Stu. Dear, loyal Stu.*

"Don't," she choked. "Don't get in trouble over me. It's not worth it."

"Of course it's worth it," Stu snapped. "And it's not just about you—it's about the integrity of the story. The integrity of this network, for that matter. Theo doesn't know dip about this and I'll be damned if I'm going to let him blunder through an interview and not ask the right questions, and, and—blow the biggest story of the decade because he's worried about how his hair looks."

The static of a flight announcement crackled over the receiver as Stu paused.

"Look. I've got to go. Do the morning show gig and don't worry about it. I managed to postpone the interview for a few days and I'll see you next week when I get back. Okay?"

"Okay," Shannon mumbled. She slowly placed the receiver back into its cradle, her eyes dazed.

Going live on the morning show was always stressful, especially for a segment so far afield from her interests and expertise. She wasn't surprised when sleep eluded her, even after Stu called to announce that he had an appointment the next afternoon, three o'clock New York time, with David Moore. As executive producer of the prime-time news, David was the first step on the management ladder leading ultimately to Jack Reardon and Rusty Parmalee. Despite the determined cheer in Stu's voice, the whole thing sounded like a waste of time. Observing how Theo preened around the newsroom yesterday afternoon, it was clear that the reassignment of her story—for that's how she thought of it, now—was a foregone conclusion. Who knew when she might get another opportunity to do something meaningful?

A few minutes after eleven o'clock she gave up, sat up, and reached for a book to try and lull herself into unconsciousness…

*She was on a train, when suddenly her grandmother appeared with a basket over her arm and a firm, almost scolding look on her face. Shannon was startled by the expression; Grammie Lib had guided by love and suggestion, always. But at the moment she was adamant.*

*"You're on the wrong one, dear," she said, with a concerned frown. "You need to get off immediately."*

*Before Shannon could ask directions to the right train, another woman opened the compartment door and sank into the seat opposite. She was young, with flaming red hair and mischievous blue eyes. "Don't tell her, Mama Lib," the woman chuckled. "Much better if she finds out for herself. Here's something to guide you, sweetheart: Espavo. It's a special word. Use it. Remember it. And you will keep looking, won't you, dear?"*

*She leaned closer to give Shannon a loving pat on the knee. Just then the conductor appeared and demanded a ticket, which she couldn't seem to find. He grew more and more impatient as she fumbled frantically through her bags and coat pockets, until finally he announced, "Well, then, I'm afraid we'll just have to toss you off, mum." Taking her by the elbow, he escorted Shannon to the back of the train. Dizzy and weak, she clung to his arm, her face bent over the tracks as they whizzed by below, the sound of his laughter echoing in her ears—*

"No!" she shouted. She was sitting bolt upright in bed, panting for breath, her heart pounding in terror. Shannon sat without moving for a minute, her ears cocked for the slightest noise around her, but she heard nothing. Everything had vanished into the fog—the train, the conductor, Grammie Lib, her mother—

Her mother? Well, the other woman had looked like the pictures of Diana in the family album. Shannon used to sit for hours when she was little, flipping through the pages, poring over the face of the woman who had given her life. She had been a beauty, this fairy-tale mother who only existed now in fading photographs and dreams …

A quick glance at the night-side table verified the time on her glowing travel alarm. Midnight. Thank God. Still enough time for a decent night's sleep, assuming she could get her brain to quiet down again. "Good Lord," she murmured to herself as she settled back into her pillow with a frown. "What was that all about? And that word again. Espavo? What the heck was that?"

"Ooh, yes, dear, the Queen Mum's awfully keen on feathers. And aren't these such a lovely color, too?" the Royal Milliner trilled. She was a trim woman, in her late fifties, Shannon guessed, with one of those unmistakable English rose complexions. She seemed delighted to show off her creations on American television.

Shannon picked up a hat rimmed with pale green feathers from the table at their knees, holding it so the close-up camera could get a clear shot.

"And this is the sample you made of the hat she wore to the Royal Wedding? Do you always do that, make a sample first?"

Shannon was trying to look pleasant as the interview progressed, but her face felt stiff, her smile mechanical. Over the past few hours her fury had dissipated to a dull ache inside. At the moment, she felt detached, a little unreal, as if she were sleepwalking through the landscape of a life she barely recognized as her own. She could only hope her inner turmoil at this latest blow to her professionalism, and her pride, didn't show on the air.

"—and of course now we're simply awaiting another Royal Wedding someday so that our little shop can spring into action again."

The milliner beamed at Shannon as she soaked up her moment of fame.

Shannon glanced past her shoulder to the floor manager, as he gave an urgent signal to wind up the interview and toss back to New York.

"As are we," she replied, trying not to let the sarcasm she felt creep into her expression. "Thank you so much for sharing your talents with us this morning." She turned to her close-up camera. "And now back to Marty and Jane in New York."

After the guest had been escorted off the set and the hot lights were dimmed, Shannon remained slumped in her chair. Her eyes were blank. Moving was too difficult to contemplate with a body that had gone numb.

She had managed to get through it, thankfully. She hadn't disgraced herself, been unprofessional in any way, no matter how much she wanted to scream. She might feel half-dead inside, but what difference did that make? The camera only cared about what it saw, and by now, she knew her craft well enough to fake her way through almost anything.

Shannon's eyes roamed to the dozens of lights suspended from the ceiling, past the massive studio cameras standing like so many gray ghosts, ready to be summoned into action. She had already envisioned how she would record her introduction to the investigative piece a few weeks from now, in front of a special news backdrop that proclaimed how important this story was. Already imagined the congratulatory phone calls from New York, the offers for a slot in the documentary unit, where she'd have the chance to report in-depth, on stories that really mattered. Now it would be Theo who got the credit. Theo's name would be attached to the story that had taken over her life for weeks, the story that had once again given her life meaning and purpose. And there was absolutely nothing she could do about it.

She closed her eyes in despair.

All at once she stiffened in her seat. Oh yes, there was something she could do. She could refuse to be part of the charade, part of a place where the Jack Reardons of the world were rewarded. Where they could use their power with no heart or conscience, with no one to stop them.

*But television is your life*, came an anguished whisper at the back of her brain. *What else is there?*

"I don't know," she said aloud. Shannon leaped to her feet, energized by her fury; propelled, somehow, to a future that might be uncertain but could hardly be worse than the one she faced here.

"But I am not doing this. I am done."

Her jaw set, she stalked into the newsroom, her long legs moving to her desk in strong, confident strides. It took less than a minute to fling her tote bag over one shoulder, scoop up her favorite lip gloss and the picture of her Dad from an inside drawer and drop them inside the smaller handbag she carried to match her suit. With a last look around to make sure she hadn't forgotten anything important, she brushed her hands together in a gesture of finality and headed for the exit.

"I won't be in tomorrow," she informed Jeremy as she swept past him. The assignment editor looked up in surprise. With Stu back in New York, he had skipped lunch to make sure the interview went smoothly. After it was over, he had expected a silent, even a sullen Shannon, but this woman looked ready to stand down an armored tank. His mouth was still open as she disappeared around the corner.

Across the room, Theo looked up from his newspaper with a knowing smile. He, too, had remained at his desk, hoping to witness a meltdown.

"Broads," he muttered, straightening the pages again with a snap.

April 11, 1982
Dear David,
By the time you get this, I'm sure you will have heard officially about my resignation. I just wanted to add my personal thanks as I depart.

You were the one who gave me my big break, an opportunity I will always remember with gratitude. It was you who sent me to the White House—and, I suspect, it was your doing that led to my getting to anchor last Christmas.

For all of that, I thank you. I don't imagine it's very easy for you at the moment, amid the new regime. But I wish you all the best and hope you can stay afloat. Journalism needs more people like you—and heaven knows, television surely does.

Sincerely,
Shannon Tyler

Shannon folded the note into a creamy envelope, licked a stamp and pushed it firmly into place. The die was cast now; all that remained of her previous life were a few loose ends.

At least the note to David had been easy to write. Another note was going to her agent, to inform him she was leaving and would let him know when she had a forwarding address. No problem with the remaining few months on her contract, she figured. If WWB had wanted her, they would have worked harder to keep her; so what if they didn't pay her? She had never been a big spender and by now had a substantial nest egg.

A longer letter to Stu had taken her most of the night to compose. She had posted it first thing this morning, before she lost her nerve. Knowing that he would call the instant word got out of her decision—even before the letter arrived—she instructed the hotel switchboard to tell anyone who inquired that she had checked out, destination unknown.

She glanced outside the window to see what the weather was doing. She was far too restless to stay in her room all afternoon; a walk would help push back the second thoughts that were jumping around in her brain.

Had it been a foolish gesture after all, leaving the only career she'd ever known—and for what? What was she going to do now? If television wasn't to be her life any longer, what would? Could she live without it—even more importantly, would she want to?

Grabbing an umbrella despite the sunshine overhead—this was London, after all, and the weather could change in an instant—she sighed as she punched the button for the lift. You have some serious thinking to do, young lady, she informed the reflection on the glass door, then stuck out her tongue at it. What the hell. She had had to reinvent herself before, hadn't she? Quitting the job in Atlanta hadn't been a sure thing, either, but then came the offer in

Washington. Surely something good would come her way again.

At the mail drop in the lobby, she hesitated, her fingertips drumming a rhythmic tattoo against the bold letters of David's address in New York. When the letter arrived on the executive producer's desk, it would mean her decision to leave the network was irrevocable. She stared at the address, waiting for something, someone, to stop her, to say, no, this had all been a dreadful mistake, that of course she belonged at the network, for the rest of a long and brilliant career. Of course they wanted her, needed her energy and her intellect.

Finally, she let the envelope fall on top of the others inside the box.

"I'm sorry, Daddy," she whispered as she turned away, biting her lip to stop its trembling. "I'm so sorry I let you down."

In another moment she was out the door and down the street, her body in motion but her brain on automatic. She walked on, faster and faster, until she was almost at a jog, with no idea where she was going or how she would know once she got there.

A few blocks from the hotel, she could see a news box at the curb and thought about crossing the street so she wouldn't be tempted to look. Yesterday she had been in such a rush to get to the studio she hadn't even read her customary half-dozen papers—and it hadn't killed her. Maybe if she didn't keep up with the news for a while her fixation with it, her need to know what was going on, would go away. After all, plenty of people didn't feel as if they had to know everything about everything, she reminded herself. Some people didn't even read a newspaper every day, although she still found that hard to imagine.

*I'll walk by it but I won't look*, she decided, turning her head as she passed. But her eyes caught a reflection in the window opposite, a reflection of huge glaring headlines. Her resolution forgotten, she stepped to the front of the news box.

"SPECIAL EDITION," the headlines screamed. "INVASION IN THE FALKLANDS—IT'S WAR."

War. Just like she'd told New York for weeks, trying to rouse the network's interest in a story about it. Now, finally, it had happened—and now she was in no position to say anything. Her platform, the front-row seat on history she had taken for granted for so long, was gone. Who knew if there would ever be another one?

Shannon shoved her hands in her pockets, lifted her chin and walked on, her steps slower and less confident now. Two blocks down the street, she brushed an errant strand of hair from her face and was surprised to discover that her cheeks were wet.

# 8

The advertisement had been running for weeks now, but Shannon had failed to pursue it. Things that sounded too good to be true generally were, in her experience, and this sounded idyllic. She had begun checking the ads not long after arriving, thinking it might be nice to have a weekend retreat in the country. Now, she urgently needed somewhere quiet to put her life back together, someplace she could be safe and anonymous, at least until she could decide what to do next.

"For someone who used to think she had it all figured out, life sure has been whipping you around lately," she sighed as she snapped open the *London Times*, trying to avoid reading news which only brought her heartache. There it was again.

*"Perfect for the writer, professor, or gardening enthusiast,"* the advertisement read. *"Quiet, private cottage on grand estate in the Cotswolds. £50/mo. Apply 01386 530900."*

Two hours later, she was speeding out of London in a rental car toward Burlingford, through some of the most breathtaking countryside she had ever seen. A mile or so before her destination, the view was so spectacular she had to pull over for a better look.

Spread below were acres of greenery, neat fields newly planted in spring crops, punctuated by quaint limestone farmhouses and long winding stone walls. The whole of it seemed untouched by time, as peaceful and serene as a medieval painting. Progress had apparently bypassed this place, leaving it much the same as it had been centuries ago. From a distance, certainly, it seemed the perfect place to heal a troubled heart, to try and make some decisions about a future that had once seemed so bright.

The rental agent looked to be in her eighties, so tiny she barely came up to Shannon's shoulder. "My daughter's business, dearie," Mrs. Satterfield explained as they piled into her car for the short ride to the cottage. "I'm just minding things for her while she's on holiday." Judging from her practiced patter, Shannon decided Mrs. Satterfield must have been showing the place a great deal lately.

"That's the big house over to your left, Braeburn House. The family was Scottish, originally, built the place in 1768. It's one of the area's finest Georgian mansions. Most of the main house is a luxury hotel now—estate taxes, such a shame, even the toffs can't afford to keep the old places up any more. The master keeps an apartment there and goes back and forth to Parliament. House of Lords, don't you know, doesn't have to lift a finger, but he's one of the few that actually works at it," she added proudly.

"Ah, and here's the Lady's Cottage," she concluded, bringing the car to a stop amid a hailstorm of gravel. To their right stood a white gingerbread Victorian cottage with a sweeping front porch and gabled windows.

Shannon climbed out of the car and tried to be discreet as she brushed off the clumps of dog hair covering her black pants. What was it with the Brits and their animals? She shook her head in annoyance, then put on a determined smile as she looked around.

The cottage was small enough to be cozy, large enough to be gracious and welcoming—exactly what she would have designed for herself if given the opportunity. Sunshine streamed into the front windows, with trees that shaded the back of the house and a lawn sloping gently down a grassy hill toward a large pond. Quiet, secluded, charming...

"What's wrong with it?" she asked, startling the agent in mid-sentence with the abruptness of her question. Mrs. Satterfield hesitated, then sighed and decided to be equally direct.

"I'm afraid it has a bit of a sad history, my dear," she confessed. "The lady who first lived here, long ago, died tragically. People have stayed in it since but no one for very long. There's talk around the village it may be haunted—but then, you know how people talk."

*I sure do*, Shannon said to herself, *and I don't believe a word of such silliness.* "Can we go inside?"

"Oh certainly, dear," replied the older woman, relieved and a little surprised that Shannon hadn't jumped back into the car with an immediate, "No, thank you." Most people heard the word "haunted" and would go no farther.

As Mrs. Satterfield pushed the front door open, Shannon drew in her breath with an involuntary gasp of pleasure and her first genuine smile in days.

A wide front foyer led to a living room paneled in dark wood—mahogany, she guessed, her new favorite—with floor-to-ceiling shelves spilling over with faded leather-bound books. Just beyond an ornate marble fireplace she could see a dining alcove and kitchen. Straight ahead, French doors opened to a stone patio overlooking the pond, and stairs to the left led to a spacious master bedroom with a sitting area and private bath. A tiny bedroom tucked under the eaves could be used for guests or as a study.

"It seems pretty lived-in for a place that's been empty for a while," Shannon commented, as she wandered through the rooms, trying to keep her excitement to herself.

"Well, since the last tenant departed, the master comes down sometimes to get away from the hustle and bustle of the big house," the agent explained. "Of course he wouldn't, once it was let."

Shannon turned to face her, not bothering to hide her amusement. "I certainly hope not," she said. "I don't mind a ghost but I'd prefer not to bump into another human."

The other woman shot an uncertain look at the beautiful woman with the sad eyes, wondering if she was making a joke. "You'll take it then?" she ventured.

"I will," Shannon replied. "How soon can I move in?"

Her first night at the cottage passed uneventfully; if there were any ghosts, she was too worn out to hear them.

She awoke to a brilliant blue sky overhead. Slipping into her favorite plaid flannel bathrobe, she padded downstairs and onto the spacious front porch. She stood there for a moment, hugging herself for warmth as she breathed in the scent of a newly awakening earth.

Stepping into the yard, she could tell by the growing intensity of a pale yellow sun overhead that spring was definitely on its way. Somewhat to her surprise, she was glad to be out of the city, glad to be away from the choking diesel fumes and crowded streets of London, glad to be here in the quiet of the country. There was nothing she had to do, nowhere she needed to be, no one she had to impress. No reason to put on makeup or straighten her hair or get dressed up. She turned back to the steps, noticing with a frown that the flowerbeds in front of the cottage seemed overgrown and neglected. What looked like rosebushes were choked with dead leaves from the winter that no one had bothered to remove. She shook her head and hurried back to the warmth of the cottage.

A quick search of the kitchen cabinets turned up a tin of tea and a well-used kettle. Figuring out how to work the Aga stove took a few minutes, but she was finally able to brew a cup before setting off to explore her new surroundings. Whoever had decorated the place had exceptional taste, she decided as she sipped. The furniture was comfortable and understated, several cuts above what you might expect for a furnished rental home. An overstuffed sofa covered in dark green velveteen sat in front of the massive fireplace, with armchairs in a subdued gold and green damask on either side. She rubbed her fingers over a creamy lampshade covering one of the porcelain lamps. Well, now. Silk. Much nicer than she would have thought. Her eyes moved around the room, taking in the round table covered in a burgundy paisley print, the neat stack of books on an end table, a collection of pastoral landscapes hanging at eye level around the room.

*Couldn't have done better myself,* she decided, *if I ever sat still long enough to actually decorate anything...*

Shannon sank into one of the armchairs, folding a leg beneath her. She pulled the bathrobe closer, shivering despite the warmth of the tea. She was so glad there was a working fireplace. She loved fires, and could imagine many a cozy winter evening sitting in front of one, here. Shannon stopped and drew up a little, startled by her thoughts.

*Whoa there, girl, you're acting like you're going to be here a while,* she scolded, *instead of just getting your life together and moving on...*

Her slim fingers tightened around the mug as she sighed. Why was it that she kept having to re-invent her life, to start all over, time after time?

"Wonder how many more tries it'll take before I finally get it right...," she said aloud, then caught herself. Uh-oh. Was she turning into one of those crazy ladies who went around talking to themselves?

Determined not to yield to the depression she felt lurking nearby, Shannon shook off her gloomy thoughts and crossed to the French doors leading to the stone patio outside. Her troubled eyes took in the lawn that sloped down to the pond, as the trees, their branches sprouting the first hopeful buds of green, rustled softly in a passing breeze.

*"Take your lesson from the trees," she remembered Grammie Lib's soft voice in her ear, "from the cycles of nature. God made the trees, my darling, just as He made all of us. Just like all the wonders of nature you see around you, we're born, we live, we wither and die--the same way the trees do every winter--and then, there they are, back again in the spring, even more beautiful than they were before. Just as we're reborn, to learn and grow, to do things better next time. It's God's lesson for us, every year. Don't you always feel happy in the spring?"*

*Ten-year-old Shannon Grace stared at her grandmother, listening intently but not really understanding what she was trying to tell her. Grammie Lib was on her knees, pressing gnarled fingers into the rich mulch around her favorite geraniums, her face turned in welcome to the warmth of an April sun.*

*"Whenever you feel sad, sweetheart, and I know you will, sometimes--all of us do," her grandmother had continued, turning to the little girl who squatted beside her, "come outside and look around. Look at all of God's wonders and mysteries, at the color of the grass, at the beauty of the flowers. If he cared enough to create all of these for us to enjoy --don't you think he cares about you, too? My darlin' girl, you were made by your Creator with the same love and attention to detail as when He flung the stars across a boundless sky, when He made the ocean rise and fall to the pull of a restless moon, and gave even the tiniest bug wings so it could fly. So don't you worry. He won't let you get so lost you can't be found ... "*

"Ah, Grammie Lib," Shannon murmured, the words choking in her throat, "I wish I could have your faith. You took everything that came with such grace, such wisdom. You embraced life; I'm barely stumbling through it, the best way I know how. Which, lately, hasn't been so hot, has it."

Downing a final sip of lukewarm tea, Shannon walked into the old-fashioned kitchen, rinsed out the mug, and positioned it carefully on the counter. Her eyes went to the clock. 10 a.m. Crossing her arms, she glared at its antique face. Only ten o'clock. An entire day still stretched before her with nothing demanding her attention, no deadlines, no wire machines to check as they clickety-clattered out an endless stream of news from around the world, no stack of newspapers to skim ... nothing.

"Okay, now what?" she shrugged, and had to laugh. "This is a new one, huh, girl." At the network, the problem had always been too much to do and too little time to do it in. Now, with all the time in the world, she had no idea how to fill it.

Then, remembering how forlorn and neglected the flowerbeds in front of the cottage had looked, she had a sudden inspiration. What the heck. She didn't want to stand around brooding all day. Maybe she would try it Grammie Lib's way. She had never done any gardening before but it couldn't be that hard, now, could it? At least it would be something to keep herself occupied, other than driving herself crazy wondering if she would ever work again.

She bounded up the stairs with more energy than she had felt in days, to finish settling in and get started on this new project. After folding her clothes into the wooden chest of drawers, Shannon lined up her toiletries inside a painted cabinet in the bathroom. Someone had added delicate stenciling around the edges, echoing the flowers on the border of the wallpaper. With its pedestal sink and lace curtains fluttering in the window, the room was dainty and feminine, with a charm that defied the passing of time. A brass pot filled with dried flowers was tucked into a corner shelf. A needlepoint sampler hung to the right of the mirror, just under the tank of an old-fashioned pull toilet, where she couldn't help but see it as she brushed her teeth.

She leaned in to examine the row of tiny stitches more closely.

"Be still," it read, "and know that I am God."--Psalms 46:10.

The verse was surrounded by two lines of carefully stitched flowers, although the scarlet and yellow of their blossoms were now faded by the years. At the bottom was a date: June, 1881, and what she supposed must have been the embroiderer's initials: A.D.

Two more pieces of needlework were framed on the wall behind her, also surrounded by flowers and with the same initials underneath.

"The truth shall make you free--John 8:32," said one; the other, "The kingdom of God is within you--Luke 17:21." Small as the squares of fabric were, each spoke of hours of painstaking effort.

Her fingers traced the letters and lightly rubbed the carving on the gilt frame. For a moment, she was spellbound by the link to whoever had created such beauty, 100 years ago.

Then, wrinkling her nose as she tried to imagine how long it must have taken her, Shannon's natural skepticism re-emerged.

"Boy," she observed, "you gals sure didn't have much to do back then, did you? I guess you didn't have much choice about being still."

She paused for a moment, wondering why these particular passages might have had special meaning to someone who lived so long ago. "Well, I agree with you about the truth part," she finally announced. "But I can't say I really get the other one. If there's a kingdom inside me, *I've* sure never felt it."

She raised an eyebrow at the thought, then shrugged and got back to work, tucking her empty suitcases into a tiny half-closet under the eaves of the second bedroom. Less than ten minutes later, she was on her way into the village to get some gardening tools and seeds for flowers.

On her first trip through Burlingford, Shannon had noticed what seemed to be a garden-supply store in the center of the little town. Getting there required some cautious steering as she tried to get the hang of driving on the "wrong" side of the road. Her first trip to the village had been from the city, on wide, well-marked roads, not these narrow little lanes that twisted and turned and terrified her. Rounding one corner, she almost slammed into a farmer guiding his sheep to pasture. By the time she pulled up in the narrow street at the front of the store, her armpits were damp with perspiration. Her fingers were clutched around the steering wheel so tightly she had to pry them away, one by one.

*Deep breath, Shannon*, she reminded herself. *Don't be afraid. You can do this. What was that word again from her dream? Oh, right. Espavo. OK, espavo. Just get on with it.*

She had to chuckle at herself as she climbed out of the car. *Really, Shannon? Magic words now? What are you, six years old? Oh well. Who cares, as long as it works...*

"I think I need a trowel, please," she said, newcomer-polite to the man standing behind a cash register, "and some advice. I'm going to be living nearby and I'd like to plant some flowers. But I'm not sure what, exactly. Can you tell me what might do well around here?"

John Sprague looked her up and down. As a rule he didn't care for Americans with their loud voices and clicking cameras, but this one seemed better than most. She had let her curly hair fall untamed onto her shoulders this bright spring morning, and the tweed sweater she had pulled on over a pair of slim jeans brought out the color in her cheeks and the bright green of her eyes. Her feet were appropriately attired in navy Wellingtons, so at least she seemed respectful of local custom. Such sad eyes, though; whatever could be troubling such a pretty lady? Whatever it was, he decided to help her.

"You must be the American, then, come to rent the Lady's Cottage," he said as he leaned across the counter, bracing his bulky frame against a pair of massive forearms.

*Damn*, she thought, unable to stop a frown. *There went her cover.*

"I am," replied Shannon, swiftly deciding to make the best of it. "But the cottage needs some color outside, don't you think? I've never done any gardening, though, and I have no idea what to plant."

"Well, then, perhaps I can help you," he said, guiding her to a display shelf loaded with seed packets.

By the time she walked out with more thanks and smiles, nods and waves, she had enough to plant the entire county in flowers. And John, somewhat to his surprise, had decided the new American lady might not be so bad after all.

Dropping her purchases into the front seat of her car, Shannon remembered that she needed cotton balls and toothpaste. Maybe by now she could even bear to catch up with the latest news magazines, she thought, as she made her way into the chemists'.

For the first few days after resigning from the network, she had continued to avert her eyes from the newspapers, resolving not to keep up with current events for a while, in the hope that it might make her abrupt decision to leave her job a little less painful. But with war now raging in the Falklands, her curiosity had quickly gotten the better of her. Every day she found herself glued to the BBC's World Service program. Being connected, after all, was what news was all about: knowing what was going on before everyone else did and then writing about it, telling the story of what was happening in her own words.

True, that was her old life and this was her new one, at least until she could figure out what to do next. But it wouldn't hurt to look, she decided, as she cautiously opened the door. She did love the chemists over here, with their colorful jumble of soaps and lotions and health tonics, all so quaint and distinctive as opposed to the sterile shelf after shelf of goods in the drugstores back home.

She was standing behind the magazine rack, having already selected the latest issue of *The Economist*, trying to decide between *Country Life* or the British edition of *Harper's Bazaar*, when a loud bang of the front door made her jump. Shannon glanced up to see a tall man, his dark hair streaked with silver, stalking toward the cashiers' stand at the back of the store.

"Mrs. Cox." From her spot halfway across the store she could hear a tense voice, whose owner appeared to be struggling to keep courteous. "I hope it isn't asking too much to ensure that your front curb remains clear of cars?"

"Of course not, sir, I beg your pardon, who seems to be there?" Mrs. Cox was almost stuttering with alarm. "It was quite empty this morning when I came in..."

"Well, it isn't now. Probably some ignorant tourist. But in any case I would appreciate very much if it could be kept open as we agreed." His voice was deep and distinct, each clipped word emphasized with an unmistakable air of authority.

Oh, God.

Shannon peeked around the magazines to the front door, her heart dropping to her knees. Sure enough, she was the "ignorant tourist" blocking the curb outside, but good heavens, why such a fuss over a parking space? She watched as he spun on his heel to depart, thought of owning up to being the offender, albeit by accident... and then decided that maybe now was not the time for True Confessions. She would be out of there as soon as he was gone, she told herself, but in the meantime, it was probably wiser to keep her mouth shut and her eyes firmly on the magazine rack in front of her. No reason to tick off the neighbors if she didn't have to.

All the same, she couldn't resist taking a look as he turned away from the cash register. Even in the midst of what sounded like a grown-up temper tantrum, he was strikingly handsome, broad-shouldered and muscular, with a tanned face that appeared too young for someone with such a full head of salt-and-pepper hair.

As he drew even with where she stood, he stopped short, suddenly aware—and chagrined—that someone else was in the store. He paused. Brilliant blue eyes locked onto emerald green ones for an electric moment; his, still sparking with barely restrained fury, hers, alive with curiosity.

She caught her breath, feeling a tug of recognition so strong it startled her, wondering if he felt the current flowing between them as strongly as she did. Perhaps so; it seemed as if one black leather riding boot hesitated for a moment. Then he was out the door, this time closing it carefully, too carefully, behind him. Shannon remained rooted where she stood, a little shaken by the encounter. Finally she lifted all three magazines off the rack and walked over to the proprietor.

"Oh dear," she said to Mrs. Cox, lifting her eyebrows in sympathy to the store's owner, "I guess I'll have to be more careful where I park next time. I'm afraid it was my car he was so angry about."

"Ah, don't worry luv, it's the only thing that makes 'im mad. Good reason, y' know, wot with the tragedy and all. Can't really blame 'im. I didn't know 'e was around today or I'd've have been more careful meself," the woman responded.

"What tragedy?"

"Well," the woman leaned forward and lowered her voice to a near whisper. "Five years ago, it was, his little Japanese wife was walking across the street with some of her pupils—she taught at the village school, don't you know—and a lorry driver came along and mowed her down, dead on the spot. Horrible thing," Mrs. Cox shuddered. " 'e hasn't been the same since. And 'e insists on keeping the entire curb, there, clear so it wouldn't happen again."

"Who is 'e—I mean, he?"

"You don't know, luv? That's Lord Michael, your landlord. You are the new tenant at the Lady's Cottage, aren't you?"

Shannon took a deep breath. What an awful story; no wonder he was upset.

She smiled her goodbye at Mrs. Cox without answering, pushed open the door to leave and then shrugged at her own foolishness. Clearly, she could forget about being anonymous here. No surprise, really, that her identity seemed already well known. Word obviously traveled as quickly through Burlingford as it did in any other small town.

She had forgotten what a novelty she must be: a mysterious American lady, arriving to rent a supposedly haunted cottage that no one else had been willing to try; a lady with no husband or children, no visible means of support, and no real reason to be here. All she had was the same deep sense she had felt since the moment she arrived, that this was precisely where she was supposed to be.

The next morning Shannon was down on her knees in front of the cottage. The warm spring sunshine felt delicious on her back as she busily turned up trowels full of dark rich soil for her new flower beds.

The clop-clop of horse's hooves and a shout made her swivel, shading her eyes to see who was disturbing her solitude.

"Hey, you there, stop it! You can't do that!"

Great. Her landlord. He sounded as if he was still in as bad a mood today as he was yesterday. He tossed the reins around an antique hitching post and covered the ground between them with a few strides to where she knelt, surrounded by piles of seed packets.

"And why not?" she replied, trying not to glare as she sat back on her heels and folded her arms across her chest. Her voice was as chilly as the morning air. Nobody spoke to her like that—not even at the White House, where people were often impatient, sometimes curt and in a hurry, but seldom really rude. And they sure hadn't been so impolite on Capitol Hill. Landlord or no landlord, damned if she was going to let this guy boss her around as he apparently did everyone else.

"Because," he explained, a little less urgently now that he saw she had stopped digging and put down the trowel, "there are flowers there already, if that's what you're after. We've had plantings there for decades. They should be sprouting up any moment now. That is," he paused, with every sign of enjoying her dawning embarrassment, "if you haven't dug them all up already."

"Oh my God, do you think I have?" she exclaimed, horrified.

"I don't think so, but let's see." Taking pity at her stricken expression, he knelt beside her, moving the trowel out of his way. His hands were strong and sure, she noticed, and much to her surprise, he even appeared to know what he was doing. Somehow she had never envisioned the local Lord of the Manor getting down and digging in the dirt.

"There, do you see?" he said, brushing away a chunk of soil to reveal the pale beige bulb underneath, then patting the earth back into place around it. "In a few weeks time you'll have the most glorious flowers in all of England sprouting here."

"I'm really sorry."

Her cheeks were still burning as she made an awkward apology. Of all people to look foolish in front of—

"I just like the inside of the cottage so much I wanted the outside to be beautiful, too. It looked pretty neglected."

"Well, it used to be quite splendid, but these days the gardening staff doesn't get down here much. They're so busy tending to the hotel they don't have time for anything else."

"Oh," she said, hoping her color had returned to normal. "Sorry."

"By the way," he continued, offering a hand to help her up, "I haven't properly introduced myself. I'm Michael Willoughby-Jones."

"I know. My landlord," replied Shannon, brushing her fingers against her jeans before shaking his proffered hand. "I'm Shannon Tyler. I guess I should probably offer you a cup of tea, now that you've saved your flowerbeds from destruction by the rampaging American."

His smile was so generous, so unexpected, that she was taken aback. His eyes seemed exceptionally warm today, a startling contrast in his tanned face, especially set off by such black and silver hair. No longer cold with anger, his eyes were a bright, almost robin's-egg blue. As blue as the spring sky, she thought dreamily, as they stood facing each other in the driveway.

Funny. She had never cared for blue eyes, especially. Jack Reardon had blue eyes. But this man's were different: welcoming, even... familiar, somehow.

"I'm afraid I can't stop today. I just came to introduce myself," he said, in a voice that had turned abrupt. Apparently he had decided to ignore the fact that they'd seen each other just yesterday. "I understand there are stories about in the village that the cottage is haunted, and I didn't want my new tenant to be frightened."

"Well, if there is a ghost, he or she has remarkably eclectic taste in literature," she responded. Okay, fine. He was just trying to be a good landlord. It had nothing to do with any interest in her. "Anyone who reads Dickens with a side helping of David Halberstam is okay by me."

"I'm afraid I'm your ghost there," he admitted. "I spent some time at the cottage a couple of weeks ago. Sometimes the activity in the main house gets to be a bit much and I like to retreat over here where it's quiet. But usually I remember to put the books back on the shelf."

Shannon said nothing but raised her eyebrows in a look filled with meaning.

"Of course, now that it's rented I wouldn't dream of disturbing your privacy," he added.

"Thank you."

"On the other hand, if you persist in rearranging the flowerbeds..." he threatened with a slight smile.

"Oh no, I promise I'll ask someone who knows what they're doing before I go digging next time," she replied, still mortified by her mistake. "But now what am I supposed to do with all these seeds?"

"Let me see, what do you have?" He bent to examine the stack of flower packets scattered across the blanket. "You've gotten good advice what to plant, at any rate. What if you put them by the pond? They should be happy in the sunshine down there."

"Where did you learn so much about flowers?" she inquired, unable to contain her curiosity. They strolled over to where his horse was waiting patiently, snuffling around the driveway in search of any grass that might be hiding beneath the gravel.

Michael's eyes turned remote, his mouth setting into a grim line.

"I spent some time with the gardeners here as a boy," he said in a clipped voice as he swung himself into the saddle. "By the way, do you ride?"

"I haven't since I was a kid, but I'd love to again."

He raised his eyebrows in mock surprise. "You were once a baby goat?"

She stared, mystified, then got the joke. Him and his damned British superiority, putting her down for a little American slang. She decided not to return the smile and this time her voice was formal. "Pardon me. I haven't ridden since I was a child."

Michael grinned as if he knew exactly what had set her off and was enjoying it. "Come up to the stables anytime you like. James will take care of you," he called over his shoulder, giving her a last wave as he set off down the driveway.

*I know you*, Shannon thought, her forehead creasing in a puzzled frown as she watched him leave. *Damn. Where do I know you from?*

# 9

Chastened by her nearly disastrous attempt at gardening, Shannon loaded up on horticultural books during her next trip to the village and asked the head gardener at Braeburn House for advice before she began planting around the pond. She was surprised by how much she was beginning to enjoy digging in the dirt. The fresh air seemed to help clear her head, and there was great satisfaction to be had, she discovered, in planting something and watching it grow. Besides, it helped pass the time. Between long walks through the countryside, gardening and riding in the daytime and reading at night, she was trying hard to keep herself occupied enough to fall asleep without too much difficulty by the end of the day.

Everyone she encountered in the village seemed nice enough, but her solitude felt comfortable and she wasn't really looking for friends. Talking about her old life was too painful and her new one felt more like a holding pattern than anything else. She could only read and garden for so long, after all, but what might fill her days from now on—what might make her busy and productive again—remained a mystery.

*Patience, patience, patience*, Shannon reminded herself, wishing she could be better at putting the idea into practice. *I feel like something good is coming. But when?*

Michael was right about the flowers. By July, she was rewarded with a dazzling display of color along the grassy slope from the house to the water's edge.

Since their official introduction at the cottage, she hadn't seen her landlord at all. Now that the Falklands crisis was over, he must be off traveling, she supposed, or serving on special committees for the Prime Minister. Or whatever a Lord did in his off time.

Although Shannon had been a whiz on Capitol Hill, quickly learning the often arcane inner working of Congress during her assignment there, she knew very little about how Parliament worked, and longed to ask. *It would be nice to talk politics with someone*, she thought. More than once she paused from her gardening to gaze across the pond to Braeburn House—but no, that would inevitably lead to questions she wasn't ready to answer and resurrect memories of her life at the network. She wasn't ready for that. At least, not yet.

Her resolution wavered when she opened the July issue of *The Economist* to find a lengthy profile of Michael inside. "One of the prime minister's chief advisers, and her main source of fresh thinking," they called him. Someone whose advice had proven especially valuable as Margaret Thatcher attempted to inject the British economic system with the same can-do spirit she so admired in the Americans.

"Oh my God," Shannon whispered, her jaw dropping as it suddenly hit her where she had seen him before. Of course he had looked familiar. He was the man she had caught staring at her outside Number 10 Downing Street last December, when she had been the human mike stand for the Thatcher press conference. Michael was part of the group waiting to go inside.

She whooped with laughter. Wouldn't he love to know that she was the person he had been admiring. Well, staring at, anyway; she only hoped it was with admiration.

On second thought, Shannon realized, her face sobering, her life in television was the *last* thing she wanted him to know. The last thing she wanted anyone here to know.

The hotel inside the big house seemed to run well enough without Michael's presence, but that was thanks to its manager, Henry Owencourt, whose crisp gray hair and ruddy face seemed perfect for the Beefeater Guards she had seen at the Tower of London. *All he needed was the red suit and a pikestaff*, she had grinned to herself the first time she met him.

Henry seemed especially well suited for the hospitality business, exuding an air of calm competence as he bustled around the grounds. She was puzzled and a little envious as she watched him, wondering how on earth he managed to get through life with such an air of ease and contentment.

Her landlord was a little more difficult to observe. One day when an errand took her inside the mansion, she paused to examine more closely the treasures collected over the past two hundred years. She wondered if Michael found it difficult to see his ancestral home and belongings ooh-ed and aah-ed over by a series of random tourists and paying guests. Maybe that was why he was so seldom around.

The ghost of Lady's Cottage she had been warned about had failed to make an appearance so far. Shannon had, however, awoken several times from extraordinarily vivid dreams of her mother. A recurring one found her on her knees in the flowerbeds outside the cottage, digging and digging for something—she could never figure out what. Her mother was standing over her shoulder, murmuring encouragement. "Keep going, dear," Diana kept urging. "You'll find it." But in the dream Shannon tossed handful after handful of dirt over her shoulder without making any progress. Finally, exhausted, she shouted, "I can't do it, mother! I don't even know what you want from me..." "And I haven't been of much help to you, have I? Forgive me," her mother said. "I'm so sorry. Forgive me..."

Her mother's pleading face and outstretched arms vanished into mist when she awoke.

*Forgive her?* Shannon wondered, once she had come fully awake. Whatever did she have to forgive Diana for? If anything, it was she who should be begging her mother for forgiveness. After all, if it hadn't been for Shannon's arrival, Diana would still be alive.

*Yes, and if it weren't for Jack Reardon and Theo Tanner, I'd still have a career—and I'll be damned if I ever forgive those two*, she frowned as she rolled over, punching the pillow into a more comfortable shape. It should only be their faces she was smashing.

As the days faded into weeks and the weeks turned seamlessly into months, her mood warmed from sadness to reflection, and even an occasional flash of joy. All were a welcome change from the anger and heartache that had been constant companions after her resignation from the network. Perhaps there really was something healing about this place, these people, who made no attempt to intrude on her life. Her new neighbors asked nothing of her, and treated her with casual courtesy instead of the awe and ass-kissing she used to get as a network correspondent on Capitol Hill. Or maybe it was just the opportunity to ponder her life in silence and solitude. "Be still," the sampler in her bathroom reminded her each morning. Good advice, it seemed. From time to time she had even felt herself smiling for no apparent reason.

She had begun taking a horse out from the Braeburn stables

every morning. She loved the freedom and exhilaration of galloping over the acres of pasture that surrounded the limestone mansion. Occasionally she would see another lone rider up ahead and her heart would quicken, hoping it might be Michael. But it never was, and she would scold herself for feeling disappointed. After all, she had only seen the man twice, and he hadn't been particularly friendly either time. There was certainly no reason to find him in her thoughts more often than was comfortable.

She would have been surprised to know that her landlord was keeping his distance deliberately, feeling as drawn to her as she did to him, but determined not to give in to it. Michael had been deluged with offers of female companionship after Mariko's senseless death. At first, to combat the ache of loneliness and loss, he had taken some of them up on it, but no one managed to capture his interest for long. Now, at thirty-six, he had no intention of starting up with anyone else. His life had settled down very nicely, thank you, and if it seemed a bit lonely and empty at times, if he found himself wondering occasionally what it would be like to have a partner again and maybe even a son to continue the legacy of Braeburn House, it was a thought that passed quickly enough. He and Mariko had tried to start a family, without success. Clearly, it seemed, children were not to be in his future.

On his weekends home, he was careful to avoid the cottage, although he kept track of his tenant's comings and goings through his hotel manager. He was not above watching her, discreetly of course, from an upstairs window that overlooked the stables. Every morning, regular as clockwork, Shannon would mount up, her hair pulled into a loose knot at her neck. For someone who had appeared so sad and reserved when they first met, she certainly seemed happy enough these days. *Couldn't be terribly intelligent, then,* he thought darkly as he drew back from the window, annoyed by his inability to stop spying.

In his experience, life was difficult, ready to break your heart at every turn, and nobody who was very smart could be that cheerful.

Oh no. Best to stay away from this woman; she was too dangerous by half.

Despite his resolution to stay away from her, Michael couldn't help himself one sultry August afternoon when he saw Shannon's name on an envelope atop a stack of letters by the front door. Phone service to the cottage had been erratic of late, Henry had informed him, and he had instructed Shannon to leave the hotel's number for messages in case anyone trying to reach her had trouble getting through.

"I'll take this one, Henry," he called to the manager, slipping the envelope into his pocket. "It could be urgent. I have to go by the cottage anyway to check on things."

*Do you really*, Henry grinned to himself, having noted for some time Michael's unusual interest in his latest tenant.

Michael knocked at the front door to the Lady's Cottage, but there was no answer. He opened it and stepped cautiously inside. "Miss Tyler?" he called softly, preferring not to disturb her if she were napping upstairs. Catching a flash of color outside through the French doors, he crossed to the patio and made his way down to the water.

The air was heavy, thick with the threat of showers. Shannon was stretched out on a blanket underneath one of the giant oaks a few feet back from the pond. A pitcher of lemonade, half full, sat on a small table nearby, the glass sweating little beads of moisture in the humid air. Bees hummed noisily in the flowerbeds nearby. He tiptoed closer, trying not to startle her awake, if in fact she was sleeping, but he couldn't resist the urge to watch her, close up, without being observed.

He paused a few feet from the blanket. As he had suspected, she was sound asleep, cheeks rosy in the heat, her head nestled into the crook of an arm. Her curly hair was fanned out around her face; her breasts rose and fell with the steady rhythm of her breath, beneath a lemon-yellow dress that fell to mid-calf of her shapely legs. A pair of sandals anchored the blanket's edge. Even from here, he could see that her feet were long and slender, with pale pink polish on the toes. A straw hat with a headband of pink and yellow rosebuds lay at her side, next to a stack of books.

Now that he was here, Michael was embarrassed to be watching her so intimately, especially without her knowledge, but found it impossible to take his eyes away. She was even more striking than he had remembered from their previous encounters. Something stirred in him as he stared at her, a deep, half-remembered emotion from somewhere, long ago...

He swallowed hard and clenched his fists to keep himself from lying down next to her, wanting to ease his body around hers as she dozed, wondering how it would feel to curl himself around her tantalizing curves, to cup his hands around the fullness of her breasts, to explore the narrowness of her waist, the soft skin of her arms and thighs, to be waiting by her side when she opened her eyes. He smiled as he imagined her reaction if she were to awaken to find him bending over her, like Sleeping Beauty coming back to life with his kiss: would she be furious? Astonished, certainly—but responsive, too?

*You bloody idiot*, he scolded himself, shaking his head to snap out of it, *aren't you a little old for fairy tales?*

Finally drawing the envelope from his pocket, he scribbled a quick message on the front and slid it onto the blanket next to her. With a final lingering glance, he backed away as silently as he had come.

An hour later when she awoke, with the strangest sensation that someone had been there with her, Shannon was only a little surprised to find an envelope at her elbow. "My compliments. MW-J," it read, in an uneven scrawl next to her name.

# 10

Shannon clicked the telephone receiver impatiently, swearing under her breath as she failed to hear the reassuring hum of a dial tone. Just what she needed, for the phone to go out—again, for the second time this week—just when she was cross-eyed with anxiety about her father.

The wait for news from home had been interminable. Ben Taylor had made an appointment with a specialist in Atlanta after a routine physical exam uncovered something that could be ominous. What, exactly, he hadn't explained when she had called in response to his message two nights ago. By now she was trying hard not to panic. Given the time difference, it was going to be impossible to find out what the doctor had said today, unless—

Her decision made, she raced upstairs to exchange her jeans and tee-shirt for something more presentable to wear inside Braeburn House. Henry Owencourt was always immaculately turned out. It wouldn't do to appear ill-kempt when she was on the doorstep of a five-star hotel begging to use the telephone, although she was sure he wouldn't mind her asking. Slipping into a pair of khakis, white oxford shirt and navy blazer, she tied back her unruly hair and set off down the long gravel driveway to the limestone mansion across the pond. For once she was too caught up in her worries to admire the fragrant greenery and twilight hush of the countryside as she hurried along.

"Thank goodness, they're still awake over there," she sighed in relief from the crest of the hill. The lights of Braeburn House beamed invitingly from the imposing floor-to-ceiling windows. Nine o'clock did seem a little late to be barging in anywhere, even if it was a hotel. And even if it was her landlord's responsibility to offer a working telephone, whether he was home or not.

Shannon was glad to see a friendly face behind the antique desk where Henry usually greeted the hotel guests. "Hi," she said to the young girl who seemed to be in charge tonight. "I'm the tenant in the Lady's Cottage. Do you know where I can find Henry?"

"Certainly, mum. He's there, in the library," the girl replied, pointing across the hall.

Despite her worry, Shannon still caught her breath at the doorway. The magnificence of this historic house never ceased to amaze her, with its elaborately carved moldings, priceless Oriental rugs and inlaid furniture, standing now as silent reminders of a slower and more gracious past. Generations might have come and gone here, but their possessions remained as silent witnesses to the power and ease that had surrounded them.

Henry sat in deep contemplation over a marble chess set next to the fireplace, so lost in thought he didn't take note of her until she spoke.

"That's a game you need a partner for, isn't it?" she asked. Her voice was gentle as she took in the droop of his shoulders. Henry always seemed so cheerful; she couldn't help but wonder what private sorrow had overtaken him.

"Oh, Miss Tyler," Henry exclaimed, leaping to his feet. "I beg your pardon, I didn't hear you come in. You're quite right, of course," he added, his voice wistful as he glanced back at the table, "I used to have an excellent partner, actually. My wife Mary. Thirty-eight years we had together, until I lost her last spring. We used to have a quiet game every night before bedtime."

"I'm so sorry," Shannon said. Imagine having someone by your side for that long. No wonder he looked downcast. "You must miss her very much."

Henry sighed, and with an effort put a smile back on his face. "Ah, well. I mustn't burden you with my difficulties. How may I help you?"

"The telephone at Lady's Cottage seems to be out again, and I really need to make a phone call to the States. Is there one here that I could use?"

"Certainly. Allow me to offer you the privacy of my office," replied Henry. "It's just across the way."

"You know...," Shannon began, as she preceded him to the door, "my dad taught me to play chess when I was little. It's been years, but if you're looking for someone..."

Henry brightened. "Would you, ma'am? I'd be delighted to have a regular game again. And I would be even happier with the company."

"You know something?" she replied, her voice surprised as she turned to face him. "So would I."

In the weeks that followed, Shannon and Henry's chess game became a nightly event. Each evening at nine, after the guests had retired to one of the drawing rooms for brandy or a book, Shannon would slip into the Big House, as she thought of it privately, and join Henry at the chessboard. Lonelier than he had realized since losing his wife, Henry declared that their game had become the high point of his day, and, she realized, of hers. History, current events, the quaint customs of each of their cultures, a detailed dissection of each of the characters who peopled the village, were all topics to be shared and laughed over.

In a shorter time than she would have thought possible, she found herself confiding in Henry about personal things as well, especially her concern about her father. Ben Taylor's letters remained cheerful and upbeat, with only an occasional reference to the limitations of his aging body. Her father insisted that whatever had concerned his doctors earlier wasn't worth worrying about. After a series of probing questions, Shannon finally decided to take his word for it. Night after night, Henry listened, and nodded, and murmured something reassuring, although often it was not his words that mattered so much as his willingness to talk about whatever might be bothering her.

Unaccustomed to reaching out to alleviate someone else's pain, Shannon found her own heartache over her botched career relieved in the process. The prospect of companionship each night gave her something to look forward to every day, and she was grateful that Henry apparently found her company amusing enough that he was willing to overlook her deficiencies as a chess player.

They had just set up the board for a new game one evening when Henry's eyes were drawn to the window. Arm in arm, a young couple outside was taking an after-dinner stroll through the manicured flowerbeds. As Henry watched, the man bent down to select a rose, then turned to his companion for her approval. Her face was luminous as she turned glowing eyes to his; despite the fading light, the very air around them seemed to shimmer. Chuckling, the man brushed the velvety pink blossom across her cheek, then tucked it behind her ear, the two of them wrapped in a cocoon of happiness so intense it was palpable. The man folded her hand into the crook of his elbow and gave it a possessive pat as they sauntered off. Even from a distance, the young woman's contented laugh could be heard wafting behind them in the soft summer twilight.

Henry sighed as he turned back to the chessboard. Shannon glanced over to see what had caught his attention outside, scowling as she took in the retreating couple. Her voice was impatient as she prompted, "Your move."

"Sweet, aren't they," Henry murmured, still caught in the spell of the romantic pair outside. "So in love..."

"Oh, yeah. Definitely sweet. At least until he sees her without her makeup on and she finds out how loudly he snores."

"Miss Shannon!" Henry stared at her in disbelief, then chuckled. "I don't believe it. You're as bad as Michael. Every female on this island has been after him for years—stunners, most of them—and all he can do is shrug and say 'Thank you very much, not interested.'"

"So? Maybe he's right."

"You cannot be that cynical."

"And *you* can't be that soft."

Turning his attention to the board, Henry was silent.

"My Mary and I were like that couple, every day, 'til the last breath she drew," he offered at last.

"Really? What was she like?"

Shannon lightened her voice, anxious to change the subject and especially eager to learn more about Henry's late wife. She had yet to hear her name mentioned in Burlingford with anything other than reverence. To hear Mrs. Cox at the chemists' tell it, Mary Owencourt—"Oh, and Henry, too, of course," she had added quickly—were the glue that held the village together.

Although they had no children themselves, Mary and Henry made all of Burlingford their family, and they loved and looked after everyone in it with a single-minded devotion. It was the Owencourts, said Mrs. Cox, who were always first on hand to congratulate the newborns and then keep a sharp eye out as the little ones grew up; to notice who was sick and might be cheered by a visit; to pop by with extras from the garden for a family having a rough time of it. They were always available to string garlands of sweet-smelling flowers and evergreens around the church, whether for holidays or the occasional wedding. And, finally, it was Henry and Mary who could always be relied upon to comfort the bereaved.

Having heard none of this directly from Henry, however, Shannon leaned closer in anticipation.

"My Mary? Oh, dear, how do I begin to describe her." Henry removed his hand from the pawn he'd been about to advance and leaned back in his chair, his face alight with memory. "Well. She was Irish, for one, and if you know anything at all about the Irish and the English you can imagine how hard it was for her to come to a little village like this, where everyone's known each other for the past three hundred years or more. Bad enough to be an outsider, ten times worse to be the kind of outsider she was. But Mary always smiled and didn't notice the slights that came her way, until eventually they stopped. People only have power over you if you let them, she would say, and she was determined not to let them. She'd forgive anyone anything."

"Really," Shannon said, with a start. That was an ability she wouldn't mind having, for sure. Maybe then she could stop having all those dreams about her mother that still woke her occasionally in a cold sweat. All those evil thoughts about Reardon and Theo...

"How'd she manage that?"

Henry regarded her steadily, wondering what might lie behind the question.

"When I asked her about it once she said that if Jesus could forgive the people who were crucifying him at the very moment they were doing it, it was little enough for us to forgive whatever hurts and slights might come our way. I don't know how she figured that out at such a young age, but she was absolutely right. It's not the other person who's wounded by your anger and hatred, Miss Shannon, it's you.

Most of the time they don't even know you're furious with them and wouldn't care if they did. All it does is eat *you* up, inside. That's why it isn't worth doing. Why give someone else the power to cause harm to you—especially when it's you that has the ability to stop it? Why let someone else spoil your life and make you miserable? Your life is precious, every day of it—every moment of it—and you shouldn't let anyone keep you from enjoying it. That's how my Mary saw it, at any rate, and over time I began to see it that way, too."

Across the chessboard, Henry noticed that Shannon's doubtful scowl had smoothed a little, although at the back of her eyes there still flickered the same wounded look he had often observed over the past months. Whatever had hurt her so badly, he thought, she managed to hide it fairly well, most times. She certainly seemed more cheerful now than she had when she had first arrived in Burlingford. But Henry could see that sometimes even her liveliest smile failed to make it as far as her eyes, and he couldn't help but wonder what had put the sadness there.

"My grandmother used to say that," Shannon murmured, more to herself than to him. "That life was a gift and not a burden..."

"Oh, well." She turned back to the chessboard and sighed. "Maybe one day I'll believe it too. Now—are you going to move or not?"

The following Friday, it was her turn to be lost in concentration over the chessboard, until a slight noise caused her to look up. Over Henry's shoulder she could see Michael tiptoeing stealthily behind the hotel manager, his eyes sparkling with mischief, one finger across his lips to silence her. This was a surprise; what was he doing home—especially acting like a ten-year-old let out on holiday?

Michael paused to examine the chessboard. Henry, deliberating over a move, was oblivious to his presence. He jumped at the sound of his employer's warning voice behind him.

"I wouldn't, if I were you," Michael cautioned. "One more move and she'll have your bishop."

Having kept one hand on the horseman, Henry was able to replace it where it had been before without penalty. Shannon registered her indignation in a loud protest. "Hey, no fair. That's two against one. Get your own game if you want to play!"

At her half-serious, half-joking rebuke, Michael's smile vanished.

"My apologies," he said, his voice cold and formal. He turned to reposition an antique inkwell one inch to the right on the table behind them, as if that were the real reason he had walked over.

"I had forgotten you Americans were so competitive," Michael added. "Perhaps I should have offered my assistance to you, instead."

About to apologize for the sharpness of her tone, Shannon could feel her face grow warm as she bit back a sarcastic reply. "That's very kind of you, I'm sure," she replied after a moment, in a tone that hid sarcasm under ostentatious good manners, "but I can't say I would have taken it. I can make my own mistakes, thank you."

"So I see." He looked again at the chessboard, then met her eyes with a pointed look.

"Besides," Shannon continued, her words sounding more hostile than she intended, "I would think you of all people would know the rules. Advice during a game isn't allowed, no matter who gets or gives it." Michael raised one eyebrow and acknowledged her comment with a cool nod.

Shannon bit her lip and tried not to glare. She was bitterly disappointed. For weeks she had tried to get Henry at a disadvantage and looked forward to teasing him about it, but now he had been alerted to the opening she had been about to exploit.

Henry's head had been bouncing from Shannon to Michael and back again during this exchange, as if he were at Centre Court for the finals at Wimbledon. He was so exasperated he wanted to smack both of them. Here they were, two of his favorite people, young and attractive, both of them; now *why* couldn't they get along any better than this? Shannon had already confided in him about how they'd met at the chemist's, so he could understand why she might find Michael's intrusion annoying and perhaps the man himself, a little intimidating. But why couldn't his employer, the young man he had helped see through boyhood into adulthood, the little boy he had loved as if he were his own—why couldn't Michael seem to behave with his usual civility? Especially to such a lovely young woman...

"It won't happen again, I assure you." Michael nodded, his face stiff. He found a chair at the far end of the library, just out of Shannon's line of sight, and loudly snapped open the *Financial Times*.

Shaking his head at the vagaries of the young, Henry turned back to the chessboard.

"Henry," Shannon murmured a few minutes later, careful to keep her voice low enough not to be overheard. "Is he still in here?"

"Who?"

"You know who. Michael."

Henry glanced over to where Michael sat, seemingly absorbed in his newspaper. "Why, yes, he is, as a matter of fact. Looking quite like a little boy who's been told by the grownups to run off and play."

Shannon sighed. That's what she had been afraid of. Although she couldn't see him, she could sense his prickly feelings radiating from across the room. He probably hadn't meant any harm. Maybe he had been looking for company, just as she had, with Henry. And here she had snapped at him and made him feel unwelcome, an intruder on their fun—and in his own house, too.

From its place in the corner, a massive grandfather clock began chiming the hour, the rich sound muted from all the decades it had echoed across this very room.

"Ten already?" Henry inquired. "Time does fly over a chessboard, doesn't it, my dear. Especially when the company is as charming as yours."

Shannon rose with a smile as she returned the compliment. "And yours. Same time tomorrow, then?"

"I shall count upon it," he replied, deciding to linger over the board for a moment longer, just in case she and Michael wished to speak again before she left the room. Sure enough, Henry noticed from the corner of his eyes, she had stopped on her way to the door. He rubbed his chin and pretended to be absorbed in studying his next move.

"I'm sorry if I was rude earlier," she said, pausing in front of Michael's chair. His face was so handsome as he lowered the newspaper that she had to restrain herself from leaning in for a closer look. Try as he might to hide it, he did look hurt, as she had suspected. Still, his sea-blue eyes were cool as he looked her over, as if he had no idea who she was or where she had come from.

"I didn't mean to run you off or make you feel unwelcome," she continued, her determination to smooth things over beginning to falter. This was turning out to be harder than she had thought. A couple more sentences and she might melt into the faded rug beneath her feet.

"I can assure you if I had wanted to stay, I would have," he replied. "It is my house, after all."

She studied him for a moment longer, wondering if he really was as arrogant as he sounded. Or maybe, without meaning to, she had hurt his feelings even more than she realized.

*You, of all people, should know how much it hurts to be left out of things*, Shannon thought—and as she did, she had a sudden inspiration.

After a swift glance around the room to make sure no one was there but the three of them, she widened her eyes, clasped her hands to her chest and put on her sweetest, most syrupy Southern drawl, the one that had never failed to bail her out of a tight spot. "Why, so it is, and what a puhfectly chahmin' house it is, too," she exclaimed, lifting her head to take in the entire library in rapt admiration. "I cain't begin to express what a pleashuh it is foah mah li'l ol' country self, jus' bein' in the presence, heah, of all you fine folks from the royalty and such. I tell you, suh, I am truly honored!"

Shannon winked at Michael's startled face, placed the back of her hand against her forehead and swept from the room with a theatrical flourish. Behind her she could hear a shout of laughter from Henry—or was it two shouts?

# 11

"Henry, I need to get to Heathrow as quickly as possible. Do you know if anyone's heading that way any time soon, or would I do better to just drive there myself? The thing is, I don't know how long I'm going to be away—or where to park—"

Shannon's face was pale as she stuck her head into the hotel manager's private office, her usually warm voice thin and strained. Henry noted both with concern as he hurried to help.

"Certainly, Miss Shannon, let me see what the schedule looks like for service to the airport today. Nothing wrong, I hope?"

"My father's having emergency surgery, I just got a call from my aunt that I need to get home right away, I've thrown together a suitcase but I don't know what time the flights are or how long it'll take to get a reservation—" She took a deep breath as her voice began to wobble.

Over her shoulder, Henry gave a slight nod to Michael, who had appeared behind her in time to catch the anxiety in her last few words.

"Is there a problem?" he inquired.

"Yes, I need to get to the airport as quickly as I can." She turned, grateful for the concern in his voice.

"I can take you to Heathrow, if you like. I have to go into London this afternoon anyway," he lied. "Really, it's no problem."

As fiercely independent as she was, as much as she hated feeling indebted to anyone for anything, for once it was easy to accept an offer of help.

"Oh, would you? Thank you so much."

"Did I understand you to say you don't have a reservation?" Henry asked.

"Yes, I figured it was more important to just get there and then I'd see when the next flight to Atlanta took off. I think there's one around eight o'clock tonight but I'm not positive."

"I'll call ahead and make all the arrangements, my dear," Henry assured her. "Just ring me once you arrive and I'll fill you in on what's what."

With a final, heartfelt, "Thank you, Henry," from Shannon, and a quick stop by the cottage to pick up the suitcase she had thrown together earlier, they were off.

As Michael's silver Jaguar rolled through Burlingford toward the highway, Shannon willed herself not to panic even as every fiber of her being strained toward Heathrow. The message from Aunt DeeCee had been brief and to the point: "Your father is at DeKalb General. Emergency surgery. Can you come?"

Noticing her clenched fists, Michael said in a voice he made as calm and reassuring as possible, "Hardly any traffic, fortunately. You'll be there with time to spare."

She nodded, turning a blank face to the window. She hated feeling so panic-stricken, so vulnerable and alone. Too much had happened in the past year; it was hard to face yet another blow to her hard-won equanimity. But here in the intimacy of the car, Michael seemed the epitome of kindness and concern. So much so, she didn't quite know how to handle it.

"Nice car," Shannon ventured at last.

"Thank you." Michael's voice was noncommittal, as if he

realized it was an effort for her to make conversation and wanted to spare her the necessity.

"It's the '68 model," he added after a moment. "A true classic. A few more years and it'll be an antique."

"Ah," replied Shannon, wondering if she was supposed to know that. The car was polished to such a silvery gleam she wouldn't have taken it for anything other than brand new.

She looked down and sighed, trying to focus on almost anything other than the anxious rumbling inside her brain. An idle glance around the car's beige leather interior landed her gaze on Michael's legs on the seat beside her, at thighs that were long and ridged with muscles. Even beneath a pair of faded khakis they seemed solid, somehow. Powerful. The rolled-up sleeves of his white cotton shirt revealed a pair of sturdy bronzed forearms and long fingers wrapped around the steering wheel. Nice nails, she noted, short and immaculately clean; a gold ring of some sort glimmered from the pinky on his left hand. He had an aquiline nose, very aristocratic, she decided, with high cheekbones and a firm, sensual mouth. Such a young face, though, to have so much silver in his hair. Other than the soft leather of the Italian shoes he wore without socks, the understated but clearly expensive gold watch on his wrist, there was little about him that told the world he was who he was... except for an indefinable—something— that spoke of generations of good breeding...

"Did you find it?" A lighthearted voice broke into her thoughts.

"Find what?"

"Whatever you were looking for at such length. Or do I have a bug in my ear, perhaps?"

"No," she replied, a fierce blush rising from her neck to her hairline. "I'm sorry. You're right, I was staring. It's just that I... haven't seen you all that much and I was curious. You're a very mysterious person in the village, you know. And Henry's as close-mouthed as they come, at least about you."

Michael laughed. "They do love to talk, don't they?"

"You don't mind?" she said, with a perplexed frown. "I'd hate it if they were talking about me."

"But they do talk about you, all the time," he assured her, still chuckling. "You're the mysterious American lady, after all. I'm old news by now. People are always going to talk about other people, especially when they don't have anything better to do. Surely you know that."

"I suppose," she admitted. "And I guess I don't mind what people say, as long as it's true. I just don't like it when people make things up about you, or judge you on what they've heard instead of what they know."

He quirked an amused eyebrow at her but didn't respond.

"You're in public life," Shannon continued. "Don't you get angry when you're the subject of idle gossip? When there are stories about you that tell the world—well, that go into your personal life, too?" The article in *The Economist* had been fairly discreet—at least by American standards—but she had been surprised by its reference to the tragedy that had killed his wife, and wondered what he must have thought of it.

His answer was a dismissive shrug. "That's just the press. You get used to it. Nosy bastards have to have something to write about, I suppose."

Shannon averted her eyes, hoping he couldn't sense her discomfort. He was probably right about her former profession—some elements of it, anyway. Still, it was difficult not to feel defensive. Good thing she hadn't mentioned what she used to do for a living.

"I have to confess, I'm curious about why you're working with Thatcher," she said, swiftly changing the subject. "She's never been *my* cup of tea, but you seem to get along with her pretty well."

"Well," he began, his eyes flickering to the side mirror as he changed lanes and downshifted the Jaguar, "she wasn't mine either, at first. But I care very much about this little island, and it certainly wasn't doing very well before she came along. I think it's time we were all roused a bit. Time we thought a little less smugly about our place in the world and more about how we might contribute to it. I suppose I could have remained on the sidelines, wringing my hands and moaning over the loss of the Empire's glory. I chose to see if I could help, instead. In the long run, I believe I'll be glad I did."

"That's admirable of you," she said.

His eyes narrowed, wondering if she was making fun of him.

"No, really, I mean it," insisted Shannon. "It's so much easier to just cut and run when things get unpleasant."

She paused, as if hearing herself for the first time. Ouch. Was that what she had done? Given up on her profession instead of trying to make it better?

"For some, perhaps. Not for me."

"But the criticism doesn't bother you," she persisted. "You really don't mind being talked about."

"Perhaps it bothered me, once. Long ago. When I was young and thought that everyone was immensely interested in everything I said or did. I finally realized that most of the world was pretty well focused on its own concerns and that what I did or didn't do, and what people said or didn't say about me, was actually of very little importance. Let life give you a real whack and you quickly put gossip in its proper perspective."

Well. He was certainly right about that. Shannon squirmed, remembering with some embarrassment how she had talked about Michael with Mrs. Cox at the chemists. Was that gossip, too?

"You see?" he continued, as if reading her mind. "No doubt

there's a great deal that people have rushed to tell you about me." He smiled as he read the answer in her face, which again had turned crimson in response.

Damn *it*, she said in silent frustration. Why was she acting like an awkward high school kid? She was a grownup now; she had interviewed presidents, and prime ministers, and kings...

"It's the penalty one pays for not being like everyone else, Shannon. Don't let it bother you, or you'll be twisted up in knots for your entire life."

She digested the comment without responding, surprised by the insight and touched by the concern that seemed to have prompted it. From their previous encounters she wouldn't have thought him capable of much empathy.

For the rest of the trip, she stared out the window in thoughtful silence as the traffic grew thicker and the signs pointing the way to Heathrow more frequent. She was surprised by how agitated and rushed everyone seemed. By now, she had grown accustomed to a more languorous pace in Burlingford. Accustomed to it, and, increasingly, fond of it.

"Ah, here we are," Michael announced, pulling next to a sign that read British Overseas Airways Corporation. "You do know what BOAC really stands for, don't you?"

She shook her head as he jumped out, beckoning to a porter, and came around to open her door.

"Better on a camel!" was the cheery answer, as Michael handed her suitcase and a five-pound note to the porter, along with instructions to make certain Miss Tyler made it to her plane.

With a laugh and a quick "Thank you!" over her shoulder, Shannon picked up her carry-on bag and headed for the door. Finally—she was here. In a few more hours, she would be home, able to find out for herself what was what with her father. From the cheery tone of his calls and letters all summer, she hadn't imagined that surgery would even be necessary, much less emergency surgery.

At the entrance to the terminal, she caught a last glimpse of Michael as she entered the revolving door. Whirling around as she exited, she was startled to see his long frame still propped against the Jaguar, arms folded across his chest. He was too far away for her to read his expression, but it was apparent that he was waiting until she was safely inside. He nodded when he saw her looking. Then, with a final wave, he was gone.

On the flight home, she replayed their conversation in the car again and again, dissecting every comment and nuance. She had been grateful at the time for what seemed like nothing more than a distraction, but in retrospect she found it even more thought-provoking. How interesting that he could be so detached and indifferent to the opinions of other people. How nice if she could do that, instead of trying to live down—or live up to—what other people thought. What did he know that made him feel so secure? Or was he just so cold and removed from everyone it didn't matter to him...

And what about his decision to work with Thatcher? Was that the wiser choice, to try and improve where you were instead of running away because it wasn't perfect? Was that what she had done at the network? Maybe she had just been in the wrong place to begin with, and for the wrong reasons. In the beginning it had been enough to be a star, to be acknowledged as someone special. But not now. Somehow, being famous for its own sake didn't seem so important any more. Still, what a shame to have learned her craft so thoroughly and not be able to practice it. Maybe one day, at the right time, in the right place, there might still be something for her to do in television—if only she could figure out what it was.

Somewhere over Newfoundland she rummaged for a pen and notepaper and began drafting a note to her old friend, now in public television. Steve Mapping would be surprised to hear from her, she knew. After all, she hadn't seen him since the Thatcher press conference, months ago. Still, it was worth a try.

"And I'll just cast my fate to the wind," she sang under her breath. Shannon nodded to the clouds outside her window as she tapped the pen against the tray table, waiting for the right words to come. A surge of excitement from somewhere deep within gave her hope that they would.

Even at 8 p.m., the sticky heat of Georgia in August felt like a furnace blast as she stepped outside the air-conditioned cool of the Atlanta airport.

How odd to be back, tooling along in a rented car down streets that seemed only dimly familiar now. After so many months in England, it even felt a little strange to be driving on the right side of the road.

*Hello, Atlanta, you've grown so much since I was here,* she thought, looking around in affectionate wonder at half a dozen new skyscrapers filling in the city's skyline. And look at all this traffic—even in August, when anyone with any sense was either on vacation or already at home.

As she pushed the elevator button at DeKalb General Hospital, Shannon studied the other occupants, feeling conspicuously foreign in her jeans and white cotton shirt. Despite the long flight, her navy blazer was still Burberry-crisp, her hair neatly tied back off her face. She chuckled inwardly that she used to worry about being unlike everybody else. She was certainly different now—probably a lot more than she had been as a child. Only this time, it suited her just fine.

Putting on her best reporter-in-command persona, she made her way to the central nursing station on the fourth floor. A middle-aged woman with frosted blonde hair and a tan that spoke of long afternoons at Lake Lanier glanced up as she approached.

"Excuse me. I'm looking for Ben Taylor's room," Shannon said.

"Oh, yes, the judge. That's what we call him, anyway," the nurse responded in a familiar drawl. "You must be his daughter. He's been expecting you, darlin'. Such a sweet man, hasn't complained about a thing since he's been here. Room 412 down the hall, take a left? Last door on the right over the garden. It's one of the best rooms we have on the floor and sure enough, he just loves to look out the window at the fountain. If he's awake you can pretty much count on him sitting there admiring the view, although of course he hasn't felt up to doing very much lately. And if he says he's hungry don't you worry, we'll have someone along directly with a tray for him. He may not feel like eatin' too much right now, but he probably should since he can't have anything after midnight, what with his surgery tomorrow and all…"

Shannon blinked, choking back the laughter in her throat. After so many years away from the South, she had forgotten how a simple question could prompt a deluge of information. At least they seemed to like her dad enough to take extra good care of him—but then, who wouldn't?

Even from the doorway, she could see that Ben Taylor's face was pale and drawn against the whiteness of the sheet. His eyes were closed, and she could hear some gentle snores. He looked so much thinner than he had just a few months ago, when they had celebrated Christmas and New Year's all at the same time. How long ago that seemed now; how triumphant she had been, fresh from her anchor debut, certain that nothing could get in the way of her success…

"Dear Dad," she murmured, her eyes misting. "My mainstay. Whatever would I do without you?"

Taking a deep breath, she tried to compose herself, knowing how upset he would be to see his poised, confident daughter in tears. Gently easing her shoulder bag onto the floor, she pulled a plastic chair next to the bed, so that her face would be the first thing he saw when he woke up. Whenever that might be.

Shannon settled in and took an inventory of the room. As hospital accommodations went, this one wasn't so bad. The furniture was standard-issue, with an adjustable bed and cabinet with blonde veneers masquerading as wood. But at least the ceilings were high, and, she had to admit, the garden below seemed as lush as the nurse had claimed.

Her father stirred.

"Thirsty," he whispered through cracked lips, his eyes still closed.

"Sure, Dad," she said, leaping to fill a plastic cup from the pitcher by his bed.

She guided the straw into his mouth and was rewarded with a hazy half-smile. "Is that really you, Grace?" he murmured. "Or am I dreaming again? I've been having the most wonderful dreams lately. Even saw your momma last night..."

"It's me," she assured him, not minding that he used her childhood name instead of the one she now preferred. "I came as soon as I heard. Where's Aunt DeeCee?"

"Sent her home for a while. She's so tired—" he said, each word formed with an effort. "She's been... taking... such good care... of me..."

"Sssh, don't talk now," Shannon whispered, grateful that he couldn't see her lower lip beginning to tremble.

Ben dropped back to sleep. As she studied his sunken face, Shannon crept one hand into his, wiping away her tears with the other.

She sat by his side all night, dozing occasionally. Her vigil was interrupted at least once an hour by a parade of nurses who bustled in to check his IV, or take his temperature, or plump up his pillow, or hand out additional pain medication. She knew they were trying to help, but she was ready to scream by seven o'clock when the doctor finally breezed through the door.

Shannon turned from the window where she had stood to stretch her stiff neck and shoulders. She extended her hand.

"You must be Dr. Angley. I'm Shannon, Ben's daughter."

"Oh yes, the TV star," he said, peering over his bifocals.

She cringed inside but tried not to let it show. "Actually, I'm retired now. When you're finished with my dad, could we talk outside for a minute?"

"Of course," he assured her. "I'll be right out."

As he ushered her a few steps down the hallway, Dr. Angley was brisk and to the point.

"Your father has a malignant tumor in his colon," he said. "As you may know, we discovered it during one of his routine checkups several months ago, and we've been keeping an eye on it ever since, trying to build up his strength for surgery."

Shannon slumped against the wall, her face pale. Cancer? And all this time Ben hadn't said a word, other than a few vague references to some tests they were putting him through. His heart was fine, he had assured her on the phone, and he was still exercising every day. Whatever it was, they'd control it with a few pills; besides, he had insisted, he felt fine.

"You didn't know?" the doctor inquired.

"No."

"Ah. Well. I had been hoping surgery wouldn't be necessary, but he was in such pain your aunt brought him here and we found some internal bleeding. It's imperative that we go in without further delay. Now—" The doctor paused, his eyes searching her face. "I've advised a colostomy but your father has refused. In fact he's been quite adamant about it. He'll allow us to remove the tumor, he has agreed to radiation afterwards, but he is refusing permission for removal of the entire lower bowel, which holds the best hope for his long-term survival. Unless, of course, you can persuade him otherwise."

Shannon bowed her head, trying to take in all the ramifications of the doctor's summary. "The best hope for survival?" How stupid had she been, taking Ben's word for it that he was fine. Talk about denial! But, God Almighty, he had always been so healthy...

All right. Think of it as a problem to be analyzed, she told herself fiercely, think of it as belonging to someone else. A problem, yes, but one that could be thought through and overcome. Don't think about it as something that could kill him. If she did that, she'd run out of here screaming, for sure.

Shannon took a deep breath and returned her gaze to the doctor's face, trying to keep her voice as matter-of-fact as his. "Why doesn't he want a colostomy?"

"I suppose he finds it unappealing, which I can certainly understand. It requires draining the body's wastes through a tube and into a bag which the patient wears attached to his body. But I can tell you that attractive or not, it's the best chance he has."

"I'll speak to him," she promised. "But knowing my father I doubt he'll change his mind."

They both turned at the sound of footsteps, and Shannon looked into the tired, lined face of her aunt, the woman who had tried so hard to take her mother's place. The woman with whom she had been at odds for what seemed like her entire life.

"I'm so glad you came, dear," Aunt DeeCee quavered, placing a trembling hand on her niece's arm. Shannon bent down and hugged her stiff body, feeling awkward as a kid again. Aunt DeeCee never had been much for physical affection.

"Of course I came. Thank you for letting me know so quickly," she said, with a reassuring pat on her aunt's shoulder. How strange, she thought; it's almost as if I were the grownup and she were the child, now.

"Did the doctor speak to you?" her aunt demanded. At her arrival, Dr. Angley had nodded a greeting and disappeared down the hall.

"Well, he told me what he thinks. I want to know what you think, and what Dad had to say about all this."

Ben stirred behind them. They tiptoed to the doorway and watched as he sighed and fell back asleep.

"Did they tell you? They're doing the surgery today. They wanted to do it yesterday but I told them they had to wait until you got here," Aunt DeeCee whispered, smoothing the hair back from Ben's forehead. Gray as he was, gray as he had been for decades, she would always think of him as her baby brother, to be fussed over and protected. "How do you think he looks?"

*Awful*, Shannon wanted to say, with the bluntness that came naturally from her professional life, but she stopped the words in time. Her aunt looked exhausted and anxious enough as it was.

"Okay," she said. "But you look wiped out. Why don't you let me stay with him until he's out of surgery? It could take hours, and no point in both of us sitting here. I can call as soon as he gets out."

"I am pretty tired," Aunt DeeCee admitted. "Perhaps I will just visit for a little while, then. Thank you, dear. You always were such a thoughtful child."

Shannon shot her a suspicious look, wondering if she was being sarcastic. After all the times Aunt DeeCee had chided her for not being as polite as a well-brought-up Southern child should be! Scolded her, for living in her own little world and never noticing or caring that others had to be considered, too...

But no, the older woman appeared perfectly sincere as she moved about the room, straightening the box of Kleenex and lining up the straws just so. As she tidied up, she cast an occasional shy glance at the glamorous stranger who to her was still a little girl, the child she had been called in to raise when Grammie Lib died. Shannon was still inwardly shaking her head in disbelief when her aunt tiptoed out, with a final, "You let me know when there's any news, now, you hear?"

Shortly before noon, her father woke up. Shannon had been dozing in the chair by his bed, but snapped awake as he called for water.

"Just a sip," she advised, handing him the straw. "And this is the last you can have before they come to get you."

"So," he said, after a quick swallow. "You really are here. Did they tell you to try and talk me into the colostomy yet?"

"Yep," she said.

"Are you going to?"

"I don't know, Dad, should I?" she asked, taking his hand. "The doctor says you'll have a much better chance of being around for longer if you do it his way. Although I can certainly understand why you'd rather not have a colostomy."

"Doctors," he snorted. "What do they know about the quality of a man's life? They're just like plumbers. They come in and poke and prod and take things out and put things in and tell you that everything is fine whether it is or not."

She smiled in sympathy. Her dad had never had a sick day in his life and obviously didn't like his helplessness now.

"I want my old life, honey, or I don't want any. I'm seventy-six years old, and I have no intention of spending my remaining days with a plastic bag of poop strapped to my body."

"But, Dad... if it means surviving..."

"Grace, I'm not afraid to die, whenever it comes." His voice was calm and strong. "I've had a wonderful life. I cherished the years your mother and I had together, even if they were cut short. I have a lovely and talented daughter, and I spent my career practicing law, just like I always wanted. Why, at this point, almost anything I did would be mere repetition, and who needs that? I've had a better life than most, and I'll exit on my own terms, thank you. I have just one regret, if it's my time to go now."

*I know*, Shannon nodded, sure of what was coming next. *You never got to be governor. I know you always wanted to be. Too bad the party turned to somebody else when it should have been your turn. You would have been a great one.*

"No, actually," Ben added, beginning to wheeze. "Two regrets. I'm sorry I wasn't a better father to you, Grace, and I'm sorry I won't be around to make up for it as a grandfather to your children. I just hope they have as much sparkle and spunk as their mother. Lord only knows where you get your courage, child. You certainly have plenty of it." Ben leaned back against the pillows, the overhead fixture casting a circle of light around his head as he gasped for air.

His daughter was dumbfounded. *That* was what he was sorry about, not being there for her? And—courage? What was he talking about, after the way she had grumped over moving to London when someone else got the weekend anchor job promised to her. And then when she had decided she'd had enough of Reardon's machinations and quit, wouldn't it have been braver to stand her ground and fight? When the good guys exit the battleground, doesn't that just leave it empty so the bad guys can triumph? And, oh, Dad... how could you possibly see me as strong and smart and brave?

"How can you say you weren't a good father?" Shannon protested. Her voice was shaking as she swiped at a tear with the back of a knuckle, but she took a deep breath and continued, determined to get the words out. "You were a great dad—the best I could have had! Who taught me how to hit home runs when I was eight, when I cried because I kept getting picked last for softball at recess? You may not remember, but I do—how you'd be out there in the yard with me, night after night, for weeks. You kept on pitching to me 'til it was too dark to see, until finally I could wallop the ball with the best of them. And who took me to football games, and let me listen in on your big cases in court sometimes, and who taught me how important it was to read? And as far as courage goes, Dad, I've always had more guts than brains—don't you remember? Like that time I walked away from the job at WSYA because I'd had enough of Jack Reardon. I know you were worried, but it turned out all right. And when I left home, that wasn't courage. I just felt like I didn't have any other choice if I was going to have a life of my own."

"You know, you broke DeeCee's heart when you left." His voice was so soft she had to strain to hear it. "She tried so hard to be like a mother to you."

Shannon averted her face, but not before he could see her mouth turn down in the sulky expression he remembered from her childhood, when he'd ask each evening how school had gone that day. Ben's hazel eyes were tender as he reached out to pat her cheek, astonishing her with the gesture. Like Aunt DeeCee, her father had never been very demonstrative.

"Grace." His voice was gentle. "It's about time you got over that, don't you think? You've been mad at DeeCee ever since you were eleven years old and Grammie Lib died. Mostly mad because she wasn't Grammie Lib, I expect."

"I know," Shannon admitted. "But she was always—so hard, Daddy. So strict. It was her way or the highway, you know? And Grammie Lib was always so—warm, and loving. Peppermint sticks and cotton candy. Aunt DeeCee was... I don't know. More like carrot sticks and spinach, I guess."

Ben reflected for a moment. "So you had eleven years of peppermint sticks and eight years of carrot sticks. Not a bad combination of the food groups, I'd say. Be fair, honey. DeeCee certainly didn't ask to take on raising a little girl who wasn't hers, but she saw her duty and she did it. I'd say overall she did a fairly good job of it."

Shannon swallowed around the growing lump in her throat. "I guess it wasn't easy, at that," she finally managed to get out.

"Maybe one day you can tell her so," he said, giving her hand a squeeze. "I expect she'd like to hear it. There's so much that becomes clear when you're flat on your back in a hospital bed, my dear..."

Ben moved feebly against the pillows, his face twisting with a stab of pain, but his voice grew stronger as he plunged on. "... so much for you to know, honey. Like how you should be grateful for every day that comes. Find yourself somebody wonderful to build a life with. And have kids, if you can. You won't believe how much you'll love them. Love, Grace. Love and joy. That's really what it's all about."

He chuckled. "I always thought I was pretty smart but it's taken me damn near my whole life to figure that one out. Money, success, power, recognition—all those things are just incidental. Gravy if you get them; nothin' to worry about if you don't."

Wide-eyed, Shannon closed her mouth with a pop, not realizing until she did that it had been open. Of all the things that Ben Taylor could have told her, this was not what she was expecting to hear.

"But, Dad," she couldn't help arguing, "I always thought you loved my success. I thought you really cared about my work. You acted like you were thrilled I was on TV, especially after I went to the network."

"Why, of course I was proud of you. You're my daughter; I'd be proud of you whatever you did. But the only thing I really care about is whether you're happy. And Grace, honey, you do look happier now—even with everything that's gone on—than you did this time a year ago. Am I right?"

Shannon stared at him, too astonished to reply. All this time when she'd been working so hard, laying her career success like trophies at his feet, trying to make up for the fact that her very existence had cost him a wife—and he hadn't valued it at all. It wasn't even what he really wanted for her.

But that's what *your* life was, she wanted to shout at him. You were the busiest person I ever saw—the hardest worker in DeKalb County! Why, you were at your law office twelve, fifteen, sometimes eighteen hours a day ... only now you're telling me it didn't matter ... it wasn't really important to you? That success and recognition aren't worth whatever they might cost?

Her thoughts whirling too fast to analyze them, Shannon's eyes were glued to his gaunt face, wondering how many more chances they would have to talk like this. Her busy, successful father seemed to be delivering the lessons of a lifetime now, quickly, in case it might soon be too late. She could hardly bear the thought. She would have done anything to ease the sadness on his face as he came to terms with the choices of his life. Choices he obviously hoped she would make differently.

"I don't know, Daddy," she quavered after a moment, "I don't seem to do this connecting stuff very well. Seems like the ones who like me I don't like back. Not enough, anyway. I think I must be one of those people who are better off alone."

"Nonsense," he said, turning his head to one side for a searching look at the face that gazed back at him with his own wide eyes, her mother's creamy skin and curly hair. She was such a blend of the two of them, his beautiful daughter, so smart and talented. And with such a good heart—more, probably, than even she knew. "You may seem tough on the outside; I suppose you'd have to be, to do what your job requires. But I believe there's a very loving person on the inside. You've just got to take a chance, honey. When the right person comes along you'll be amazed at how it'll fall into place...."

"Yeah," Shannon muttered, "I wish."

Ben's eyes focused on a spot somewhere over his daughter's shoulder. "Did I ever tell you about how your momma and I met?"

Shannon held her breath. Diana was a topic seldom mentioned in the Taylor household, especially after Grammie Lib died. Ben had never brought up her name and Shannon was afraid to ask, worried about her own role in her mother's death, afraid of resurrecting memories she knew were painful for her dad. It seemed easier, somehow, to go about their lives without ever mentioning the gap in their household that Shannon felt every day of her life, an empty, hurting place that even Grammie Lib's boundless love couldn't fill and Aunt DeeCee's more stringent manner hadn't even tried.

For years, Shannon would sneak off to sit by herself with the family photo album in her lap, studying its contents like an archaeologist exploring ancient ruins. On page one, there was her mother, as slim as a model as she struck a pose on the spacious lawn outside their home. Her father, so dapper in his Army uniform, his face younger than his years as he and his best friend Jonathan flashed V for Victory signs and marched off to Korea together. Ben carrying Diana piggyback across the lawn, both of them convulsed with laughter. Who were these people, Shannon would wonder as she got older, this couple so obviously crazy about each other? This lighthearted man with the mischievous eyes bore no resemblance to the somber father who crept into the house late each night, his briefcase stuffed with legal papers. And who was this woman who had captured his heart long after everyone else had given up on him? Ben had been the confirmed bachelor, the last one left in his old crowd, Grammie Lib had confided. Even Jonathan and DeeCee, who had been circling each other since first grade, finally settled down together. And then Diana Randolph appeared and Ben was a goner.

"I didn't think I'd ever fall in love, either." Her father's voice was lower now. "Your grandmother used to tell me I was going about it the wrong way—that sometimes you just have to wait until love comes to you, 'cause all your struggling and searching and pushing for it isn't going to bring it any faster. That first you have to be comfortable with who you are, to celebrate and love yourself, before there's room in your heart for someone else. And then you have to believe you deserve a good partner before you can find one..."

*That sounds like Grammie Lib*, Shannon smiled. Her throat ached with memory and longing; wishing, not for the first time, that she had been old enough to hear her grandmother's advice about love direct from the source.

"And, finally, she told me....," Ben rasped, determined to finish his story. "She said if you want love in your life you have to give your own away first. You can't just hug it to yourself like a miser hoarding his gold, all worried and afraid there won't be enough to go around. You have to send your love into the world—to everyone you meet, from the cashier in the supermarket to the fellow who parks your car—like ripples in a pond, without worrying or even thinking about whether you might get it back. Until one day those ripples touch the very person you need, and all the love you've sent out comes back to you—"

"Times three," Shannon finished the sentence for him.

"Times three," Ben echoed. "How'd you know that?"

"That's what she used to tell me, too. How everything good you do comes back to you three times over. Same way with the bad. So, she said, it was just good sense to pay attention to whatever you did since you were going to get it back in triplicate." She paused in remembrance. "But tell me the rest of the story."

"That's about it. I finally got where I was comfortable with myself, felt okay about being alone, and I said one night, 'Lord, if you've got somebody good for me I think I'm about ready, and if you don't I believe I'll be just fine all by myself.' The very next week your Uncle Jonathan dragged me to a party at Agnes Scott, pretty much as a joke. I was just finishing law school and thought I was too old for any of those giddy college girls to pay attention to. But I looked up, and there was your momma. That was that, for both of us..."

Shannon's eyes welled, but she was silent as she brushed the tears away. That was it, was it? Decide you'll be okay alone and the person you want will appear? Give your love away with an open heart, knowing one day you'll get it back without any effort on your part?

She shook her head, doubt written clearly across her face.

"I know." Ben's voice was fading to a ragged whisper. "It sounds too easy. But you have to be open to love, Grace. You can't just turn up your nose at it, or try to hide from it, or you'll be missing the best that life has to give. That's why we're here, you know, to love each other and be kind to one another. And to learn. If you can just manage that—and that's not so hard, is it?—you don't have to worry about what's waiting when you die. You'll accept it, welcome it even, knowing it's not the end of who you really are..."

"How can you say that? Everybody's afraid to die."

"Not everybody. At least they wouldn't be if they knew what I know." She looked at him with suspicion in her eyes but his face was calm and content. Complacent, even. He looked—he looked like Clare, she thought, remembering the serenity in the spiritualist's face as she talked about what lay beyond the grave.

"Yeah?" she teased. "How'd you get so smart?"

"An angel told me," he winked. "I've been seeing them a lot lately." Ben closed his eyes again, his breathing deep and regular, and didn't stir until they woke him for surgery.

# 12

Stepping from the artificial cold of the hospital lobby, Shannon was startled to see that it was still light outside. The air was so thick with late-summer humidity that it was like stepping into a steam shower, but the blast of heat actually felt welcome after the chill of her father's room. It was astonishing, she thought, how differently time seemed to pass inside a hospital, especially in the anxious days that followed Ben's surgery. Mornings flowed seamlessly into noontimes, afternoons into evenings and nights and then into morning again, with no reminder of the progress of time other than the intensity of light—or the lack of it—outside the window. With the curtains usually drawn to help Ben sleep, it was easy to forget there even was an outside world.

Shannon flung an affectionate arm across her aunt's shoulders as they made their way to the parking lot. Despite the closeness that had come with their shared worry over the past two weeks, she wondered as she did so whether the older woman might flinch or pull away. As a group, the Taylors had never been particularly demonstrative. Hugs and kisses from anyone other than Grammie Lib had not been a memorable part of her childhood. Now, however, Aunt DeeCee seemed pleased by the warmth the gesture had implied.

"I imagine you'll be glad not to have to make this trip anymore," Shannon said.

"I surely will," Aunt DeeCee replied, "although I don't think your father is likely to be a very good patient once he gets home. I'm going to have to hire a nurse big enough to sit on him just to keep him quiet."

Shannon laughed. "I don't imagine he'll be very easy, at that. He sure hasn't been happy with any of this. Not that I blame him. He was always so active, it's going to be a challenge, having to take it easy. But at least the doctor said they got the tumor, so once he's done with the radiation he can start getting his strength back."

"Yes, thank the Lord. It surely helped having you here. He's been worrying that he didn't do right by you when you were little."

"I know. We talked about it some. I don't know what he's worried about, though. I thought he was great. And then I had you and Grammie Lib, too."

"Well... you had Grammie Lib. I'm not sure that I figured in all that much." Her aunt gave Shannon a sidelong glance.

"I guess you did have to be the strict one," Shannon replied. "I probably didn't appreciate you like I should have. Grammie Lib was always fun, but she used to say you were the one that held the family together."

Aunt DeeCee's head swiveled in surprise. "She told you that?"

"Sure did. She said I wouldn't be alive if it weren't for you." Shannon's eyes misted. "Funny. I haven't thought about that for years..."

Aunt DeeCee's stern face softened at the words, as memories rose that she had grown accustomed to pushing away. Memories that had haunted her for what seemed like her entire life...

"She ever tell you why?"

"No. But I think it's time somebody did. Don't you?"

Aunt DeeCee fished in her handbag for the car keys, stalling for time as she tried to get her thoughts together.

"Let's get in and turn on the air first," she said.

As they reached the car, Shannon automatically headed for the passenger side. Funny how they always reverted to their old roles when she was home, another reason why she didn't like to visit very often. Her independence had cost too much for her to relinquish it easily, even for a little while.

Within a few minutes, the accumulated heat of the day had dissipated enough that they could climb inside Aunt DeeCee's yellow Mercedes and sit down. Despite the lateness of the hour, the cream-colored leather seats were still sizzling from an entire day beneath the hot Georgia sun. Shannon fanned the stagnant air around her, wincing a little from the heat that scorched the back of her thighs straight through her linen pants. She turned to her aunt with an expectant look, only to find DeeCee hunched over the wheel, her eyes focused on a past only she could see.

"It was November," she began.

*"... you were due any minute and I had just dropped by for a visit, after teaching school all day. The front door was wide open. I knew right away something must be wrong. It was terrible outside, cold and rainy, you know, the way November can be. I looked at the hall table and there it was, all crumpled up, a telegram from the War Department. Said my Jonathan and your daddy were missing in action in Korea. I looked around but there wasn't any sign of your mother—Diana always was hard to keep track of. So I ran to the back of the house where Grammie Lib was doing her needlepoint, with Beethoven's Ninth Symphony cranked up as loud as it could go. I used to ask her why she played it so loud and she said it was for him. "Poor man," she'd say, "he couldn't hear it himself when he wrote it, so I figure Mr. Beethoven might like to hear it now." Anyway, she came running when I screamed out about the telegram and said I couldn't find Diana. We both ran out in the rain to look for her. Down by the pond we found her clothes, all stacked up, neat*

*as you please, with a rock on top to keep them from blowing away. By then there wasn't much light left, but we could see your momma, naked as a jaybird, floating in the weeds near the shore. By the time we reached her she was just barely conscious, moaning about how she wanted to be with Ben; she said she wanted to die, too. Grammie Lib grabbed her by the arm and said she wasn't going anywhere until she had this baby, first, and we wrestled her out of the water and got her on up to the house. By then she had started into labor, and it moved fast, I guess, because she had been thrashing around in the cold pond.*

*Anyway. By the time the doctor got there you had already been born. Your grandmother and I delivered you—how, I'll never know. We just did it, somehow. Somehow knew what to do. The ambulance came, finally, and took your mother to the hospital, but by then it was too late. She lived through the night but the next morning she was gone. Three weeks after we buried her, we got another telegram, saying your father's battalion had been holed up in the mountains but that he had gotten out alive. My beloved Jonathan was gone and Ben was shot up pretty bad, but ... he was alive. We had to wait 'til he came home to tell him about his little baby girl ... and his wife ... "*

Aunt DeeCee's trembling voice stopped. Shannon looked up from the fists she had clenched in her lap to find tears streaming down the face of her normally cool, composed aunt. It was the first time she had ever seen her cry.

"I'm so sorry," Shannon said, wanting to lean over and hug her again but not sure if she should. "I had no idea. I mean, I knew I had an uncle who died in the war, but not much more than that. I guess I was never very fair to you, was I?"

Her aunt wiped her eyes and took a deep breath. "Well, I suppose I could have been a little easier to live with, too."

"Do you mean to tell me ... ," Shannon said, the words coming out in what felt like slow motion, " ... that my mother basically threw her life away? I always thought *I* killed her ... "

"Oh, Lord, no, child. You didn't have a thing to do with it. It was her own weakness that killed her. I guess she just loved your Daddy so much she couldn't imagine life without Ben. There was a time when I didn't think I could go on without Jonathan, either."

Shannon closed her eyes, stupefied. "Leaving him like that—and with a baby to raise, too—how could he forgive her? I mean, it's not like he ever talked about her much, but when he did it was always with love ... "

"Well, he didn't forgive her at first. And he didn't get over it, either, not for a long time. Your grandmother carried most of the burden when you were little. And then when you were, oh, seven or eight, I'd say, she just sat him down one day and told him it was high time he stopped feeling sorry for himself and got on with his life. He had a daughter who needed him, she said, and it was an insult to Diana's memory for him not to pick up and go on. That she'd be so upset at how he was treating her baby girl. Their baby girl."

Aunt DeeCee sniffled, pawing through her cavernous bag for another tissue.

Her discomfort at the heat forgotten, Shannon sat and tried to absorb what she had just heard. How bizarre, seeing your parents as young and foolish and heartbroken; at least as foolish, in their own way, as any one of your contemporaries ... as foolish as—you.

"Here." Shannon located a tissue in her own bag and handed it over. DeeCee blew her nose, gave Shannon a wobbly smile and turned on the ignition, flooding the car with music from the tape inside the dashboard cassette deck.

" ... I once was lost, but now I'm found ... was blind, but now I see ... " floated through the air on a rich soaring soprano.

"Oh, God, Aunt DeeCee, is that 'Amazing Grace?' I hate that song," Shannon scowled.

Her aunt turned to her in astonishment. "You do? But it's so beautiful, Grace—I mean Shannon. You probably haven't heard it since you were little. Just listen to the words for a minute."

Shannon folded her arms, her face stony as the melody continued.

"Who is that, anyway?"

"Hush up and listen. That's Jessye Norman. That pretty colored girl opera singer. Doesn't she have a gorgeous voice?"

Shannon winced inwardly at the description, wondering whether to make an issue of it. No, she decided a second later; Aunt DeeCee probably thought she was only delivering a compliment.

"... through many dangers, toils and snares... I have already come... 'twas Grace that brought me safe thus far... and Grace will lead me home."

Lead me home. Where had she heard that phrase before? Oh yes, Clare, again. The woman in London who said she could talk with the dead. She had told Regina's friend—what was her name?—that her mother would be there to lead her home, when her time came. Sure was a nice idea, anyway: that someone you knew and loved would be there to greet you when you died. It would be comforting, to think that you went on, somehow. That death wasn't something to be so scared about. If only you could believe it, as her Dad seemed to...

"Do you believe in that?" Shannon blurted, so abruptly that Aunt DeeCee jumped a little.

"What, dear?"

"What the song just said. You know. About God's grace and everything. About being led home when you die."

Aunt DeeCee turned to blink at her niece, too astonished to try and hide her reaction. She had always been an ardent churchgoer, but Grace's refusal to attend Sunday School once she became a teenager had been the source of some of their fiercest arguments. Since then, they had carefully tiptoed around anything religious, or controversial, during her trips home.

"Why, I don't know," she replied, then paused to consider the question more fully. "Well, yes, I guess I do believe it. That's what the preacher's been telling me all these years, anyway."

"I'm not interested in what the preacher says. I want to know what you think."

"Then...I suppose...I do," Aunt DeeCee's hesitant voice made it less than a ringing endorsement. "Can't say I'm in any hurry to find out, though."

She smiled, as did Shannon, and they rode on without saying anything as the tape segued into "Ave Maria."

"Grace, honey? I mean Shannon—sorry, dear, I just can't seem to think of you by your first name..." Aunt DeeCee said tentatively, afraid of disturbing their newfound harmony.

"It's okay. What?"

"Why don't you like Amazing Grace? I've always loved it, and so did your grandmother. That's why we wanted you to have the name. Well, actually, I guess it was me who wanted it more than she did." *And why I was so hurt when you quit using it, first chance you got,* Aunt DeeCee added to herself.

Shannon was staring out the window at the new subdivisions they were passing and didn't notice the pause. Suburban Atlanta was now jammed with sprawling developments, grandiose faux Tudors and Tuscan villas and English manors, all of them brand-new and wedged into a quarter-acre of land. Every mile, it seemed, there was more freshly blackened asphalt sprouting off the main road, stretching like giant Daddy-long-legs across the pastures as they gobbled the dairy farms that had surrounded her childhood home. When she was growing up, this part of Atlanta had been so rural that only the main roads were paved. Now, all the old country lanes had become four-lane highways to accommodate the cars and malls and cookie-cutter subdivisions housing the city's newcomers, erasing the peace and greenery of her childhood.

"Shannon? Was there some reason you didn't like that song?" her aunt prompted.

Shannon remained silent, wondering how to answer. Talk about long-held secrets! The hateful nickname she carried as a child had gnawed chunks from her soul for so long that one day she decided never to think about it again—and had largely succeeded. On the other hand, she was past thirty now, which should make her a genuine grownup. Maybe it was time to open up a little. Put all that behind her. After all, Aunt DeeCee had finally confided in her, so maybe this was a day for secrets to come out. Still, she couldn't help a sigh from escaping as she began to speak, as if she could release twenty-five years of pain with the outward motion of her breath.

"Do you remember when I was little and Grammie Lib used to know who was calling on the telephone, before anyone had answered? And you'd tell me not to tell anyone, because they'd think the whole family was strange?"

"Yes...," Aunt DeeCee replied with a puzzled frown.

Shannon took another deep breath and plunged on. "Well, I did it, too, sometimes. Something like that, anyway. It was before you came to live with us. I was six years old and I told a kid in my class not to be sad, that his grandmother was just fine and waiting for his grandfather to join her. I have no idea why I said it, or where it came from. I just blurted it out, trying to make him feel better, but instead—boy, howdy, all hell broke loose. I got in a ton of trouble when his mother called Dad about it. And then—when his grandfather suddenly had a heart attack and died a couple of weeks after he'd lost his grandmother—well, you would have thought I was one of the Salem witches come back to life."

By this time Aunt DeeCee had pulled into their driveway and turned off the ignition. Rolling down the window, she turned to face her niece, confused and concerned. Shannon finished the story in a rush, with a blind stare at landscaping she didn't really see.

"... and that's when the kids all started calling me Crazy Grace. Remember when you kept wanting me to have a friend over, after school? I didn't ask, because nobody would come. Nobody played with me at recess, or sat with me at lunch, so why would they want to be with me afterward? I guess they really did think I was crazy. Or in league with the devil or something."

The words were streaming out now in a flow that she couldn't have stemmed if she'd tried. "They called me Crazy Grace until a teacher heard them one day and got on them about it. But they just chimed in, all sweet and innocent, 'Why, no, Miss Adams, it's just a nickname from church—*Amazing* Grace.' From then on whenever I'd get up to read or have to recite in class I'd always hear somebody humming it from the back of the room. As if I'd ever forget how I got the name. Or what they really meant."

Shannon finished telling her story to the window. When she didn't hear any response, she glanced over to the driver's side of the car. Her aunt was weeping, for the second time that day. Shannon was so astonished she just stared.

"Oh, honey," Aunt DeeCee finally whispered, reaching into her bag again in the off chance that she had missed a fresh tissue somewhere. "Why didn't you ever tell me?"

"I don't know. I guess I was too embarrassed to say anything at first, and then as time went on I just tried to forget about it. Besides, there was nothing anybody could do ... "

"Why, of course there was," her aunt said, her voice thickened by tears and indignation. "Your father and grandmother and I would have snatched you out of there in a minute if we'd known and put you right into private school."

"You would?" Shannon was incredulous. "But how could I ever ask such a thing—me, the person who killed my mother. That's what I always thought, anyway: I was scared to breathe, almost, for fear I'd use up too much air. My being here was an accident, a fluke, that took away the person Daddy loved most. And, then, he was always talking about how important a public school education was—especially after he was going to run for governor. It meant a lot to him that I was still in public school after desegregation came."

"Shannon Grace Taylor, the very idea! There isn't anything we wouldn't have done for you. Campaign or no campaign. Don't you know that?" Aunt DeeCee gave her eyes a last swipe and twisted sideways in the seat. "Just wait 'til you have children of your own. You'll see. Why, you were as much mine as if I'd given birth to you, myself. Your Uncle Jonathan and I tried to start a family before he went off to the war, but I guess it just wasn't meant to be. I sure loved you like a daughter, though. I worried about you, cared about what you were doing... although, I guess, maybe... I should have told you that, shouldn't I?"

*Well, yes, you should have,* Shannon agreed, but thought it best to keep that to herself. Whatever her methods, Aunt DeeCee had meant well and had done the best she knew how. Anyway, it was pretty useless at this late date to keep holding onto the grudge she had carried for so long...

Her aunt's voice was soft as she continued. "I don't think any of us have any idea how much we were loved 'til you see how much you love a child yourself. I surely didn't, anyway."

"Guess I'll have to take your word for it," replied Shannon, trying to lighten the mood. She was still taken aback by the love and heartbreak she had seen in her aunt's eyes. "I don't think you'll find me knitting booties any time soon."

"Maybe not soon, honey, but don't you miss it, you hear? I believe it's one of the greatest experiences life has to give."

Shannon smiled and reached for the door handle. "That's what Dad said."

"There now, you see? Your Daddy's a smart man."

"I guess."

Aunt DeeCee closed the door, still shaking her head. "You know, I just can't get over that story. No wonder you were so—so—"

"Tough?" Shannon suggested, trying not to sound defensive.

"No," her aunt corrected her. "I was going to say strong. I guess you had to be, to get yourself up and go to school every day with the other kids making fun of you. Gracious, child, no wonder you were in such a hurry to get out and make a name for yourself. I imagine I would have been, too."

Shannon smiled. "But you know what's interesting? For some reason, I don't feel like I have to do that anymore. In fact, I don't miss TV nearly as much as I thought I would. It's still the thing I do best, I suppose, but it isn't how I'm starting to define myself now."

She took a deep breath. "Wow. Never thought I'd say that. I used to live and die for my job."

"By the way, speakin' of TV, I keep forgettin' to tell you. There's some man who keeps callin' here trying to reach you. Stuart somebody? He says you owe him a phone call."

Shannon started guiltily at the name. Trust Stu to figure out a way to track her down. "Yeah, I guess I do, at that. His name is Stu Siegel and he's a great guy, but I don't know... I'm not sure if I'm ready to talk to anybody at the network just yet..."

"A special friend, is he?" her aunt inquired with a mischievous smile. For a moment Shannon caught a glimpse of the girl who had inhabited that face, once; a girl who had giggled and traded secrets with her friends, just as she would have liked to—if she'd had any friends.

"No. Sorry. Just an old pal."

"Oh," Aunt DeeCee said, trying not to sound disappointed. It wasn't easy being supportive without sounding nosy.

"Knock it off," Shannon said with a grin. "I hear it'll happen when it's supposed to happen. *If* it's supposed to happen."

Her aunt's face was sheepish. "Can't blame me for tryin'. Just—don't do what I did, honey. Don't live your life with nothin' to show for it at the end."

"Hey. You have *me* to show for it."

Her aunt tilted her head and smiled. *My goodness*, Shannon thought, startled, *she really did have a nice smile, when she used it.*

"I guess I do, at that," Aunt DeeCee admitted.

They approached the front door together, with their arms around each other's waists. Shannon reached over and kissed the top of her aunt's head as she turned the key in the lock. After all these years of anger and estrangement, what a relief to tell the story at last. What a comfort to find that Aunt DeeCee would have been on her side all the way—if only she had had the nerve to confide in her.

"Shaaaaaaaaanon...."

A thin thread of a voice, wispy and insubstantial as it called her name, but insistent enough to rouse her from a deep sleep.

"Shaaaaaaaaaaanon..."

In the four-poster bed that had been hers from childhood, Shannon rolled to one side and pulled her grandmother's wedding-ring quilt higher against her chin. "What?" she mumbled into her pillowcase.

*She was standing at the edge of a pond, perhaps the one outside the Lady's Cottage, she thought at first. But no, there was no Braeburn House in the distance, strain as she might to see it through the fog. She heard a splash and turned, startled, to find a young woman with a haggard, pleading expression emerging from the weeds at the water's edge. The woman's hair was dripping wet and she was nude. As she came closer, Shannon could see that her hands were clutched around a hugely pregnant belly.*

*"Mother?" she said, her eyes wide with disbelief. She ran over and caught her by the elbows to keep her from falling, as the other woman's eyes rolled back into her head and her knees buckled beneath her. Shannon laid her gently on the ground and knelt at her side.*

*"I'm so sorry," the woman was saying over and over in a ragged whisper. "So sorry, so sorry ... I didn't mean to ... didn't mean to hurt you ... never wanted to hurt you ... "*

*Shannon pushed the tangled hair from her forehead. She was so young, this woman. Her skin was almost translucent in the semi-darkness, her suffering so palpable that Shannon could hardly bear to watch.*

*The woman opened her eyes, struggling to bring Shannon's face into focus. "Forgive me?" she said, her voice hoarse with effort. "Please ... please ... you must forgive me ... "*

*Why, she's no older than I am, Shannon thought in a daze. She snaked one hand behind the woman's shoulders, lifted and cradled the wet and swollen body, rocking her against her chest in an unconscious gesture of comfort, her own cheeks wet with pond water and tears. "Forgive me ... ," the woman whispered again.*

*"Of course I forgive you," Shannon assured her.*

She awoke with a start, her arms clutched around the pillow as if she were rocking a baby.

Propping herself up on one elbow, she made a befuddled survey of the room as the pictures and voices vanished into the mist. Only the familiar silhouettes of her childhood furniture were there to greet her. "Good Lord, Shannon," she murmured, shaking her head. "What is it with these dreams of yours?"

She flung one arm over her head and tried to settle into a position comfortable enough for a return to sleep. Within seconds, she became aware that a feeling of peace was stealing over her body, a feeling that embraced her with the ease and comfort of one of Grammie Lib's quilts, stitched inch by inch with love. The feeling was warm, sweet, relaxing, and all the more welcome because it was so unexpected. This time as she closed her eyes and drifted off into unconsciousness, she felt light enough to float on top of the mattress, as if she had been relieved of a burden she hadn't known she was carrying. When she awoke to daylight and the sound of doves cooing outside her window, she extended her arms overhead into a delicious stretch and realized that she was smiling.

The next morning, she stayed long enough to see her father safely home from the hospital and settled into his old bedroom. Once Ben was sound asleep, she took Aunt DeeCee aside for one last instruction at the door.

"You call me, now, if he needs me. I'll be here on the first plane," she said in a fierce whisper.

"Of course I will, darlin'," her aunt replied. "But the doctor says he'll be fine. It's just going to take a while 'til he's up and around again. So you run along now, you hear? You get back to that pretty little place you like so much. And don't you worry about a thing."

After one last hug and wave out the window, Shannon backed

out of the driveway and made her way to the airport, the tape of "Amazing Grace"—a gift from her aunt—in her handbag. Back she flew to London, and from there sped to a white gingerbread cottage by a still, peaceful pond, which much to her surprise was beginning to feel like home.

# 13

Shannon stifled a yawn as she wandered into the living room, setting down her tea so she could fling wide the French doors. It was mild outside, even for September, but a hint of crispness in the morning air made her wonder how many more such opportunities she would have this fall.

Snapping on the television, she nestled into a chair just as the sound came up, followed by the serious face of a BBC newsreader.

"... have pictures now of that massacre at the Palestinian refugee camps of Sabra and Shatila south of Beirut... the death toll, we are reliably informed, is in the hundreds... Men, women and children, all slaughtered by Christian Phalangist gunmen..."

Shannon bolted upright, the tea splashing onto her forearm as she leaned forward to get a better look. "Oh my God," she muttered, her stomach twisting with nausea. Usually the most horrifying images were edited out before they hit the air, but these appeared taken straight from the camera.

The announcer's dispassionate voice droned on crisply over grainy shots of bodies, piles of them, heaped on top of one another like logs for a giant bonfire. The camera zoomed in for a close-up at one corner of the stack where a hand was poking out. A child's hand, apparently, its delicate fingers still clutching a doll. A wide shot displayed what looked from afar like piles of blood-soaked rags.

Shannon turned away, unable to watch any longer as the announcer's voice faded to an indistinguishable buzz. Remembering with a shudder how she had almost lost her composure during the plane crash story the night of her anchor debut, a thousand lifetimes ago, she wondered what was happening to her detachment. She was used to death by now, reluctantly used to it. The sudden, inexplicable loss of hundreds was hard enough to take when a plane dropped out of the sky—but this was worse, somehow. Worse, because it was deliberate. How could people do such things to each other?

She swallowed hard, imagining for a split second that she was standing at the edge of the massacre, forced to witness the bloodshed. A merciless sun scorched her head as a group of soldiers—human beings—swung machine guns to their chests and fired into another group of human beings. She could hear the cries of the children as they died in the arms of mothers trying to shield them with their own bodies. In front of her horrified eyes, fathers crumpled to the ground, powerless to defend the families they loved... their eyes fixed and staring, stripped of dignity as they lay, their bodies bloated and rotting in the sun...

Shannon blinked to erase the pictures in her mind and glared at the television set. "Anything else you can tell us? Like, *why* this happened? So we can maybe figure out some way to stop it...?"

But the announcer had moved on to the next story, and the next, and then there was a commercial break, leaving her to fume over questions that seemed to have no answers. None to be had on Britain's new breakfast television, at any rate.

"You know what?" announced Shannon, her lips set in a firm line as she marched to the set and snapped it off. "I have a life to put back together, and I refuse to start my day by dwelling on everything that's wrong with the world."

She folded her arms across her chest as she regarded the blank screen. "If you're not going to tell me what I need to know, then what good are you?" she continued with an impatient frown. "Don't just tell me that it happened, tell me why it happened. And at least give us some idea how we might fix it."

*That was it.* Her eyes widened. That was what she wanted to do—explain *why* things happened the way they did. Get different perspectives, reach for genuine understanding. Point the way toward solutions and not just show a relentless parade of problems. But where? And for whom?

Since returning to England, she had eagerly checked her mailbox each day, hoping to hear something from Steve Mapping, her friend at PBS. Surely he had had time to respond to her letter by now. Surely he would have some ideas. Perhaps he could point her toward more substantive work, offer some direction for her life. But—so far, nothing. Not a word.

She stood in front of the set, one foot tapping impatiently on the carpet.

"Well, to hell with it. If you don't need me, I don't need you," Shannon finally declared. She yanked the plug from the wall and pushed the whole apparatus, cart and all, into the closet.

"So there," she said, closing the door with a firm click.

Her eyes caught by a flash of white outside, Shannon crossed to the window to observe a family of ducks as they marched down to the pond from Braeburn House across the way. Despite her fierce mood, she couldn't help but smile at their heavy bottoms waddling from side to side. They were so self-important as they strutted across the gravel driveway and into the water with a splash, content with themselves and their own little world. As she leaned against the window frame, it seemed almost incomprehensible that a planet that held such peace and simple beauty could also contain such unreasoning hatred, the kind that could explode into a fusillade of bullets and gore thousands of miles away.

*Heaven knows how I'm going to fill the hours I used to spend watching the tube,* she thought, with a final glance at the closet. *Not to mention getting over my news addiction. But given the choice, I believe I would rather watch the ducks.*

Kicking the television habit was more difficult than Shannon had anticipated. By the end of the first week, she had devoured twice as many books as usual and decided she had better find some additional ways to occupy her time, if only for the sake of her eyesight.

The library, she thought as her eyes popped open on Monday morning. Libraries always needed volunteers, didn't they? That would be something helpful, maybe even fun to do. After all, she had always loved being around books ...

Tossing back the covers with an enthusiasm she hadn't felt in some time, Shannon hurried through breakfast and into her clothes. By nine-thirty she was pacing outside the doors of Burlingford's quaint stone library, whose faded Victorian lettering promised it would open at nine. Finally, the elderly Mrs. Satterfield came puffing up the walk, an umbrella tucked under her arm and clutching a grease-stained paper bag.

"Miss Tyler, now, isn't it?" the tiny lady said, shading her eyes against the sun as she squinted up at Shannon. "And how are you liking the Lady's Cottage, dearie? You do remember, I'm the one took you there first."

"Yes, of course I remember," replied Shannon, trying not to sound annoyed by her tardiness. "Your daughter was on holiday and you were showing the cottage for her. Are you the librarian, too?"

"Indeed I am," said Mrs. Satterfield, grabbing Shannon's arm for balance as they navigated their way up the narrow steps. She fumbled for a massive brass key and after several tries finally pushed open the wooden door, flooding the dimness with sunshine before it shut again. "The light, the light, now where's that blessed switch?" she muttered, patting one hand along the wall. Shannon blinked as shelves of books sprang into view beneath the fluorescent glare.

Mrs. Satterfield hobbled to an ancient wooden desk and sank into the chair with a sigh of relief. "Ah, me," she lamented, "I do believe that walk gets longer every day."

Shannon shifted her weight from one foot to another, uncertain how to begin, and beginning to wonder what she was doing there.

"Beg pardon, dearie," Mrs. Satterfield said, tilting her head with a rapid series of blinks and nods, looking for all the world like a bright-eyed bird. "Here you've come all this way and I haven't even begun to help you. What would you like—fiction? Or a magazine? We get the latest novels from London once a month but you'll have to sign up for those—big demand, don't you know … "

"Actually, I'm looking for work. Volunteer work, of course. I thought perhaps I could help out here, maybe a few times a week … " began Shannon, her words trailing off as the woman began to shake her head vigorously.

"I wish you could, dearie, wish you could but no, no, no, it wouldn't do. Wouldn't do at all. If they think I can't handle the job on my own, first thing you know they'll want to put new staff in here and then what would I do? Then what, eh? I'm in charge of the Burlingford Library for 47 years now, rain or shine, and so I intend to keep my post, don't you know."

"Oh—well—I certainly wasn't trying to take your job away," Shannon stammered. "I just wanted to help out somehow."

Mrs. Satterfield shot her a shrewd glance. "Not enough to do with yourself, eh, dearie? You young people don't have to worry about your next meal, do you, now. When I was your age it was work, work, work. No time to be bored." She plucked a piece of lint from her skirt and began muttering to herself.

Shannon backed away. "Ah, thank you anyway," she said. Mrs. Satterfield looked up, startled to find Shannon still standing in front of her.

"Eh? Eh? Still here, then? Need something to do, is it? Well, try over t' the schoolhouse. The reading lady's at home with a new baby this year and mayhap they haven't replaced her."

With one hand reaching for the doorknob, Shannon thanked her and fled. Good Lord. This volunteering business was more complicated than it looked.

Outside, she breathed in the crisp fall air and began to chuckle as she made her way down the driveway. The schoolhouse was less than half a mile away, and it was certainly worth a try. They'd lost their reading lady, had they? Whatever that was. Well, if there was one thing she was pretty sure she knew how to do, it was read aloud.

"I'm sorry," the woman behind the glass in the tiny administration office said with a puzzled frown. "Might you repeat that, please? You want to know about the leading lady? Dear me, I can't think whom you must mean... we don't really put on theatricals here..."

"No, your reading lady," Shannon corrected her, feeling a little foolish. "I understand from Mrs. Satterfield you've lost your reading lady. That she's home with a new baby. Or something."

"Oh, our *reading* lady," the woman repeated, comprehension dawning at last. "Yes, of course. We actually call her the story lady. She comes in two mornings a week and reads to the little ones.

And yes, indeed, you're quite right, we don't have her services at the moment."

"Ah," Shannon said, her face brightening. "Then—do you need one? I'd be happy to volunteer."

"Well," the other woman said, in a voice filled with doubt. "I don't wish to be rude, but there is the matter of your accent..."

"Thank you for not saying 'my awful American accent'," Shannon responded with a smile, determined not to be turned away. "I'll make a special effort to speak clearly, if that will help." The other woman smiled, too, a little less certainly.

"And do you have any experience reading aloud?"

*Only to twenty million people at a time*, Shannon thought.

"I do, actually," was all she said.

"Well then, that's lovely. We'd be delighted to have you," said the woman, her face suddenly breaking into a smile. She held out a hand for Shannon to shake.

"I'm Mrs. Holden, assistant to the school administrator, but just between the two of us," she lowered her voice to a whisper, "I'm the one who makes certain things are run properly around here. Now. When would you like to begin? The children have been missing their story hour and I'm sure they'll be happy to see it resume as soon as possible."

"Oh, um, whenever you'd like," Shannon said. Who knew she would have to talk her way into a volunteer job? But this seemed perfect. And it would certainly help pass the time...

"Well, the usual schedule is Tuesday and Thursday mornings, nine to eleven. The littlest children come in first, and then it's a new group at half past the hour—four classes in all, time you're done." Mrs. Holden gave her a doubtful look. "Are you quite sure you want to do this? There's no pay at all, you know."

"I'm sure," Shannon said, her voice firm. "I'll see you tomorrow, then."

"Wait!" Mrs. Holden held up a cautionary hand as she reached for a stack of picture books behind her with the other. "No doubt you'll want to go over these tonight. You won't want to stumble in front of the children, now, do you?"

---

Forget anchoring, or live shots from Capitol Hill. Reading in front of a group of children, Shannon decided within the first week, felt like the hardest work she had ever done. And... the most enjoyable.

On her first Tuesday morning, as she stacked the books next to her pint-sized chair, she realized that her palms were sweaty with nervousness. *Shannon,* she scolded herself, *what is your problem? They're only little children, after all—*

And with that the library door was flung open and a cyclone of six-year-olds descended. "I claim the lady's lap!" shouted a little girl with blonde ringlets, flinging herself into Shannon's arms.

"Oh, but, dear," replied a startled Shannon, trying to keep from tumbling over backward as the child squirmed into a more comfortable place on her knees, "I only have one lap and I have to hold up the books so that all of you can see the pictures."

The child's lower lip began to tremble and her blue eyes filled with tears. *Oh, God,* Shannon panicked, *what have I gotten myself into?*

"How about this, instead," she suggested quickly. "What about if I sit on the floor and you can stay right here, next to me. Would that be all right?"

The little girl thought it over for a moment and then her face cleared as she announced, "All right, then." She plopped down next to Shannon, her flowered cotton dress frothing around her in a sea of ruffles. "Jillian, you go there, on the story lady's other side," she ordered another little girl with an imperious gesture.

Shannon looked at her willful new friend with a smile. This was one little person who clearly knew what she wanted and how to get it.

"What's your name?" Shannon asked.

"Lily," she replied, popping her thumb in her mouth and snuggling as close as she could get to Shannon. Touched, Shannon hesitated, then put her arm around Lily for a quick hug.

Children in the abstract had never interested Shannon very much, but as she looked into the circle of faces assembling around her she began to realize how very individual they were. A red-haired little boy with freckles splashed across his face looked like mischief, for sure. Another little fellow at the front with sad brown eyes and shaggy hair bore further investigation, too. Despite repeated "shushes" from their teacher, the children were too excited to settle down very easily. In almost every face, a big smile and sparkling eyes signaled what an adventure it was for them to abandon their familiar classroom for something as delicious as this. Mrs. Holden had been right: story time was one of their favorites, and they had sorely missed it. Within a few minutes more, with the help of their harried teacher, each child had found a place around Shannon and seemed ready to listen.

"Now this story," began Shannon, "is about a gigantic—what?" as she pointed to the picture.

"Lorry," the children shouted.

"That's right," she said. "Now where I grew up, in America, we use a different word. We call these trucks..."

"Miss Shannon, are ye quite certain ye wish to go ridin' today?" the groom inquired in a soft burr that sounded more anxious than usual. "I hear we're in for a bit o' bad weather later on."

"I know that's what they said but I don't believe it," she replied. "Just look at how sunny and beautiful it is—finally. It feels like it's been raining for weeks. No way I'm staying inside again!"

"Are ye quite sure ye're dressed warm enough? It is November, you know. The weather can be more than a mite changeable this time o' year," he persisted with a worried frown, his eyes scanning the horizon for the snow clouds he felt sure were lurking just beyond.

"Really, James," she scolded with a smile as she turned to canter down the driveway, "You're starting to sound like my Aunt DeeCee."

Michael watched her leave from the window upstairs and couldn't help smiling as well. Business in London had kept him largely occupied and elsewhere since her return from Georgia. From here, he couldn't make out what she said to the groom, but he admired the smile that accompanied her words and the bounce of her curls as she set off. That one, he grinned to himself, must be a handful. He turned back to the defense minister's study on NATO troop strength with a sigh that, if overheard, might have been described as wistful.

Shannon was indeed in high spirits as she left atop Black Thunder. It had taken weeks of determined pleading and several additional lessons before James would let her out with the stallion, who was known for his independence as well as his strength. Still, he was a beauty, powerful and sleek, and Shannon couldn't have been happier as they moved along in the crisp air of mid morning. With the bright sunshine overhead, it had to be forty-five degrees, at least, far too warm for snow. She couldn't imagine what James had been so worried about.

At noontime she spread a plaid wool blanket for her picnic lunch and allowed Black Thunder to graze in a nearby pasture as she got out her sketch book. She had always loved to draw and scribble as a child, but never took art lessons and hadn't thought much about art during the frantic days of her television career. Now that she had more leisure time than she could have ever imagined, drawing—like riding—was another connection to her childhood self that she was taking pleasure in rediscovering.

She was so absorbed in trying to get the exact shading of the fir trees next to one of the meandering stone walls she loved about this part of the Cotswolds, she failed to notice that the sun had disappeared behind thick gray clouds—until, suddenly, something wet touched her nose. Fat, heavy snowflakes began to fall, just a few at first and then faster and faster until the ground around her was rapidly turning white. Black Thunder, who had been grazing peacefully nearby last time she had looked up, was nowhere to be seen. And it was apparent that while her black jodhpurs and wool hacking jacket might have been fine for a sunny fall day, they offered scant protection against a snowy one.

"Way to go, Shannon, you dope," she muttered to herself, gathering up the blanket and sketchpad. She tried to think of the shortest way home. She wasn't sure if she could find her way back at all, she realized, having assumed on the way out that the weather would hold and it would be no problem retracing her way to the road. But now—dear God, where had her horse gone? She hoped that he had decided to amble back without her and wasn't wandering around in the snow, as lost as she was. Shannon set off down the hillside toward the woods, her head lowered against the splattering snowflakes, swearing under her breath every step of the way.

Once she was inside the woods, the trees seemed to offer a little protection. The heavy wet snowflakes pelted her less mercilessly, but she was still shivering, more miserable by the moment. Shannon pulled the picnic blanket like a shawl over her head, wishing she had had sense enough to wear a hat and warmer clothes and hoping she could remember how to get out of here. She had heard stories of people getting totally lost in woods no thicker than these.

"Oh, don't be so dramatic," she said out loud, hoping to quiet a growing sense of alarm. So what if she got drenched and wound up in bed for a few days. After everything else she had been through, getting a little wet hardly seemed anything to worry about.

Michael had been casting anxious glances out the window since shortly after noontime, when the morning's sunshine abruptly gave way to a series of grey, scudding clouds. When there was still no sign of either Black Thunder or his rider by two o'clock, he tossed aside the position paper he had been trying to analyze and began to pace. A few minutes after three, as the courtyard disappeared beneath a blanket of white, he heard the sound of horse's hooves. Michael leapt to the window in relief, only to frown at the sight of Black Thunder's empty saddle. He could sense the groom's dismay, too, as he ran outside. He watched as James grabbed the bridle to lead the horse into the warmth of the stable, all the while craning his neck as if he expected Shannon to leap out from behind one of the hedges.

Michael could stand it no longer. He grabbed his car keys from the porcelain dish by the door, shrugged into a green weatherproof slicker and took the stairs two at a time, almost crashing into Henry at the front door.

"Miss Shannon—" Henry began, a worried frown puckering his forehead into deep creases. His shoulders were covered in snow. He had been standing on the front steps for the past ten minutes, the concern in his eyes becoming more pronounced with each second that ticked by with no sign of her.

"I know," Michael snapped. "I'm going to go look for her. Any idea which way she went this morning?"

"None." Henry's voice was sad. "I regret to say I wasn't here when she left."

"She can't have gotten far. Get a fire going upstairs for me, would you," he shouted as he drove away.

Henry bustled off, grateful for something to do.

After more than an hour of trudging through the woods, her head lowered against a driving snow that erased any recognizable landmarks, Shannon's teeth were chattering so hard she put a knuckle between them, afraid that otherwise she might bite through her bottom lip. Even with the blanket wrapped around her, she was soaked. Her hands were numb, her feet had lost all feeling some time ago, and her entire body was shivering uncontrollably. Still she walked on, a fierce argument raging in her head over the wisdom of stopping to rest for a while.

*You can't stop*, she told herself, *that's how people die of exposure. They go to sleep and never wake up. But I'm so tired*, came the counter-argument, *can't I sit down for just a moment and close my eyes?*

*No. It won't be just for a moment, it'll be forever if you give in. C'mon, girl, move those feet. You're not a quitter. Sooner or later you'll come to something you recognize.*

"The shed," she said suddenly, raising her head in fresh hope, the one where—. The thought vanished as quickly as it came. She must be hallucinating. There was no shed on the property, not in these woods at least. Not so far as she knew, anyway. She paused to concentrate for a moment, willing the elusive image of a shed to return. She shook her head. No. It was gone. She kept walking, more slowly now, each step dragging a bit more than the one that preceded it.

Michael kept the hotel's battered Land Rover in first gear, creeping along the narrow rutted lane that circled the woods. Occasionally he stopped to sweep the area with a flashlight, hoping the beams might pick up a trail his headlights missed. It was no use; the snow was falling too quickly for footprints to remain visible for long. He had already searched all the obvious places. If she had stuck to the road she would have been back hours ago. It only made sense, then, that she was somewhere deep inside the woods. But where?

*Bloody hell,* he swore to himself. *Damned idiot. What did she mean wandering off and getting lost like this?* He certainly couldn't mount a thorough search all by himself, and in the time it would take to rouse enough people to do one properly she could be dozing off, quietly freezing to death somewhere. God only knows where she might have gotten off to. He shut his eyes for a minute and sent up a silent prayer that wherever she was, she had enough sense to keep walking.

Shannon stumbled along, dully observing the half-moon marks her riding boots were leaving in the snow with each weary step. The numbness that had begun in her toes was halfway up her legs by now. She was beginning to wonder how long she could command her exhausted body to keep moving.

Suddenly a dark shape rose up in front of her, a dozen yards off to her right. It appeared to be some sort of shed, open on one side. *Even if it isn't warm,* she thought in relief, *at least it'll get me out of the wind and snow.* She hobbled over as quickly as she could on legs that had gone stiff with cold.

Peering cautiously into the gloom inside, she could barely make out what appeared to be some scattered bundles of hay. She tried not to think too much about what little creatures might have already set up housekeeping inside them as she sat down on one of the bundles, packing loose bits of hay around herself for insulation. *Now if I were really smart,* she told herself drowsily, *I'd have a match with me so I could set the place on fire. I bet that would help somebody find me. Assuming, of course, that anybody's even looking.*

Now that she was away from the assault of the snowflakes, the temptation to close her eyes was almost irresistible. "Stay awake, damn you," she commanded. This is no time to give up, not now, when there are people depending on you. Dad. Aunt DeeCee. All those children who've come to rely on your being there twice a week at the village school, to tell them stories and make them laugh. Lily, especially. Shannon had never been the object of such adoration as she saw in her tiny friend's eyes—not since Grammie Lib, anyway. And what about Henry? Think of how upset he would be to lose his chess partner. Keep those eyes open, girl!

Let's see, now. Who else? Michael. Um, maybe. He'd be sorry to lose a good tenant. At that thought, she had to pause. Don't sell yourself too short, she smiled to herself. She still remembered the jolt of their first meeting, and suspected from a few of the glances she had intercepted since then that maybe he had felt something, too. Hadn't he delivered that message from her father personally? And hadn't he driven her—well, dropped her off, anyway—at Heathrow last summer? Even if she hadn't seen much of him since then.

But, God, this is pathetic, she thought; only those few to care about her? What value could you put on your life, if your leaving it would mean so little? If you've affected so few people that almost nobody will care all that much whether you live or die? What's the point, if your life is only about you? She frowned into the gloom, hugging her knees to her chest in a vain attempt at warmth. No question, that had been her main focus over the years. *My* career, *my* advancement, *my* ambition. It's only lately that I've begun to think about giving back, even a little bit. And then it was mostly to keep myself busy, she had to acknowledge. At least in the beginning.

She blew on her fingers, wondering when her body heat might begin to kick in again. Her eyes fixed on the snow-laden trees outside, their branches sagging beneath this unaccustomed burden...

*"DeeCee, honey, come out here and help me with these groceries, would you please?" Grammie Lib's arms were filled with a huge box of canned goods as she headed toward the back of the Taylor's station wagon, letting the screen door slam behind her.*

*"Oh, Mother, for heaven's sake, are you visiting those no-count Fergusons again?" Aunt DeeCee's face was cross as she appeared at the side door, wiping her hands on a dish towel.*

*"Just because they haven't been blessed with the material goods we have is no reason to be rude, DeeCee. They're God's creatures the same as you and me. Now, bring that basket of fruit with you from the kitchen table, would you, dear?" Grammie Lib was serene, her expression purposeful as she hoisted the heavy box onto the car seat with a little groan.*

*Aunt DeeCee did as she was told, muttering all the while. "For the life of me I do not understand why you feel it necessary to keep goin' over there all year round,"* she complained, placing the fruit basket on top of the cardboard box.

"*Because, dear,"* Grammie Lib replied equably, with a pointed look at her daughter, "*people get hungry all year round. Not just at Christmastime when you and your ladies group show up with food baskets from church."*

"*Well, at least I go to church, Mother. That's more than I can say for you."*

"*I know, darlin', and I'm sure God is delighted you're able to make time for Him one day a week. Seems to me you'd do even better to remember Him in what you do every day."* Grammie Lib's smile was bland as she beckoned to her granddaughter. "*Grace, honey? Are you ready?"*

"*Sure, Grammie,"* the eight-year-old had answered. *She loved going anywhere with her grandmother, even to the Fergusons, whose ramshackle house smelled of pee and had a wooden floor so old and cracked you could see straight through to the bare ground beneath it.*

"*Shannon Grace,"* Grammie Lib said as she began backing down the driveway, "*if there's one thing you ever remember from your grandmother, I want you to remember this: the quickest way to happiness for yourself is by doing something to help someone else. Not just at Christmas, either, but all the time. If you see a need, you step in and do something, you hear? Even a little something is better than nothing at all."*

"*But that's not what Aunt DeeCee says. She says if you don't go to church you're going to go to hell and burn forever, and you don't go to church, Grammie,"* the little girl pointed out with a worried frown.

"*Never you mind what she says,"* her grandmother replied, giving her knee a comforting pat. "*I get along just fine with God. I don't have to go inside a building to talk to Him. Every time I reach out in love to one of His creatures, animal or human, it's my way of saying thank you, Lord, for putting me here. For letting me have so much that I have something to give to someone else. And every time I say thanks to Him in that special way, why, He blesses me right back. You try it, honey, when you get a little older. You could say it's entirely selfish, you know—the quickest way there is to make yourself feel good. You'd be amazed how it works."*

"Well, I'm trying, Grammie," she said aloud. "And you're right. I probably enjoy reading to those children at least as much as they like hearing it..."

She stared into the deepening twilight at an icy wonderland, breathtaking in its beauty. A slight smile came to lips numb with cold, as she realized how much happier she had been, lately. How much she had to look forward to, in the peaceful little world she had begun to establish for herself. It might not be what she had thought she wanted, ten or twenty or even two years ago, but it was what she wanted now. At last, she settled back, warmed by the hay and worn out by the long walk. In another moment she was fast asleep.

Slowly, cautiously, Michael turned the Rover around, careful to stop short of the ditches on either side as he retraced his path along the edge of the woods. For some reason he kept thinking of a shed. *Go to the shed*, a voice kept hammering from somewhere deep in his brain.

"What shed?" he finally said aloud. He looked around, feeling a little silly, as if he might have been overheard. Then he remembered, snapping his fingers at his own stupidity. There *was* a shed, about half a mile off the road: he had played there as a child. Surely if Shannon had walked anywhere near it she would have sought shelter inside. In fact there was even a pathway, he recalled, just below a sign pointing the way to Burlingford.

He pulled to one side of the narrow lane and started down the path, then came back for the spare blanket that was always kept in the trunk. If indeed Shannon had made it to the shed, she was likely to be frozen through, and would need to be warmed as soon as possible. Grasping the flashlight in one hand, the blanket in the other, he broke into a half-run, all at once confident of what he would find.

Shannon blinked awake to a blinding beam of light in her face and an exultant, "I knew it!" from Michael.

"Hullo," she said, her words fuzzy with sleep. "I was just dreaming about you..."

"Scare us all again like that and it'll be more like a nightmare," he said, his face stern, as he wrapped the blanket around her damp body.

"Here, put your arm around my neck," he commanded, hoisting her off the ground. Nestled against his chest as they made their way down the path, she could hear Michael's heart racing. She wondered if it was only exertion that was making it hammer so.

"Thank God, thank God, you found her," Henry beamed as Michael headed for the staircase leading to his private apartment.

"Really, Michael, I'm all right, you can put me down now," Shannon protested, feeling more than a little self-conscious.

"No."

She couldn't see his expression but the reply was clipped enough for her not to challenge him again.

"Henry, I want Dr. Miller here right away to examine Miss Tyler for frostbite and exposure," added Michael, his long legs taking the steps two at a time despite his burden.

Henry was puffing up the stairway after them. "I already called him. He's in hospital delivering a baby, but there is a Dr. Rossman among our guests this week. I took the liberty of inquiring as to his specialty. He's an internist from Cleveland and says he would be happy to be of assistance if we should require it."

"Is the fire going good and hot upstairs?"

"Oh yes, indeed. We put another log on as you pulled into the driveway."

"Send up some hot tea as well, please." Michael swung around to close the door with one foot, either ignoring or failing to see Henry's astonished look at being so quickly dismissed.

Peeking over his shoulder, Shannon made no attempt to hide her curiosity as Michael deposited her on a green damask sofa in front of an ornate marble fireplace. Henry had given her a tour of most of the rest of the house but of course had never intruded into Michael's private apartment.

Such a handsome room, she decided, with another glance behind him as he set her down: bookshelves all around, a massive antique desk set at an angle across one corner, an oversized sofa facing the fireplace with armchairs on either side, all with the look of faded comfort she had come to associate with the best of English homes. Very handsome, indeed, and totally masculine. In fact, very much like its owner, who had begun to unwind the blanket around her as if he were unwrapping a giant present. She tried not to giggle as he abruptly stopped.

"Don't move," he commanded, returning a moment later with a flannel shirt, thick socks, and a soft navy bathrobe. "They'll probably swallow you but they're the best I could do," Michael said, tossing the clothing on the sofa and stepping back a few steps. He folded his arms and frowned, as if trying to decide what to do next.

"Th—thank you, I'm sure they're f-fine," replied Shannon, her teeth chattering as steam rose from her wet clothing. She rubbed her hands together, waiting for him to leave so she could get undressed.

"Oh. Pardon me." He finally understood why she was hesitating, and turned in some embarrassment toward the bedroom door. "Call me when you've finished."

No sooner had she pulled on the last sock and tied the bathrobe snugly around her waist than there came a discreet knock at the front door.

"Henry," she exclaimed with pleasure. "Since when did you start delivering the tea trays?"

"Ever since my favorite chess partner went and got herself lost in the woods," Henry winked. "Are you quite all right?"

"Just cold and wet, that's all. And very sorry to have scared all of you."

"Well, all the same the doctor will be up in a moment to check you over..."

"No, really, that isn't necessary," she protested. "I promise, I'm fine."

"I insist." At the sound of their voices, the bedroom door had opened. Michael's face was set and unsmiling, and Shannon felt guilty all over again for causing such trouble.

"Is Black Thunder all right?"

"Yes, indeed, it was his return without you that set us off looking. But don't you worry, he's having a nice dinner of oats and hay in the stable with not a care in the world."

Another knock.

"Ah, Dr. Rossman. Here's your patient now. Mind you take good care of her."

"Thank you, Henry," Shannon said. What a nice man he was. She glanced over to see if Michael's expression was still as rigid as it had been a moment ago. It was.

Dr. Rossman had been a handsome man, twenty years and forty pounds ago. His brown eyes seemed kind as he quickly took note of Shannon's color. Pale, but evidently not in shock.

"Well, young lady, come over to the light and let's have a better look at you," he said, waving her ahead of him toward the fireplace.

"And you, sir?" he said with a pointed look at Michael, who took the hint.

"I'll wait in here," he said, unnecessarily, as he retreated into the adjoining room.

"Now then, let's see those fingers and toes..."

When the doctor had left, after pronouncing her in remarkably good condition considering the length of her exposure, Shannon tapped gently on the bedroom door. She was startled when it opened immediately to reveal her landlord, his mouth still in the same grim line as when he found her, his eyes stern and cold.

It didn't help her self-confidence any that she was barely clothed, while Michael had changed into a white oxford-cloth shirt and gray flannel trousers. One hand was cupped around a crystal glass containing an inch of brandy.

"I want to thank you for rescuing me," she began. "I hope you know this isn't my usual style, to make trouble for everybody."

Aargh. Nothing. She knew she had caused all of them some anxiety, but he didn't have to act quite this nasty about it.

*Damn her, anyway*, Michael thought, as he tossed off another swallow of brandy. *What business did she have scaring all of them like that. And what business was it of his to care, one way or the other.* His brows drew together in a frown, as he tried without success to look away.

Shannon had no idea how appealing she looked at that

moment, with the flames behind her casting a reddish glow around her drying chestnut curls. Her green eyes were more vivid than usual against her pale skin, her mouth a delicate pink.

Still holding her gaze, Michael had to mentally shake himself to keep from grabbing her and crushing her into his arms, remembering how good her body had felt against his only a few minutes earlier. He turned away, forcing himself to concentrate on how foolish and careless she had been.

"Please," she said, "I feel as if I'm keeping you from this nice fire." She extended a hand as if to lead him there.

Michael ignored the gesture, unwilling to trust himself to stop with a touch of her hand, and settled into an armchair next to the crackling flames.

Shannon followed him with a pang of puzzled disappointment. For someone who had seemed happy to find her he was certainly acting indifferent now.

He eyed her over the top of his brandy glass.

"The doctor's verdict was encouraging, I trust?"

"Yes, thank you, he says I'm fine," she replied, splaying out her fingers in front of the fire, greedy for the warmth. "I'm just supposed to take it easy for a day or two—"

Just then the electricity in the room flickered, lowered, and went out altogether, leaving only the fire to cast dancing shadows around the room.

"What the—"

Annoyed, Michael started for the door, then stopped and raised a quizzical eyebrow when he saw Shannon break into a delighted grin.

"This is great!" she crowed. "When I was a kid in Atlanta, we used to get these huge ice storms every few years. All the power lines would get knocked out and we'd be without electricity for days, sometimes, and we would gather around the fireplace for Scrabble tournaments and tell stories..." She trailed off, her cheeks reddening as she realized how idiotic she must sound.

Michael settled back with a thoughtful expression, deciding that whatever was going on with the electrical system, it could wait. Such glee over the power going out was a new one, in his experience, and probably worth hearing more about—especially from someone who could well have frozen to death a few hours ago. She seemed remarkably resilient; he'd give her that.

"You are welcome to use the shower, here, once you are warmed up," he offered, trying to suppress the images that rose to mind of a naked Shannon, soaping up in the marble and mahogany of his bathroom.

"I would love to," she replied, grateful for a change of subject. "In fact, I should probably do it now before the water has time to cool off. If the electricity is out for a while it may be a while before there's enough hot water for a shower again."

"Oh, I shouldn't worry. The hotel has an emergency generator. I imagine it will kick in momentarily. In the meantime, however, do go ahead if you wish. You'll find candles and matches in the lower right hand drawer."

"Thank you, kind sir, she said," Shannon laughed, picking up the soft flannel of the bathrobe as she dropped into a curtsey. She was pleased to see his somber expression finally relax into a smile.

What a little actress she was, he thought, first a Southern belle that night in the library, and now an English maid. He was still chuckling to himself as she closed the bathroom door behind her.

*Candles in the lower drawer, eh?* Shannon frowned into the mirror. *Wonder who used them the last time a shower by candlelight had been called for?*

# 14

Sure enough, by the time Shannon had finished her shower the lights were back on.

"My apologies," Michael greeted her as she emerged from the steamy bathroom. "I suppose we'll have to be citizens of the twentieth century after all. Of course, if you prefer, there's no reason why we can't turn the lights off again in favor of candles and firelight."

He gestured toward the fireplace, where two dinner plates topped by heavy silver covers stood waiting. Small wooden tables had been set up in front of each armchair, and a bottle of champagne was chilling in a bucket nearby. "I took the liberty of having Henry send up a couple of trays," he explained.

"Oh, Michael, this is lovely," she smiled, surprised and touched. Who would have imagined this gruff man capable of such a thoughtful gesture? "Thank you. And yes, I would like it very much if we lit the candles."

"Certainly," he said, his voice pleased.

She settled into the armchair opposite his and peeked underneath the plate cover to see what it contained, trying to suppress how self-conscious she felt about her clothing. His clothing, actually. She choked back a giggle.

"What's so funny?"

"Just—how elegant all this is, and how silly I must look sitting here in your bathrobe. And your socks," she added, holding out one foot and wiggling it, abandoning the attempt to hold back her laughter.

"I don't think you look silly at all," he said.

Coloring, Shannon reached for a fork.

She was hungrier than she had realized, and made short work of her chicken breast stuffed with rice, spinach and ricotta cheese. The roasted potatoes and glazed carrots disappeared almost as rapidly.

"Mmm, whoever said the English can't cook never ate here," she said at last, settling back with a sign of satisfaction.

"My mother's influence." He acknowledged the compliment with a salute of his wine glass. "She was Italian, and always insisted on good food and fresh ingredients. None of this boil-the-roast-for-nine-hours business for her."

"Italian?" Shannon said, her reporter's curiosity piqued. "How did she get all the way out here?"

"War bride," he said, then continued when he saw that she seemed genuinely interested and wasn't just making conversation. "My father was wounded at Anzio and they met in a hospital in Rome where she was volunteering, as many of the ladies did in those days. When the war was over he brought her back here."

"Really," she said. "Was it a difficult adjustment for her?"

"I suppose," he said, turning back to the fireplace. His voice was even, his words clipped and precise. "I don't really know. Both my parents were killed in a plane crash when I was three. They were on their way back to Italy to see if they could locate any of my mother's relatives who had been displaced in the war. Their plane went into the side of a mountain." His eyes never moved from the fire but she could see a muscle begin to twitch in his jaw.

"Oh," she said, her eyes glistening as she pictured Michael as a lonely little boy. As sad in his own way, as little brown-eyed Sam in her reading group, whose father had left the family at midsummer. What was it Michael had told her once? Oh, yes. "I spent a lot of time with the gardeners," were his words shortly after they met. And then, he had to face another heartbreaking loss in Mariko, the mysterious wife whose name was only mentioned in a whisper around Burlingford.

"How awful for you," she finally said. "I wish there were something more I could say than—I am so sorry. I can't imagine all you've been through."

The face that he turned to her was carefully blank, but his eyes were bleak and unguarded. She caught her breath at the pain she could see there; the pain—and loneliness, too—that seemed to permeate his entire being. As she watched, she could see his expression soften, without knowing that it was in response to the moisture he could see welling in her eyes.

"You know about Mariko, too, then."

"Yes. I was curious, that first time I saw you, why you were so upset about a parking place. Remember? At the chemist's. You were livid because a car—I regret to say, mine—was blocking the walkway for pedestrians."

"Indeed. Well, imagine how you might feel if it were your own negligence that killed your wife, your own blasted focus on your career to the exclusion of everything else, even something as basic as a caution sign and a crosswalk."

Michael's face was dark. He drained the contents of his wine glass in a single gulp, his long fingers circling the fragile stem as if he were debating whether to refill it or throw it into the fireplace.

"But you weren't driving the truck that ran into her," she argued.

"No, I was just the bloody fool who kept on promising her I would do something about all the cars in the village. She would come home from school and complain in her sweet quiet way about having to cross the street with a string of rambunctious children, and nothing to slow everyone down. And I would listen and nod and say yes dear, right away, dear, I'll take care of it, dear. Until the day that a driver who had one pint too many over lunch at the pub failed to see them crossing until it was too late. I was the rising star in London, you see, the dashing young Lord who was oh so concerned about acid rain and overpopulation in the Third World and troop strength amongst the Warsaw Pact—I couldn't be bothered with anything as mundane as traffic control. Until... one day the lack of it wiped out everything I cared about. At least with my parents, I was so little I barely knew them. Mariko... Mariko was—" he said, and swallowed hard, his words suspended in mid-sentence. He pressed his lips together and was silent, looking around the room as if wishing he were anywhere other than here.

Shannon stared, feeling his misery and guilt as acutely as if they were her own. She wanted to walk over and cradle his head to her chest, smoothing back his hair as a mother might comfort a child, but she didn't dare risk such an intimate gesture. *Love is the answer, Shannon*, came the words from a faraway corner of her brain. Love must include helping people, comforting them when you could— but how could she ever reach out to this remote stranger? Was it even possible for him to make peace with himself?

As she sat, frozen with indecision, Michael sighed, the reserved mask he usually wore settling back into place.

"More wine?" he asked, his tone deliberately light. "I do apologize. I had no right to dump all of that into your lap. It was a long time ago, after all. It simply comes back and smacks me in the face every now and again."

"You had every right, Michael. I'm honored that you would confide in me," she said in a low voice.

"Yes. Well." He pushed aside the tray table and stood up, as remote again as if they had been discussing the weather. "Let me get someone up here to clear these trays."

Crossing to the telephone, he clicked the receiver twice, then swore under his breath.

"The lines must be down somewhere," he announced. "I will need to check again with Henry. He said earlier the hotel was completely booked and if that's still the case you'll stay here tonight, in my room. I can take one of the couches. I won't have you out in the cottage in this weather with no electricity and no telephone."

Shannon blinked as his broad back retreated across the room, wishing she could come up with the right combination of words or gestures, the right thing to say or do that might soothe and comfort him.

*Whew*, she thought, when the door closed behind him. *And I thought I was hurting.*

That night, as she snuggled under the goose-down comforter covering her landlord's antique mahogany bed, she dreamed of a man trapped in ice. His eyes were closed, his fingers frozen into claws, as he tried to break free of the bleak prison that held him captive. "Help me," he was pleading. The face she saw was Michael's.

The next morning she awoke to a world that was pristine white, brilliant sunshine sparkling off blinding snow. After a quick splash of water on her face, she cautiously opened the door to the living room and peeked around it.

"Worst snowstorm in thirty years," Michael announced from his place by the fire, his expression surprisingly cheerful as he lowered his book. "School's closed, roads are impassable. No one is going anywhere."

A fire was blazing away behind gigantic brass andirons, and Henry's signature domed covers were lined up again on tables next to the armchairs. Through the open door to the study she could see sheets and a blanket neatly folded over the sofa where he had spent the night.

"You're just in time. Henry's brought up eggs and tea and scones. There's even a pot of coffee—I assume you still drink the dreadful stuff, although I'm sure I don't know how," he said, pretending to shudder.

"Actually, believe it or not, I've become a pretty serious tea drinker," replied Shannon as she made her way to the fire.

"Wow," she added, admiring the cozy setup. "With service like this, I may never go home." She slid into an armchair and shook the folds from a crisp linen napkin before smoothing it onto her lap.

"Well, you're probably stuck here for another day at least, if you can stand it. The electricity is out all over the district. Henry said they hope to have it restored to the cottage sometime tomorrow," he continued. "Would you care for a scone?"

Michael had decided long ago that the true test of beauty was how a woman looked first thing in the morning. As he held out the bread basket, he had to admit this woman passed the test and then some. Her thick chestnut hair was in cheery disarray over her shoulders but her face was freshly scrubbed, without the pallor of the night before. In fact, she appeared to be glowing with good health.

"Ahem," she said with a gentle cough, helping herself to a scone. "As the wise man once said, do I have a bug in my ear?"

He leaned back in his chair, folding a pair of muscular arms across his chest, and gave her a cocky smile. He felt suddenly, inexplicably, quite pleased with himself.

"I was merely congratulating myself on having a tenant with such a strong constitution," was all he said.

She returned the smile and began to spread the clotted cream. "Speaking of tenants, past and present, what's the story with the ghost? Is there one, really, or is that just how you chase away the undesirables?"

"Of course there's a ghost," he said. She took a bite and looked up to find his eyes were playful. "Did you think we made him up?"

Her mouth was too full for a reply, so she shrugged and raised her eyebrows by way of response.

"Actually, to give you a more serious answer," he continued, "I'm told there was a great deal of talk about a ghost in my father's day. Then, more recently, the young man who rented the cottage began complaining of some odd events right after Christmas: lights going off and on, that sort of thing. The last straw was sometime in March when he said he woke up to a voice saying 'Get out,' and off he fled to London. And then, a few weeks later, you showed up. You haven't heard anything, really?"

"Not a thing," she assured him. "Maybe the ghost likes me. Although I have been having some pretty interesting dreams."

"Oh? Anything you might like to share?"

"I ... can't remember anything specific right now," she said vaguely, embarrassed to tell him how often she had heard her mother's mournful voice begging forgiveness, until—it suddenly struck her—until that morning in Atlanta when she had said she did forgive her, after her talk with Aunt DeeCee and the dream that had followed. The moment when she had understood, finally, *why* Diana might have wanted her forgiveness. Why she seemed to think it necessary. From that day on, the dreams had stopped—the ones featuring Diana, anyway...

Michael gave her a sharp look, aware that she was concealing something, but reluctant to push.

"I'm glad you haven't found it annoying," he finally said. "Now.

Seeing that you seem to be stuck at Braeburn House today, what would you like to do?"

"Well," she laughed, looking down with a rueful smile, "without my clothes, I'm afraid my options are pretty limited. "

He chuckled. "Let me see if they've been able to salvage any of what you were wearing yesterday. If not," as he threw up his hands in a gesture of surrender, "I'm afraid you'll have to settle for a long nap by the fire."

"Oh no," she said. She wagged a finger at him that he could tell meant business. "One way or the other, I'm getting out of here to build a snowman. Even if I go out looking like Charlie Chaplin—in *your* Sunday best!"

That evening, after the trays had been removed at the conclusion of another cozy dinner, Michael issued a challenge.

"You and me, one game of chess, winner take all," he proposed.

"Be careful," she warned. "Henry says I'm getting pretty ferocious."

"Yes, I rather supposed you might be," he replied, enjoying the gleam in her eye, his own alight with anticipation. If nothing else, the game gave him a perfect excuse to sit and stare at her without seeming rude, which, at the moment, struck him as a good way to pass the time. What a fascinating woman she was; funny, serious, lively and sympathetic by turns. He couldn't quite put his finger on it but there was something compelling about her, something that made him want to watch her every expression for as long as possible without calling attention to himself. It seemed beyond belief that he had only known her for such a short time. She was a total stranger, really. And yet—there was a connection there, something about the two of them together, that made it seem as if they had been chatting by the fireplace forever. *Soulmates,* the thought hit him. Was that the word for it?

A little more than an hour later he was forced to concede defeat. Truth was, he'd spent so much time watching his guest, he had hardly paid any attention to his own game. He still couldn't work out why she seemed so familiar, but it was a mystery he was in no hurry to solve.

"Checkmate," she announced with a triumphant smile. "Hey, I thought you were supposed to be good at this. That's what Henry claims, anyway. You must have parked your brain somewhere else tonight."

"Even the best players lose sometimes," he said, not caring in the slightest. He certainly wasn't going to admit how distracted he'd been. "Henry was right: you are tough."

"And for my prize—I get to pick the next activity."

"Fair enough, it would be your turn anyway. So what shall it be—cards? Swords? Anything but more snowman-building. You quite wore me out today." He stretched, yawning, and laced his fingers together behind his head.

"No, this one requires brains more than brawn. I'm curious about how well NATO could withstand an invasion from Eastern Europe. Assuming that's not top-secret, of course. "

With an effort he snapped his jaw shut before it became too obvious that it had dropped. "Not to sound condescending, but how do you know that's even on the defense minister's mind?" he parried.

"Old reporter's trick," she explained, her face bland. "I saw a position paper lying on your desk and read the title—upside down of course. Any reporter who can't read upside down at twenty paces has to turn in the trench coat."

He continued to stare at her, more than a little nonplussed. Of all the things that could have come out of her mouth, he had certainly not expected this. "Really," he said. "You're a journalist, then. I wondered what you did before now."

"I am. Or at least I was. I'm not sure what I am at the moment," she confessed. Her face was pensive as she wrapped a curl around her finger and gazed into the fire.

"It's a long story," she said, her mood shifting as she turned back to him with a determined smile. "I won't bore you with it now. But I really do want to hear what all of you think about NATO."

"Well..." he said, leaning forward to gather his thoughts, "it's a bit tricky for Europe, actually...," as he launched into a detailed analysis of the minister's report—at least what parts of it could be safely disclosed.

Surprised as he was by her interest, he was even more amazed by her grasp of the subject.

"How is it you know so much about this?" he broke off his explanation at one point to demand.

"As in: most Americans don't know and couldn't care less about foreign policy?" she couldn't resist teasing.

"Well... yes."

"Oh, I don't know. I suppose I've always been intrigued by politics, and now that I'm here I find that I'm a lot more interested in how people in Europe see things. Somehow the world looks different from over here. The American perspective seems a little limited, somehow."

"Really. I must say I'm impressed."

"Hey. I read *The Economist*," she said, her eyebrows arching in mock belligerence, then added more gracefully, "Thank you for the compliment. *I'm* impressed by your knowledge."

They exchanged another smile and then she rose, stifling a yawn. "And now if you'll excuse me, I'm going to wander off to bed before I start to snore."

"Thank you for warning me," he grinned. "Good thing I need to check in with Henry downstairs."

Shannon stopped by the window to admire the snowman they had constructed that morning, now listing slightly to his right on the lawn outside.

"He looks a little drunk, doesn't he?" she said, and turned to smile over her shoulder as Michael strolled over to investigate. She caught her breath, feeling her heart leap as he wrapped his arms around and over hers, cuddling her against his broad chest in a warm embrace, his cheek resting against her head as they gazed at the snowy lawn.

"Thank you for today," he said, a note of tenderness turning his voice deeper and more husky than usual.

Her head reeling, she was almost afraid to breathe. As much as she longed to, she didn't dare turn around, afraid of what might happen next. Afraid she might scare him away completely. It felt so good to be held by someone who didn't seem to regard her as a casual conquest.

Shannon closed her eyes, feeling the blood start to pound through her body as she warmed to his touch. Wishing he wouldn't move. Wishing the two of them could just stand like that forever...

"I—enjoyed it too," she finally whispered.

He planted a swift kiss on the top of her head and gave her a last affectionate squeeze.

"Good night then. I'll see you tomorrow." With that he was gone, quietly closing the door behind him.

She stood at the window for a moment more, pressing her hands to her cheeks. Her heart was racing madly in her chest, a hot flush pulsing from her toes to her hairline. On a sudden impulse she leaned forward and blew on the frosted windowpane, watching as her breath formed delicate crystals on the glass. She traced a tiny heart in the fog with her forefinger, then quickly erased it and drifted off to bed.

At 2:46 in the morning, Shannon awoke with a start. A column of golden light was glowing at the bottom of her bed. She rubbed the sleep from her eyes, stunned and incredulous at what she was seeing—dreaming? As she watched, a face appeared faintly in the glow. Thin and insubstantial as a hologram, the image moved slowly as it examined the room up and down, side to side.

She realized all at once that it was her father's face she saw. Not the drawn and wasted one she had last seen in Atlanta, with deep lines etched by pain and suffering. This face was young, robust, healthy, brimming with energy and excitement.

"Dad?" she whispered.

"Here you are," the figure said, looking pleased. "Good, good."

Did she hear his voice? Or did the words form themselves, somehow, inside her head?

She stared at the glowing apparition, too fascinated to be afraid.

"I can go then," he said, the gold light beginning to fade, "your mother's waiting for me." She felt a faint cool breeze along her cheek, soft as a caress. She reached up her hand and touched the skin where the sensation had been, her eyes filled with wonder.

Another moment more and the light was gone, the room restored to its usual darkness, except for the faint gleam of moonlight reflecting off the snow outside.

For more than an hour, she sat up in bed, hugging her knees to her chest and dissecting the mysterious message. Had she been dreaming? She didn't think so. Dreams were one thing, even ones as vivid as she had been having back at the cottage, but this was different. This last was the sort of thing she wouldn't want to tell anyone about—although, for some reason, it hadn't been at all frightening.

If anything, it had been comforting. Reassuring, even. But why would she be seeing her father now? Unless... unless perhaps he was indeed on his way somewhere else...

Shortly after noon a telegram arrived from her aunt. "Tried to call," it read. "Your father took a sudden turn for the worse and died in his sleep last night. Cremated this morning as per his instructions. Call when you can. Love, Aunt DeeCee."

# 15

The steady staccato of raindrops splashing down from the eaves and drumming onto the stones of the patio were a fitting accompaniment to the bleakness of Shannon's mood on this mid-November evening. Monday's storm had been followed by unseasonably warm temperatures that melted all trace of snow around Braeburn House—except for the snowman that Shannon and Michael had created so gleefully on the lawn. Their joint creation had lasted two more days, shrinking and becoming more misshapen by the hour, until finally he was only a giant puddle. And now it was raining, one of those steady, determined downpours that kept everything here so green.

Shannon stared pensively into the fire she had lit to chase away the gloom of early winter. Was it really her father she had seen the other night, at just the time Aunt DeeCee's telegram said he had died? It had certainly seemed real enough, at the time...

And why had he seemed so pleased to find her there, in Michael's bed? She had come to Burlingford in search of a new direction for her life, not for romance. Obviously, Michael hadn't been looking for anyone, either, if his standoffishness was a reflection of his true feelings. Here it had been three days since she had returned to the cottage and not so much as a telephone call from him.

"Are you sure love is worth the trouble?" she asked the ceiling in exasperation, aiming the question at the heavens in general and her father in particular—then clapped her hand over her mouth in dismay when she realized what she had said. Love? Who had mentioned anything about love?

Well, she had to admit, maybe that's exactly what this was all about. Why else would she be moping around, feeling sad about her father, certainly, but also gloomy and irritable because she hadn't heard from Michael. Between the mysterious visit the other night and the dozens of communications from beyond she had been reading about in Clare's book, the thought of death—even the death of someone she loved as much as her father—no longer seemed quite so frightening. No wonder the book had been a best seller. Weren't all of us looking for some hope, some evidence that dying was not the end of everything, as people feared? That somehow, in some way, the unique energy that was "us," continued, in a different form? That those we love could still watch over us, even if they might not be able to communicate directly?

No, she decided. These feelings weren't about grief; somehow she knew her Dad was fine, wherever he was. It was heartache that was troubling her on this gray and gloomy night. Heartache, and loneliness.

She sat up straighter on the sofa, struck by a sudden thought, her eyes widening as she considered the possibilities. Maybe it wasn't just bad luck and bad timing that had kept love from her door all this time; maybe she had raised the barricades around herself so high that no one could get in. She had no friends at school; her father had been caught up in his law practice; Aunt DeeCee was too strict—and too busy—to offer much loving companionship to a lonely little girl. "Maybe," she mused aloud, her eyes narrowed at the thought, "Maybe *I'm* the one who kept people out—pushed them away even when they would have been there for me, if only I had asked. Maybe I didn't want anyone to get too close for fear I'd get hurt."

Maybe Grammie Lib was right. Maybe reaching out to someone else was, absolutely, how you made your own life better. She thought back to when she had been touched by Henry's loneliness, months ago in the library; how fully she had been repaid by her efforts to understand Michael's painful past, even if she hadn't been able to help him with it. Why, if it hadn't been for him, she could have frozen to death out there in the woods. As for Henry, she couldn't ask for a kinder friend. And her story-time children, for she thought of them, now, as "hers"—they had also brought an immeasurable richness to her life.

Shannon began to pace around the living room, too excited to sit still. You can't hurry love—she knew that much from The Supremes—but maybe her Dad was right. Maybe you did have to allow yourself to be open to it, ready for it, willing and able to welcome it when it appeared. Maybe it really did come along when you quit trying to force it, when you finally surrendered and said *Okay, fate, ready when you are.* Maybe you had to get out of your own way, first. Figure out who *you* were and what *you* wanted instead of letting other people dictate the course of your life. Like Aunt DeeCee had attempted to do, throughout her teenage years. Like she had allowed her old bosses at WSYA and then the network to do, for far too long.

She crossed to the French doors to measure the progress of the rain. The patio stones were at least two inches under water and the showers showed no sign of letting up. "This isn't a shower, it's a monsoon," she muttered. Making her way to the tape player, she popped in the cassette of "Amazing Grace," hoping the music might soothe her. Funny, how a song she had always hated had come to be such a comfort over the past few months; the simple faith of the words as well as the beautiful melody. "'Twas Grace hath kept me safe thus far..." she sang along as the rich notes filled the house. Wouldn't it be nice to think that something—anything—was able to keep you safe these days...

Maybe a book would help the evening go by faster. Her restless steps took her to the bookcases lining either side of the fireplace. She ran her fingers across the voluminous selection: everything from the classics to a smattering of the most recent best sellers. Shakespeare, she decided. Something timeless that might help her figure out the puzzle pieces of her life. Almost without thinking, she pulled out a slim leather-bound volume of *Romeo and Juliet*.

*Now there's a pair of star-crossed lovers for you*, she couldn't help but smile: *sure puts your life into perspective, doesn't it? You might be unhappy from time to time but there's certainly nothing bad enough to make you want to kill yourself.*

She opened the volume and sniffed the pages. She loved the smell of old books, that musty combination of print and ink that signaled adventure was ahead—and was startled when a piece of creamy notepaper fluttered out.

"Hello," she said, stooping to pick it up. "Where did you come from?"

Even a glance told her that it was very old. The paper was yellowed around the edges, the handwriting an elegant copperplate she had always associated with Victorian times. Unfolding the paper carefully, she was astonished to find the page filled with a series of aphorisms and Bible verses.

"In Adam's Fall We Sinned All," the first one read, crossed through with a decisive stroke of black ink.

"Ask, and it shall be given you. Seek, and ye shall find; knock, and it shall be opened to you.—Matthew 7:7" was the next entry.

"Be strong and of good courage; be not afraid, neither be dismayed, for the Lord thy God is with thee wherever thou goest—Joshua 1:9". That one had a question mark in the margin next to it. No wonder, Shannon thought; what an inspiring idea.

And, then, the verse that fairly leaped off the page at her, so familiar had it become from the needlepoint in her bathroom. Eight simple words she saw every time she brushed her teeth. "Be still, and know that I am God.—Psalms 46:10."

Below it on the notepaper were two more verses that by now seemed implanted in her brain: "The truth will make you free—John 8:32," followed by, "The kingdom of God is within you—Luke 17:21."

Shannon began to smile. The woman who stitched the samplers upstairs must have been mulling over a number of choices before settling on the three verses she wanted, the ones she would labor over for so many hours before pronouncing herself satisfied. How long it must have been before she was ready to stitch her initials, A.D., at the bottom, and frame the ideas she had chosen. Why, this must be her handwriting, then, the original lady who had inhabited the Lady's Cottage. Shannon felt chill bumps along the back of her neck as she examined it eagerly, looking for some hint, some clue about the character of the woman who had lived here so long ago. What was it Mrs. Satterfield had said: that she had died, tragically. Perhaps it was her ghost that had been shooing people away, ever since.

"Can't say I blame you," Shannon told the notepaper. "I wouldn't want anybody here, either." But wait, she reminded herself. The only person she had seen in her dreams was her mother. Certainly not some romantic Victorian lady.

Shannon smiled at the thick black line drawn with some vigor through the first saying. "Guess you didn't much go for the concept of Original Sin, did you, A.D., whoever you are," she laughed. "You must have been a rebel in your day, too."

She bent her head to examine the bottom verses more closely. "Well, lady, you must have been pretty smart. You were right to choose this one: the truth does make you free. Free to be who you truly are, not what somebody else wants you to be. I was certainly freed by finding out the truth about my mother—and about what my Dad valued most in life. And, 'be still'," she mused. "You're right. That's important, too."

Shannon's eyes drifted to the window, where the trees were outlined against the barren expanse of lawn. "In my old life, I didn't have much time to be still, did I? No," she corrected, "didn't take the time. Maybe you can't absorb anything worth knowing until you can do that. If you're always so busy running around ... if the rush of living distracts you from the sound of your own heart, how can you ever discover what you want?"

She stiffened at a muffled sound at the front door. Was that someone on the porch? As she reached the foyer, she heard a firm knock and saw a shadow on the translucent door, too tall to be Henry.

"Coming," she called as she slipped the notepaper back inside *Romeo and Juliet* and replaced the book on the shelf. Her discovery was too private, too intriguing to share with anyone just yet.

"Michael—come in before you drown. What a nice surprise," she said. Her voice was warm as she opened the door, a much different greeting from the sulky and indignant hello she might have given him had he arrived an hour earlier. "Here, let me take your coat."

He stood in the foyer, as awkward and unsure of himself as a little boy. As he held up a basket of fruit in one hand and brandished a bottle of wine in the other, she guessed from the look of mingled guilt and relief on his face that he must have been expecting a very different reception from the one he was getting.

"I am so sorry I haven't been by before now," he said, holding out the peace offerings. "Just as you got the news about your father, I got called back to London for an emergency session—the Middle East again. It's been non-stop ever since."

"You don't have to apologize," she assured him. "I understand."

"I thought you might enjoy some fresh fruit. Henry said these just came from the greengrocer," Michael continued, handing her the basket.

"Thank you, really, that's so nice," she said, touched by the gesture. "I haven't been out much the past couple of days, certainly not in this downpour."

"I'm not intruding?"

"Not at all. In fact, I'm grateful for the company. I was just sitting here feeling a little lonely and sorry for myself, so you're just in time. Would you like some tea?"

His face was skeptical as he followed her down the hallway. "You—lonely? You strike me as the most self-sufficient of women."

"Well, I suppose I am when I have to be," she admitted, "but, as your little mission of mercy has just reminded me, it's nice being around other people, too. I'd say it's all your fault—yours and Henry's—for making me feel so welcome last week," she added with a laugh.

His eyes followed her as she set a kettle on to boil and reached into the cabinet for a tin of tea. Not for the first time, he was astonished by her candor, by her disarming American way of admitting straight out what she thought and felt—even that she was lonely sometimes. He had missed her, too, but found that fact difficult—no, impossible—to admit.

Arriving back from London, his apartment in Braeburn House had never seemed so empty and echoing. He found himself haunted by pictures of Shannon in the armchair across from his in front of the fireplace, waving her fork in the air and laughing. Haunted by those images and now, damn it, almost tongue-tied. Yet here she was, confessing simply and directly, without a trace of coquettishness or embarrassment, that she had enjoyed his company and missed him once he was gone.

"Well done. I'm not sure that many of your countrymen could

do this properly," was all he said, however, as she shook tea leaves into a silver strainer over each cup, then carefully poured the steaming hot water to let them steep.

"You can give Henry the credit for that one. If it hadn't been for him, I'd still be using tea bags."

Michael shuddered. "Dreadful invention."

"Yeah, yeah—purist. Do you want to take these in by the fire?"

"I'm yours to command," he said, trying to sound as agreeable as possible as he fell into step behind her. *That'll be the day*, she smiled to herself, patting her hand on the sofa to indicate there was plenty of room for him there.

"Actually, I'd rather take the chair, if you don't mind. I can see more of you than your right ear that way."

Her face went pink at the compliment. The iceman *had* thawed since her visit. "I have been known to turn my head, especially when someone asks nicely," she said, trying to subdue a widening smile. "But you should sit wherever you're most comfortable."

Michael settled into his chair, his expression puzzled as he looked around.

"What?" Shannon said at last.

"Something seems different in here," he announced. "I'm trying to decide what it is."

She followed his eyes around the cozy living room, at her growing collection of Victorian inkwells and the antique pillows she had purchased on one of her occasional forays into London. She had even acquired a burgundy cashmere lap-robe to fling over one corner of the sofa—but dollars to doughnuts, no man alive would ever notice that kind of subtle decorating touch. No, it had to be something else he was looking for.

"I know," he announced, in the voice of a man who had triumphed against incredible odds. "It's the television. Did you move it upstairs?"

Shannon stifled a grin. Trust a man to notice when the TV was missing. "No," she said with a perfectly straight face. "I took it into the city and pawned it. I got these lovely pillows instead. Do you like them?"

Michael closed and opened his mouth a couple of times in an obvious struggle for an appropriate response. "Ah—," he said, then read the truth in her dancing eyes a millisecond before she burst into laughter.

"You can tell the most ridiculous story with the straightest face I've ever seen," he marveled. "Are you quite sure you aren't British?"

"Cross my heart. I'm as American as they come."

He shook his head with a rueful grin. "I see. What did you really do with it?"

"I . . . ," she hesitated, wondering how honest she could be with him. How strange it might sound if she told him the real reason she had locked the television away. She took a deep breath and decided to risk it.

"I put it away. It's in the closet. After the massacres at Sabra and Shatila I decided to see if I could live without it for a while. I figured best if *I* were in charge of the pictures that got inside my head. Besides, it was taking up too much of my time. I've found other things to do that I like better."

He absorbed her explanation with a grave nod of his head. "You're probably wiser than the rest of us, then," he added after a moment. "There's precious little worth watching anymore."

They sipped their tea in silence, then Michael put his cup aside and leaned forward. "I haven't had a chance to tell you privately how sorry I was to hear about your father. I wasn't sure I would even find you here today but Henry told me there wasn't a formal service."

Shannon shook her head. "That's my dad. He decided years ago to be cremated and he insisted on as little fuss as possible. Instead of having people waste their money on flowers he couldn't smell, he said, he would much prefer it if they contributed to a scholarship fund he set up. I spoke to my aunt last night and she said the money's been pouring in. He would be very pleased by that."

"His death was somewhat sudden, I take it? I know he had been ill, but it didn't seem as if he was in imminent danger..."

"Yes and no," she replied, circling a finger around the rim of her teacup. "We all hoped for the best after his surgery last summer, and the doctors seemed to think he was recovering well even if they couldn't tell us how much more time he might have. So, yes, I suppose I was prepared for it to a certain extent. Although it's always a shock when it happens. Mostly I'm trying to remember him as he was when he was vigorous and healthy, not all gaunt and wasted like the last time I saw him in the hospital." She fell silent, remembering their conversation about life and love, about his regrets from the past and his hopes for her future. Remembering, too, his strange appearance the night he died, wondering if she would ever get up the nerve to confide to Michael what she had seen. Or—her reporter's brain reminded her—what she thought she saw.

"If it wouldn't be too painful for you... I wonder if you might tell me a little about him."

"I think I would like that very much," she replied softly, a little surprised by the invitation. Then it dawned on her. Of course—he had grown up without a father or mother around. No wonder he was interested. Or was he interested because it was *her* story he wanted to hear?

Shannon began to speak, the words coming out slowly at first, then quickly, almost tumbling over each other in a flood of remembrance.

"Growing up, I took my Dad for granted, I suppose like all children do. He was just—always there, usually stretched out in his favorite reading chair in the living room with a stack of books piled beside him or a tower of files from whatever case he was working on. He wasn't just an intellectual, though: he taught me how to throw a baseball and hit a home run. He spent hours teaching me how to play chess, and was as excited as I was the first time I managed to beat him because he insisted that I win fair and square. He taught me the finer points of football and grammar and good manners, and he pointed the way toward becoming the kind of person I wanted to be. My dad pushed me to see the other person's point of view, always, even when I didn't want to. He said it was much better to go through life with an attitude of, 'How may I help you?' instead of, 'What's in it for me?' He told me I could do anything, be anything I wanted to be, as long as I was willing to work for it—pretty radical advice for a girl child in those days.

"Not everything in his life was happy, certainly. My mother died when I was born and he was very lonely for a long time—tried to bury himself in his work, apparently. I don't remember him much when I was little, but by the time I was seven or eight he had snapped out of it, so that's when my memories of him really begin. He got involved in politics for a few years—even thought about running for governor one day—but it didn't work out. Maybe he was too nice a guy to have succeeded, anyway, but by the time he was ready, the party had decided to look elsewhere. Still, he lived his life pretty much the way he wanted, and when it was time for him to go, he went with no complaints. And as awful as it was when he got sick, at least I got to tell him how much he had meant to me—how much I learned from him. I honestly don't think he had any idea. We were a pretty quiet family and didn't tend to have those kinds of conversations."

She stopped, suddenly realizing that what she had intended as a few appreciative comments had turned into quite a monologue. "Sorry. I've probably told you far more than you wanted to know."

"Not at all."

"I wish he had been able to visit me here so you could have met him. I know he would have loved the cottage. And I think you two would have liked each other."

"No doubt. He sounds like a remarkable man."

"Yes, he was. Thank you for letting me talk about him. I do feel better," she replied, aware, suddenly, how much lighter she felt having shared her sadness. And now it was her turn to lean forward, cupping her chin in her hand as she studied him.

"If it's not too intrusive, I would be interested in hearing about Mariko. If you feel like talking, of course," she offered. "Not about how she died—I already know that part. I'm more interested in knowing how she lived, who she was, what she cared about."

He drew back, startled, but knowing she meant well. Mariko was such a silent inner ache in his soul, a private anguished part of himself he had kept tucked away for so long, he wasn't sure that he was even able to talk about their life before the accident.

"Well...," he said, hesitating for a long moment. Baring his soul went so completely against how he had always conducted himself. On the other hand—well, what the hell, he thought, feeling a little reckless. If Shannon said it had made her feel better to talk about her father, perhaps it might work for him as well.

"We met at the London School of Economics," he began, turning his face to the fire as if the words he wanted might appear somewhere in the flames.

Shannon sat back and began to breathe again. She had been afraid for a minute there that she had gone too far, overstepped her bounds; that he would retreat again into careful correctness, brush away her newly urgent effort to understand him.

"Mariko was tiny, so small and delicate. I know it's a cliché, but she really was like a dainty little doll, all jet-black hair and red lipstick and porcelain skin. But she had a spirit and intelligence that let you know she was a lot tougher than she looked. She was half-Japanese, actually. Her father was an American businessman who had gone there after the war, met her mother and stayed. Her very traditional mother was horrified that Mariko wanted a degree in economics, which of course made Mariko all the more determined to do it, just as her grandparents' opposition had made her mother all the more determined to marry an American. I wouldn't know from personal experience," Michael added with a rueful smile, "but I gather that people will do a lot to spite their parents."

Amen to that one, Shannon sighed to herself. Not to mention some of their other relatives. "Almost makes you wonder why people have kids, doesn't it?" she said, trying to lighten the conversation a little.

"Oh, I hear there are compensations," he replied, his tone lightening in response to hers. "Especially in their creation."

Shannon's eyes widened. He had always been extremely proper around her, at least until his hug the night they'd built the snowman. Maybe he was just being friendly; on the other hand—

She prompted, "Go on with your story," as her face grew warmer under the scrutiny of two piercing blue eyes.

"There's not much more to tell. We fell in love, we got married, I took my place in Parliament, eager to apply all my new economic theories to government, and Mariko began teaching at the village school. The rest you know."

"What was she like as a person? Was she happy here?"

"I wish I knew. Sometimes it was hard to tell," he said.

"For all her rebellious streak, she was quiet and reserved, very much the dutiful daughter, from what I gather, and then the dutiful wife. I seldom had a clue what she was thinking about and usually she wouldn't tell me when I'd ask; there was a very private part of her I never felt I could touch somehow. In fact ... " he hesitated, "now that I look back I wonder how well I did know her. Perhaps not very well at all. We both had our separate lives, you see. And, I suppose, one can get bogged down a bit in married life."

"But, Michael, don't you think if she were miserable here she would have told you about it? Maybe she was happy with the choices she made."

"Yes, of course, but—" He stopped, shaking his head in amazement. "Isn't that odd. Here I've been carrying around this mythic portrait in my head all these years of Mariko the Martyred Wife, sacrificed on the altar of her husband's stupidity, but as far as Mariko the person..." His words trailed off.

From her place on the sofa, Shannon finished her tea and sat quietly, watching him. There seemed to be little she could add, so she was content to let the silence stretch from one minute into two.

"Would you like some more tea?" she inquired at last.

"Thank you, no," he said, rousing himself from the armchair. He was so comfortable, and the conversation had been so interesting and illuminating, that he would have been happy to sit where he was for hours if there weren't so much yet to do. "I have to be going. I'm meeting Henry this evening to go over plans for the Christmas Revels."

"Revels? That sounds like fun."

"That's right, I had forgotten you haven't been here for the holidays before. It feels as if you've always been around..."

From her perch on the sofa, Shannon held back a double-take, trying not to look as startled as she felt. *Two* personal comments in one night?

"... the Christmas Revels have been celebrated in the Great Hall at Braeburn House for nearly two hundred years. They're quite something. Music and dancing and treats for the children and wassailing all around, just as they did in the village long before there even was a Braeburn House. Do say you'll be there—or are you planning to go home for Christmas?"

Shannon shook her head. "No, I thought about it but there's just my aunt now, and she wanted to visit some cousins in Savannah, so I've decided to stay here. I would love to come to the Revels."

He took her hand in a warm clasp at the door. "I'll count on you then. I think you will enjoy it immensely. We even have a fortune teller who comes in. Who knows, perhaps she'll give you a head start on the New Year."

"Really? Do her fortunes come true?" she asked with an impish smile.

He gazed over her shoulder, trying to recall the predictions from last year. Ah, yes, the woman had said he would have two great loves in his life: one that had come and gone (no great surprise there) and—now he remembered—one that was yet to come, a love far greater than the first...

Michael looked at Shannon, his face alight with an expression she couldn't decipher as he reluctantly let go of her hand. Reaching for his hat and coat, he forced himself to stop looking at her mouth as it widened to an infectious grin, her earlier gloom now only a memory.

"You'll have to come and see for yourself. By the way," he added, "come to the Revels in costume if you like. A great many people do."

Shannon closed the door gently behind him, then turned to lean against it, hugging herself in anticipation. Thank God. Here she had been dreading Christmas, especially this year. Michael and the Revels sounded like the perfect antidote to torturing herself with thoughts of how completely her life had turned upside down in the past twelve months. How it had skidded from the triumph of her anchor debut in New York to the days of despair in London to—well, whatever it was these days.

Now. All she needed was something wonderful to wear.

# 16

Fiona McPhail's cornflower-blue eyes snapped open in the gray light of early morning. Startled out of sleep by a loud snore emerging from the tousled blonde head on the pillow beside her, for a moment she didn't have the slightest idea where she was. Her gaze took in the elaborate plaster molding around the ceiling, wandered down to framed botanical prints on the wall opposite, then over to a silver bucket on the desk where a bottle of champagne floated upside down. The green circle of a second bottle, also drained of its contents, sat upended in the trash can. *Two* bottles. No wonder her teeth felt so furry, her mouth as parched as if she had spent the night in the Sahara.

Fiona stifled a moan as she propped herself up on one elbow, her nose wrinkling at the sour smell of last night's final brandy wafting from a glass on the bedside table. Now she remembered. The blonde head belonged to that handsome reporter from American television—oh, what the devil was his name. The fellow who had flung a leg over her desk late Monday in that casual way the Americans had, leaning in with an intimate smile as he invited her to tea at the Ritz. Her—Fiona McPhail—at the Ritz! She stifled a giggle at the thought of what her mum would say about her new, ever-so-fancy boyfriend. *That's sort of what he was*, she told herself defensively, *didn't he come 'round to ask her out, even after he'd gotten what he wanted?*

*Oh, blast, what was his name again.* She closed her eyes, trying to remember. *Tom? Ted? Theo? Yes, that was it. Theo... Tanner.* Of course, he had no way of knowing that she had given him the defense minister's report last week on orders from the press attaché. *He* thought he had weaseled it out of her after days of pleading and flirtation. Fiona stretched her arms overhead, her full breasts rising with the gesture. Her lips curved into a complacent smile as she glanced again at the sleeping body beside her. He certainly had to hang around a fair amount before she had come across with it. That had been Dennis Montgomery's idea too. He hadn't wanted it to appear too easy.

Fiona extended her toes toward the foot of the bed, tentatively feeling around for her knickers. That's where they usually seemed to turn up. Either there or on the floor someplace. At any rate, she'd better find them fast or she'd be late for work this morning. Little enough was going on at Number 10 Downing during these last weeks before Christmas, but they'd be looking for her, all the same.

She eased herself out of the covers and stumbled toward the bathroom, yawning, her strawberry-blonde curls in a mad frizz around her shoulders. The reporter was still dead asleep on the other side of the bed. Maybe he'd come by again this afternoon. Maybe he'd even take her back to the Ritz.

Shannon could see Braeburn House coming alive as she dressed for the Revels, the sky sinking from silver twilight into the dark embrace of a winter's night. From across the pond, candles were lit from room to room until the old limestone mansion glowed like a canary diamond against a black velvet sky.

For the past hour, a long line of cars had been purring slowly up the driveway. Shannon closed her eyes and imagined with a shiver of pleasure the sound of horse-drawn carriages clop-clopping to the honey-colored entrance, pausing to discharge their gaily dressed partygoers.

*I wish I could have seen it for myself,* she thought, propping her chin on her elbows as she leaned against the windowsill. *Life must have been so much more pleasant in those days, without the distractions of telephones and television, without the relentless pace of modern life. Without all the hard choices we have today...*

*Whoa, there, Shannon,* she shook her head to remind herself, *don't get carried away with your romantic notions.* She knew well that life was only good in those days if you were a member of the ruling class—and even those women had far fewer choices than she. Hard as it might be to make her own decisions, she knew she had the luxury of options they couldn't have imagined.

*Besides,* she grinned as she turned away from the window, *you would have been lousy at needlepoint.*

Shannon returned to the dressing table for a final critical look. She had decided to wear makeup tonight, for a change, and didn't want to overdo it.

No, that was about right, she thought, turning from side to side to gauge the effect. She offered up a silent prayer of thanks to the makeup artists at the network who had taught her how to highlight her cheekbones with a slightly darker shading underneath, topped by a final dusting of blusher; who had demonstrated the best way to feather her eyelashes with mascara until her green eyes seemed enormous; the wizards who had shown her how a lipstick brush could add just a dash of color and shine to her generous mouth.

She smiled into the mirror in satisfaction. After all these months, it was fun to be reminded that she could still appear glamorous when she chose. *Not bad, kid,* she nodded in appreciation to her reflection. She crossed the room to pat the deep burgundy velvet of the dress suspended from a padded hanger on the closet door. After Michael's invitation to come in costume, she had asked Mrs. Cox for a second opinion on proper attire for the Revels. The chemist's wife, who was something of a frustrated artist as well as a lover of all things Elizabethan, had promptly come up with a drawing even better than Shannon had been imagining, then had steered her toward a seamstress who could be counted upon to work quickly. Even Shannon, who wasn't all that interested in clothes, had to admit that the result of their combined efforts was both simple and stunning.

The dress had a scooped neckline that left uncovered the top swell of her breasts, with long sleeves ending in a point over her wrists. The dropped waistline accentuated the slender curves of her body, gently hugging her figure until it broke into graceful swirls from her hips to the floor. A simple rope of burgundy intertwined with gleaming gold thread circled her narrow waist as it fell to a knotted "v" in front, then swung provocatively from her knees with each movement of her hips.

Her chestnut hair had been swooped back from her face with a simple headpiece in gold filigree dotted with pearls—a relic saved by Mrs. Cox from one of the previous Christmas Revels—then cascaded in thick curls over her shoulders and down her back. She fastened a pair of diamond studs on her ears, studied the effect in the mirror, then shook her head and took them off. No. No modern jewelry tonight, she decided. No jewels at all, in fact, except for the antique ruby ring she now wore regularly. Instead, she freed two wispy curls from her hairline in front of each ear to frame and soften her face.

Stepping back to survey herself in the full-length mirror in the bedroom, she hardly recognized the regal stranger staring back at her.

"Regina Lancaster, Georgie Moran, eat your hearts out," she

laughed aloud as she lifted her skirts for a triumphant pirouette, "look at what your Crazy, Amazing Grace has become!"

All at once the smile fell from her face and her eyes turned reflective. Funny how the thought of her childhood classmates didn't seem to hurt any longer, why those memories didn't seem as awful as they once had. How odd. Speaking their names seemed so easy now. Painless, even. Come to think of it, even running into Regina in London hadn't bothered her, once she had been able to see her as a person in need of comfort, instead of the impossible-to-live-up-to icon of her childhood.

*Maybe being so different actually helped me*, the thought came to her. *Maybe that's what gave me the strength to make my own way in the world. It got me here, didn't it? Instead of being angry because I wasn't like everyone else, maybe I should be grateful for it. That's how Grammie Lib lived, anyway, and look how happy she was.*

"Here's to you, Shannon Grace Taylor," she saluted herself in the mirror with a grave little smile. "You, my dear, are a survivor. And you are going to be just fine."

With that happy thought, she gathered up her skirts, lifted her chin, and stepped confidently out the door.

"Welcome, Miss Shannon!" Henry's booming voice greeted her. His eyes were alight with pleasure. "You look like—like royalty, my dear, a duchess at the least. I won't say a queen," he added with a wink, "you're far too young and pretty for that particular title."

"Duchess will be just fine," she smiled in return. "As I recall, you people aren't very nice to your queens. I'd rather keep my head, thank you."

"And so you shall, at least if I have anything to say about it. May

I offer you champagne?" he added, as a waiter swung by with a tray of glasses.

"It's a bit crowded in here, I'm afraid," Henry continued, handing her a slender flute. "Everyone in the district turns out for this. Perhaps you'd prefer to see the view from the stairs?"

Shannon nodded, guarding the glass against her chest as Henry steered her through the crush to the central staircase. "I'm afraid I shall have to leave you here while I check in with the kitchen for a moment. Lord Michael is about, somewhere...," he said, turning his head to scan the crowd.

"That's all right," she replied, trying not to appear too obvious as her eyes followed his search. "Thank you for getting me this far. I'll just watch from here for a while."

"Lovely. I shall see you later then," Henry beamed and hurried off.

Gathering her long skirts in one hand, cradling the champagne in the other, Shannon inched her way to the landing. Henry was right; it did appear as if everyone in the whole district had turned out for this, and little wonder. Her eyes were eager as they swept the entryway.

The Great Hall was ablaze with light, with colorful holly and fragrant pine branches festooning the room. About half the women were in costume; others wore holiday dresses that swished when they walked, the men solemn as penguins in black tie or tails. Either way, she realized in relief, her outfit was perfectly appropriate.

Sipping her champagne, she placed a graceful hand on the banister and surveyed the sea of faces below, still on the lookout for a dark head streaked with silver. The scene below was so perfect it was almost surreal. She felt as if she had wandered onto a movie set; at any moment the cameras would begin to roll and the handsome star would appear. But Michael must be in another room, she realized with another crane of her neck, trying to dismiss a pang of disappointment.

A tug at her velvet skirt brought her attention downward.

"Lily!" she exclaimed. "Happy Christmas!"

The little girl who had become her favorite at story time licked the stickiness from her lips and solemnly held up the remains of a peppermint cane. "Mummy gave me this and told me to stay on the stairs. She said I'd get runned over down there."

Shannon laughed. "She's probably right. Are you having a good time?"

Lily patted a pocket of her dress with a conspiratorial smile. "I have three more sweeties in here. Don't tell!"

"No, of course I won't," promised Shannon. "Now, let me see your dress. You look pretty as a princess tonight."

Giggling, Lily held out a pair of arms clad in green velvet and twirled in an exuberant circle, sending her full taffeta plaid skirt flying over several layers of petticoats and a pair of white tights. Her patent-leather shoes were polished to a gleaming black. Narrow green and red ribbons anchored a knot of blonde curls atop her head, then fell in a colorful cascade down her back.

"Beautiful!" Shannon applauded.

Lily stopped twirling and gave her an appraising look. "You too. May I see your crown?"

Shannon dropped to one knee and lowered her head so that Lily could inspect the design more closely. The little girl gave a curl that had fallen over Shannon's shoulder a gentle, almost reverent pat, then got on tiptoe to study her "crown" as intently as if it had been the queen's own jewels. "Diamonds," Lily breathed, her eyes alive with wonder.

"Mostly pearls, actually—not real ones, though, just make-believe. Would you like to have it when I'm done?"

Lily's blue eyes grew so wide they threatened to pop out of her face. "Could I? Really? Do you mean it? "

From over their heads came a disapproving growl. "Come, now, Lily, what'r'ya beggin' for y'self this time?"

Shannon straightened to find herself on eye level with James, the groom. Away from the stables, he looked awkward and uncomfortable. His suit was too tight around the middle, his tie yanked too far to one side. His face was flushed with the warmth of the room and the several glasses of champagne he had flung down his throat in the past half-hour. James tugged at the collar of his shirt with one calloused finger as if desperate for air, his other hand grabbing for his daughter to stand at his knee. The sparkle vanished from Lily's eyes as she anxiously gazed from her father's glowering expression to the face of her dismayed story lady.

"Oh, no, not at all," Shannon assured him, wishing he hadn't come along to spoil the moment. "It was my idea, entirely. I would love for Lily to have the crown, when I'm through. If that's all right with you and her mother, of course. I certainly won't need it, not until next year, anyway."

She directed a smile toward the apprehensive little girl. "Will you let me borrow it, if I do?"

"She will if she knows what's good for her," James responded, his voice sharp with reprimand. "Come on then, girl. It's time we went."

With a last imploring glance over her shoulder, Lily stumbled along behind him.

"I'll see you again at story time, after the holidays," Shannon called to her with an encouraging smile. "I'll bring it to you then, okay?"

She could just catch a glimpse of Lily's nod before she disappeared into the crowd. Shannon stood looking after them, a puzzled frown etched across her forehead. Lily was such a delightful little girl; why couldn't her father see that as clearly as she could? No wonder she seemed so starved for affection, if that was the treatment she got at home...

Shannon sighed, some of the luster of this festive night dimming as she peered over the staircase.

From where he stood in the downstairs library, Michael was trying to extricate himself from a conversation with his nearest neighbor, Ackerly. *Good man, really, probably can't help being such a bore*, he reminded himself for a third time, trying to be charitable. No use. He was on fire with impatience, suspecting that Shannon must be somewhere in the house by now and anxious to find her. But Ackerly seemed pleased to have an audience for his plans for spring planting. It wasn't going to be easy to get away from him.

By the time Michael was finally able to make his escape, the lights in the Great Hall had been dimmed for the carolers bringing in the wassail bowl and locating anyone quickly was impossible.

Wanting to get closer to the action, Shannon had moved to a doorway downstairs. As she stood on her tiptoes, she could see the bowl lifted high above the shoulders of the singers, their voices ringing through the hall in three-point harmony. The mesmerizing scene was heightened by candlelight that cast an orange glow upon all who had gathered there. Together they stood, a community that for centuries had been joining hands at just this time, generation after generation, to chase away winter's darkness and celebrate the return of light.

*This is how it must have looked fifty, a hundred, even two hundred years ago,* Shannon thought. Her eyes misted as she considered the history of this beautiful old hall and the people whose lives had been woven together for so long. The magic of this time and place was part of why she loved it here, why she felt so at home with the simplicity she had found in Burlingford. Here, everyone seemed to care and look out for one other, with an unspoken warmth she wouldn't have understood or perhaps taken time to appreciate twelve short months ago.

The scene was so engrossing that Shannon didn't know that Michael was near until she felt his warm breath in her ear as he leaned down to murmur, "You approve of our quaint English customs, then?"

Spinning around, she whispered an enthusiastic, "Oh, yes!"

His heart leaped at the sight of her smile. She was so beautiful, tonight even more than usual. His eyes traced the contours of her mouth, frustrated that the press of the crowd prevented him from drawing her into a dark corner where he could take her in his arms and kiss her thoroughly, as he'd been wanting to for weeks now.

How had it happened, he wondered, as she turned back to the singers. When had politeness turned to interest, interest to curiosity and then—in a swooping, scalding rush—become desire and longing? When had it become important to him whether she was happy or not, what her mood might be? When had his eyes begun to linger on her face a fraction of a second too long, when had each casual handshake begun to last for a good two beats beyond the usual? He couldn't decide whether it was love that led to paying attention, or paying attention that had opened his heart to love…

Even lost in thought, Shannon and Michael remained acutely aware of the other's presence; aware, as well, that something important had changed between them, an awareness so heightened they could feel the very air around them crackling with anticipation. Both were startled with the burst of applause as the song ended and the crowd began inching back to make room for the Morris dancers.

"You look… magnificent," Michael said, taking advantage of the pause in the music to take her hands in both of his. "Whatever made you decide to come as a medieval princess?"

"Only a princess?" she replied, pretending to be insulted. "Henry said I look like a queen. Oh, no, sorry, I'm wrong; he said I looked like royalty. A duchess—that was it. Not quite a queen."

"Well, let me see," he smiled, as she backed up a step to gather up her skirts and twirl, just as Lily had moments before, making the rich velvet float in a seductive swish from her hips to her ankles. Two spins and she stopped, laughing, a little embarrassed by the obvious appreciation in his eyes.

"I think ... Henry was right." Again taking her hands in his, Michael raised them to his lips with a meaningful look. Neither noticed that the couples standing around them had begun to bend their heads together for whispered consultations, trying not to be too obvious with their stares. Despite the best efforts of every unmarried female for miles around these past years, Michael had always appeared at the Revels unaccompanied. And now here he was, flirting—in public, no less—with the American!

Henry, who had seen the couple from across the room and had started to join them, stopped dead in his tracks when he saw the gesture. *As far as those two know*, he grinned to himself, *there's no one else in the room at the moment.* He was certainly not going to intrude.

Shannon's heart was racing as she reclaimed her hands at the sound of music rising once again behind her. She turned to see a quartet of Morris dancers enter the room, red sashes crisscrossed over their chests, ribbons of bells on their legs jingling merrily as they skipped in and began a series of intricate loops and whirls.

"The Morris dancers have been performing in this hall every Christmas since it was built," Michael bent to whisper in her ear.

"They've held up remarkably well for such old people, don't you think?" He rolled his eyes at her lame joke, shook his head and grinned.

"What are the bells for?" she turned to ask, mostly for the

pleasure of having his face bend so close to hers again, close enough to inhale his strong masculine scent, close enough to lift a hand to his cheek—if only she dared.

He shrugged. "They've always worn them. Perhaps to scare the darkness away."

She nodded, the butterflies in her stomach still turning backflips at the direction of her thoughts, and forced herself to turn back to the dancers. Under any other circumstances, their graceful split-second precision would have been absorbing. Their faces were focused and intent, waiting until they had finished with a flourish before they broke into wide smiles. The hall erupted into a tidal wave of applause as a waiter came to whisper an urgent message into Michael's ear.

"You'll have to excuse me for a moment," he frowned, turning back to Shannon. "I've seated you next to me at dinner, but first I need to take a quick phone call. Perhaps you might want to visit the fortuneteller while you're waiting. You'll find her through the door," he added, pointing.

Shannon made her way into the ballroom where a tented booth had been set up in one corner. Two stout, middle-aged women were standing next to it, whispering about the fortunes they had just heard, as they apparently waited for someone else. A heavyset man with thinning white hair lifted the flap to exit just as Shannon arrived.

"Marvelous, just marvelous. Even better than last year," he beamed, rubbing his hands together enthusiastically as he rejoined his companions.

"Don't be shy, you're next, young lady," he boomed at Shannon.

"Go on, now," he added with a shooing motion, as she paused by the entrance.

Shannon took a deep breath. She supposed this couldn't be all that different from Grammie Lib's strange ability to predict the future, sometimes—or her own occasional flashes, for that matter. And then there had been that woman in London, the one she and Stu had gone to hear. Clare. The lady who said she could talk to the dead, and didn't seem at all surprised when family members had confirmed the details she relayed from the loved ones they had lost. That had been bizarre, too, although in a different way. Journalist that she was by training, a professional skeptic as most reporters were, it was hard to take the whole business very seriously. So why the sudden shiver, now? And why was her pulse going at ninety miles an hour?

Squaring her shoulders, she lifted the flap of the canvas tent. A turbaned woman with kind brown eyes looked up expectantly as she came in. Half a dozen votive candles on the table were barely able to penetrate the gloom. Incense smoldering in one corner carried the heavy scent of patchouli through the stagnant air.

"Don't mind the surroundings, luv, it's just for effect," the woman chirped. Her voice sounded normal. Cheery, even, as if she could feel Shannon's unease and wanted to put her fears to rest.

"They wanted me to wear this silly outfit tonight since it's the Revels," she continued, "but actually I've been doing intuitive work for years now. There's nothing to be afraid of, my dear."

She patted the chair next to her, indicating where Shannon should sit, and began rifling through a stack of Tarot cards on a small table at her knees. As she approached, Shannon could see that it was draped in a cream-colored shawl with angels dancing around its fringed edge. Well. That was a good sign, at least.

"What do I do?" she asked.

"Well, we might start with the cards," the woman began, then gave Shannon a penetrating look. "No, actually, perhaps a reading, instead. May I have something you keep close to you, something you wear all the time. A ring is usually good at helping me tune in."

Shannon slipped off her ruby ring and handed it over. The woman took it between a thumb and forefinger, then closed her eyes for a moment as she rubbed her fingertips over the stone. "Mmm," she said, her eyes popping open again for an instant, her smile as cheery as ever, "and now your hand, luv?"

Shannon sat motionless, almost afraid to breathe, as she watched the other woman's eyes flicker behind her eyelids. Her brow was furrowed in concentration as she brought the ring to her forehead. Shannon's already strained nerves stretched taut as the moment of silence pulsed on.

"Well. Welcome back, milady," the woman said at last. "It's good to have you here again."

She opened her eyes and smiled at Shannon, who couldn't help letting out a small sigh of disappointment. Here she'd been hoping for—almost expecting, really—some sort of guidance, or insight. Hadn't Michael said she had made a good prediction for him? But this woman obviously had her confused with someone else. One of last year's Revelers.

"I'm very sorry, I'm afraid you must be mistaken." Her voice was polite but her face was stiff with dismay. "This is my first year here, at the Revels."

The woman laughed and leaned forward as if confiding a delicious secret. "Of course it is, this time around. I meant welcome back to Braeburn House. I saw you were mistress here, oh, around a hundred years ago, I would say. I got such a clear image of you in long skirts standing all regal-like in the Great Hall."

Shannon felt a cold prickle along her neck as the little hairs stood on end, could feel the color rising and then draining from her face. The galloping of her heart sent tremors into hands she pressed together and folded into her lap. She studied the woman for a moment, trying not to look as stunned as she felt.

She took a deep breath. That had always worked before—on television, at least. She tried to calm herself, tried to decide how to respond. Tried to figure out if she was crazy, or the fortuneteller was, as her heart sang, "I knew it!" and her reporter's brain scoffed, "Don't be ridiculous."

"I'm not sure how this stuff is supposed to work," Shannon finally replied, pleased and a little surprised that she was able to keep her voice steady, "but let's say you're right. Why would I come back? And why here?"

"I don't know, dear," the older woman admitted. "Unfinished business, perhaps, from last time. The need to balance the scales: if you harmed someone in your last life, you might want to make things right. Or if someone harmed you, they may need to even things out so they can move along in their path. Perhaps there's something important you've come to do, something you weren't able to complete before. Or perhaps you're just here to be happy this time—I did feel as if this lady was terribly sad..."

Happy? Shannon thought, her face blank. That was a new one. When had she ever thought of happiness as a major achievement in life? Success, sure. But happiness? Her father was the first one to make her think *that* was important, and even he didn't figure it out until he got sick.

"Give me another moment," the woman said, closing her eyes again. "I'm getting a picture of the letter D. Deborah, perhaps? or Diane? At any rate, she's telling me she's sorry...."

"Diana," Shannon interrupted, "my mother. And I know she's sorry. She already told me." The words were out of her mouth before she had time to think. She drew back and blinked, astonished at herself. Good Lord. What was she saying?

"Well, you know how mothers are," the woman smiled. "They'll tell you as many times as it takes, if need be, until they're certain you heard it. At any rate, she says she's very proud of you, of how far you've come, and she's happy to see you all dressed up tonight. About time, she said. Apparently she doesn't like your boots very much. The ones you wear for gardening."

"Oh, come on." In spite of herself, Shannon began to laugh. "That's too easy. You must say that to everybody, at least everyone around here..."

"Indeed, I do not. This woman—your mother, you said?—has been watching over you for a long time. Watching you from babyhood until now, watching as you grew up. She's saying she's so pleased and excited for you... but I can't... quite... get why...."

She paused a moment and frowned, as if listening to a phone call from far away that had become swamped with static. "I'm sorry, dear. I'm not getting anything more."

She glanced over at Shannon, who sat slumped into her chair. Part of her longed to believe the fortuneteller's words; how lovely if they were true. How comforting to think that she was here in Burlingford because she was supposed to be; that something—someone?—had been pointing her in this direction, all along. If her mother had truly been watching over her—why, that would mean that Clare was right. That death wasn't really the end, that people didn't die; they still existed, only—somewhere else. And if that was true, then maybe she *had* seen her father the night he died... as he made his transition, moving on from physical life to wherever he was going...

Oh, Shannon, her logical mind snorted in response, don't be absurd. Spooks and spirits that know where you are and what you're doing? Loved ones that keep an eye on you from—wherever? Or perhaps this was all a gigantic joke. A lucky guess from someone good at picking up on what people wanted to hear, comforting nonsense for lost souls, desperate in their search for meaning.

Shannon scowled and folded her arms across her chest.

*Come on. You—mistress of Braeburn House a hundred years ago? Ridiculous. Out of the question.*

And yet... and yet... preposterous as it might sound, there was so much that seemed, suddenly, to fit:

—how comfortable she had felt in London, how familiar it seemed as she walked its streets...

—how much the Lady's Cottage had seemed like her own place, right from the start. Almost as if she had designed it herself. How comfortable it was living in Burlingford; how easily she had slipped into the rhythm of life in this small community...

—her father's words the night he died. How pleased he had been by where he had found her. And Clare, whose demonstration that night in London had opened her mind enough that her father's appearance had been reassuring instead of terrifying...

—how she had been feeling for months as if she were looking for something, waiting for something—something she couldn't quite grasp, couldn't really imagine—but *knew*, somehow, was coming into her life... coming to change it, and her, forever...

And now this. She bowed her head, trying to sort it all out.

Those odd flashes she had experienced since childhood, the strange ways that fate had bumped her along to this moment in time, this place, with these people—this man? Was Michael part of this, too, part of a destiny that had led her here?

"I'm sorry, love, this isn't easy for you, is it." Shannon jerked upright, startled by the sound of the fortuneteller's voice. Her face was earnest and sympathetic, as if she knew exactly how Shannon was feeling. "It must be a bit startling. Give it time. I'm sure it will come together for you..."

"I hope so," Shannon said, her voice unsteady as she slipped the ring back on her finger.

"Thank you," she added. "I think."

She lifted the flap of the tent and groped for a nearby armchair. Her heart still thudding painfully in her chest, she tried to digest this startling new information, process it, the same way she would organize a particularly complex news story.

All right. What the woman had said would certainly fit with some of the bizarre things that had been happening lately—especially the nagging sense she had felt from the moment she met him that Michael was important to her somehow, that she knew him from somewhere. Maybe their encounter outside No. 10 Downing was only a partial explanation; perhaps there was far more to it than that.

Or was it simply that now, with no work to keep her busy and preoccupied, with no father to count on for support, she was going a little crazy ... just as her mother had, all those years ago ...

Shannon's eyes darted around the room, frantic with questions she could hardly form. "Be still, and know that I am God"? Or be still, and lose your mind ... tormented by what you can't explain?

# 17

Michael gave a polite nod without really seeing the half-dozen stragglers who were chatting by the fireplace, champagne flutes glittering in their hands, as he entered the downstairs library. Crossing to a gilded desk, he waited until Henry had ushered them outside and closed the door before picking up the receiver. Phone calls from the prime minister were almost always bad news. He devoutly hoped it wasn't the Middle East falling apart again that had prompted this one.

"Willoughby-Jones," he said, in the crisp voice he used for official business.

"Oh yes, Lord Michael, it's Dennis Montgomery calling. I do apologize for having to disturb you..."

"Montgomery," Michael replied, surprised. Montgomery was the newest press attaché. Michael didn't know him well but what little he had seen of him wasn't impressive. Montgomery was one of those oily, ingratiating sort of fellows who seemed to pop up around the powerful, holding briefcases, keeping press briefings on schedule—and taking particular satisfaction in being the bearer of bad news. "I was told it was prime minister calling."

"Well, it was important to get you on the line, and actually I am calling on her behalf," replied Montgomery, his voice rapid and apologetic. "It seems one of the American networks has broadcast a story on our new concerns about NATO and she wants to make certain everyone's copy of the defense minister's report is present and accounted for."

"Why?"

"Well... from the sound of it one might think the reporter had obtained an actual copy. There's at least one direct quote. And as you know the report had a very limited distribution. You still have yours, I take it?"

"Certainly I still have mine," Michael said, in a tone that made it clear he considered the question to be impertinent as well as unnecessary. "And I am hardly in the habit of handing over confidential information to the press."

"Of course not, sir. The PM merely wanted to put everyone on alert. Can't have confidential documents floating about, now can we?"

Michael rubbed one hand across his eyes, considering the implications. With the prime minister meeting in Washington next week with the American president, the leak could hardly have come at a worse time.

"When did the story air?"

"Last night's broadcast. We just obtained a transcript a little while ago. And of course the Yanks are clamoring for a response."

"Get me a copy, will you?"

"Certainly, sir. It will be on your desk on Monday. Sorry to disturb you."

"Quite all right, Montgomery," Michael replied, reminding himself that the man was only doing his job, after all. "Happy Christmas," he added.

"And a very happy Christmas to you, sir," Montgomery replied, glad that Lord Michael couldn't see his smirk as he hung up.

Still slumped in her chair, Shannon was staring blankly into space when Michael appeared in the ballroom foyer.

"Oh, there you are," he said, hurrying over until he was close enough to see that something had upset her terribly, something that had turned her eyes dazed, her face paper-white.

"What is it? You look as if you've seen a ghost."

With an effort she brought her eyes back into focus on his worried face. He should only know... if only she could tell him. He would surely think she was insane if she just blurted it all out—assuming, even, that she could. How could anyone possibly explain this one? "Oh, hello. Guess what. I just found out I was once your great-grandmother! In a previous life, of course." Oh, yeah. Right. Just—lovely.

"I'm... not feeling well all of a sudden, " she said, barely moving her lips. Her voice was so subdued he had to stoop to catch the words over the distant roar of the party. "I think I'd better go home."

"Did the fortune teller say something to frighten you?" he asked, angry and alarmed.

"No, no, I'm fine, really," she lied, not wanting to upset him, especially not in the midst of the holiday celebration that meant so much to him. "I just don't feel up to being very social just now. I'm sorry. I know I'll miss a wonderful dinner."

"Not nearly as sorry as I am," he said, trying to coax a smile. "Now I'm the one who'll have to amuse old Ackerly, who's deaf as a post and twice as boring. I was hoping you might spare me that."

"I'm sure you'll be able to manage." Noticing the concern in his eyes despite his light tone, she attempted a smile of her own, but while her mouth curved into the acceptable shape that was where it stopped. Her eyes remained distant, focused on a place he could not see.

"Are you quite sure you can make it home?" he inquired, covering her cold hands with his own warm ones. "If you're unwell, I can have a bed made up for you here in the house..."

"No!" she said, more strongly than she had intended, then cursed herself for his wounded expression. "I'm so sorry. Really, I appreciate your kindness, I just... need to get home."

Shannon got shakily to her feet.

*Home*, she thought. Why *did* the Lady's Cottage seem like home—her real home, the one she'd been looking for, longing for, all her life.

Michael put a comforting arm around her waist and walked her to the door.

"Martin," he called to one of the hotel's most trusted waiters, busy collecting abandoned champagne glasses from the front hall. "Would you be so kind as to drive Miss Shannon home? She's not feeling well at the moment and I would prefer that she not make the walk by herself."

"Certainly, sir," Martin replied, as if it were perfectly normal for a guest to be escorted home before dinner. "I shall pull up the car right away."

They stood in the doorway, waiting, his hands moving over hers in a warm caress, thumbs brushing against her knuckles. His blue eyes were dark with concern as they tried to read her still, set expression.

"If you're feeling better tomorrow, will you come to luncheon? It's very small, just a few old friends," he coaxed, unwilling to let her go without some assurance she would be back soon.

"Yes, of course," she said, forcing a smile to lips that felt stiff and cold. Still, just standing next to him, with their hands intertwined, made her feel better, stronger, somehow. "I really—I'm so terribly sorry—I hope I haven't spoiled dinner for you—" she began, as Martin braked to a stop a few feet away.

"Not at all," he said, raising her hands to his lips for a second time that evening, relieved to see some color beginning to return to her face, "although of course I'll miss you. May I ring you later and make sure you're all right?"

"Yes, of course," she said, with a last grateful look as she started down the steps.

Michael stood silhouetted against the light of the doorway, one hand raised in a wave, until the vehicle pulled out of view. He put the other hand to his chest to quiet the sudden feeling that his heart was disappearing down the driveway with her.

"Thank heaven that's done for another year," Michael said, reaching over to take Shannon's hand as they waved goodbye to the last of the luncheon guests. It was a glorious day, unusually warm for December, with not a single cloud to mar the perfection of a Wedgewood-blue sky.

"I thought you loved this," Shannon tilted her head at him and smiled. Except for hollow circles under her eyes that signaled a sleepless night, there was little to suggest her panic from the night before.

"I do, I do," he sighed. "I'm always happy to see the Revels come, and always happy to see them go. But more importantly, I want to know how you are. Shall we go upstairs, perhaps, and build a fire?"

"I'd love that, but first I have a favor to ask. Would you mind if we took a look at the family portrait gallery? Henry showed me all your ancestors once, but it was a very quick tour. I'd like to see them again, if I could."

"Certainly," he replied, puzzled but obliging. Whatever had set her off last night, it was a relief that she seemed to be herself again. "Let's see. Shall we start at the beginning and go forward, or begin with my father and work our way back?"

"Oh, let's start at the beginning," Shannon decided, "that seems the most logical way to do it."

She resolutely kept her eyes fixed elsewhere as they strolled the length of the hallway to the oldest portrait still hanging. No fair peeking ahead to 100 years ago, the time period she was most interested in. She was determined to take this tour with no preconceptions. Surely if the fortune teller had been right, there would be some evidence to confirm it. A hint in a picture, perhaps; *something* to make Shannon stop feeling like she was still in the grip of an improbable dream.

"Now this one is my great-great—oh, however many greats it was—grandfather, the original Lord of Burlingford, so named by Queen Elizabeth the first, apparently because he either loaned or gave her a great deal of money. I believe those lines were drawn somewhat indistinctly in those days. His son proceeded to squander a fortune at the gaming tables, but his grandson—no fool, he—was an industrious lad who went on to make a fortune in the wool trade. A few generations and some fortuitous marriages later they were doing well enough to build a new residence, the one still here today…"

Shannon listened in admiration. However much Americans enjoyed their own history, it seemed all brash and brand-new compared to the English version. And while Henry's tour had been fascinating, it had been headlines compared to all of Michael's details.

"What an incredible heritage," she interrupted. "You must feel so proud to be part of all this."

"I suppose. Proud. Humbled. Inadequate. It certainly makes one think a great deal about the accidents of birth, about how I landed here instead of being born in the slums of Calcutta. You're right, it is an impressive history, a huge house filled with beautiful things that all the many generations who came before me managed to collect and acquire. Yet, I've often thought I'd have cheerfully traded in the lot for parents and brothers and sisters. All the basics of a more normal childhood."

Shannon squeezed his hand.

"Perhaps there's no such thing as a normal childhood," she suggested. "I didn't have one either. But—maybe the challenge is to do our best with whatever we've been given. When you become a father one day, I would hope that you can give your children what you never had. What you've missed so much."

Michael's eyebrows lifted at her comment but he stifled what would until now have been an immediate disclaimer. When he became a father. It was a startling thought. And yet, hearing the words from her mouth, it no longer seemed as impossible as it would have even a few months ago.

"Spoken like a true optimist," was all he said aloud, but his hand tightened on hers as they continued their stroll.

"And now to the late 19th century...," Michael began, then stopped when he saw Shannon frozen in front of one of the portraits, her eyes wide, fingers against her mouth to stifle a gasp.

"What is it? What do you see?" he asked urgently, looking from her face to the haughty face of Lord Geoffrey Willoughby-Jones, who gazed back at Shannon with Theo Tanner's brown eyes, Theo's high cheekbones, Theo's golden hair framing an erect white collar and perfectly knotted cravat. Even his aristocratic sneer was carved in the same sulky, dissatisfied mouth. Substitute Lord Geoffrey's silk waistcoat with a navy blazer and replace the riding whip with a microphone, and the transformation would have been complete. It was all there, plain as day. How could she not have noticed it before?

"Oh my God," she whispered.

"What?" Michael demanded again.

"Before I explain—are there any pictures of Lord Geoffrey's wife?" she turned to ask.

"Only one that I know of," he said, utterly mystified. "It wasn't a very happy marriage, apparently. He was a confirmed bachelor until late in life, if I remember the story correctly, when he became desperate for an heir. Alexandra, I believe her name was. She grew up in London and was quite young when they were betrothed. No choice, of course. In those days, young ladies did as their parents decreed."

"Why isn't her portrait here with the others?"

"There was some scandal about how she died. I gather Lord Geoffrey wasn't the most loving of husbands and I'm sure the age difference didn't help. The official version is that she was prone to fits of melancholia and killed herself. The story told in the village is that she ran off with a lover and was drowned. Although she seems a bit young to have acquired one of those."

"May I see her picture?" she said, unable to control her eagerness.

"Certainly. Not sure if I remember where it is—perhaps we should check the third-floor gallery. That's where we keep the less illustrious relatives. Now. Once we find her will you kindly tell me what this is all about?"

"I promise."

Grabbing his hand, she began to run.

"Are you sure this is the right one?"

"Yes, I'm quite certain," Michael replied, looking from her face to the portrait in growing puzzlement. "Really, Shannon—"

"Just a second," she said, with an absent expression.

The woman in the portrait was a haughty blonde, with dark blue eyes and hair wound into an elegant chignon at her neck. As she examined her more closely Shannon could tell that she was indeed very young, perhaps no more than her late teens. Despite her brave posture and the jaunty cut of her riding habit, her eyes looked sad.

"This was probably painted shortly after their wedding," Michael suggested, after letting her study the portrait in tactful silence for some moments.

"But—she doesn't look at all like me!" Shannon exclaimed.

He gave her a long look. "Pardon? Why were you expecting her to?"

"I know, it sounds ridiculous," she said. Her face was heavy with disappointment. She had gotten her hopes up and probably made a complete fool of herself—and now, she was going to have to tell him something. But what? How much of the truth could she tell? How much did she know, even?

Shannon gave him a wary look, trying to gauge his expression. "Tell you what. It's freezing up here. Let's go sit by the fire and I'll try to explain."

A few minutes later they were settled in his private apartment, teacups in hand, scones and biscuits on a plate beside them.

Michael leaned forward expectantly as Shannon began, her eyes riveted on the crackling flames.

"I don't know how to try and explain this without sounding like a complete fruitcake," she said, pausing to choose her words carefully. "When I first came to England—no, wait. Strike that. I'd better start back when I was a little kid..."

As rapidly as she could, she retraced her childhood for him: the loss of her mother, the eccentric grandmother and austere aunt who raised her, the startling predictions that led to her awful nickname and subsequent isolation in school, her job at the local newspaper writing up weddings and engagements while going to college at night...

From time to time she glanced over to get Michael's reaction to her story but his expression remained carefully blank.

"... and so finally I wound up here. Well, no, not here, exactly, I was in London, first..."

Shannon paused as she became aware of how much of her past she was leaving out. Still, this was no time to start talking about the network. That part would have to wait; her story was complicated enough as it was. Besides, given his low opinion of the press, she would have to think hard about how to frame that part of her past. If he didn't like the print media, she couldn't imagine what he thought of television. And now didn't seem the time to go into detail.

"So, anyway," she continued, feeling a little guilty over what she was omitting, "When I lived in London I kept feeling as if I'd been there before, and in some mysterious way I seemed to know my way around. And then I wound up here, in a cottage that felt like home from the very beginning, so much so that within days I was out on my hands and knees, trying to put in flowers—me, who never planted anything in her life. And then—remember when I was lost in the woods and you found me? All of a sudden while I was walking along, wet and shivering, I thought of a shed. And sure enough there was one."

Shannon put down her teacup and swiveled to face him.

"Michael," she said, "I promise you, I had never seen that shed before—never knew there was one out there—but I know that finding it saved my life. I would have gone to sleep under a tree and probably frozen to death otherwise. Something—wouldn't let me. Something kept urging me on, until I finally got to the shed."

At the mention of the shed, Michael straightened in his chair. Until now everything she had said, while interesting, could be dismissed as mere coincidence. But something had pointed him toward the shed that day, too, an insistent feeling he had finally given in to—and indeed, that's where she had been.

"Okay, so here's where it really gets weird," she continued, speaking more slowly now. "Michael ... do you believe that our spirit lives on after we die? That someone who's dead can come and say goodbye?"

He pondered the question, aware that a flip answer wouldn't do.

"Well, centuries of Christian doctrine have been telling us we have an immortal soul," he replied at last. "And centuries of British folklore have been filled with tales of supernatural occurrences, of people who are supposed to be dead who reappear from time to time. So I suppose it isn't too large a leap to believe that something about us lives on, once we're finished with our bodies. Why?"

She turned back to the fire as if there might be an answer in the flames. "I could swear that I saw my father the night he died. Only ... he looked young and healthy. He was here—in your house, in your bedroom—and he seemed to be glad that I was here, too. He was looking around like he approved. He even said, 'Good, good' ... and then he disappeared."

"There are, I suppose, any number of stories about that sort of thing," he said. His voice was mild, his expression noncommittal. "Anything else?"

She sighed, reluctant to continue, but in too deep to stop.

"Last night when I saw your fortune-teller, she told me I had been here before. That I had been mistress of Braeburn House around a hundred years ago. When I asked her why I would have come back, she said perhaps it was to correct mistakes from the past. Or maybe—because it was time to finally be happy."

She swallowed hard, gazing around the room for something

that would ground her in reality. Make her story sound a little less preposterous.

Winter sunlight streamed through the window, warming books and furniture and photographs and all the conveniences of modern life, things that were solid and substantial. Here she was, a reporter, by habit and inclination and training one of the world's major skeptics. But what was a reporter if not a seeker of truth, argued her heart. How could a reporter, of all people, *not* have an open mind—*not* be willing to admit that perhaps life was more magical and mysterious than most of us had imagined? If life wasn't some sort of random accident—then what was it?

*I don't know what to think anymore*, flashed the thought. *I only know how I feel.*

Shannon stared at her hands, as a rising tide of certainty from somewhere deep inside insisted this was right, this was absolutely right, and oh so much more—amazing, and wonderful—than anything she could have ever imagined…

"I see. Is there more?"

"Yes. One more thing. Your ancestor, Lord Geoffrey, is the spitting image of someone who's caused me a lot of trouble in my life. Or maybe Theo was the spitting image of him. I just don't know anymore," she said. "Honestly? I don't know what to think. All I can tell you is, I sure don't look like—what was her name again?"

"Alexandra, I believe. We can look it up if you want to know all the particulars."

"Oh. I almost forgot. You said she may have drowned, right? Well, I've been petrified of water all my life. I can hardly bear to even fly over it. In fact," she smiled for the first time since sitting down, "I got a kid in horrible trouble one time in Sunday School when I was little. Georgie Moran. He was trying to baptize me during a church picnic at the lake—I must have been eight or nine—and when he tried to dunk my head under the water I went completely berserk. Not one of my better moments."

Michael chuckled, relieved to see her mood lighten.

"What happened to Georgie?"

"The teacher scolded him severely, as I recall. But he got back at me later."

"Oh?"

"Oh, yeah," she replied with a rueful smile. "He was always the first one to start singing 'Amazing Grace,' in class. That's my middle name. Grace, that is. But they weren't exactly using it as a compliment."

"It doesn't sound so terrible."

"I guess you had to be there."

Her heart lifted as she looked into his eyes, which—she realized, with a start—were merely curious. Not condemning. Not even judgmental, despite the incredible nature of everything she had just told him. So there it was: Georgie Moran. A name that had caused her so much grief, now merely another story that could wait for details.

She had so much to tell Michael, so many stories to share. Hoping, no, *knowing*—that at long last here was someone who would listen, who would make the effort to understand. He sat watching the expressions flickering over her face, a half-smile playing around his mouth.

"So." She looked at him, her eyebrows lifting in expectation as she awaited an answer she no longer feared. "Do you think I'm crazy?"

"Well. I have to confess, it does sound a bit strange," he replied after a moment, his face turning serious again. "Although I'm probably the last person to have any answers about why we're here on this earth, or what happens to us next. Mariko and I once did a turn with the Eastern mystics who wouldn't find any of this surprising.

In fact, I heard a young woman lecture in London last winter who sounded quite convincing about communicating with people 'on the other side' as she put it, which would make it fairly plausible that something of us lives on. She offered some remarkable detail, as I recall. There was a woman who said she had been watching her daughter plant flowers at her grave. She told her not to be sad, that she had watched her do it and that she was with her all the time..."

"Michael!" Shannon interrupted. "Was it an American woman she was talking to?"

"I'm not sure if I remember. Why?"

"Was the lecture at a spiritualist church in the West End? With a woman named Clare? And another fellow who prayed over people at the beginning?"

"I came in late so I didn't see any praying... but yes, the woman's name was Clare. She wrote a very popular book about her work, I believe."

"Yes, she did. And I was there, sitting up at the front. You were there that night, too?"

"Yes. Interesting coincidence."

"What were you doing there?"

Michael stared into the distance. Why *had* he gone? What had led him to that place?

"I don't really know," he said at last. "I had been hearing about this woman, and I suppose I wanted to know if Mariko... if Mariko was all right. If—wherever she was, she forgave me. But why that place, why that night... I have no idea. How strange that you were there as well."

"More than strange."

She took a deep breath, risking everything to say what was in her heart.

"Unless something, somehow has been trying to get us together.

Unless that's what all of this is about. Remember a few minutes ago when you spoke of the 'accident of birth' that put you here instead of Calcutta? What if there are no accidents? What if there's a reason why we're here, the two of us, together, even if we may not understand it..."

"That's a little egocentric, isn't it?" His voice was bland but his blue eyes were alert.

"Maybe," she admitted. "Or maybe it happens to everybody, only they're smart enough to get it the first time. Me, they had to beat over the head."

What was it Stu used to call her—"Show-me Shannon"? She smiled, remembering. She had certainly been shown. Her path could hardly have become clearer if skywriters had appeared overhead to proclaim it.

"I guess I must be a particularly hard case," she added, her eyes sparkling with mischief.

Michael rose, as if summoned by a magnet pulling his body to hers. In two strides he was towering over her, lifting her from the chair until her face, alight with longing, was only inches away. His arms circling her body, he drew her so close that her breasts were crushed against his chest, her legs against his powerful thighs.

His voice dropped to a husky rumble. "At the moment, I really couldn't care less why we're here..." he said. Confident, now, that she wouldn't move away, he loosened his grip enough to cup her face with his hands, his fingers moving up to comb through her hair, the heat of his palms cradling her temples as he continued. "And it doesn't matter in the slightest whether you or I or both of us or neither of us were here before or not. All that matters to me is ... now."

The last word was muffled as his mouth lowered to hers. She strained to meet his embrace in a gesture as old as time, man and woman molded together in a way that was both breathtakingly new and sweetly familiar, the electric current of desire flowing from his body to hers and back again until they were connected in an endless loop of blood and muscle and heat. Her head swimming with the unaccustomed feelings pulsating through her body, she clung to his neck, half-afraid that if she let go of him her legs would buckle and she would drop to the floor. As if reading her mind, Michael bent down to place a muscular arm behind her knees. His mouth still consuming hers, he scooped her up and carried her to the comfort of his bed, where all thoughts of whatever had come before, what might be yet to come, gave way to the fierce urgency of the here and now.

# 18

Shannon propped herself onto an elbow, her face wreathed in a mischievous grin as she gazed across the pillow.

"Well," she said. "You look mighty pleased with yourself, Lord Michael."

He stretched luxuriously beside her in the rumpled bed, then crossed his arms behind his head and smiled at the ceiling.

"I suppose...," he said with a lazy chuckle.

"In fact," she continued, her eyes gleaming wickedly, "I'd say you look like the cat that swallowed the entire birdcage as well as the canary."

"Didn't taste like a birdcage," he murmured, "but perhaps I should check just to be sure."

Michael pulled her close for another long kiss. "Mmmn. Not a single feather," he announced as they drew apart.

Shannon pulled the sheet over her breasts, still grinning. "I'd better get out of here before Henry suspects what we've been up to."

"My guess is, he would be delighted. And, knowing Henry, not the least bit surprised."

She swung her legs over the edge of the bed, then turned to glance at him over one shoulder.

"You could come with me if you'd like," she offered. "I was thinking of making fettucine alfredo tonight for dinner."

"Without the help and supervision of a genuine half-Italian?"

Michael exclaimed in mock horror. "Whatever were you thinking?"

"Well, come on then," she laughed, tossing a pillow at him. "But you'd better put some clothes on first. My landlord is a very proper Englishman, you know!"

Henry was checking the day's mail as the two came bounding down the stairs and into the foyer. Flushed and exuberant, their high spirits were a clear signal that their relationship had taken an important step forward. It wasn't difficult to guess what that step might have been.

"What do you think, Henry? I have a dinner invitation to the cottage," Michael informed him, keeping his voice solemn with an effort.

"I would say it's about time, sir," Henry replied, equally grave.

"Henry!" Shannon scolded, with a light tap to his shoulder. "You're supposed to be on my side."

The hotel manager looked at her face, rosy with the afterglow of her afternoon encounter, and bowed.

"As ever, madam, as ever," he replied, waiting until she had turned away before breaking into a gigantic grin of his own.

Shannon paused at the top of the hill as the gabled roof of the cottage came into view.

"It was built for Alexandra, wasn't it?"

"I don't know for certain but I would imagine so. The architecture would be correct for the period, certainly. You really do fit in there, don't you?"

She considered the question as she took in the darkening sky and the stark outline of the trees, the grandeur of the mansion in contrast to the coziness of the cottage.

"I never imagined I could live somewhere like this, with all its history. The cottage, especially, feels like such a healing place. I feel so peaceful when I'm there. As if I belong. I've never felt that way about anywhere my whole life until now. All these years I've been bouncing around, trying to figure out where I fit in. Where I want to be. Where I want to stay. Where I might be able to build a life for myself."

Michael surveyed the landscape as she spoke, seeing through her eyes the inheritance he had largely taken for granted. For the first time, he felt as if he truly appreciated its beauty and was grateful, instead of seeing the historic house as a burdensome backdrop to the losses of his life. Grateful, and wanting to say more about sharing it, together.

Knowing it was still too soon, he kept silent, willing himself to be patient. The lines around his eyes relaxed into a look of contentment as he tucked her hand beneath his. They continued the short stroll to the cottage in companionable silence, their breath coming out in white puffs that mingled and danced in the chilly December air.

"Here you are, sir: home again, home again, jiggety-jig, if I'm remembering my Mother Goose correctly," Shannon announced the next morning as she pulled up with a flourish to Braeburn House. "Shannon's Taxi Service—no charge."

"I should think not," Michael countered. "Although I would hardly describe you as a fat pig, which you may recall is what that trip to market was all about."

He looked over with a lazy smile, his eyes intent on her face as he brushed a runaway curl over her shoulder. Even after nearly 24 hours of togetherness, he was in no hurry to leave. "In any case, it's less than a kilometer."

She raised her eyebrows in mock indignation. "Yes? And how many cabbies do you know who also provide dinner? As well as—" she added with a suggestive leer—"Well, no, let's not get into that."

Laughing, he reluctantly reached for the door handle, then paused. "Do you still want to check on Alexandra's full name? I could probably put my hands on the family Bible rather quickly."

She checked her watch with a frown. "Well..." she hesitated. "How quickly? I'm supposed to be at the Connaught for lunch at 12:30. A friend of mine from the States is in town."

"Perhaps we could give it a try," he suggested. "If I can't find it in five minutes you can go ahead and I will continue to look."

"Deal."

Passing the manager in the front hall, they caroled in unison, "Good morning, Henry."

"Good morning, Miss Shannon, Lord Michael," Henry replied, careful to keep his face straight.

His eyes followed them as they laughed their way up the stairs, still engrossed in each other. Henry sighed. He had been young once, and in love. The signs, as always, were unmistakable. He had a feeling his evening chess games with the young American were about to be put aside in favor of livelier occupations. Ah well, he thought as he hurried off to the greenhouse to check on centerpieces for the dining room. Rubrum lilies might be nice tonight. They would be so lovely for a wedding, too, it suddenly struck him.

"1920, 1903....here it is, May 3, 1881. Lord Geoffrey Willoughby-Jones, married Miss Alexandra Victoria Danbury," Michael's forefinger, which had been moving rapidly up and down the page, stopped at the entry they had been looking for. "Yes. Their son, Andrew Philip, born March 7, 1882. And look—here's when she died. When they say she died, at any rate. September 10, 1882."

"Good Lord," Shannon said, appalled. "She had a baby?"

"Well, yes. How do you think I got here?"

"Oh. Of course. I thought perhaps a previous marriage—but that's right, you said he married because he needed an heir. But Michael, how awful, if she ran away she was going to leave her baby..." Shannon's voice trailed off.

It was difficult to imagine a mother so unhappy with her marriage that she would be willing to leave a little one behind. Not that different from her own mother's abandonment, prompted by a different reason but with the same result. Shannon ached for this unknown child. How hard had life been for this little fellow, with an absent mother and an elderly, indifferent father? She at least had Grammie Lib to love and fuss over her. Had little Andrew Philip had anyone to care about him?

"Well, I suppose she was very young," she said at last, trying to give the unknown Alexandra the benefit of every doubt. "Poor thing. To be so unhappy and to die without having ever lived, really. Not even twenty, from what I could tell from her portrait."

Shannon moved to the window and narrowed her eyes, trying to imagine the view as Alexandra would have seen it from there, editing out the cars parked in a neat row alongside the stables. Everything else would have looked much the same, she decided.

"Alexandra Victoria," she said, drawing out the words. "Beautiful name."

"Only for a hopeless romantic," Michael teased. He snapped the book shut and consulted his watch. "You had best be on your way if you're planning to be in the city by noon. Oh, and—hurry back," he ordered in a low growl, giving her a light smack on the bottom to speed her along.

Shannon flashed him a dazzling smile and saluted smartly. "Yes, sir, your lordship," she laughed, then took a half step toward the door. "Race you to the front door—loser provides dinner tonight!"

Two elderly ladies registering at the front desk looked up, startled by the noise, as Shannon and Michael came clattering down the stairs. The pair caught sight of them and slowed to a more decorous but still hurried pace to the door.

"I win!" Shannon said in a triumphant stage whisper as she turned the massive brass handle, a point Michael had to concede as the door began to shut behind her.

"Six o'clock, then, here," he called, opening it wide enough to catch her confirming wave.

Making his way across the foyer, he nodded to the ladies who were standing with their mouths open, luggage piled untidily around their feet.

"Was that—was that Shannon Tyler?" the one closest to him gasped.

Michael stared. The woman was quite absurd, he decided. Even her hair was a most peculiar shade of silver blue. Still, he had to ask.

"You know her?"

"Why, of course I know her. Everyone in America knows her. Although I must say she looks very different. Much thinner and younger than she looks on TV, don't you think, Mildred?"

The other woman nodded in agreement.

"Do you know," she confided, "my granddaughter Jennifer went to journalism school because of her. She used to watch Miss Tyler every night, standing outside the White House for her reports, and she'd say, 'I want to be just like her, Nana.'"

Michael stared at her in disbelief, trying to smooth his face into an expression of mild interest instead of the sick devastation he felt. Shannon—on television? At the White House? The most famous newswoman in America? An identity she had somehow neglected to mention?

"If you'll excuse me, ladies," he gave them a polite nod and began to back away.

"Oh, wait, if you're a friend of Miss Tyler's you probably know if she's going to take the job or not," Mildred said, eager to find out what she could from this handsome young man.

"Pardon?"

"Why, they want to put her on the news every night with Jeffrey Patterson. It's all the thing in America, now, two anchors instead of one. We were just reading about it on the plane ride coming over. And oh my goodness, here she is, Joan, can you believe it? She just dropped out of sight, you know..."

"I'm afraid I can't help you there," replied Michael, in a voice that dripped icicles. "I haven't the faintest idea."

He turned on his heel and began to stalk upstairs—then paused on the landing as he was struck by not one but two awful thoughts. All at once it came back to him where he had seen her before. It wasn't in some previous life, as she would have had him believe, he thought, with an angry snort at his own gullibility. No, it had been on the steps of Number 10 Downing Street, about a year ago. She had been holding a microphone. Which meant... which meant she must work for an American network, just as the ladies had said. Then what the devil was she doing here?

His eyes narrowed as he tried to reconstruct his conversation with Montgomery the other night. "I am not in the habit of disclosing confidential information to the press," he had informed the press attaché. No, not when he knew with whom he was speaking. How clever of her to have somehow failed to mention it.

He turned and made for the stables, his mouth in a grim line. What he needed was a long pounding gallop over the countryside to clear his head and keep him from exploding. If he didn't ride off some of his fury before she got back, he couldn't answer for the consequences.

"No, no coffee, thank you. Sparkling water for now and then tea, please, later."

Shannon closed the elegant leather-bound menu and handed it to the hovering waiter. Their orders placed, a fragrant basket of warm rolls wrapped in white linen before them, it was time for some serious conversation with the man who had been her friend as well as her agent for half a dozen years now.

Sol raised an inquiring eyebrow into the shining expanse of his balding forehead.

"Tea instead of coffee? You're becoming very British," he observed.

"I guess," she confessed with a smile. "But then, I really like it here."

He gave her a sharp look, then leaned across the table and lowered his voice so they wouldn't be overheard.

"Enough to give up the chance of a lifetime?"

"What do you mean?"

"I mean, WWB wants you back on the air as of yesterday. There are rumblings—more than rumblings, actually—that they want a co-anchor for Patterson. A *female* co-anchor," he emphasized.

As he'd intended, that got her attention. Shannon straightened and gave him a look he couldn't quite read.

"Not me."

"Of course, you," he responded, his face as indignant as his voice. "Who have they got better than you? You have the brains, and the credibility, although," Sol paused to glare at the waterfall of curls down her back, "you'll have to do something about that hair. You're starting to look like someone out of a Gothic novel."

Shannon exploded into laughter, then tried to turn it into a cough and stifle it in her napkin, remembering that she was sitting in the dignified dining room of the Connaught Hotel, a place where raucous laughter would be considered, at best, extremely ill-bred.

"I do love television," she said, once she had managed to control herself. "It's just all about the hair, isn't it? Number three on the list of how to be successful on TV—have great hair. Or maybe what I should say is: straight hair. Come to think of it, I'm surprised it's as low as number three."

"Shannon," Sol said, his voice as urgent as his expression. "Don't be an idiot. This would make your career. They want you, and they want you badly. Don't you remember the days when the joke was that WWB stood for, 'We're Without Broads?' Well, not any more. They've hired a new talent scout, a woman, who's bringing in some very competent women correspondents. Before you know it, the edge you had as their senior woman in Washington is going to be gone. You have to grab this now."

"Right. And spend every minute of every day waiting for Reardon to pounce?"

"God, no. How isolated *are* you, here? Reardon's out, as of a week ago. Your old buddy David Moore is going to be running things now. With, I might add, ample help from Rusty Parmalee, who found forced retirement in the chairman's office not to his liking after all."

Shannon didn't even try to hide her shock, although the news gave her less satisfaction than she would have thought. "Reardon's gone? No. What happened? I thought they loved him."

"Turns out the guy was too sleazy even for the new owners. The clincher was when three of the network's main advertisers pulled out after a five-part series on teenage drug-addicted prostitutes. Needless to say, there were plenty of lurid details."

Shannon couldn't help but grin. "That was his favorite series in Atlanta, too. But they didn't buy it in the big time, huh?"

Sol shrugged. "It didn't help him, that's for sure. That and falling ratings."

"Ah, well, now you're talking. Wonder how long he'd be there if the numbers had stayed up."

"Who knows. And who cares. The important thing is, you can come back now. David wants you. So does Rusty."

"And what would I be doing, exactly?"

"What do you mean, what would you be doing. You'd be co-anchoring the show every night."

"Any reporting? Any chance to get out in the field? How about some international pieces? Or documentaries? Or long-form reporting of any kind?"

"Oh, Shannon, come on. You know how it works. The big rating periods are getting to be almost year-round, now. Your value is to be there at the anchor desk, not chasing some penny-ante piece about God-knows-what in Swaziland. All you have to do is sit there and read."

"That's what I'm afraid of," replied Shannon, with a grim edge to her voice. "And what about Jeff Patterson? Is he still managing editor of the broadcast? Do I get to be a managing editor, too? Or do they just want me there as window dressing on the set—to look pretty and read, and bring up the numbers of our female demographic?"

"It's hard to imagine you as window dressing, Shannon. My guess is, the job will be whatever you make it. Jeff's used to running the show but he's not an unreasonable man. I'm sure he'll want to hear what you have to say."

"Oh, I'm sure he'll be willing to hear it. But will he listen to it? I mean, please, Sol. I'm getting too old to spend my days combing my hair and waiting for the lights to go on so I can read somebody else's words, collect an enormous paycheck and go home. That's not even what I wanted a year ago and for sure it's not what I want now."

Shannon stared past Sol's shoulder at the green silk wallpaper, remembering how the possibility of a different future had appeared as she walked with Michael to the Lady's Cottage the day before. She dragged her eyes back with some reluctance to the face of her disappointed agent.

"I can't do it, Sol," she said. "I'm sorry. I know you'd like me to. But I just can't."

"I don't get it. Half the women in America—and everyone of both genders that works in television—would cheerfully run each other over for an opportunity like this. There has to be more than what you're telling me."

"Well...," she hesitated. "The thing is, I think I've finally figured out what I'm doing here."

"In England?"

"In England. In life."

Sol lifted a skeptical eyebrow.

"That sounds cosmic."

She laughed. "It does, doesn't it? What I mean to say is, I think I've finally figured out where I belong. And who I belong with."

"A guy, huh. I should have known. Well, fine," Sol said, his mouth turning down impatiently. "He'll love New York."

"I doubt it. He's a member of Parliament. And one of the main people the prime minister likes to consult on economics. Not a job that allows for a lot of movement in and out of the country."

"You could always commute. Or he could."

"New York to the Cotswolds?" Shannon hooted. "I don't think so, Sol."

He sighed.

"Shannon. Do you have any idea how much money we're talking about here?"

"No, and I don't want to know. The last time I did something because I thought the money was too good to turn down, I made myself miserable, back in Atlanta. Besides, my dad left me enough to live on for quite a while. I don't think I'm going to go hungry any time soon."

"That's nice. I'm glad to hear you won't starve," Sol said, not bothering to remove the sarcasm from his voice. "So how long do you plan on not working?"

"I don't know. I guess until something comes along that I really want to do."

"And you can afford to do that."

"Whether I can afford to or not, I'm doing it," she replied, with the same stubborn look he remembered from the past. "I told you. I have an inheritance, and I have some savings. I've always made more than I could spend. I'll be fine."

It was obvious from his disgruntled expression that was not the answer he wanted to hear, but Sol merely shook his head and said nothing.

"Oh, Sol, don't be mad," she pleaded, putting a hand over his. "I know it's aggravating for you, after you've always been there for me, and believed in me. I know it's hard to see an opportunity like this slipping away. But I have a life to live, too, not just a career to be concerned about. I want my life to matter, to count for something. I don't want to spend every breath I take in the service of people who probably wouldn't bother to show up at my funeral one day. I want to be more than a footnote in the annals of broadcast history—one more woman who broke through one more barricade."

Sol sighed, sensing defeat but not ready to fold.

"Look around you at the network, Sol," she continued urgently.

"I know what I used to see: dozens of hardworking, talented women giving their all for 12, 14, sometimes 18 hours a day. Running themselves into the ground until they wake up at forty wondering when their real life is going to begin, when they're going to spend some time doing what they want to do, which might include getting married and starting a family. Most of them are spending so much time on the job they don't have time to look for Mr. Right. I don't want that, Sol. I don't want to wake up one day when I'm forty or forty-five saying, 'Oops, I forgot to have a baby.' That's assuming the network would even want me when I was that old. Probably not, is my guess."

"All the more reason to go after it now," he reminded her. "You don't have forever."

"Maybe," she smiled. "Maybe not. Who knows what forever is?"

Seeing his look of confusion, Shannon became serious. "No, you're right, Sol, it is my career. But even more than that, it's my life, and for the first time I'm beginning to understand what I want to do with it. What *I* want. Not my dad, or my bosses, or the world at large. It's been about television for a long time, as you know, and I'm not saying there's no place for TV any more. But I think it's time to start making room for other things, too."

Sol shook his head. He knew Shannon well enough to understand how immovable she could be when she had made up her mind. Clearly, her decision had been made long before they sat down for lunch. Come what may, she would always dance to her own tune, whether or not the rest of the world approved.

"Okay, okay," he grumbled. "I just hope you won't regret it."

"I won't," she promised with a sunny smile. "How could I regret following my heart?" She rose to plant a kiss on the top of his head, then paused for a more practical question. "By the way—just in case, mind you—how do you feel about giving away the bride?"

Arriving back at the cottage with barely enough time to change for dinner with Michael, Shannon found a fat envelope from the States waiting for her. She turned it over, noting an elegant logo of the globe in the upper left-hand corner.

"WGBH?" she thought, her heart leaping as she began to tug at the flap. "Mapping" was scrawled in black ink above the return address. Steve Mapping, her old producer friend who had landed at the premier public television station in Boston. WGBH generated the kind of programs for national broadcast on PBS that she had always admired. Finally! She had been wondering why she hadn't heard from him. When was it that she had written—August? She ripped the envelope open with a silent prayer, her hands shaking as an airline ticket fluttered to the floor.

Dear Shannon,

I'm sorry it's taken so long to get back to you but I finally found a project I think you might find interesting. We have managed to secure funding for a 13-week series similar to what you suggested in your letter last summer, covering U.S. issues from a European perspective, since—as you observed—things often look very different from over there. I'd like for you to meet with my executive producer in Boston as soon as possible. How fast can you be here?

We'll also need to decide very soon where to tape the program. We can tape all of them in London, or divide them between London, Rome, and Stuttgart.

The money isn't great (welcome to public television!) but I can promise that the program will be interesting and intellectually worth your while. Please say yes. It would be great to work together again.

Cordially,

Steve Mapping
Senior Producer
"As Others See Us"

Shannon's eyes misted as she gazed across the pond to Braeburn House. *One door closes, another one opens,* she thought as she began to dance around the porch, her arms flung wide as if to embrace the entire world in glee and gratitude. "Maybe it isn't television that's the problem," she said aloud, "it's what I can do with it...."

And this sounded like the perfect vehicle, she thought, nearly exploding with excitement. A substantive program on US-European issues, taping an hour away, in London? I can't wait to tell Michael!

Physically worn out after a long afternoon of riding, Michael was still far from being calm by the time Shannon rapped at his upstairs door. The clock was just striking six.

"Michael, you'll never guess," she bubbled as he swung the door open, then stopped as she saw his glare.

He nodded for her to enter without saying a word, then closed the door and leaned against it, his blue eyes glittering with anger. Folding his arms across his chest, he said in a voice cold with accusation, "Why didn't you tell me who you are?"

# 19

Shannon froze. Except for the steady ticking of an antique grandfather clock in the corner, the room was silent. Her heart thumping painfully in her chest, she felt as trapped and panicked as she had when Georgie pushed her head underwater at the church picnic all those years ago.

She tried to keep her voice casual. "Who do you think I am?"

"Don't play ignorant with me, Shannon. I know exactly who you are. Now."

He fixed her with a pointed stare.

"The 'most famous newswoman in America,' I believe was the phrase. An inspiration to female journalists everywhere. A woman so well thought of, in fact, that she's about to become co-anchor of her network's major news programme, any moment now."

She sighed, then spotted the tea tray by the fireplace. "May I?" she asked.

He nodded curtly and gestured for her to help herself.

The tea was tepid by now but pouring it gave her a moment to try and calm her racing pulse. She considered how to answer him, wondering what she could say that might take that black look off his face.

Teacup in hand, she sank into her favorite armchair. "Do you want to sit down?"

Settling deliberately across from her, Michael surveyed the toe of his boot for a long moment.

"Well?" he finally snapped.

"Well," she echoed, trying to summon a smile. "I suppose being famous, as you put it, isn't quite as bad as being an ax murderer. But yes, I am fairly well-known in America. And no, it was not something I especially wanted to trumpet when I came here. Does it really bother you that much?"

"Certainly not," he replied, sarcasm dripping from every word. "Why on earth would it? Merely because I know what you look like asleep, and about the little freckle on the inside of your left thigh, just because I'm coming to know the texture of your skin and your favorite authors and how you make fettuccine? Why should I care in the slightest that everyone in America seems to know what you do for a living and until a few hours ago, I didn't have a clue?" His voice rose as he spoke, until he was almost shouting by the time he got out the final question.

"I did tell you I was a reporter," she reminded him, remembering with a clutch of conscience that she hadn't been very explicit, actually, after describing her first newspaper job.

He remembered, too. "Indeed you did, so modestly I assumed it must have been some extremely insignificant position which I refrained from inquiring about for fear of embarrassing you. So much for my perceptiveness," he added in a bitter aside, leaping to his feet and beginning to pace around the room.

"How stupid was I," he continued, "assuming that you were still writing up ladies luncheons and the like back in the States. I should have been tipped off by your reading habits and your interest in NATO, even if you didn't see fit to mention your years at the White House."

Michael stopped his agitated walk in front of the fireplace. Leaning one arm across the carved marble of the mantel, he stared off into the distance, his jaw clenched with the effort to control himself.

"Michael, I wasn't trying to mislead you," she began, bewildered and anxious. "It just didn't seem that important to me. I came here to get away from my old life, not to announce to everyone that I met, 'Hey look everyone, back home I used to be on TV.'"

"I'm not everyone."

"No, of course not. But you of all people should know the downside of being a public person, how careful you have to be if you want to maintain any kind of private life. Good God, Michael! I even quit dating in my twenties because of all the men who would ask me out so they could brag to their friends that they had taken me to bed when all they had done was invite me to dinner. Is there any wonder I wouldn't want to flaunt it now? Especially not to someone like you. Compared to what you do, being on television is no big deal. Besides, you said yourself that the press is just a bunch of 'nosy bastards.' Remember? So why wouldn't I want to pick the right moment to tell you about what I did on TV?"

His face was impassive.

"Michael," she began again, "please listen to me. Television was my job, something I enjoyed and was good at. But God knows it's part of the reason why I've never had any kind of normal relationship. And now here it is again, threatening this one—for entirely different reasons. I'd be tempted to laugh, except at the moment it doesn't strike me as all that funny."

She rose to stand beside him, her eyes bright with appeal. He remained silent, staring into the tapestry over the fireplace as if he could find the answers he needed within its faded threads, if only he looked hard enough.

Studying his unyielding profile, Shannon shook her head, sadness sweeping through her heart.

"I must be missing something here," she said. "I can understand how you might be a little surprised, perhaps even a bit upset. But why are you so furious about this, Michael? You can't even look at me."

He turned his head to glare at her. "Of course I can look at you. But for how long? How long will you be content to be buried out here in the country, away from your exciting career? How long before you decide that you're quite rested now and ready go to back to your adoring multitudes? I can't compete with that, Shannon. I can't and I won't."

"I'm not asking you to," she replied, careful to keep her voice even, despite how unfair he was being. "If I wanted to go back, I would. But here I am."

"Here you are. Until there's an incredible opportunity that would be impossible to turn down."

"You sound like Sol," she muttered.

"Who's Sol?"

"My agent. That's who I had lunch with today."

"You have an agent?" Michael's eyebrows rose in disbelief. "Like a movie star?"

"I know," she said, with a gesture of resignation. "I used to wonder why it was necessary, too. But believe me, it is."

"I see. Well, I'm sure you couldn't wait to hear all the lovely details about your new job." His voice was cold. "All right, then. When should I begin looking for a new tenant so you can go be a star again?"

She sighed.

"Michael, I have already had enough ego gratification to last me a lifetime. It's true that, at one point, being on television helped me get over some of the pain I felt as a child— being different, not one of the gang, left out of all the fun it seemed the other kids were having. When I first went on TV, I felt important, really special, for the first time in my life. Yes, it was wonderful. Yes, it was exciting.

But I can tell you that success, by itself, is pretty thin gruel when it comes to living on it. It certainly doesn't bring happiness, or even contentment. I want a life, now. A real life. I want to be somewhere that I can put down roots. I want work that's interesting and worthwhile, and a place I can call home, and—and—people who care about me. Why is that so hard to understand?"

"It isn't hard to understand, I suppose," he said, rubbing a weary hand across his eyes. "I've just heard it before, from someone else who thought she meant it. Mariko said she wanted all those things, too. Until she got here and realized that perhaps she might never finish her degree, that perhaps she would be stuck teaching kindergarten in a little village school until the end of her days..." He swallowed hard and was silent.

"I see." Shannon's voice was small and sad. "So this really isn't about me at all, is it? About what made me who I am, or why I might want a future, here, my choice, with no regrets. This is a discussion about Mariko. About the past. And you've said yourself you don't know if Mariko was happy with her choice or not."

There was a long silence as he considered her words.

"That's part of it," he admitted at last.

"Only part? What else is there?"

"The NATO report," he said, playing his last card, wanting to hurt her as much as her deception had devastated him. But his words brought no satisfaction, only a reminder of her betrayal, a betrayal so deep it felt like a heat-seeking missile aimed straight for his heart. Until he saw her face. Puzzled, confused—innocent?

"The what?"

He returned her stare. "I told you not to play ignorant with me, Shannon. The NATO report you asked me about the last night you stayed here. The same NATO report that turned up on one of the American networks. Yours, I'll wager. Complete with direct quotes.

To the great embarrassment of both our governments. Isn't that what really brought you here? To lie low until you could get your hands on a really big story, straight from the one person who'd be foolish enough, unguarded enough, to give it to you?"

Clenching her fists so tightly she could feel her nails digging into her palms, Shannon didn't speak for a long moment. Couldn't speak, until she was sure she could form words and deliver them in a voice that wouldn't quiver.

"And you think I gave it to them," she said. Her voice was quiet, each word dropping like a grenade between them. "You actually think I would stoop that low. That I would take a report from your desk. That I would pass along something—anything—that you had told me in confidence."

Michael paused, as a flicker of doubt crossed his mind. Still, he could not stop the words from spilling out. "You're a reporter, aren't you? Isn't that what you people do?"

Shannon's eyes were bleak but she held her chin high.

"And you wonder why I wasn't in a hurry to tell you what I did. Yes, I'm a reporter. It's a profession I've been proud of, most of the time. But I'm hardly the kind of reporter you're describing. And if you think it's even possible that I would do such a thing, you're not the person I thought you were, either."

"You lied to me once, Shannon." Michael's voice was ice as he met her gaze, stare for stare. "Why should I think that this is the truth now?"

"The truth?" Shannon echoed. "How should I know what truth is? I'm the woman who's just been told she was here at Braeburn House a hundred years ago. Is that the truth? Or is that some silly story we'd both like to believe because, maybe, it makes how we feel about each other a little less scary? Is the NATO report what's really upsetting you, Michael? Or are you just looking for a convenient excuse to push me away, like everyone else you won't let get close to you?"

*Careful, Shannon*, she thought, her voice taking on the shrill tones she disliked hearing from others and cringed to hear coming from her own mouth.

"I don't know what 'the truth' is, any more than you do," she continued, after a deep breath. "Seems like I've been chasing what's true all my life, past all the secrets I grew up with, all the buried things that nobody wanted to talk about at home. I thought becoming a reporter meant that I was *in* the truth business now. If I just looked long enough and worked hard enough, I would find it out there somewhere. But the news isn't the truth, not really. It's just our best guess on whatever random events we decide are important on any given day. A snapshot. One moment in time. Whatever people tell us, colored and spun by their own perceptions, plus whatever else we manage to find out, and then it's usually on the run. Truth only becomes clear over the passage of time, something we have to leave to the historians. I used to think my job was the only truth I needed to live by. I didn't need love, or friendship, or other people. Until one day my job let me down, and I had to find something else to keep me going. So what is truth? I can only tell you what I think it is: it's naming things as they are, with a clear mind and an open heart. Investigating for ourselves, even if what we find doesn't fit into the neat little box of things we've been taught to believe in."

Shannon turned away from the window to face him in one last appeal. "The truth is, Michael, I do believe we are supposed to be together. That this time, for whatever reason, we have a chance to get it right—to make it work—if we don't mess it up in the meantime by not being able to trust each other. I'm telling you the truth, as best I can, and I am sorry if it isn't enough. Sorry for myself, absolutely, and even sorrier for you, for being unwilling to hear it."

Her eyes sought his averted face, only to find the same stony expression as when she began. Her shoulders drooping with resignation, Shannon made her way to the door before he could notice that her eyes had filled with tears. With each step, she hoped that he would say something to stop her, find a way to admit that he had been wrong to doubt her. When he did not, when the room remained still, the air between them heavy with pain and regret, she turned the knob.

Very quietly, the door closed behind her.

The yellow legal-sized envelope was atop a stack of correspondence when Michael arrived at his office on Monday. He tore it open and began reading the transcript of the WWB report from the previous week.

> Jeffrey Patterson:
> "President Reagan meets with British Prime Minister Margaret Thatcher next week in Washington, amid grave concerns among the British cabinet about NATO's ability to withstand an invasion from the Warsaw Pact. As Theo Tanner reports, what the British say publicly and what they worry about privately are two very separate matters.
>
> Theo Tanner:
> It was just two days ago, in a speech to a group of business leaders in Ohio, that President Reagan expressed the full confidence of the United States in its European allies:
> (Reagan) "Our relationship with NATO has never been stronger. Together with our NATO allies, we stand ready to meet any challenges posed by the Soviet Union."
> Prime Minister Margaret Thatcher, who arrives in

Washington next week for a meeting with Reagan, said much the same thing in a recent speech in London.

So much for what both sides say publicly. But a confidential report written by the British defense minister raises some serious questions about NATO's capabilities, especially in the face of a full onslaught of Warsaw Pact forces. According to that report: "Without increased funds for training troops along the Eastern borders of the NATO allies, the alliance is in serious danger of collapse. NATO funding has fallen well short of Soviet spending, especially in materiél—including tanks, missile launchers, and short-range weaponry—along the front lines of the Iron Curtain..."

Michael scanned the rest of the report, his forehead creased in a frown. The quote sounded authentic enough, although he didn't remember reading anything like that, exactly. The defense study had been more of a general assessment of troop strength, not a call for more funding. At least, not as he remembered it. Well. He would take it home and look at it again tonight, when he had more time to spend. At the moment he was late for a meeting.

In the days that followed the Christmas holiday, Michael resolutely turned his thoughts elsewhere: to the coal miners in the north country, out on strike again—

... Shannon's hair was shiny as coal, wasn't it, as he remembered how it spread across her pillow at dawn...

—to the growing threat in Eastern Europe, and the unlikely but seemingly genuine friendship between Margaret Thatcher and the American president—

...not so strange then, perhaps, the intimacy, the kinship and comfort he'd felt around Shannon almost from the first, even though they too came from such different worlds...

—to the renewed undercurrent of mutterings about a unified Europe, with no borders and a common currency sometime in the not-so-distant future--

...the future. How could he imagine a future without Shannon: digging in the dirt outside the cottage, shrieking with laughter as they constructed their ungainly snowman, graceful as a princess in her burgundy velvet gown.

By the end of the week, he could stand it no longer. When she had failed yet again to appear for her morning ride—a fact he had noted from the upstairs window—he decided to saddle up, himself, and see what was what. Perhaps she had changed her schedule to the afternoon, when he was usually away, hoping she wouldn't run into him. Or perhaps she was already gone, to claim her exciting new job.

"James," Michael said, careful to keep his voice casual as he swung a booted leg over Black Thunder's broad back a few minutes later, "I'm wondering how far to ride. Do you know if Miss Shannon will be wanting him this afternoon?"

The Braeburn House groom loosened his grip on Black Thunder's bridle and gaped up at his employer.

"Why, why no, sir," he stammered. "She—she's gone to America."

"Quite right, how silly of me to have forgotten," Michael mumbled, turning the stallion's head toward the driveway so rapidly that the puzzled groom didn't think to add, "But she said she'll be back in a few days."

Michael rode off down the long driveway, Black Thunder's hooves kicking up a small spray of stones behind him. His face was a study in bleak despair.

# 20

Shannon's eyelids fluttered and closed. The magazine she had been leafing through aimlessly a few minutes ago slid unnoticed from her lap, landing with a soft *plop* on the floor. Her chin sank to her chest. On the television set across the room, big-band music from a ballroom somewhere segued into an excited shout.

"... thousands, no, hundreds of thousands of people are here in Trafalgar Square as the minutes tick ever closer to midnight this New Year's Eve..."

The reporter on the scene was shouting, apparently forgetting that he held a microphone, as he tried to hear the sound of his own voice over the clamor of the crowd.

The noise was enough to make Shannon startle awake, her head jerking upward from the awkward angle it had fallen as she dozed off. She blinked, vaguely registering the sound from the television.

It took a moment to figure out where she was. A soft pool of lamplight. Blue and yellow flowered chintz on the sofa. Now, that looked familiar.

Oh. Of course. London. Not in the cottage, after all, the cottage that had come to feel like home. She was back at Claridge's, after a whirlwind trip to the States that had ended with her acceptance of the PBS offer to host "As Others See It" in the coming year. The show that she had thought—in her first flush of excitement at Steve Mapping's letter—would give her something interesting to do while she and Michael began building a future together.

She drew in a ragged breath at the painful flood of memories that came roaring back with full consciousness. A future together?

"Not bloody likely," she said aloud.

She turned to the night-side table, where the hands on her travel alarm clock were pointing to six minutes before twelve. Good Lord. Not even midnight yet, and she was dozing off like an old lady. Another few minutes and she would have missed the beginning of 1983 completely.

"And a Happy New Year to you, too, guys," she said, raising a glass in sarcastic salute to the television set opposite. Catching sight of herself in the mirror above the dressing table, she swallowed a sip of champagne and extended the salute to the woman in the glass, watching her mouth twist into a smile that held no pleasure.

"Well, here you go again," she announced to the sleepy-eyed woman opposite, "starting over. One more time. And just when you thought you finally had things figured out. Knew where you were going."

She sighed and took another sip. "Damn, girl. You think you'll ever get this right?"

Shannon made a face as she lowered the glass, the champagne suddenly tasting sour and flat.

Tossing the magazine onto the coffee table, she rose, yawning, intending to go splash some water on her face. A wave of nausea forced her to abruptly sit down again. She dropped her head between her knees and took several deep breaths, willing it to pass. Her eyes were closed tight against the onslaught as she tried to stop the room from spinning, her breasts tender and sore where they pressed into her thighs.

Her eyes went blank with disbelief.

Oh, no. Please, God, no. Not now. Later, maybe... but not at 32.

The same age her mother had died having her. After all these years of pushing those fears away, all the times she had tried to laugh at the superstitious hold it had on her. Here it was again. Looming. Inescapable. Was this her destiny, after all? Was this why fate had brought her here, to kill her off? Surely she had done nothing to deserve this.

No. She couldn't be. Pregnant—and alone. Not after she had tried so hard to be different from her mother, been so determined to avoid her mother's fate. Not after she had fled from love for so many years, fearing what else it might bring.

"What about it, Grammie Lib?" Shannon demanded. "You're the one that always knew about this stuff. Is it all a stupid joke? Is that why we're here, to play out some ridiculous game, only we can never figure out the rules so it's impossible to win?"

She stared into the distance as words from a half-remembered conversation came flooding back to her, words she had tried hard to file and forget as she approached and then passed her thirtieth birthday. Words she hadn't really understood then, but that seemed cruelly appropriate now that she had finally reached the age she had been dreading. Now that she was 32 and, most likely, pregnant. Pregnant, on top of everything else that had gone wrong in her life. Well, thank God her father wasn't alive to see it. His only daughter pregnant, with no husband in sight, was surely not what Ben had in mind when he spoke of the joys of family life.

*"I swan, it's like the whole family's cursed." Aunt DeeCee's voice, in a hushed and deadly whisper to Grammie Lib. "I told Ben not to get tangled up with the Randolph girl. Flighty as June bugs, the whole family. And that little girl's just like her momma. Got her head in the clouds just like Diana always did. She'll live like her and die like her. You mark my words."*

*"Hush, DeeCee, she'll hear you." Grammie Lib's voice was low*

*and soothing as always, but it held a sharp note of command that helped it carry to where eight-year-old Shannon Grace was crouched behind the library door, too fascinated to move.*

*Silence.*

*"There was nothing wrong with Diana, not really. She was just weak, that's all. You know how your brother loved her. And she loved him. If only she had valued her own self, more." Grammie Lib's voice trailed away, then resumed with new energy. "Anyway, that child of theirs is a precious gift to all of us."*

*"Easy for you to say, Momma." DeeCee's tone was bitter. Accusing. "You can float around the house, talking to plants and spirits and God-knows-what-all. I'm the one who has to make sure the laundry's folded, that dear brother Ben has fresh shirts for court and there's dinner on the table. I'm the one who has to see to it that child behaves herself, and leaves the house looking like a lady. She could waltz out of here naked as a jaybird and you wouldn't even notice."*

*"Now, DeeCee," Shannon heard her grandmother say, over the angry click of high heels across the gleaming wood floor. The child ducked down behind an antique sideboard where she couldn't be seen.*

*Aunt DeeCee paused at the doorway to deliver a final blast. "You and Ben can moon around about Diana, and fate, and love, and the meaning of life, all you want. But I don't have the time. I'm too busy havin' to pick up after her messes. And yours."*

*She stomped off toward the kitchen, still muttering to herself. Grammie Lib came to the doorway, her flowered chiffon dress rustling as she glided across the floor, the faint scent of lavender preceding her. "How did I raise such a mean-spirited child?" she murmured, with a sad shake of her head. "Doris Cecilia. I know it broke your heart to lose Jonathan, but you could mend it if you wanted to. You seem to want to wallow in your misery. No wonder you're so unhappy, honey; you just bring it on yourself..."*

Shannon opened her eyes, returning to the cheery hotel room. *But I didn't choose to be unhappy,* she thought past the lump in her throat, *I just can't seem to find my way out of it.*

"No," she said aloud, slamming her hand on the coffee table so hard it made a forgotten teacup rattle in its saucer.

"No!" she shouted, this time, her face contorted with determination.

Crossing to the window, she shook a fist at the bleak winter sky. "I am *going* to have this baby, damn it, and I am *going* to live to raise it! If I really was Alexandra, before, I will *not* be cheated out of this again."

Catching a glimpse of herself in the mirror, panting and a little wild-eyed, she looked at her clenched fist and had to laugh at her own theatrics.

"Yeah? And who do you think you are, lady," she inquired, "Scarlett O'Hara, out in the garden patch?"

"As Gahd is mah witness," she mimicked, in the falsetto drawl she used to put on to amuse herself and the cameramen while waiting to shoot a standup outside the Capitol or anchor a newscast. Her play-acting always got a laugh, which was why she did it. Why she had done it for Michael, too, all those months ago.

Michael.

"As God is my witness," she said again, in a normal voice this time. Slowly, she straightened her fingers and dropped her hand to the windowsill. Her eyes blurring with tears, she gazed out again, this time in supplication.

"Please, God?" she whispered. "Please—can't I have a little happiness, for once? Please let me have this baby. Please don't let me die."

Her feelings still too raw to risk a return to the Lady's Cottage just yet, Shannon decided to stay on in London. A brief search turned up a furnished flat near the BBC studios where her new program for public television was to be taped. The apartment was tiny, but the location was perfect: walking distance to her new job but far enough from the WWB bureau that she felt in little danger of running into any old colleagues from the network.

A week into the new year, with hours of agitated pacing from the kitchen to the living room to the bedroom and back again, had done little to calm Shannon's mood. The nausea that began shortly after she woke up each morning was evidence of a pregnancy she more than suspected but was not yet willing to confirm.

"Dad—wherever you are—if you're out there," she muttered as she walked the floors late one night, "I could really use a little guidance, here. Grammie Lib? Mom? Anybody? Are you sure I'm supposed to have a baby, now? Isn't my life complicated enough as it is?"

No sooner had she put the thought into words then, suddenly, she had an inspiration. Of course. "You idiot," she scolded, racing for her old Filofax with the calendar she had kept there. What about that spiritualist woman she had seen last winter—Clare. Clare would know what to do. Clare would have the answers she needed. Maybe she could even put her in touch with somebody so she could ask them directly—

Shannon paused in her frantic rummaging. "Shannon," she said aloud, "for a skeptical journalist, you are losing it. Do you really believe..."

Yes. There it was. February 18, the night she and Stu had visited the little church in the West End almost a year ago. Well, why not?

It was certainly worth a try. Thank God she had written down the address, in the one place she could easily find it a year later.

She was out the door first thing the next morning.

The building was much the same as she remembered it, although at this hour the double front doors were bolted shut. Racing up the steps, she rattled the handles, not ready to give up on the hope that they would open.

"Of course there's nobody here," she muttered, with a scowl of disappointment. "On a Thursday morning, why would there be?"

Her shoulders slumping in defeat, she turned away, then decided to try around back, where a narrow alley led to what appeared to be a rear parking lot. A man was sweeping up between the cars as she rounded the corner. He looked up in surprise as she hurried over.

"Could you tell me—" she began, then paused at the vacant look in his cloudy brown eyes, " ... where I might find Clare ... "

Her words trailed away uncertainly as the man held up his broom and grunted.

"Miss? Is there something I can help you with?"

Another man emerged from a back door. His face was friendly and open, one hand shielding his eyes against the sun. She recognized him immediately; it was the same person who had prayed over her. Had it been only a year ago?

"Yes, please," she replied. "I'm looking for Clare. It's very important that I find her. I heard her lecture here last spring and I need to speak with her right away—"

Nick McAllister blinked, both at the rush of words and the panicked look on her face. "Oh. Well," he said, his voice kind as he swung open the screen door. "I'm afraid Clare's not here, actually.

She's on holiday in Greece at the moment. But why don't you come in for a cup of tea? Perhaps I can be of assistance."

In a daze of disappointment, Shannon followed him up the steps and into a spacious kitchen flooded with sunlight. Fat red tulips sprang from a white porcelain pitcher on the kitchen table, a splash of color that spoke of the pleasure someone had taken in their beauty.

"Do you take lemon? Or milk?" Nick asked, giving her a sideways look of assessment as he poured two cups of tea. "There's sugar on the table, if you care for it."

"Thank you," Shannon whispered, cupping her hands around the steaming mug. She had to get hold of herself; she couldn't sit here bawling in some stranger's kitchen. Even if it was a church. Even if she was pregnant. And terrified. And alone.

They sipped in silence for a few minutes, as Shannon tried to calm herself. There was something very soothing about sitting with someone who asked no questions, someone who merely—sat, his calm face radiating goodness.

"Feeling a little better?" Nick inquired at last.

"I think so," she gulped.

"Would you like to talk about it?"

"No. Yes. I—I don't know," Shannon said, her voice beginning to break. She took a deep breath. "I've always solved my own problems. I don't even know what I'm doing here, really..."

"Perhaps I can guess," he replied. "You're a pilgrim of sorts, I would say—"

Her response was an angry snort. "Wrong. I'm not exactly religious and I am certainly not on a pilgrimage."

"I do apologize. I didn't mean for it to sound pejorative; I merely meant that you seemed like someone on a quest. Looking for something you don't think you can find on your own. It's not unusual, you know."

Shannon considered his comment, and finally had to smile at how ridiculous she must have sounded. "I see. So I'm not the first person to come pounding on your doors demanding answers about the meaning of life."

"No indeed," he replied. "As I say, it's actually fairly common."

"And what do you tell these poor questing pilgrims of yours?"

"That depends entirely on what they're looking for. Some want to know why love isn't working out for them. Others want power, or riches, or fame." He paused. "And you? What do you want?"

"Well, I've already had fame, and I can tell you it didn't do much for me. Quite the contrary, in fact."

She turned to the window and sighed.

"I'm just—tired of banging my head against brick walls. I'm tired of feeling lost, and afraid, and alone. I keep feeling like there's something I'm supposed to know, or do, but I don't have the slightest idea what, or where, or with whom—"

Nick held up a hand like a policeman directing traffic to halt the flow of her words. "Please. In my experience you do much better to focus on what you do want, instead of what you don't. So let me ask again: what do you want?"

"What do I want? Damned if I know," Shannon responded with some impatience, then caught herself, her expression clouding with guilt and embarrassment. However unorthodox, he *was* a minister. Aunt DeeCee would faint if she heard her talking like this.

"Sorry," she muttered, ducking her head for a detailed examination of her shoes.

He smiled and gestured dismissively.

"Actually, that's not true. I'll tell you what I want," she said after a moment. "I want to know why my life keeps falling apart. Why, no matter how hard I try, no matter how much I struggle, things never seem to work out—"

She choked off a sob.

"I just don't know what to do," she finally managed.

Flattening her fingertips against her mouth in the hope that the pressure might help her regain control, she locked her eyes on his in expectation and trust. Surely *he* would know...

"Oh, dear me," he replied. "If you don't know, I surely don't."

Well, hell's bells, she thought, giving him an indignant stare. If *you* don't know, then what am I doing here?

Reading the question on her face, he added, "But there is someone who knows. You. Even if you haven't allowed yourself to hear it yet." He tapped his chest. "You have all the answers you need. Right in here. That still small voice each of us has within can always be relied upon for good advice. I imagine you've heard it yourself, more than once."

"Oh, I've heard more voices than you can shake a stick at, from the time I was a kid. And most of the time they've gotten me in trouble."

"Perhaps those voices were just trying to get your attention," he suggested.

She sat back to consider the idea. Was that what her bizarre experiences had been about—something from somewhere inside that was trying to help her see the truth of her life? "Shannon the Skeptic," they had called her at the network. Was she so hard to reach that dramatic measures were required?

"I suppose I'm speaking more metaphorically, here," Nick went on, "about the 'voice' that comes from your own internal guidance system. The one that lets you know, very clearly, when you're on track in your life."

"Really? How?"

"By paying attention to how you feel. By getting quiet long enough so it can register above the clamor in the rest of your life."

"Be still," the words tumbled out, "and know that I am God."

"Exactly. Very good advice indeed. Psalms—"

" 46:10," she interrupted. To his questioning look she added, "It was embroidered on a sampler hanging in my bathroom. A message from the past. Maybe even from my own past..."

Nick straightened, his expression changing from thoughtful to alert. "Oh? How's that?"

Shannon took a deep breath and launched into an abbreviated version of her story: how the career that she had relied upon to give her life meaning had been cut short, how she had landed at the Lady's Cottage, the fortuneteller's words about how she had lived in Braeburn House as Alexandra.

"So here I am, after an extremely weird year," she concluded, "pregnant, most likely, at age 32. The same age my mother was when she died right after I was born. Now, I know it sounds completely ridiculous, but I have been petrified for years thinking I wouldn't live past 32, either. It was one of the reasons I was always in such a hurry at work. I figured I might not have much time, and I had better make the most of whatever I did have. You know? The clock was ticking, so I was able to be tough and aggressive and get the stories no one else was willing to get.

"You said to be quiet and still, a minute ago. Well, I've been doing that for months now. My life has slowed to a crawl, compared to what it used to be. And, you're right, it has helped, some."

After another moment of thought, she admitted, "Actually, I have to say it's helped a lot. Only, I'm no closer to the truth now than I ever was. About who I am, what I'm doing here, whether I might have been here before, or if I'm just kidding myself. And even if I were here before, what difference does it make? What am I supposed to do with that? All I know is, I don't want to die. Not now. I really want to have this baby..."

She bit her lip, hard, as Nick rose and strolled to the window.

"What is 'truth'? That is the classic question, you know. Pontius Pilate tried to get an answer from Jesus about what truth is. Of course he didn't succeed. Wasn't really interested in the answer, is my guess." From where she sat, she couldn't see Nick's expression, although his words were coming out so slowly it sounded more as if he were thinking aloud instead of talking to her.

"I would say it's the great underpinning of the universe, part of what keeps everything else propped up. Anything that isn't built on truth invariably crumbles and collapses. Not right away, of course; there are those who get away with lies and assorted chicanery for quite some time. Sometimes for centuries. But eventually anything that doesn't have truth as a foundation just doesn't hold up. It's a process that seems to be accelerating, lately, as if all of humankind is slowly, inch by inch, making its way toward some great truth. Perhaps, even, the truth of our collective existence here."

He turned back to Shannon, as if suddenly remembering she was there. "Have you noticed?"

"Can't say I've thought a lot about it," she muttered, wondering what any of this had to do with her. Why he seemed to be avoiding the issue at hand.

"No," Nick replied with a smile. "I suppose you have more pressing concerns. What you really want to know—at the moment, anyway—is whether this is it for you. Whether your life is likely to end as your mother's did, at the same point and under the same circumstances."

Shannon gave him a reluctant nod. Put that way, her fears did sound a little—well, dramatic.

"There are two answers to that one. The first is, yes, of course, we're all going to die at some point. Our physical bodies, anyway. The second answer is no, you won't die. None of us do—at least, not our spirit, that special God-spark that makes us who we are. That never goes away. The life force that is the real 'You' keeps coming back to gather new experiences, from a different point of view. New bodies to experience it with. New wrappings for the package, if you will."

"Funny you can be so, I don't know, calm and matter-of-fact about it," replied Shannon. "Most people don't want to talk about death. It's like it terrifies them so much they don't even want to say the word. For years I found the whole thing too heartbreaking to think about, no matter how much of it I saw in my job."

"Of course," he agreed. "Most of us are afraid of the unknown. If more of us knew what really happens to us when we die, we'd be a good deal less afraid. Especially if we knew—absolutely knew—that we would be here again."

Shannon looked at him somberly. "I think I've always felt that was true, deep down, although I never really put it into words. I can remember my grandmother saying that life goes in cycles. That rebirth always follows death. But then she was pretty strange. At least all the neighbors seemed to think so...."

She shrugged and took another swallow of tea.

"Life is always more of a challenge to the people who ask questions, who don't accept whatever might be the conventional wisdom of their day," replied Nick. "It's more challenging, but far happier, too, living the truth as you see it. Your own truth—not what others tell you it is. When you are able to free yourself from the straitjacket of other people's fears and expectations, when you can finally live your life guided by what *you* want, what *you* believe to be true, you'll be amazed by what begins to happen."

She was silent for several moments, trying to take in what he was telling her. Then she turned to face him and narrowed her eyes into a hard stare, what Stu used to call her "bottom line" look.

"Okay," she said. "Do you think I'm going to die now, or what?"

"I shouldn't think so." He looked a little amused by her intensity but his voice was very gentle. "As for your mother, perhaps it was her choice to go when she did. It usually is, you know. People often die when they decide there's nothing to live for. Or, when they have completed what they came here to do. Some do it quickly, and others take a while. That doesn't mean you're on the same timetable, that you have to depart the same time and in the same way that she did. It's important to distinguish between faith and superstition, Miss—"

"Tyler," she supplied. "Shannon Tyler."

"The future is not absolute. We have free will, all of us, and we have our own script to write. You are the one in charge of your life. You and you alone have the power to create whatever you desire. To be, and do, and have whatever you want."

"*Anything* I want?"

"Absolutely. It's completely up to you."

"My grandmother used to say that, too. I wish I could believe it," she said, in a small sad voice.

"Perhaps you should try. It is the truth—"

"And 'the truth will set you free,' right?" she blurted.

He raised his eyebrows and smiled at the interruption.

"I know it sounds like a cliché, but that's right. The truth is inside you all the time, directing your steps. Like a compass, almost. So you won't get lost."

"Must be a little crowded in there," Shannon couldn't help but quip. "Isn't the kingdom of God supposed to be within you too?"

"Indeed. It *is* the little part of God you carry inside, the part you brought with you when you came. Miss Tyler—"

"Shannon—please."

"Shannon, then." Nick smiled and began again. "Do you know who you are?"

"I ... guess so," she said after a pause. "I mean, I've always been pretty introspective."

"No, I mean who you *really* are. Perhaps I should put it the way Teilhard Pierre du Chardin did. He was a Jesuit scholar of the early 20th century who said, 'We are not physical beings having a spiritual experience. We are spiritual beings having a physical one.' What that means is that everyone here is actually a spirit being—an angel, if you will—pretending to be human."

"No. Really?" Shannon laughed. "We're angels? Come on."

"I know, it sounds unusual, but it's not a joke," Nick continued, his voice earnest. "Whatever you want to call yourself, the real you is eternal, with a vast reservoir of power you haven't even begun to tap. It's only because you very much wanted to be here that you are. You are spirit compressed into a physical body, just like every other person who happens to be here at the moment. Not as the punch line to some cosmic joke, or the victim of some random game, blundering about in the dark. You are here, we all are, to learn and grow. And most of all, to be joyful while you're doing it. Being happy is how you fulfill your purpose. Not by being miserable."

Nick's gaze never wavered as he looked at Shannon. Her rapt face was soaking up his words as if every syllable could penetrate the pores of her skin.

"The standard of success in life isn't what you accumulate, Shannon, whether it's money or position or power. It's how much joy you feel while you're here. And that's not so hard, is it? Being joyful. "

His quiet voice resonated through the kitchen as he continued. "Think about it. There is so much to physical life that is absolutely delicious: feeling the sunshine on your face. Holding someone you love. The softness of a baby's hand curled around your finger. The majesty of the mountains and the timeless mystery of the ocean. You came here because you *wanted* to have a physical body, so you could better experience the joy of all these things. You wanted to add more learning, more love, to yourself and to the planet."

Shannon tilted her head, fascinated, but unable to resist challenging him. "And I'm in charge of what happens to me."

"Absolutely."

"Well, if I'm in charge of it, why do I keep messing it up? Given a choice, of course I'd rather be happy."

"Probably because, like most of us, you didn't understand how it works. It's hard to play the game of physical life if you don't know the rules—like my personal favorite, the law of attraction. Like attracts to like. If you make a conscious effort to focus on what makes you happy, if you concentrate on what makes you feel good, you will have more of it. If you focus on what you don't want, you'll get more of that."

Shannon gave him a skeptical look. "I don't want to sound rude, but—that's impossible. How can you control what you think?"

"You're right, of course," Nick replied. "You can't choose each and every thought that comes into your head—you would probably go crazy if you tried—but you *can* choose the ones that linger. You can choose whether you're living the life that you want or the one someone else thinks you should have. Your emotions will guide you. If most of the time you're in a good mood, happy and in love with your life, you're getting it right."

They sat in silence for a moment, until finally a tentative smile began to form at the corners of her mouth. "Um... could I have chosen to be here because there was someone I especially wanted to be with?" she inquired.

"Certainly. Why not? The two of you may have even agreed about it before you came. There is no such thing as coincidence, you know. What we think of as coincidence is more divine guidance than anything else."

Her forehead puckered into a frown. "Sorry to be the eternal naysayer..." she began hesitantly, "but you sound so sure about all this. How do you know what happens when we die? You haven't done it. Not lately anyway," she couldn't help but add with a grin.

"You're exactly right: not lately." Nick leaned back and folded his arms across his chest. "But week after week, for years now, Shannon, I've sat in my church and listened as Clare made the most remarkable connections with the spirit world for people who have lost someone they loved. You've heard her yourself, didn't you say?"

At Shannon's nod, he continued.

"Those connections are so vivid and detailed, so exact in their descriptions it couldn't just be a lucky guess. Beyond that, studies are being made now of people who've been clinically dead for some period of time and then restored to life. In fact, there's a doctor in the States who's been researching this sort of thing for years. Near-death experiences, they're called. Almost universally, these people tell the same story about being bathed in love and light as their spirits departed their bodies. They experienced feelings so strong and wonderful that most didn't want to return to life on Earth at all and were disappointed when they did. And what's more, I suppose, I've learned to trust in how I feel. Sometimes, you know, we can think with our hearts better than with our heads. And my heart tells me this is so. That our lives continue forever, and that death should truly hold no fear. There is no death as we think of it, only a transferring of our consciousness from physical to non-physical. The same way we go from being conscious to unconscious every night when we fall asleep. Death is nothing more profound or scary than that. *You are eternal.* So am I. So are we all."

"But—why now? If you're right, why has it taken us so long to figure this out? Clare's connections, near-death experiences, spooky things we can't explain. Why is this happening now?"

"I'd say there are two explanations. One is, that these things have been occurring for centuries but only a brave few were willing to talk about them. Everyone else was afraid, understandably so, of being shunned, or worse. They used to torture people who were different, and hang anyone suspected of witchcraft, remember? And, we didn't have the communications technology to begin putting together all these stories before now. The second is that we are getting closer and closer to a cosmic turning point, when all of us on planet Earth get to choose a world that's more in alignment with love and peace—or not. It's up to us to decide."

"Maybe both are right," offered Shannon. "Sounds good to me, anyway. Although I have to say it's a little hard to try and absorb it, all at once."

"Of course," Nick replied. "Remember, I've had years to mull this over, and at the moment I'm only giving you a very broad outline of how I think it works."

"If you're right that I had a plan before I got here—how will I know whether I'm doing what I meant to, then?"

"You will always know, if you take the time to listen and use your emotions as a guide. When you're not certain of what to do, ask yourself: is this something that will make me more joyful, or not?"

"I don't know," Shannon said, with a defeated sigh. "All this sounds good but—at the moment it seems like my life is more about fear, and loss, and, I don't know, shattered dreams, than anything else. Nothing ever seems to work out for me. I try and I try, and then just when I think I've about got my hands on it, what I want gets snatched away. And there's not a thing I can do about it."

"On the contrary. Things do always work out, one way or the other. But *how* they work out is very much up to you."

"Right. Like I can control it."

"Indeed you do. That's what I've been trying to tell you."

"Well, sorry to be such a slow learner. But I still don't get how, exactly."

"Again, by what you choose to focus on—the trash in the gutter or the beauty of the trees. The one who's sick, or the thousands who are well. Well-being abounds on the planet, Shannon, if only you can look for it. The more you look for reasons to feel good, the more reasons you will find. And in that moment when you are feeling good, you are also attracting whatever else you want. Love, wisdom, good relationships, whatever you may be looking for. It's like sending out a radio signal to the Universe that says: 'I'm glad to be here. I feel really good. Send me even more reasons to feel this way.' I promise you, the Universe will rush to oblige. You are not alone. We human angels have more spirit guides and cosmic buddies than you can imagine, all ready and eager to be of help. All you have to do is reach out your hand the tiniest bit..."

Shannon sighed and turned away from his beaming certainty.

"I don't know. It would be nice if there were something in my life to be happy about, at the moment," she muttered to the window.

"Something? It appears to me you have a great many somethings to be glad about. Look at yourself. You're young, and healthy—"

"Oh, sure, that old chestnut. Pollyanna 101." She made a face and raised her voice into the false cheer of a bedside nurse. "'Now, now, dearie, don't complain. After all, you still have your health.'"

"Try getting sick," he replied. "I imagine then you might appreciate the good health you're taking for granted. But all right, let me see if I can approach this from a different angle. Most of us have the whole thing backward, you see. We think that once we get the new car, or the big promotion, or have this much money, or that big house or wonderful partner, *then* we'll finally be happy. When actually, the way to bring about everything you truly want is to get happy first."

"But how? I already told you—"

"Yes, I know. You keep insisting there's not much in your life to be happy about at the moment."

He eyed her in silence for a moment, then leaned forward with a knowing look. "Tell me. When you go home today, will there be heat on in your flat?"

"Yes, of course."

"And when you go into the bathroom in the morning, is there hot water that comes out of the faucets for you to wash your hands or bathe?"

"Yeeees," Shannon replied, giving him an unwilling grin.

"Ah. Amazing, isn't it. Think of all the centuries that humans didn't have such wonders at their fingertips. What an incredible miracle: heat and hot water, right there in your own home whenever you want them. In other times, you would have had to fetch your water from a village well, and then lug it back to your home and heat it over an open fire. There's something you can appreciate, is it not?"

"Mmm..."

"Well, then. It isn't difficult to look for things to appreciate when you begin making a conscious effort to do it. I promise you, Shannon—begin very simply, just by looking for the good that's around you. Then your appreciation grows and multiplies until your life becomes so amazing you can't wait to wake up every day. And the best part is, it's so easy once you get the hang of it."

"You're right about one thing: it does sound simple. Too simple."

Nick smiled. "The student came to the Buddha and he said, 'Master, how will I know that what I have found is the truth?' And the Buddha said, 'Because it works.' Shannon, this works."

"Well, I have to confess what you're saying isn't entirely new to me. My grandmother used to say it, too."

Shannon's voice shifted into the soft cultured tones of Grammie

Lib. " 'Appreciate what you have, darlin' girl, all the wonders and marvels around you, because you cannot be grateful and unhappy at the same time. It simply cannot be.'"

"Bravo," Nick applauded. "Your grandmother was obviously a very wise woman."

"It's fair to say her head was on straighter than mine seems to be," Shannon confessed, examining her hands with a sigh.

"Well," he said in a brisk voice, "so much for metaphysics and philosophy, for the moment. Perhaps we should try something practical. Would it help if you knew more about this woman you believe you were, before? What was her name, Alexandra?"

"Oh. Well, yes, it might, I suppose. But how?"

"Ever hear of regression therapy? It's discovering, under hypnosis, information from past lives that people find helpful in dealing with their current ones."

She was intrigued enough to forget her fears for a moment. "Really? I've never been hypnotized before."

"Have you ever done any meditation?"

"Years ago, in Atlanta. I was working a very early shift on television and it helped relax me enough to get to sleep. I didn't keep up with it, though."

"That's a pity. Perhaps you might try again. I think you might find it helpful, especially as you try to work through everything that's going on right now. It's particularly useful as a way to make the connection to the eternal you, the spirit part of you that's been here so many times before. Actually, hypnosis and meditation are very similar; hypnosis in some ways is a kind of guided meditation. I help you get quiet inside, and then I ask you questions to focus in on what you need to know."

"Okay," she shrugged. "Who knows? Maybe it'll help."

"In here," Nick directed, nodding toward a dimly-lit parlor lined on three sides with bookshelves. Overstuffed chairs flanked the marble fireplace; heavy lace curtains filtered the noise from the street. A curved Victorian sofa appeared big enough to seat six people with ease.

"Make yourself comfortable and close your eyes when you're ready."

Shannon swung her legs onto the cushy sofa, trying to suppress the shiver of excitement crawling down her spine. She plumped pillows for her head and pulled a nearby lap robe over her legs.

"If you're settled, then, close your eyes and take a deep breath. I'm going to slowly count backward from ten, and with each count, take a breath and feel yourself sinking into a warm and comfortable place. It feels so good to be here. You are totally relaxed, safe and warm, with nothing that can harm you. Breathe. Ten... nine..."

By the time he got to the final number, her breathing had deepened enough to let him know that she was in the quiet state he had asked her to find.

"Go back in time now," Nick said, his voice gentle and calm. "See yourself strolling through a beautiful green garden, peaceful and relaxed. Up ahead, you can see a stone bridge. The bridge is there to connect you to a time long ago. When you are ready, look at your feet. What do you see?"

"My shoes have buttons on them. And heels. Oh. I'm wearing a long skirt..."

The words came out slowly, but with precision, as if she were describing a movie only she could see.

"I'm wrapping something. Jewelry. I'm winding it into muslin strips and hiding them in the hem. Oh," she said, her lips curving into a smile of recognition, "it's burgundy. My favorite color. Velvet, I think ... so elegant ... "

"How do you feel?"

"I'm really sad. My chest hurts with the pain of it, like a heavy weight holding me down. But I know I have to go, to get away ... there's someone I want so much to be with ... "

"See if you can focus in on his face. Is it anyone you know from this lifetime?"

Her eyelids flickered. "Michael. He looks different, but I'm sure it's him ... it *feels* like Michael, somehow ... "

"Can you tell where you're going?"

Shannon paused. "I'm not sure. Somewhere on a ship. Uh," she grimaced. "There's a storm. I feel really seasick. The air is terribly stuffy. I feel like I'm suffocating, I've got to get up to the deck—I have to breathe—"

"What do you see now?"

"I'm walking along the railing, hand over hand. Someone's yelling at me to get back below ... "

"Is it anyone you recognize from this lifetime?"

A long pause. "No."

"What else do you see?"

She caught her breath. "I'm—I've been swept overboard. I—I can't breathe. My chest hurts. I'm spinning down in the waves ... sinking. Oh," Shannon's voice was filled with wonder. "Look at the light. It's so beautiful ... the brightest, most beautiful light I've ever seen. It's like I'm floating on cotton balls, just resting ... "

"Can you see anything else? Or anyone else?

"Michael," she whispered. "Oh, Michael, I'm sorry. He's furious. And so sad. He's standing at the dock, waiting for me in

America... and I never got there. He doesn't know.... he thinks I changed my mind... that I don't love him, after all."

A tear slipped from the corner of each eye, tracing a silvery line across her temple.

"Go back to the light," suggested Nick in a gentle voice, "remember how loved you felt at that moment, how safe and comforting it was to be there."

He waited for a moment to let her continue the experience without interruption. Then, as her sorrow changed to a look of contentment, he began bringing her back up to full consciousness.

"Well," he said, once she had reopened her eyes. "That seemed fairly vivid."

She blinked. "Wow. It was."

"Did you learn anything?"

Shannon thought for a minute. "Michael believed I abandoned him when I was Alexandra. Maybe that's why he's having such a hard time trusting me now. Just like Alexandra abandoned her baby, just like my mother abandoned me in this lifetime. Oh my God, Nick, that's it!"

"Ah...?"

"Alexandra left her baby to fend for itself, right? So maybe in this lifetime it was important for me to grow up without a mother, to understand how painful that would feel, to *be* the baby who was left behind." Shannon continued, her words tumbling over one another, trying to keep up with her racing thoughts.

*And maybe now I've been given another chance*, she thought as her hands rubbed her belly. *To be the kind of mother I wasn't, last time. To be the kind of mother my own mother couldn't be to me. Which must mean I'm going to be okay. But what kind of mother can I be all alone?*

"Nick," she said after another moment's reflection, "do you think Michael will come back to me? Should I go to him, maybe? Try again to explain?"

He shook his head regretfully, wishing he could give her the answers she longed to hear.

"The best thing I can suggest is that you meditate on it," Nick said. "You'll get the answer you need. It sounds as if you're already fairly intuitive. Didn't you mention earlier that you've made some interesting predictions from time to time?"

"Yes, sometimes, starting when I was a kid. I always figured everyone else could do that, too, until the other kids started making fun of me. After that I just tried to forget about it."

"Don't. It's a wonderful gift you have, if you choose to use it. In fact, it could be a clue that you're being summoned to a higher calling in this lifetime. We choose to come here for a reason, you know; perhaps this is yours."

Nick paused to regard her thoughtfully.

"Have you ever heard the term 'Lightworker'?"

"Can't say as I have. If you're talking about me, 'Darkworker,' might be more accurate."

To Nick's puzzled look she explained, "Back in the States I had a career in television. I'm not sure there's a lot of light there. I used to think that doing the news was a higher calling of some sort, telling people important things they needed to know. But now it seems like it's mostly becoming glitz and infotainment. That's one of the reasons why I decided to walk away—that, plus all the horrible stuff it brings into your home. I couldn't even watch it any more, after the massacres at Sabra and Shatila. I will never understand how people can do things like that to each other and I just didn't want those pictures in my head."

"You did news on the telly, eh? Well, I understand your concerns.

But perhaps there's another way to think about it. Perhaps you have been given a megaphone, one you can use to amplify whatever you wish. All the evil *or* all of the good there is in the world. Perhaps you can turn people's attention to some of the marvelous possibilities we have as humans instead of the many ways we can hurt one another."

Shannon blinked.

"The world is changing, Shannon, it's shifting in ways we can't even imagine. I can't tell you how or when, but I believe we are reaching a crucial juncture in time, when everyone on the planet will have to decide whether they're on the side of light, or darkness. Love, or fear. And when we do, we're going to need people—Lightworkers, if you will—to point the way toward how the world could be, if we choose to let it. How peaceful and happy humanity could become, once we understand that we're all in this together. That all of us are connected—to each other, and to the divine intelligence from whence we came.

"Perhaps you're a Lightworker, Shannon. That could be why you're here. Or," Nick shrugged, "perhaps not. It's really not for me to say. It's totally up to you whether you want to light a match in the darkness or just enjoy a happy life. Either is fine, and you get to choose."

"I'd rather you just tell me," she confessed.

"Ah, but that's the whole point. *Nobody* should tell you what to do with your life. It's past time for us to play 'follow the leader.' The new game is to follow ourselves, and tune in to our own inner wisdom."

"Right. Easy for you to say."

"Of course. But not that difficult to do, either. Once you begin to understand who you really are, you can't help but change how you approach the world. Gandhi urged us to 'Be the change you wish to see in the world.' What that means to me is that we can create heaven right here on earth, bit by bit and heart by heart. We create heaven in our own experience and for everyone else here, by cooperating with one another, playing well together, and nurturing one another every chance we get. And that's not so hard, is it?"

"Not when you put it that way, I suppose."

"To answer your more urgent question, though: perhaps it's Michael's job, now, to come to you. To find his own way back to the woman he lost the last time. If he discovers that he's sufficiently unhappy without you, perhaps it will become clear to him what he must do to be happy again. The best thing for you, I'd say, is to become clear about what *you* want. After all, it's your life, too. This isn't something for him to decide and you just go along with it. Do you want him? Are you sure? How confident are you that Michael will be able to accompany you on this journey, or at least not put obstacles in your way? If you are certain you want him, then my best advice is to get into as joyful and appreciative frame of mind as you can, as often as you can, and then..." Nick eyed her eager face as he took a last sip of tea.

"Yes? And then?"

"Well, then comes the part that can be challenging. To have enough faith, enough trust in the essential goodness of the Universe, that you can relax and wait, knowing that what you want will come to you in its own good time. If I may, I would strongly recommend that you try not to fret about it—that only slows down its arrival. *Know* that it is coming and it will."

Shannon contemplated her empty mug. "Well. It does sound good, so I hope you're right about all this. I remember a long time ago, when I got my first job working for a newspaper and it opened up a whole new world for me, I thought I was the luckiest person God ever made."

She turned back to Nick, willing strength and energy into her voice.

"Maybe I can feel that way, again. You're right about one thing; my life's not so terrible. Even with everything that's happened this past year, I'm still better off than that poor baby of Alexandra's. And even though my childhood may not have been the greatest, at least I had my dad and Grammie Lib and Aunt DeeCee to love me. Now it looks like there'll be a baby of my own to love. I guess I'd better find out for sure."

"Probably a good idea," he observed, a smile lifting the corners of his mouth.

"Okay, so ... I'm in charge of my life. Wow. That really is an amazing thought," Shannon echoed. "Although I guess better me than anyone else."

As she heard her own words, a surge of energy rippled through her body, as if in affirmation. How incredible, to no longer feel like a puppet on someone else's string, her life at the mercy of forces beyond her control. She felt like running outside and tossing her hat into the chilly winter air, like the opening of the old Mary Tyler Moore show she used to watch on TV, spinning in circles until she was dizzy, arms outstretched in thanks for whatever miracle that had put her in this place, at this time ...

"Make no mistake, my dear," Nick added, with a nod to her sudden exuberance. "Whether you describe yourself as a pilgrim or not, you are indeed on a journey, and once launched you won't be able to turn back. Seekers are never satisfied until they find out what they need to know, and each answer leads you to a new question. But the answers you will receive are more marvelous than you can imagine. You'll see. For lack of a better word, I would say your life might well become—miraculous."

"Sounds good to me. I could use a miracle right about now," she grinned.

"Ah, well. Couldn't we all?"

At the door, Shannon held out her arms for an impulsive hug, forgetting for the moment that hugging strangers had never been part of her repertoire. "Thank you, Nick. Thank you so much."

He held her close as a brother might, as if they had known each other forever. After a moment, he broke the embrace and stepped back. His hands still clasping her shoulders, his penetrating eyes searched her face.

"I'm glad to help, but don't thank me. Thank God, or Spirit, or All-That-Is, or whatever else you want to call it—the fairies of the universe who look on and applaud every time one of us reaches for, and discovers, the joy we all have access to. All you have to do is to be kind. Be compassionate. And when you need anything: ask, and it is given. Remember?"

"Got it," she smiled, turning for a final wave as she bounded down the steps.

# 21

"You're really sure? There's no chance of a mistake?" Shannon said, her voice trembling with suppressed excitement. In the days since she had made the appointment, it had become clear how much she wanted the answer to be "yes".

The young National Health Service physician stared, unable to conceal his curiosity. He didn't think that was a wedding ring on her left hand, but surely it must be; he had seldom seen anyone so excited about the results of a pregnancy test. So many of his clients were despondent at the news.

"It's a bit early yet, but the test did come back positive," he replied, fussing with the charts in his hand to hide his guilty expression. As pretty as she was, he had no business staring at a patient—probably a married woman, no less!—as he was doing.

"Here's a brochure telling you what to expect in these early months—dietary advice, that sort of thing. Will you be seeing us here in London before the birth?"

"I—I'm not sure," Shannon said. Now that her fears had been put to rest about her pregnancy leading to a premature death, her mood had shifted to a rush of anticipation without much thought about logistics. During her meeting in Boston with the executives at WGBH, it had been decided to tape "As Others See It" in Rome, Stuttgart, and London. Maybe they should change all the tapings to London now. She swiftly considered the possibilities and came to a decision.

"Yes, actually, I suppose I will. Does that mean you'll be my doctor?"

She was so lively and appealing, he thought, leaning in for a closer look without realizing it. Then, recovering himself, he cleared his throat in embarrassment and began flipping through her file.

"Um, actually, you'll see any one of us in this office. As long as everything is routine they'll want to move you in and out fairly quickly, so I'd advise you to take notes and write down all your questions in advance."

"Oh, I can do that," she assured him. "I'm a reporter, so I have lots of practice taking notes."

"Indeed? Are you with one of the American papers?"

"No, I'm hosting a program on American issues from a European perspective. It's for public television in the States—our version of the BBC," she explained. What a pleasure to feel proud about her work again, to know that she was doing something important, something meaningful. It wasn't something that everyone would enjoy, perhaps, but it felt perfect for her.

"I see. Well. Right, then," he replied. Taking a quick glance at his watch, he realized that he had just burned up fifteen precious minutes of his day in idle chitchat. He would have to move even faster than usual for the rest of the afternoon.

"We'll see you again then in four weeks time," he said, his voice brisk. "Very nice to meet you, Mrs. Tyler."

"Actually, it's Ms. Tyler," she replied with a wink, leaving the young doctor red-faced yet again as she shook his hand and reached for the doorknob.

Passing by Harrods on her way home from the doctor, Shannon's stomach reminded her it was time to eat. She slid onto a chair at the snack bar for a glass of milk and a hefty slice of chocolate cake, adding a crisp apple for the rest of the walk home later. She allowed herself a smile of satisfaction as she placed the order: what a treat to view food as a baby-building necessity instead of an enemy to her camera-ready figure!

She was savoring the last bite of creamy icing when a sharp smack followed by a wail swiveled her attention down the counter to a young woman and a little boy, half a dozen seats away. From the looks of it, more bread and cheese had spilled over the plate and onto the floor than had gone into the boy. Within seconds his shrieks rose to a roar, impossible to ignore.

"Down," he was insisting, tears spurting out of his frantic eyes as he twisted off the stool and away from his angry mother. "Jeffie want *down*."

A row of heads along the counter took in the scene, glanced at each other, and quickly turned their attention back to their plates.

"Jeffrey, do sit down and be quiet," commanded the red-faced mother. She closed her hand around his tiny arm, gave it a shake and hissed, "Don't make me have to spank you!"

A moment of silence ensued as three-year-old Jeffrey drew in a deep breath, opening wide for an even louder howl.

"Down, mommy, down..." he sobbed.

"I said quiet!" insisted his mortified mother, as the other diners frowned their disapproval. She grabbed the wriggling little boy by the waist and set him emphatically in front of his plate. "Food costs money, you know. You're not going anywhere until you finish what's in front of you!"

Shannon's stomach clenched as she watched, horrified and helpless. Should she say something? Do something? But what? Children got cranky and difficult and mothers ran out of patience all the time. This wasn't child abuse, exactly, but still...

Jeffrey flung back his head, screaming, until finally his furious mother yanked him from the stool and marched him to the door, one arm propelling him forward, the other smacking his bottom with every step.

Her eyes following them as they left, Shannon placed a hand on her stomach and made a fierce, silent vow. *Whoever you are in there, I promise, I will never, ever, treat you that way.*

The ugly scene was still in her head as she slowly made her way home. If only she could have helped them somehow, the tired little boy and his angry mother. If only such a thing were possible.

The calories helped power her through the afternoon, but by evening some of her elation at the confirmation of her pregnancy had worn off and the sobering realities of single motherhood began to settle in. Would she be able to handle this new responsibility any better than the woman at Harrods had, today?

Snapping on a light to chase away the twilight gloom, she curled up in the window seat overlooking the handkerchief-sized garden outside. "Well, at least I should be okay for money," she mused aloud, comforted by the sound of the words, "and maybe I can hire a nurse or somebody to be with me when the baby's due. It would be nice not to have to face this alone."

Henry would probably be there for her, too, if she asked. No. She shook her head decisively. Despite their friendship, it didn't seem quite appropriate. Besides, she hadn't spoken to him since her abrupt departure from the Lady's Cottage. Knowing how devoted he was to Michael, not wanting to make him uncomfortable about their rift, she thought it best to simply let Henry be for a while. Maybe they would talk later, when she had gotten a little better at creating some happiness and serenity for herself. Nick had made it sound so easy. Perhaps it would be one day, but she didn't seem to have the hang of it quite yet.

Shannon sucked in her breath as another thought made her stomach turn a cartwheel. Aunt DeeCee. She still had to tell her aunt about the baby. Her aunt, whose stern and unbending rectitude had caused her to frown on Shannon's every move, from adolescence through her teenage years. Until finally she had fled, as soon as she got her first job and could afford to move out.

God knows, she hadn't done the family proud lately, between her failure to get the promised weekend anchor job followed by her decision to quit the network altogether. But at least she hadn't done anything disgraceful. Not until now, that is. Oh, the tabloids would have a field day with this one. A celebrated network correspondent, pregnant and single? Please. Thank heaven she was over here, where nobody knew her history and she was a lot less visible than in the States. She would be done with the PBS program before her pregnancy started to show on camera, so she could keep it a secret from the world if she wanted. But not from her only remaining family.

Aunt DeeCee. It was hard to imagine what she would say, or what she would think even if she didn't say it. As Shannon remembered all too well, there were few shades of gray in her aunt's world. Only the strictness of black and white. And even though their relationship had improved considerably during her father's illness, Shannon doubted that Aunt DeeCee would be anything other than horrified and disapproving at this latest bombshell from her unpredictable niece.

Not, of course, that unwed motherhood was unheard of, even in Aunt DeeCee's cloistered society. Every year she and her garden club ladies had at least one or two cases of teen pregnancy to cluck over. Every year at the local high school there was at least one girl who disappeared for a while amid a storm of gossip, only to reappear months later, sad and subdued, her reputation gone forever. Those girls were trash, in the narrow world of Atlanta's matrons. Now here she was, about to be one of them.

*Oh boy*, she thought again with a sigh, then squared her shoulders, picked up the old-fashioned rotary telephone and began to dial. *Thank God I'm over here so Aunt DeeCee can still hold her head up around town. But I sure do hate to disappoint her.*

She glanced at her watch as the phone began to burr. Six o'clock London time meant it was one o'clock in Atlanta. Aunt DeeCee was probably just finishing lunch. Well, this ought to give her a good case of heartburn.

"Taylor residence," came her aunt's voice in a soft drawl. Even after she had gotten her own place, she preferred her old style of answering the phone. To Aunt DeeCee, "Taylor residence" made it sound like a whole swarm of people lived there, instead of one little gray-haired lady. At least it might discourage any burglars who had the courtesy to phone before stopping by.

"Aunt DeeCee?"

"Grace—I'm sorry, Shannon, darlin', is that you? How are you, sugar? I am so glad to hear your voice!"

*Well, enjoy it. You won't be for long*, Shannon thought, as she took a deep breath.

"I'm fine, Aunt DeeCee, but there's something I need to tell you. Nobody else there has to know, but I thought you should. I'm going to have a baby." She got the words out as quickly as she could, then braced herself for the gasp of horror she knew was coming.

She was not prepared for a squeal of delight from the other end of the line.

"Oh, my goodness, that's wonderful! A baby, just like I was hoping."

"It is? I mean, you were? But I'm not married or anything..."

"Oh, so what. Who's the daddy? Is it anybody I know?"

Shannon pulled the receiver away from her ear and looked at it suspiciously. Either she had dialed the wrong number or her aunt had had a personality transplant in her absence. She couldn't actually be *happy* about this, could she?

"Ah, no. Well, sort of. The father is my landlord. You know, the man who drove me to the airport last time I came home. I told you about him, didn't I? The guy who owns Braeburn House?"

"Oh, yes, I still have that hotel brochure you gave me. Why, that's wonderful, darlin', what a beautiful place he has. Is that where you three are going to live?"

"Well, actually, it's more like we, two, instead of us, three. Michael..." Shannon's voice faltered, her heart constricting at the sound of his name. "He doesn't know about the baby yet."

"He doesn't?" A note of concern began creeping into Aunt DeeCee's voice.

"No. We, uh, we had a big fight. That's another reason why I'm here in London. Not just to do the show for PBS. I thought it was best if I got away from Burlingford for a while."

"Oh, honey. Well, are you all right? How are you feeling?"

Shannon sighed. "I'm okay. Physically, I feel fine. And otherwise—well, I'm working on it. One day at a time, y'know?"

"Now, are you sure you can manage this all by yourself? You know you're always welcome here... or I could come there, I guess..."

"You're sweet to offer, Aunt DeeCee, but I think I'm okay. Remember when you said I had to be strong when I was a kid? I guess that's coming in handy, now."

"What about your new job? Are you worried about ... ," her voice lowering to a whisper, "you know, what people are going to say about you?"

"Well, I'd prefer not to be causing you embarrassment, but otherwise I am trying hard not to care anymore about what people think. Or say. Seems like I've spent my whole life worrying about other people's opinions, trying to get them to approve of me, and I have decided it just doesn't matter. After all this time, I am going to live my life my way, and to heck with them. Easier said than done, maybe, but it actually feels kind of liberating."

Aunt DeeCee cackled. "You know, you're sounding more like your Grammie Lib every day. She never gave a lick about what anybody thought of her, either. I always wished I could do that but I never quite made it. So I guess you're in good company."

Shannon's smile was rueful. "I guess I am."

"Well, now, you rest up, you hear? Don't lift anything heavy, and make sure you eat right, and take your vitamins, and, oh, what else? I can't remember. I reckon I'll have to read up on it."

"You really don't mind?"

"Mind? Honey, I'm thrilled. There's going to be a baby in the family." Her aunt's voice was filled with wonder. "I'm going to be a great-aunt. That's almost as good as being a grandmother, now, isn't it?"

Shannon tightened her grip on the receiver. "Seems to me you *will* be the grandmother. You're the one that finished raising me, after all. And this baby will be darn lucky to have you, too."

Shannon was still shaking her head in disbelief as she hung up a few minutes later. Then, overwhelmed by hormones and emotion, she lowered her face into her hands and sobbed. All this time she had been surrounded by love, from her aunt as well as her father, only she had been too blind to see it. It was love that accepted her as she was, ready to rejoice with her, glad to be there for her, no matter what. Love that, in its own way, was as simple and all-encompassing as Grammie Lib's welcoming arms and tender guidance had always been.

"I will take no less from you, Michael. If you ever do come back into my life, I will accept no less," she promised herself in a fierce whisper.

As the long winter nights and short winter days of January ticked by, Shannon and Michael each threw themselves into their work. Each tried hard not to think of the other. Both found it impossible.

Buoyed, now, by the reality of her pregnancy, Shannon spent her days doing research for the new PBS program. She was delighted to find that doing work as substantive as this was as satisfying as she had hoped, as enjoyable as it was stimulating. It was only temporary, she knew. Thirteen weeks worth of shows, at best. But the work helped make the hours go by, and she was grateful for the diversion.

Remembering Nick's advice, each morning when she awoke she took a few moments to look for reasons to feel good. And every day she found them: the sunshine streaming through the bedroom window, the warmth and comfort of her bed, the excitement of the new life that was growing within her. Nick was right, she discovered. Beginning each day by focusing on what made her happy seemed to set the tone for the rest of the day, causing the hours to whiz by far more enjoyably than she might have imagined under the circumstances.

Research for the new program occupied her mornings. During the afternoons, she began a walking pilgrimage around London, rejoicing at how familiar everything seemed, instead of finding it disconcerting. "No need to dwell on the past," Nick had advised, "spend your time enjoying this life." All the same, she took pleasure in imagining how the city must have looked through Alexandra's eyes a hundred years ago.

In the evenings, as darkness fell and she longed for the comfort of a cottage by a pond, her thoughts often turned to Michael and what he might be doing or thinking. She pushed them away before sadness could overtake her, dreaming instead of the daughter or son forming inside her body. What a miracle the whole thing truly was. How could it be that a few tiny cells, too small at the outset to be seen with the naked eye, could form themselves into a heart and lungs and teeth and toenails? Would this little work of art have her mother's curls, she wondered, his father's blue eyes? She found her steps slowing by each perambulator in the park, captivated suddenly by a peek at babies she had once thought boring. *One good thing about being a loner as a kid*, she sometimes had to remind herself, *it should make life as a single mother a little more bearable*. Although it wasn't going to be easy. She hadn't decided when or even whether to tell Michael about the baby.

Each morning as she stripped for her shower, she examined her figure in the mirror, cupping her swelling breasts and running her hands over her belly to see if she could feel a bulge. She consoled herself with the thought that even if Michael couldn't overcome his fears and come to her, at least she would have the baby, and her work. She tried to relax, as Nick had counseled, and stay focused on everything that was good about her life.

When staying cheerful seemed beyond her no matter how she tried, Nick himself, calm and reassuring, was only a telephone call away. "Remember that you are able to create what you want through the power of your thoughts. Focus on what you want, and then relax," he reminded her. "Relax into good health, relax into feeling good. Remember that until *you* feel good, you have nothing to give to anyone else. The best thing you can do for your baby and everyone around you is to be happy, yourself."

"I'm trying, Nick, I really am," she wailed one night. "It's just so hard, sometimes."

"I know it's challenging. You're brave to even make the effort. Tell you what—if you need a shortcut, Shannon, try telling yourself, 'I want to feel good. Bring me the thoughts that will help me feel that way,' and then see what comes up for you," Nick suggested one night. "That alone will help guide you to what you want. I know it sounds simple—maybe even a little simple-minded—but give it a try and see what happens. And while you're at it, keep looking for opportunities to show kindness to others. You're still reading to those children every week, correct? That's doing good work in the world. The more good you do, the kinder you are to everyone you encounter, the better it will make you feel."

"Worth a try, I guess," she conceded. "Anything else?"

"Well, you're a journalist, yes? You might find it helpful to write about the beauty you see in the world, and all the things you have to be grateful for. Anything you pay attention to, grows. So, notice. Pay attention to what makes you happy, reflect on it again as you write about it, and you'll soon have more of it."

"I haven't kept a diary for years, but okay, Nick, if you think it will help ... ," she said doubtfully. Shannon took a deep breath as she made the promise, comforted and ready to try again.

Shannon twisted off the shower nozzle, then stiffened at a faint noise from the next room. Was that the phone? She didn't get many calls, so it might be important. Michael certainly could have tracked her down by now, if he had really wanted to...

She snatched a thick towel from the rack and raced into the living room, trying to subdue the hammering of her heart as the bell shrilled again. Could it be—

"Oh, hi, Nick," she said, trying to conceal her disappointment as she picked up the phone and headed back into the steamy bathroom.

"Not the voice you were hoping for, eh?"

"No, no. I'm always happy to hear from you. How are you?"

"Right as rain. But I was thinking of our conversation the other day and thought I might offer another shortcut to your feeling better again."

"Well, that's good to hear. What do you have?"

"Have you ever encountered the idea that we're all surrounded by an energy field? What some people call an aura? "

"Vaguely. I remember reading something about how the Soviets had even photographed it, right? With Kirlian photography, or something?"

"Exactly. So it's not just wishful thinking or supposition. I've been experimenting with the implications of this for some time, in fact, and I wonder if you might be willing to experiment with it as well."

Shannon wrapped another towel around her shoulders and sank onto the plush floor mat. Knowing Nick, this conversation could take a while.

"Always glad to be a guinea pig. What do you want me to do?"

"Well, first of all, if you can think of yourself as surrounded by an energy field, consider this: what if your soul isn't something inside your body, as we've always thought. What if your body is actually inside your soul? In other words, what if you came into physical form with a bubble of energy that spreads itself out, all around you. Think of what that might mean, and what you could do with that idea. Are you with me so far?"

"It sounds a little out there, but, okay..."

"If that energy is your soul, the best and highest part of you, what do you suppose might happen if you began to consciously direct that energy to others?" Nick continued. "As you went about your business every day, you could send them a –beam, for lack of a better word— of love and compassion. You could consciously send blessings, if you will, to everyone you encounter. Imagine the good that would do, to them and you. Remember when we talked about Gandhi's direction for us to 'Be the change you wish to see in the world?' What if instead of just being it, you could consciously create that change, by blessing everyone and everything in it?"

"Everything? But what about the bad stuff? There are lots of people doing all kinds of things that I don't approve of." Shannon flashed back to the unpleasant scene at Harrods, the whiny child and furious mother. Instead of feeling helpless and horrified, wouldn't it have been nice if she could have helped soften their anger and frustration... especially without them knowing it.

"Indeed. But see if you can suspend your judgment long enough to send those people, too, or those situations, love and blessings. Imagine embracing them with your own energy, your own field of compassion. See if you can feel their anger dissipating, their discord dissolving. Uncomfortable situations turning out differently. I think you'll be surprised by what happens."

"A happy surprise. What a concept."

"Think of the power it would give you," Nick continued, "to consciously create what you want in your life. Imagine if you could help improve the things you found troubling. Imagine if you could actually help create the kind of world you want to live in."

"Gosh, Nick, I've been wanting that forever," Shannon sighed. "And, I have to confess, the personal power idea doesn't sound all that strange. My grandmother used to say we get back everything we send out, times three."

"Yes! That's it, exactly. We reap what we sow, correct? So why not use the power we have to create what we want, by showering everyone else we meet with silent blessings. From a totally selfish standpoint, just think what you would be getting back if you did that."

"Yeah, but what about the people who've done you wrong? Like those jerks at the network who stole my story and cost me my job. Them too? I'm supposed to bless them?"

"Let me ask you a question. Are you quite certain that's the job you truly wanted? Were you completely and totally happy there?"

"No. Not really," she had to acknowledge. "Although they did pay well."

"Making a great deal of money can be lovely, as I'm sure you know, but it's clearly not the only thing that matters. Sometimes our greatest gifts can arrive wrapped in dirty old newspaper, not the fancy velvet bows and shiny paper we might prefer. But make no mistake, they are gifts all the same. We haven't talked about your old job very much, but it certainly sounds to me as if you are happier now than you used to be. Perhaps your getting forced out of the network—or feeling as if you had no choice but to walk away, as I believe you mentioned—was just that sort of blessing in disguise."

"That's one way to look at it, I suppose."

"Which is probably why a very wise man suggested a couple thousand years ago that we should bless even those who curse us.

That says to me there's something very powerful about all this."

"Okay, okay, you've got me. What do I do? Just go around smiling at people?"

Nick chuckled. "That's part of it, I suppose, but you can be even more focused. When you see a beggar on the street, for example, what do you feel?"

"Terrible. Repelled. And, truth be told, really glad that I'm not them."

"Ah. But what if you could gaze at them with total compassion, total acceptance, knowing that whatever path they're on, they might have chosen it for the learning it would bring them. What if you looked at them as the powerful angels they are—just like you—and instead of being repelled, just honoring and blessing them for whoever and wherever they are in their journey. Smiling at them instead of averting your eyes, sending them a blessing and trusting that they will get out of the experience whatever they came here to discover. And then, of course, if you would like to purchase a sandwich and ask if they would like it, that's all right, too."

Shannon laughed. "That does sound better than just thinking 'ick' and moving on."

"It does, doesn't it? Imagine if you were the one experiencing that lifetime. Wouldn't you like to think that someone might acknowledge you as a fellow human traveler instead of simply turning away?"

"Sure."

"And now here comes the challenging part. Are you willing to actually do it? To send blessings to people whether they seem to need it or not? To become sort of a walking lighthouse, beaming love and light everywhere you go, as odd as that may sound?"

"I imagine it will take a bit of getting used to, but I'm not averse to trying it even though it sounds strange," Shannon replied. "It's always irritated me when people seem to think that we've already discovered everything there is to know. I've often thought about what would have happened 150 years ago if you had gone around telling people that there was an invisible force that one day would heat our homes and cook our food and bring light into the darkness. You'd probably be carted off to the nearest asylum. Electricity had always been there, we just hadn't learned how to use it yet. So who knows, maybe this is another power that's always been there, just waiting to be discovered."

"And that's why you might be a good person to help discover it. Thank you for having such an open mind."

"I'm a journalist, remember?" she replied. "Shouldn't we have the most open minds of all?"

"Should, perhaps. In actuality, I'm not so certain. In any case, I'm delighted you're willing to give this a try. Do let me know how it goes."

"Sure," Shannon replied, feeling comforted as she always did by Nick's sound advice.

With Michael or without, at no time did she consider ending the pregnancy, despite the difficulty of raising a baby by herself. It had been so long since she had had a man in her life she really cared about, she had been taken by surprise when desire had joined with love to create their child. She had even wondered if perhaps it was the baby who was the reason she had been drawn to Braeburn House, to fulfill whatever destiny might lie ahead. To balance the scales and learn whatever lesson she was trying to master in this lifetime. Or whatever the heck she was doing here.

Despite her present state of flux, she was more convinced than ever, somehow, that she was doing what she was supposed to, now. Although she did wonder from time to time why the love she wanted so much seemed to be taking its own sweet time about finding its way to her.

"No," she would remind herself in those moments, "*I want to feel good.*"

And just as Nick had promised, a feeling of peace and well-being would wash over her to help chase away the lingering clouds of doubt.

She certainly had plenty to write about in the journal she had begun to keep. Her possible past life, for one. Alexandra had been so young, Shannon realized; how awful to have been forced into marriage with a man much older than herself, so desperate to get away that she had been willing to abandon her baby. A woman whose public desertion—if indeed that's what it had been—would have been the worst possible blow to her cold, proud husband.

In idle moments, she continued trying to put the pieces together. If she was Alexandra, and Theo was Lord Geoffrey, if she had wounded and disgraced him in that lifetime, then it probably made sense that Theo had been so determined to cause her problems in this one. Poor Theo. No wonder he was always trying to trip her up. Had been, from the moment they had met back in Atlanta. When seduction had failed, mischief and malevolence had taken its place. He, himself, probably didn't understand why he was doing it.

"Boy, would I like to know what you guys were like together," she grinned to herself one evening. "That must have been some awful marriage."

And were the scales finally balanced now? Or was there something else she needed to learn before they could all move on? What if Michael didn't come back to her? What then?

Each time the fretful thoughts took over, she noticed, the heaviness in her chest grew to the point that it became hard to breathe. Who knew that heartache was an actual physical feeling and not just something you read about in books?

"Okay, knock it off, Shannon. There is nothing to be afraid of, remember?" she said aloud, remembering Nick's caution about pushing happiness away by holding on to thoughts about what you didn't want to happen.

She took a deep breath. "Everything will turn out fine. However it turns out," she added firmly, hoping that Nick's words of reassurance would resonate all the way into her heart. Maybe even into Michael's heart, too.

All she wanted to do these days, it seemed, was sleep and eat. From the instant she opened her eyes until the minute she sank into her bed at night, Shannon was ravenously hungry. Feeding the beast, she privately thought of it, an urgent gnawing hunger that could only be appeased by what seemed to her like enormous quantities of food. She had always been a light eater, careful to keep her weight down since the television camera added ten extra pounds to even the thinnest person. Now she didn't care what she looked like. Fresh fruit was what she usually craved, followed by eggs and bread and potatoes and tea. By now the very idea of coffee nauseated her. Even a whiff of it could make her gag. What she seemed to want more than anything was pasta, al dente, with butter and freshly grated Parmesan cheese on top, and a sprinkle of nutmeg to finish it off.

"You definitely have an Italian grandmother, pal," she announced late one morning, rubbing the slight swell of her stomach as she did so. "I've never seen anyone who wanted so much pasta."

She bustled around the kitchen of her new flat, setting a large saucepan of water on to boil and rummaging through the refrigerator for a last chunk of cheese. Outside, a watery sun was doing its best to poke through the usual London haze. She paused by the window for a moment, her eyes on the still-bare trees below, her mind faraway, at the Lady's Cottage. Remembering how blue the sky seemed there, how clear the air compared to the diesel fog that hung over the city, she allowed herself a brief sigh of remembrance, then shook her head and turned back to the stove to stir the noodles.

Her stomach gurgled with impatience at the delay. "Oh, hush," she chided it with another pat. "I'm almost done. You'll be fed again before you know it."

Tomorrow she would be shooting the first show in the new PBS series, and as she hoisted the pot of boiling water from the stove, her mind was focused on which of her old television clothes she could still get into. The orange cashmere jacket was always good, especially against the blue of the world map that would be behind her. If only she could still squeeze into its matching orange and black pleated skirt. Maybe, if she didn't button the top button and covered the gap with a wide leather belt, she could still get away with it.

Absently resting her left hand on the colander in the sink to steady it while she drained the noodles, she wondered what other skirt might work if the first one didn't fit. Then she let out a gasp and a muffled scream as she realized she had just dumped scalding hot water—straight off the stove—all over her hand.

"Oh my God," she whispered. Frantically, she turned the cold water tap to full blast. She shoved her injured fingers underneath, remembering from a distant corner of her brain that ice-cold water, not the butter remedy of her childhood, was the best thing for a burn.

"Please, God, let this be all right," she said over and over, her knees weak with fright at her injury, a part of her brain furious with her own absent-mindedness. It was certainly going to cost her this time.

For fifteen long minutes she stood in front of the sink with her trembling fingers immersed in the running water, wondering if she should give it up and just get herself to the hospital. She tried to decide if she would be able to hold a script with her burned hand tomorrow or if the bandage would be too bulky, look too awkward on the camera. Was there any way they could shoot around it?

"Damn, damn, *damn*," she groaned. Of all times not to be paying attention. What was she trying to do—sabotage herself, today of all days? She still had research to get through before she would feel completely prepared for tomorrow's taping.

She pulled her hand from the cool water, frowning as she examined it. After only a few seconds the pain was so fierce she put it back in. A few minutes later, it occurred to her that she was wasting a lot of water; she could be standing there for quite some time trying to decide what to do.

Seized by a sudden inspiration, Shannon pulled a large bowl from the cupboard and ran some water into it. Then, fumbling with her good right hand, she dumped half a tray of ice cubes into the bowl and immersed her throbbing fingers once again. Ah. Better. *Although*, she thought grimly, *this bowl is going to look mighty peculiar on the set tomorrow.*

Carefully balancing the bowl filled with ice water against her chest, she made her way into the living room with a plate of buttered noodles. Normally, she didn't prefer them that way, but plain they would have to be. Grating fresh cheese over the top was impossible with only one hand. She settled into her favorite reading chair in the corner with a wince of pain, still not sure if she was being brave or stupid in not rushing off to the doctor. For some reason she couldn't explain, she didn't think it was necessary.

*I'll wait and see*, she decided. *If it's absolutely unbearable I'll go in, otherwise I'll just stay here and get my work done for as long as I can.* From time to time she would lift her hand from the water. The skin was still an angry, puffy red. Considering what she had done to herself, it didn't seem too bad. But each time she removed her fingers from the frigid water, they began to throb so painfully she would have to immerse her hand again all the way to the wrist bone.

Finally, at 3:30, she pushed aside the pile of research and stood up to stretch. Since her first conversation with Nick McAllister, she had gotten into the habit of taking some time every afternoon to meditate, to find that peaceful place somewhere between full consciousness and sleep, to quiet the chatter of her mind and just—be—for a while. What was it Nick had said? We are human beings, not human do-ings; meditation helps make the connection to the inner self, the one that remembers what's truly important.

She smiled, remembering. He was right. Over the weeks, meditating had become the high point of her day. Now, as she tossed a blanket over her legs, having discovered that it was important to stay warm as she quieted her mind, she was struck by another thought. Weren't there people who believed that the mind and body were so connected that you could help yourself heal? She closed her eyes, trying to recall what she'd heard from that doctor she had interviewed in Atlanta a few years ago, the one from Harvard who wrote a book about what he called the relaxation response. Her eyes flew open again as the details came back to her. That's right, she thought, beginning to get excited. The film clip he had brought with him showed Tibetan monks wrapping wet sheets around themselves in a 45-degree cave, then going into a deep meditative state and steaming the sheets dry. And then the doctor had talked about how your mind has tremendous powers to help your body heal.

She looked at her reddened hand, still blistered and throbbing from the scalding hot water she had dumped on it so carelessly that morning, and sighed. Well, it was certainly worth a try. If this didn't get better soon she would definitely have to get herself to the hospital.

Closing her eyes again, she snuggled under the blanket and imagined herself lying on the beach under a warm sun. She began counting backward from ten, slowly, finding herself sinking into the embrace of an ever-deeper relaxation that flowed through her body like a warm current. It felt so good, so comforting, almost like— love, she decided. Her expression grew dreamy as she began to focus on a warm healing light, saw it move down her arm into her poor scalded fingers, visualized the fingers straight and whole again, the skin its usual healthy pink, her entire hand restored to its normal functioning. She held the thought for several minutes, painting her fingers over and over with radiant light.

When she emerged half an hour later from the quiet place her mind had taken her, blinking a little against the fading afternoon sun, she was astonished to find that the pain in her hand was gone. Vanished. So much so, it was as if she had never injured it in the first place.

Her forehead puckered in a frown, Shannon carefully examined her fingers. They were still pink and a little swollen, but they didn't hurt anymore. Less than an hour ago, the painful throbbing had eased only when they were numbed beneath the icy water. Now there was not so much as a twinge.

Wait a second, she thought, cautiously flexing her hand. How can this be? I know what I did to myself. I know how much it hurt. How can it be that after a half-hour's meditation, the pain is gone? Absolutely, completely, gone, without so much as an aspirin to dull the pain? Less than four hours after dumping a pot of scalding water all over it, my hand is fine.

Her eyes narrowed as she re-ran the day's events and considered all the possibilities. Finally she gave up. "Wow," she said out loud. What was it Nick had said about expecting miracles? Wait until he heard about this one.

"I'll take it," she smiled, turning her head to address the sunshine streaming through the window. "Thank you very much."

As soon as her eyes flew open the next morning, she raised her hand for another look. Apart from three spots of slightly roughened skin on her forefinger, her ring finger and at the base of her thumb, there remained no signs of yesterday's traumatic burn.

"Whoa," she said, laughing out loud. "This is amazing." Who could have imagined such a thing? Shannon sat up in bed, hugging her knees to her chest. Good Lord, she thought with an excited smile, if I can do this, what else must be possible? And if I can do it, everyone must be able to. We just need to figure out how to tap into it. What was it Grammie Lib had said, all those months ago in New York, when I was so lonely and upset and looking for answers, that night in the cab...

*Look inside. Everything you want—everything you need is right there, inside you. And what was that funny word she used—es-something. Oh, right, espavo ... whatever the heck that is ...*

"Yes," she whispered. *That's exactly what she said, only I didn't understand it at the time. What an incredible thought, what amazing power we all must have, sealed away somewhere inside us. Now, if only we could find the key to unlock it. Nick says we can have whatever we want by focusing on that and blocking out the rest. But is that really it? Can it truly be that simple?*

Then, remembering her frantic prayer of the previous day, as she had stood at the sink asking over and over that her hand be all right, she recalled Nick's words in a sunny London kitchen. They were words that Shannon had heard again and again during her childhood, although they had barely registered at the time: Ask, and it will be given. Seek, and you will find.

*Oh*, she thought, incredulous at how easy it was. *I got quiet and I asked. And look what I received—more than I ever could have imagined—power beyond anything I could have thought I had.*

"Thank you, whoever you are. Whatever you are. However this works," she exulted to the world beyond her window. All this time when she was trying to figure out what to do, and the instructions were right there, all along. The answers were exactly where she had been told they would be, inside her.

"Thank you so much," she said again, her heart brimming with gratitude and certainty. The tears began to slip, unheeded, down her face. No matter what happened, whether Michael found his way to her or not, she was certain at last that she—and their baby—were safe, and protected, and loved.

# 22

"If everyone is quite ready, then, we will commence rolling tape for the programme in approximately one minute," came the crisp tones from the BBC floor manager.

From her place on the set facing a panel of international journalists, Shannon had to stifle a grin. God bless the Brits. They were so polite. None of this brusque "Stand by!" business for them.

The makeup artist emerged from the shadows next to Shannon's close-up camera where she had been scrutinizing the image in the viewfinder. "Just a quick touch-up, love," she murmured, whisking a fragrant brush filled with powder over Shannon's nose, forehead and chin. "Your lipstick is fine and you look beautiful," she announced after a final appraisal. "Thanks to you," Shannon replied with a grateful smile.

God bless PBS, too. From Steve Mapping on down, everyone involved in the show had been wonderful to her, from the moment she had walked through the door. What a pleasure to feel so welcome here, to be treated as if she truly had something to contribute.

"I have been advised that we are rolling tape now, and we shall be at speed in thirty seconds' time," announced the floor manager.

Shannon took a deep breath as she gazed into the shadows beyond the cameras, realizing to her surprise that she wasn't nervous. Excited, yes, but not terrified. That was something of a miracle in itself, considering how much she wanted to do a good job here and how long it had been since she had appeared on the air.

Her eyes dropped back to her script, her forehead wrinkling in puzzlement. Not nervous—now, that really was bizarre. She had always been petrified at WWB. As time went on she was so adept at hiding it that anyone watching her would have laughed at the very idea. Only she knew that every morning at the network she woke up, her stomach clenched in panic as she contemplated the hours before her, wondering if this would be the day when she was finally found out. Wondering when it would finally become clear to all the powerful people around her that she was an intruder here, unwanted, unwelcome—that it had all been a dreadful mistake and now it was time for her to crawl back home.

*I'm not afraid any more.* The thought hit her all at once, with such clarity that her entire body snapped to attention with the force of it. *I know I can do this. If I can heal myself from a hideous burn, I can do anything.*

She stared at her script, the words a blur as her mind raced over the implications of this astonishing new idea.

*I'm free. Free of my fears. Finally! Free to be who I am, just like Nick said.*

Within seconds she felt a surge of joy so intense she didn't even try to stifle her smile, her newfound confidence radiating around the table like ripples in a pond. Even the British newspaperman, whose hands had been trembling as he fussed over a stack of notes in front of him, seemed calmer. He took a deep breath and returned her smile. With a last reassuring nod in his direction, Shannon turned her attention to the floor manager, waiting for the drop and point of his hand that would tell her to begin speaking. Then, in the darkness just beyond, she saw it again: a picture of something crashing and falling to the ground, the same thing she dimly remembered seeing last night just before she fell asleep. Despite the crash, whatever was falling didn't appear to be ominous. In fact, she could see people shouting in celebration, all around it. But what could it be? And of all times to be seeing things, again...

"In five, four, three..." she heard from the floor, followed by a pause and then a finger pointing at her. Just as she remembered from all those other cues, all those years.

Shannon lifted her eyes for a warm gaze and a pleasant smile into the camera. "Hello, and welcome to 'As Others See It,' the new PBS series on issues in the United States from a European perspective," she said, totally at ease, completely in control.

She couldn't help noting the irony when Steve had told her the topic of their first show: "The Future of NATO in a Cold-War World." Of all things to be leading off the series, after the trouble it had caused with Michael. He would have been so interested in seeing a show about NATO being taped, she had thought as she made her way through the stacks of research about it. What a shame not to have been able to share it with him. *Well*, she told herself, determined to keep her spirits up, *maybe one day.*

Twenty minutes into the taping, it was clear that all her homework had paid off. The discussion was going very well, so well that she was astonished when the floor director showed her they had only four minutes more until the close. With a slight flicker of her eyes she let him know she had picked up on his cue. Then she turned back to the correspondent from *Paris Match*, who was winding up a lengthy argument in favor of more American funding.

"... because whatever else happens, France knows better than anyone the need for NATO as its bulwark against the tanks and troops of the Warsaw Pact. As long as there's a Berlin Wall reminding us every day of the threat we face, the governments of Western Europe will spend as much as they have to, to keep themselves safe," he concluded, with a decisive nod.

Carlo Fierovanti, the London bureau chief for Italian national television, galloped off in pursuit of an opposing point, as Shannon's eyes widened. Of course! That was the image she had seen—last night and again this morning—something gigantic falling amidst a great celebration. But the Berlin Wall? It had been there for so long; surely there wasn't a chance it would come down. Not in this century, anyway, no matter how much she or anyone else might wish it. *Plant the seed*, an insistent thought formed in her head.

As Fierovanti paused for breath, Shannon jumped in. "We're almost out of time, gentlemen, but I want to return to a point that was made a moment ago, about the Berlin Wall. It's a radical idea, certainly, but let's just say, for the sake of argument, that one day communism did crumble, and the Berlin Wall along with it. Would we still need NATO? How different might the world be if the Soviet Union—if communism itself—were no longer perceived as our greatest enemy; what then?"

Alan Altonstall of the *Financial Times* leaped in. "Well, we would have to find another enemy, I suppose. Have to keep the arms industry in business one way or the other. Either that, or perhaps we'd have everyone join NATO, Warsaw nations and all!"

Merriment all around, followed by a final comment from Fierovanti.

"It's a lovely idea, to be sure," he said, his brown eyes dolorous as they peered over a pair of heavy black glasses. "But not likely in our lifetimes, I regret to say. Communism is too deeply entrenched, its hold too intractable upon its people to just—go away. Perhaps our children might see it—yes?—but we surely will not."

*Wanna bet?* Shannon thought, but contented herself with thanking them all for their comments and then segueing smoothly into a tease for next week's program. Microphones were silenced as music and closing credits rolled, over a wide shot of handshakes and animated discussions around the table.

"Studio's clear," announced the floor manager as Steve Mapping burst from the control room and extended his hand in congratulations.

"Gentlemen, thank you so much. That was just great. Exactly what I was hoping for. And Shannon, good job. I loved the bit at the end, about the Berlin Wall. That ought to make some headlines, back in the States. I can't imagine anyone there has even contemplated such a thing, much less talked about it on television."

He pumped Shannon's hand enthusiastically as her guests wandered off to continue their animated discussion. "Really, it was very thought-provoking. Where in the world did you come up with that one?"

"I don't know," she said, ducking her head to hide her smile. "I just thought it might be interesting to talk about."

Steve laughed. "A world without the Soviet Union. That's great. It'll never happen, of course. Or at least we'll never see it. But what a way to get the series launched. I loved it."

Shannon grinned. "You're welcome."

She was still floating three feet off the ground when Nick called that evening.

"I just arrived home and found a message to ring you right away." His usually calm voice was anxious. "Is everything all right? The note said it was urgent."

"Oh, Nick, so much better than all right. You won't believe what just happened," she bubbled. "I scalded my hand the other day and it was really awful and painful and then I did a meditation and it healed all by itself and then I got this amazing vision during the program today and it was so real, Nick, and I feel so incredible, and so happy, and everywhere I go I smile at people and they smile back and everyone is so nice and I'm loving my work again and I started thinking about how great the whole world could be if everyone could do that..."

"Whoa, whoa, whoa, lady," he laughed. "Slow down. Take a breath. But it's great to hear you so happy and excited."

"Nick, it is truly amazing. You were so right about how this works. I'm just blown away by the possibilities."

"Well, congratulations, dear one, and Espavo...." Nick began, then stopped when he heard a loud gasp.

"What did you just say? What was that again?"

"Espavo. It comes from an ancient civilization, thousands of years ago. It means hello and goodbye and most of all, 'Thank you for claiming your power.'"

"That's it, Nick, that's the word!" she exclaimed. "That's what my grandmother—wait, come to think of it, my mother, too—has been telling me all this time. I kept hearing it in my head but I didn't have a clue what they were trying to say."

"It is a good one, isn't it? And what a revolutionary concept, reminding us of the power we all have within. Our job is to claim it, and use it, to create what we want for ourselves—health, love, joy, abundance. Saying 'Espavo' is a wonderful way to remember to do that."

"Power. Hmmn." She paused to mull it over. Power—power*ful*—wasn't exactly the way that polite little Southern girls were taught they should be. Obliging, yes. Powerful, no. "I always thought my power came from the network. They're the ones who put a microphone in my hand and put me on television and made me famous, even when that was uncomfortable sometimes. I did feel powerful, though. And then they took it all away. Or I guess I decided I didn't like their kind of power."

"I can understand how this might sound confusing," Nick empathized, "but step back and think again. It was always your power, to use as you pleased. You just thought it came from elsewhere. Your power is part of your birthright as a human being living on planet Earth. Your power is yours alone, ready and waiting for you to claim it, to use in whatever way you choose. Sounds to me as if you've not only found it, you're directing it in the ways you want, if all these good things are suddenly happening for you and to you."

Shannon fell silent.

"Wow," she finally managed. "Thank you, Nick. I think I need some time to process all this."

"I'm sure you do. Please, take all the time you need. If I may make one more suggestion, though: try not to think about it too much. Try to just feel it. I believe we would all do better as humans if we thought with our hearts more than our heads."

"Not quite sure what to make of that one. But I'll work on it. Stay tuned, as we say in my business."

"One more thing before you go. As much as I hate people who say 'I told you so,' you may remember—ahem—that we spoke of your life becoming miraculous?" he teased. "What do you think so far?"

"Remember, you are dealing with a skeptical journalist," she reminded him with a laugh. "But I have to say ... I think I'm starting to get it."

At Braeburn House, Michael's shortness of temper was becoming a major topic of conversation among the staff, who whispered behind their hands at how grumpy and hard to please he had suddenly become. Only Henry understood when Michael found the towels too scratchy, the tea bitter, the hallway flower arrangements insufficiently colorful, the roast overdone and the potatoes too salty.

Henry missed Shannon, too, missed her cheery presence, missed the camaraderie of their chess games. He missed seeing her face in the glow of the fire, and watching the lights go on every night at the Lady's Cottage across the pond. He sighed when he saw how much Michael seemed to miss her, too, although pride was keeping him from acknowledging his feelings or doing anything about the situation. Henry wished he dared broach the subject with his employer, whom he regarded as almost a son. The one time he had tried, however, Michael snapped at him so fiercely that he had held his tongue ever since.

"Sir," Henry stopped him one morning for a worried inquiry as Michael strode scowling through the foyer, bound for Parliament. "May I have a word?"

"Certainly, Henry, what is it?" Michael paused. Being courteous required a conscious effort these days, but he was trying.

"I hate to trouble you with this, sir, but the third-floor chambermaid says one of the family portraits seems to be missing, the one of Miss Alexandra that was hanging in the hallway," Henry said, his anxiety clear. Any theft was serious at Braeburn House. The theft of a family heirloom was doubly so.

"I'm sorry, I should have told you. It isn't missing; I've removed it to my rooms," Michael explained. "It's, ah, it's a very handsome painting. I like to look at it," he added uncomfortably, shifting his briefcase to his other hand as Henry stared.

"Very good, sir," the astonished manager managed to recover.

Michael nodded and continued on his way, leaving a bemused Henry in his wake.

The portrait of Alexandra, the black sheep of the family? The one that had been banished to the third floor? Whatever could he want with that?

Michael had thought the passing of time would have made his life a little more bearable by now. It had been nearly eight weeks, after all, since his final confrontation with Shannon. But time had slowed to a crawl, no matter how much he willed the hours to go by faster.

Each night when he opened the door leading to his private apartment, the empty, echoing space seemed to mock him with its silence. Everywhere he looked he saw her. He remembered the grace of her long fingers as she warmed her hands by the fireplace, and how triumphant she had been when she beat him at chess. How warm she had felt in his arms the first time he had dared to hold her, as they admired the snowman they built together. How soft and vulnerable she had appeared in his bathrobe; how amusing instead of frightening she had found the entire adventure of being lost in the snow.

He wished she had never been in his apartment at all. Damn her, anyway. The pictures in his head of Shannon here, in the space that had been only his for years, played over and over in an endless loop until now they seemed impossible to erase.

Michael flung his briefcase into the armchair and paced around the room, his hands clasped behind his back. As he passed the desk, his eyes were caught by the defense minister's report on NATO, the one he had been meaning to read again. Day after day, however, whether by accident or on purpose, he kept forgetting to bring the transcript of the WWB story home with him. Well. He had it in his briefcase now, he suddenly remembered; this was the perfect opportunity to compare the two and confirm his suspicions. Perhaps then he could get the blasted woman out of his head, once he could verify how she had betrayed his trust.

Three readings later he raised his head to stare into the distance, appalled and ashamed of himself. Try though he might to find it, the quote wasn't there. Which meant Shannon couldn't possibly have been the source, even if she had secretly read his copy without his knowing about it and passed along her notes to someone else. So where had the quote come from? Had it been inserted into another report? Was there another version that Tanner had obtained, one that Michael had never even seen? Who knew, he reflected, his expression bitter at the thought. He was well aware that people at the highest levels of government leaked information all the time, often for purposes so obscure that only they knew the reason for it. This news leak certainly played into the hands of those who wanted more funding for NATO. Tanner's report had the ring of absolute authenticity, especially on the eve of a meeting between leaders of the two governments. And in fact, he suddenly realized, that's exactly what *had* happened: the Americans promised more money and equipment for the alliance at the meeting's conclusion.

Yes, everything had worked out exactly as the leaker had wished. *Too bad my stupid suspicions destroyed any hope of my own happiness,* Michael thought.

He stared at his reflection in the glass, hardly recognizing the haggard stranger who stared back at him. The woman he should have believed in was gone to America now, having taken a large chunk of his heart with her. Perhaps one day, years from now, he would have the courage to look her up at the network and explain how wrong he had been. How foolish he felt not to have trusted her.

Perhaps they would even be able to laugh about it, about the strange twists and turns of fate that had seemingly brought them together only to tear them apart. Maybe they would laugh. But he doubted it.

Her head down as she hurried from the village schoolhouse, Shannon was so absorbed in her thoughts that she didn't notice James leaning against the fence until she was almost on top of him.

*Aargh*, she groaned to herself. Just what she didn't need, to run into someone from Braeburn House. It was getting harder and harder to sneak into Burlingford twice a week to read to the children at story time, but she enjoyed her time with them too much to give it up. It certainly wasn't their fault her life had suddenly shifted to London; why should they have to do without? Still, it was hard to ignore the hammering of her heart each time she took the back way to the schoolhouse, hoping to see—no, hoping to avoid seeing Michael's car as he left for the city each day. So far, she had been lucky.

One gray day as January drew to a close, she even dared to drive past the Lady's Cottage . There it was, standing proudly across the pond, as graceful and intriguing as it had been for a hundred years. The place she had once dreamed of calling her own—hers and Michael's, that is—forever. But the cottage seemed forlorn in her absence. Piles of brown leaves had been allowed to collect around the front steps; the windows were shuttered and dark. From her vantage point at the end of the driveway, the whole house seemed to be in mourning. She found it too painful to linger for long.

"I want to feel good," she had reminded herself as she downshifted the Rover and sped away, her knuckles whitening on the wheel. "And I *can* feel good, no matter where I am, no matter what I do," she added as she hurried on to the schoolhouse. She knew that just a few minutes with Lily and the rest of the children would bring a smile back to her face and into her heart. Somehow, they always did. She didn't even have to work at sending blessings to these beloved children; love seemed to well up inside her, every time she looked at them.

"Hello, James," she said now, her voice a little cool. "Are you here to pick up Lily?" Remembering how he had treated his daughter at the Christmas Revels, it was a challenge to be cordial to the Braeburn groom.

*Blessings, Shannon, blessings, remember?*

She gritted her teeth as the words floated into her brain.

*Send him love and light. Bless him, and see what happens.*

She took a deep breath and kept her eyes on the children's antics until she could offer him a genuine smile and silent blessing.

James turned with an inquiring look as if he could feel her good wishes, his glum face softening ever so slightly. She flushed and pulled her jacket a little tighter around her waist. *Oh, don't be ridiculous,* Shannon scolded herself; *he may know a lot about horses, but the man doesn't have X-ray vision. You're barely showing; there's no way he could guess your secret.*

"Aye," he confirmed. "Her gram's vis'tin' so she's to be fetched early. I'm lettin' her run around a bit so she won't be such a hellion when she gets home."

"She's hardly—" Shannon began, then drew up short as she caught sight of Lily over her father's shoulder. James turned, too, only to find his daughter in the beginning of what looked from afar like a spirited argument. Broom in hand, Lily had been busily sweeping when Shannon first looked—part of her favorite game of playing house, no doubt—but now another little girl appeared to be trying to wrest the broom from her. Only, Lily was having none of it. Her stocky legs planted firmly on the ground, blonde ringlets bouncing around her head as she shook it in a determined 'No', she held on to the broom with both hands. Her friend Jillian, Shannon realized, seemed equally determined to grab it away.

Too far away to hear what the children were saying to one another, James turned to Shannon with a disapproving shake of his head. "Such a headstrong lass, that one. Doesn't know how to take her turn, a'tall. And to behave such a way with her betters, too."

"Oh, I don't think Lily has any 'betters'," replied Shannon loyally, her eyes still on her little friend. "And I've seen her share things very well at school. Maybe she just wasn't finished with the broom yet."

They turned back to the girls in time to see Lily point to a corner of the schoolyard, her other hand in firm possession of the broom. Jillian looked but didn't appear to see whatever Lily was trying to show her. As the two grownups watched, Lily scampered off with Jillian at her heels. When they returned a few seconds later, both girls were carrying brooms. Together, they began sweeping the boundaries of their imaginary house, chattering as if there hadn't been a moment's disagreement between them.

Shannon couldn't help but laugh as she turned back to James. "I'd say your little girl solved that one very nicely, wouldn't you? She had the broom first, after all, and wanted to keep it, but she was happy to show her friend where to get one of her own."

"That 'un is headstrong, I tell y'—knows what she wants and does whatever she needs to get it. I fear for her, Miss Shannon. I fear for what she'll become. She'll get trampled on one day, if she keeps on, and that's a fact."

He cleared his throat noisily. It had been a remarkably long speech for a man whose words were usually saved for horses.

Shannon's triumphant expression eased as she saw the naked emotion that lay beneath the groom's stoic face. Perhaps he wasn't mean, after all; just afraid, with the same kinds of fears any father might have for a daughter he loved and wanted to protect. How foolish of her not to have realized that. Anyone who had such devotion for the beasts he tended must have a soft heart, far softer than he was willing to show. And now what should she say? How could she reassure him, as Nick had been there to reassure her, about how pointless it was to be afraid? About how your fears could drive away everything you wanted most…

"I suppose every parent worries about their child, James," Shannon began, after a moment's thought. "But I don't think you have to be afraid about Lily. It's great that she knows what she wants and doesn't back down. I have to believe it will come in handy as she gets older and her friends want her to do something she knows she shouldn't. Would you prefer to have a child so weak that she went along anyway? Or to have her become a teenager, aimlessly drifting along, with no idea what she wants in life? Seems to me it's much better for her to feel powerful enough to make her own decisions. Find her own way."

"I s'pose," he admitted.

Shannon turned from the playground with a wistful glance. "They are so beautiful, aren't they? All so different, so special, each in his own way. They have so much to teach us, if only we'll listen."

"Y'mean, we have so much to teach them," he corrected.

"No. I meant exactly what I said." Shannon propped one foot on the fence, leaning on her elbows as she gestured toward the schoolyard. "Look at them out there, James, running around and having a great time. Nobody had to stop them at the door to remind them that this was supposed to be fun. They knew that, all by themselves. None of them is worrying about what's going to happen tomorrow, or next week, or next year. They're just laughing and having a good time with whatever they're doing right now. We grown-ups have to remind ourselves, sometimes, of all the reasons we have to be happy. But these little ones jump out of bed in the morning, ready for each new day, without having to think twice about it."

"Umph," James grunted, unconvinced. They watched the children in silence for a moment.

"Do you remember the first time Lily was put in your arms?"

"Aye," he mumbled, so quietly she wasn't sure at first that he had spoken at all. She gave him an encouraging smile as he tried again. "That I do," he said, this time loud enough to be heard. "That 'un was a beauty, she was, even as a wee thing."

"I'm sure she was. And I would guess that you were watching her then with hope and love, instead of fear and worry. Why, I'll bet you thought every inch of that baby was absolutely perfect. My guess is that you loved her unconditionally, exactly as she was. Just as she loves you, then and now."

She glanced over to find that the groom's expression hadn't changed, although he did appear to be listening. Encouraged, she plunged on. Who knew if she might ever get another opportunity.

"You and her mother are the center of Lily's universe, and you will be, for years. She cares more about the two of you than anyone else in the world, and it's incredibly important what both of you think of her. That you approve of her all the time—not just when she's doing what you want her to. Every time you look into that little face I hope you can remember what a miracle it is that she exists at all. Right under your nose is a living breathing person that *you* helped create. You may be here to protect her, for a time, but she's here—all these children are—to teach us. Oh, sure, we can set a good example, ourselves, and give them some guidance, like which fork to use and to sit up straight in church, but they show *us* what truly matters. They remind us what love is. They teach us how we can live, if we choose to. If we can learn to be happy in the moment, as they are, we don't have to worry about living happily ever after. It'll happen all on its own."

*Wow, Shannon, some speech*, the thought crossed her mind. *Where the heck did that come from?*

James surveyed the cheerful chaos of the schoolyard for a few more moments, new respect beginning to dawn in his eyes as they followed Lily and her friend, happily playing together. "If it'd been me, I'd have flattened 'em, anybody tried to take what I had," he muttered at last, a reluctant smile tugging at the corner of his mouth. "And prob'ly gotten meself sent home for another thrashin' from me Dad."

Shannon grinned. "I told you she was smart. Smart enough not to hold a grudge; smart enough to solve her own problems, her own way. Not bad for a six-year-old, wouldn't you say? And just look at that smile of hers. When was the last time you saw a grownup looking that happy?"

James conceded the point with a wry salute of his fingertip to the brim of his cap, then turned to give her another appraising stare. "You," he blurted. "You look that happy. It's like—y'r glowin' with it."

"Really?" She could feel her face grow hot at the compliment. "Well, thank you. I've been working on it," she added with a laugh. "Didn't know it shows."

He ducked his head, almost as embarrassed as she was.

"I'd better get going," said Shannon, after a quick glance at her watch. A few steps away from him, a sudden thought brought her up short. "James," she added, turning to face him once more. "Do me a favor? Please don't tell anyone you saw me here."

The groom's weathered face was puzzled. "But Lily knows you're here twice a week. It's all she ever talks about 't home."

Shannon's face clouded. "I meant at Braeburn House. Promise?"

"As y' wish, m'um," he shrugged.

# 23

Michael splashed two inches of brandy into a snifter, swirling it carefully as he stared with thoughtful eyes at Alexandra's portrait. Two nights ago had come his discovery about the NATO report—one more element of an excruciating week filled by long and tedious meetings on topics he had once found enthralling. Now, he found it an effort to summon up any enthusiasm for them.

*Perhaps I need a vacation*, he thought. His eyes traced the somber black broadcloth of her riding habit up to the jaunty feather in Alexandra's hat. *Perhaps I should go someplace exotic and faraway. Someplace where I can get my mind to stop telling me every moment of every day what a damned idiot I've been.*

"Who are you, woman?" he said aloud, as the brandy began to soothe the raw edges of his nerves. "Do I know you? Or have I been bewitched by talk of ghosts and past lives?"

Michael set the snifter on a nearby table and lifted the portrait off the wall. He wanted to examine it as closely as possible, to look carefully into Alexandra's cool face. If only there were some hint that Shannon's incredible theory might be correct—that fate, destiny, God, whatever, had truly intended them for each other. That despite everything, their relationship could be retrieved from the ashes of suspicion and mistrust between them.

Surely he hadn't fallen in love with a charming and beautiful fruitcake who might be here one minute but gone the next. Surely one day he could safely surrender to the overpowering desire he felt for her, the need for her presence that made him more ill-tempered with each week she was gone, the lust and longing that pounded through his body no matter how much he tried to bury himself in work. Surely there was some way for them to be together, even if he had to follow her to New York. Could he do it? Was it worth the risk? Even if he did, would she still want him? After all, her life there must be so busy, so glamorous.

He sank into a chair and propped the portrait on his lap, still searching for the answers he wanted so desperately. The picture smiled back at him, an enigmatic half-smile that revealed nothing. Finally he tossed it aside and rose to his feet. In an uncharacteristic fit of rage, he hurled the empty glass into the fireplace and stalked off to bed.

The insistent tapping of the chambermaid on the door awakened him from a deep sleep. He had been having a vaguely unpleasant dream, in which Alexandra was snapping her riding whip across his palm as she scolded, "Michael! You can't have forgotten about me already!"

He snatched the clock from the bedside table and groaned, realizing he must have turned off the alarm and gone back to sleep. The knocking at the door surely meant that his breakfast was here. Michael shrugged into a bathrobe and hurried to the front door where a chambermaid was waiting with a large silver tray. A domed cover kept his usual eggs and sausage warm on the left; mail and newspapers were stacked neatly to the right.

Mumbling his thanks, Michael closed the door with one foot and brought the tray to a table by the fireplace, where he had started taking his meals since he and Shannon had dined there by candlelight one snowy evening. The portrait of Alexandra was propped on the sofa in silent reproach.

"Oh, shut up," he said, and turned it face down.

As he snapped open the morning's *Financial Times*, a small clipping with a note attached fluttered to the floor.

"I thought you might find this interesting," read Henry's precise script.

The six-inch story was from the *International Herald Tribune*, which Henry read each day as an aid to conversation with his foreign guests.

"Network names Brittany Winter as first female anchor," the headline read.

Michael scowled. What the bloody hell did he care about who the bloody Americans picked to read their news. Just the same, he scanned the rest of the story until he got to the last paragraph, which he read over and over until the words finally penetrated his brain.

"Another leading candidate for the prestigious anchor slot was longtime White House correspondent Shannon Tyler, now living in London where she is hosting a new program for PBS. 'I'm flattered to have been considered, but I'm very happy where I am,' Tyler said."

Michael sat staring at the clipping, his face blank, then let out a whoop loud enough to startle anyone passing by in the hallway outside. Shannon hadn't gone back to America to take the network job after all, he realized, his eyes dazed. She was still right here. She had been all along, just an hour away. He had to find her. Had to tell her—

He crossed to the sofa and turned Alexandra's portrait to face him once again.

"Sorry, old girl, I shouldn't have doubted you, should I?" he said by way of apology.

And then he froze.

He had been so busy studying the portrait's face, her eyes, her expression, searching for some trace of the woman he loved, some affirmation that would tell him they were meant to be together, that he had paid no attention to her hands. On the slim aristocratic finger of a woman long since dead, there glowed a dainty square-cut ruby ring, an exact duplicate of the one Shannon had worn from the first moment he had met her. He had privately admired it since the morning when they knelt together in a search for flower bulbs outside the Lady's Cottage. But how had she come to have the ring? That preposterous tale she had spun—could she possibly have been right about that, too?

His eyes darting to the grandfather clock, he sprang into action, calculating the exact number of minutes it would take him to get to London if he left now.

Henry thought he had seen everything in all his years of hotel management, but he was unprepared for the sight of an unshaven, tousle-haired Michael clattering down the front steps two at a time, pausing at the bottom long enough to clap him on the shoulder with his left hand, enthusiastically pumping his right one.

"Henry, I'm off to London," Michael shouted over his shoulder. "Wish me luck!"

Henry peered from the front window at his employer's car streaking down the driveway in a cloud of dust and gravel, his face creased in a smile of satisfaction. How fortunate indeed that he read the newspapers so carefully.

Even the usual rush hour traffic couldn't faze Michael's cheery mood as he made his way into the city. His only worry was how to make amends to the woman he now realized he should have trusted all along. How foolish of him not to have believed her, believed *in* her, too. He cursed his own stupidity and stubbornness that had made his last weeks so miserable.

As he wove through the cars he considered what whether a little something from Bond Street might ease the conversation. A cashmere sweater, perhaps. Or a silk scarf. No, one of those expensive handbags from Paris. Or perhaps something antique. What was it she collected? Oh yes, Victorian inkwells, he remembered with a smile. No wonder she seemed to like everything from that period, from architecture to antiques.

His eyes flickered over the expensive shops as he considered what might constitute an appropriate apology. Half a block from Sotheby's he craned his neck to see why there seemed to be a crowd gathering outside the auction house. He was paralyzed by the sight of a head with a cascade of curly chestnut hair bobbing up the steps.

*Oh, no, no*, he thought. *It's impossible. It can't be Shannon—life doesn't present us with that kind of coincidence. Does it?*

Michael pulled up on the opposite side of the street, oblivious to the irate chorus of horns blaring behind him. He read the banner proclaiming, "Public Auction Today" and strained again to see if he could make out the face of the woman with the dark curly hair. No use. He could only see the back of her head as she disappeared into the building.

He shut off the car's ignition and jumped out. His Member of Parliament license plates would protect him for a few minutes, even here, and he wasn't going to run the risk of losing her now.

"I promise, God, if it's really Shannon I will never doubt you again," he muttered, directing a fervent prayer to the sky as he dashed across the street.

Michael shouldered his way through the crowd inside, looking eagerly into a maze of rooms jammed with display cases. Sterling silver tea sets and brass candlesticks were carefully arranged on tables next to serving spoons and crystal decanters, alongside oil paintings of landscapes that no longer existed and portraits of people long since forgotten.

As he stood surveying the crush on the second floor, the crowd parted long enough for him to see at last the face he had been looking for. Shannon was studying a case of antique baby spoons, oblivious to the noise and crowds around her. Elbowing his way through the dealers and the tourists, Michael arrived at last behind her. He shifted his weight from one foot to the other, awkward and indecisive, until he was able to gather his courage and lean close enough to inhale the vanilla scent of her hair.

"I know where there's better stuff than this lot," he whispered in a teasing murmur just above her ear, "and it's all yours—if you want it."

She spun around, her eyes widening, her face alight with joy and astonishment.

"Oh, Michael," she whispered, "Finally! Where have you been?"

"Well, let's see. I've been a damned fool and a complete idiot, for starters," replied Michael, folding her into arms that trembled with relief. Her cheek pressed to his chest as he continued the apology. "Also foolish beyond belief not to have trusted you."

"Well, yes," she conceded with a shaky laugh, drawing back to drink in his face. "All of the above. But I didn't ask *what* you'd been, I asked you where."

"Ah. Well, then, that's easy. Same place as always. Our house. Yours and mine—if you're willing to share it with me."

"It's what I've wanted for some time now, Michael. I've been hoping for it, and wishing for it, and visualizing it like mad for weeks. But are you absolutely sure that's what you want?"

He hesitated, hoping he could keep his voice steady long enough to get the words out.

"*You* are what I want. What I need. Every blessed bit of you.

More than you could ever imagine," he finally answered. Pressing his lips into her hair, Michael closed his eyes in a silent prayer of thanksgiving as he embraced her once again.

He was startled when Shannon pulled away. Had the face she turned to his appeared any less tender, he would have been terrified.

"I'm so glad," she said, her voice soft. "But you do realize we have a lot to talk about before we can begin to make any decisions. About anything."

He nodded, afraid to trust himself to speak. He pulled her close against him, unconcerned about the stares from the crowd around them. It was some time until he could let go of her long enough to lead her down the steps, into the car, and back toward home.

Outside, the London bobby who had been scratching his head as he eyed the expensive silver Jaguar—apparently abandoned right where it stood—looked up with relief as they approached.

"Sorry," Michael murmured by way of apology as he opened the door for Shannon. "Emergency, you know."

"Quite all right, your Lordship," the bobby responded, his face brightening as he recognized whose car it was. "I'm sure you don't make a habit of it."

Shannon managed to wait until they had pulled away from the curb before she began to laugh. "I can't believe you just left your car practically in the middle of the street like that," she sputtered.

Michael didn't seem to find it quite as amusing as she did. In fact, she could have sworn his face was turning red.

"Yes, well, it was important," he managed after a moment, then gave his full attention to maneuvering the car through the crowded streets of London's shopping district.

As they pulled onto the main highway to Burlingford, Michael glanced over at his silent passenger, wishing he could stop the car and just look at her for a while. God, she was gorgeous. Absolutely glowing with health and vitality—and something else he couldn't quite put his finger on. Confidence, perhaps? A serenity he had never noticed before? Something was different about her, that was certain.

Whatever it was, it was making him nervous.

His eyes flickered self-consciously to the rearview mirror. Shannon looked a hell of a lot better than he did at the moment, he frowned, passing one hand across the dark stubble on his jaw.

"My apologies," he said when she looked over at him inquiringly. "I ran out so quickly this morning I didn't take the time to shave."

Shannon smiled. "Oh, well," she said. "Let's just enjoy this beautiful day." She turned back to the window, soaking up the sunshine and scenery.

Shannon was right: it was a glorious day, but at the moment he had too much on his mind to notice. *Easy enough for you to say*, Michael thought, again aware of how much she had a right to be angry with him. Furious, even.

Actually, at the moment he would have preferred her fury. That at least would have seemed more predictable, more manageable. Anger was something he knew how to deal with: he could apologize and promise to do better, as his fellow man had been doing for centuries. He didn't know what to do with this calm creature sitting next to him. Especially not one emitting waves of happiness—waves that on further reflection seemed to have very little to do with him.

Michael drummed his fingers on the steering wheel. For one of the rare times of his life, he did not have the vaguest idea what to do or say. He turned to Shannon again, only to find her lips turned up in a smile; friendly, yes, but a little distant, too. Impossible to read.

His heart turned over in his chest.

Six miles from the Burlingford cut-off, he could stand it no longer. He took an abrupt turn off the main road into the gravel driveway of a pub, an imitation Tudor sort of affair that would have been jammed with tourists had it been summer. Now, however, the place looked deserted.

Shannon raised her eyebrows as he braked the Jaguar to a stop.

"I could do with something to eat. And drink," he said, pulling the keys from the ignition.

Ducking his head to keep from bumping into the low ceiling, Michael blinked as his eyes adjusted to the gloom. Good. One hour before lunchtime, they had the place to themselves, except for someone wiping down a well-worn bar.

He gritted his teeth, steeling himself for what was to come. If they were going to have it out—if Shannon was going to tell him goodbye and good riddance—at least he wouldn't have to add that painful memory to all the other ones rattling around Braeburn House.

He nodded toward a high-backed booth in the corner, standing aside to let Shannon precede him. They settled themselves onto the plump leather seat cushions as the man tending bar bustled over to take their order.

"Brandy for me," Michael growled. "A double. And whatever you have in the way of eggs and toast."

Shannon tried not to let her surprise register. Brandy? At eleven o'clock in the morning? He really must be upset.

"Tea, please, with milk," she smiled up at the bar man, sending him a silent blessing of thanks for this quiet spot where they could chat.

"Certainly," he replied, giving her a puzzled look as he backed away.

Michael leaned across the table as soon as he was out of earshot. "Damn it all, Shannon," he burst out. "If you're going to break my heart and send me packing, I do wish you'd get on with it."

"Michael," she replied softly, touched as well as shocked. "I don't want to break your heart."

They sat in silence until their drinks arrived, Michael lifting his for a deep swallow before the glass even touched the table. *I don't want to break your heart*, she had said. That didn't mean she wasn't planning to. And he noticed she had said nothing about sending him packing. He took a deep breath and tried again.

"You look wonderful." His eyes swept over her face as if his assignment for the day was to issue a detailed report on each feature.

"Thank you," replied Shannon, studying him in return. "I wish I could say the same. Are you all right?"

"You mean, am I all right despite my guilt and remorse over some incredibly bad judgment?" Michael's lips were smiling as he said the words but his eyes were somber, searching hers for some sign of forgiveness.

"And how, exactly, did you figure out that your judgment was so bad?" Shannon was careful to keep her tone light.

"Henry. He discovered a news article about your decision to stay here, in London. I thought you had gone back to the States already to take the anchor job. I read it this morning and … here I am."

"So I see. What about the NATO report?"

Michael's eyes fell to the droplets of brandy clinging to the bottom of his glass. He picked it up in his palms, rubbing the snifter from side to side, as if the gesture could warm his fingers as thoroughly as its contents had warmed his throat.

"Two weeks ago I was at home one night. Miserable. Missing you. And I read the bloody thing again. The quote wasn't there. So obviously you couldn't have been the one who leaked it. What I find horrifying is how I ever could have thought you would. Or could. I am so deeply ashamed of myself, I don't know how you can forgive me."

He summoned the courage to look into her eyes and was astonished to find them clear, her brow serene.

"That's not so hard, Michael. Of course I forgive you. My guess is, you were afraid—of me, of how we felt about each other, of what all that might mean to your comfortable life. After all, you haven't had to accommodate yourself to anyone else for quite some time now."

Shannon reached across the table and gently touched his hand, hoping to relieve the anguish in his eyes.

"I forgive you," she repeated. "The question is, can you forgive yourself?"

"No. The question is, can I salvage what I threw away so foolishly? What I now realize I really want."

"Are you absolutely sure I'm what you want?" Despite her best intentions, Shannon's eyes began to fill. "Because wanting is the first step toward having, Michael. You see, the fairy tales aren't all wrong. You really can live happily ever after. But before you can do that, you have to understand how valuable you are. How special, and worth loving, just as you are. If you don't love yourself, first, you won't be able to love me or anyone else for very long."

"I certainly don't feel very lovable at the moment," he admitted.

"Ah. But you must. You are capable of so much happiness, if only you'll allow it."

"And you—are you happy?"

"Happier than I was, certainly. And more importantly, I'm learning how to get myself there when I need to."

"And that is..." he prompted, as his food arrived. He unwrapped the silverware from his napkin and began to dig in.

Shannon waited until the bar man had moved away to continue. These days, you never knew. The last thing Michael needed was for *this* conversation to show up in London's tabloids.

350

"Well, as best I can figure it, step one is accepting the fact of who we really are. We've been here many times before and we'll be here many times again. Last time I was Alexandra, this time I'm Shannon, who knows who I'll decide to be next time. Which means... what fun. We get to do this over and over and over again."

"You sound so sure. I wish I could believe it as much as you seem to."

"I know. It's taken me a while to get there, too, and I even had a head start, thanks to Grammie Lib. But once you get that, you understand why there's no reason to fear death. I used to be so scared of dying. And now I'm not, because now I know that when we die, we reconnect with the spirit version of ourselves, and it's wonderful. Once you stop being afraid of death, it makes you appreciate life a lot more. You wake up and start to realize that you've been marching along, pretty numb, when there is so much more available to you. Being awake and truly alive makes all the difference in the world."

"I can see where it might," he nodded, trying to be agreeable.

"And the other way to get happy is by appreciating everything you already have. My grandmother knew that. She used to say it all the time. I don't know why it's taken me so long to figure it out. She used to say that you couldn't be grateful and unhappy at the same time, and she was absolutely right. Until you're happy with who you are, until you're able to fall in love with yourself and value yourself, you don't have anything to give to anyone else. That's one more reason why all of this is so important. Because until you make a conscious decision to be happy, it's just too easy to let your fears take over. To whisper in your ear all the reasons why you don't deserve and will never get what you want. Listening to your fears—letting them run the show—just about guarantees you won't be happy. Ever."

Shannon eyed him over the edge of her teacup, wondering if any of this was sinking in. His face seemed puzzled, but hopeful.

"So," she said after a moment. "I don't know what the future may hold for us, Michael, or if there even might be an 'us.' But I can tell you this much. I have decided to be happy, every day of my life. I'm going to enjoy and appreciate all the wonders and marvels—all the beauty—that's around me every precious moment that I'm here. And part of my being happy is surrounding myself with other happy people who won't let fear rule their lives either. Nick says that happens anyway once you've made a decision about what you want—"

"Nick?" he interrupted.

She gave him a severe look. "Down, boy. He's a minister. Someone I went to see at that spiritualist church in the West End."

"Oh." Ducking his head, Michael resolved to keep his mouth shut.

"Anyway, Nick says that the happier you are, the more you draw what you want to you. So maybe..." she paused to consider the implications of what she was saying. "Maybe the fact that you were suddenly inspired to come find me means it's working for us, now."

She gazed tenderly across the table at his downcast eyes. As haggard as he appeared at the moment, she really could look at that face forever.

"Anyway. That's what I plan to do with my life," she announced. "I am going to be happy. And as for what you do, my dear and handsome landlord..."

Shannon's voice broke and her lower lip began to tremble. She leaned toward him and cupped his unshaven cheek in her hand. Michael rubbed it against the soft flesh of her fingers without breaking his gaze from her tremulous face. Too moved to speak, he held his breath to hear what might be coming next.

"Well, darling, that's up to you. You're the only one who can possibly know what you want. Who or what can make you happy.

Whether you want to listen to your fears or listen to your heart."

Michael placed his hand over hers to keep it anchored against his face and took a deep breath.

"I know I was miserable after you left," he finally managed. "And I'm sure I was miserable before you came, although at the time I was probably too busy to notice. So if you're telling me that I need to get over my fears and remember to trust you, God knows I'll try. And if being happy is as important as you say, I suppose there's no remedy but to work at it so I can have you back in my life again. That is, if you'll have me."

"I think we'd both like to have you." Shannon's voice was so low it took a moment for her words to register. His eyes widened as they flew to her midriff and then back to her face. Shannon nodded.

"Guess what we did," she said with a shaky laugh. She patted her belly, her throat so choked with happiness she could barely breathe.

"How—I mean, wha'—I mean," Michael sputtered. "Oh, my God." He dropped his face into his hands for a moment, then fanned his fingers sideways so she could see his dazed but rapturous expression.

"I guess this happiness thing isn't so tough after all, is it?" she grinned.

"I think...I could get the hang of it," replied Michael, leaning across the table to plant a fervent kiss on the soft lips that were waiting for him.

# 24

"Lovely wedding," Mrs. Satterfield chirped from her post overlooking the grand foyer of Braeburn House.

"Indeed," Henry beamed, pleased by how quickly the staff had been able to spring into action. Every greenhouse from here to London had been stripped of its best blossoms. The hall was fragrant with rubrum lilies and glossy gardenias arranged carefully in vases. Elegant white peonies floated in crystal bowls on tables throughout the house. The weather might still be chilly outdoors, but inside, the hall had exploded into spring.

"Pardon me while I claim a dance from the bride," Henry said. He strolled toward Shannon and Michael, noting how their faces seemed to light up the entire room. Ever the original, Shannon had chosen to get married in her burgundy velvet dress. "It's still close enough to Valentine's Day to wear red, you know," she had informed Michael with a laugh. "Besides, this is my destiny dress. I would insist on wearing it even if we got married in August."

"Mrs. Satterfield, will you do me the honor?" Michael gave up his place next to Shannon and took the hand of Burlingford's oldest resident. "After all, you were the one to bring Shannon to the Lady's Cottage in the first place."

She simpered, her wrinkled face as coy as a girl's. "Certainly, sir. Just as my family has been tending to your family for well over a century now."

He drew back to regard her with amusement.

"Really? As far back as that?"

"Oh yes, sir. Why, when I was just a wee little thing, my grandmother used to tell me all about Miss Alexandra. Such a tragedy for her, you know, having to marry Lord Geoffrey when she was in love with her young man—" Mrs. Satterfield broke off in confusion, suddenly remembering to whom she was speaking.

"Do go on. I always like to hear the old stories," he prompted, carefully steering the elderly lady around the floor.

"Well," Mrs. Satterfield said, delighted by the drama of this particular tale, "My Nana said she was supposed to be with Miss Alexandra at all times—Lord Geoffrey's orders. Sometimes she would be told to stay by the edge of the woods, there, between the cottage and the village road, while the missus gathered wildflowers. Near the old shed, don't you know. Well, one time she got suspicious about what was taking the missus such a long time, so she followed Miss Alexandra. There she was, with such a handsome young man it would break your heart. Childhood sweethearts, they were, back in London. So sad, the two of them. Well, Miss Alexandra saw her spying from the woods. To make sure she wouldn't tell anybody, she gave Nana the ruby ring she always wore. Said they were going to run off together, first chance they got. Miss Alexandra loved that ring, you know. Her young man gave it to her when they were engaged. Secretly, of course. Her family never knew; they just handed her over when a good offer came along. She tried to put the wedding off as long as she could, Nana said. Insisted that he build the cottage for her first, so she might have a quiet place all to herself, to read and dream and do her needlepoint. That was fine with Lord Geoffrey. Very particular he was about his house, you know, didn't want a young lady mucking about trying to change things. She still wore the ring, too, even after she was wed. She told her husband it was an old family heirloom."

Mrs. Satterfield paused to catch her breath. "Oh dear, excuse me sir, I'm just an old lady rambling on."

Michael's face had stiffened as he absorbed her incredible story. "She gave her ring to your grandmother?"

"Yes, although Nana didn't want to take it; she knew how special it was to her. Miss Alexandra just laughed and said she wouldn't need it anymore, because she would have everything she had ever wanted once they got away. Especially once Nana brought the baby to her. He was too little to make the journey by boat just then; she was going to bring him over later. And then of course she drowned, or so it's said, and her little boy had to grow up without her."

"What happened to the ring?" Michael said, trying to keep his voice casual.

"Nana kept it tucked away for years. She was afraid to tell a soul what she knew, especially after Miss Alexandra was lost. She held onto it until after the Great War. My father never came back from France, you know—shot through the heart, he was—and the family was quite desperate. It was Nana's dearest possession, and she was right unhappy when she had to sell it. But it was either that or the family go hungry, since she was too old to find another position and the rest of us were too young," she added, her voice matter-of-fact.

They danced on for a moment. That would explain how the ring got into an antique store in London, Michael supposed, but how to explain what divine act of providence, what amazing intervention had led Shannon to it? And she to him?

"Whatever happened to the young man?"

"Oh dear me, nobody ever saw him again. I would imagine when Miss Alexandra never showed up he made a new life without her in America. That's where the two of them were planning to go—off to the Wild West or somewhere. She had such an adventurous spirit,

Nana said, no wonder she couldn't be content to live out her days with such a stodgy old husband. Begging your pardon, sir."

"Mrs. Satterfield," Michael said slowly, "how is it I never knew about any of this?"

Cheeks flushed from the unaccustomed exertion, she considered the matter, her expression grave.

"I suppose, sir, because you never asked," she said at last.

"Ah," Michael replied, enigmatically enough that Mrs. Satterfield, worried that she had offended him, hastily cast about for a change of subject. "I do want to thank you, sir, for endowing the scholarship programme. It was quite generous of you."

"The what?" he said.

Mrs. Satterfield looked confused. "The one Miss Shannon asked me to set up through the library. The essay contest, with a scholarship to the winner—someone from the village who might not be able to continue their studies without a bit of help. The first one's going to the Cox lad. Such a smart boy, you know, and beside himself thinking he couldn't afford going off to university. Why, it was the very sort of thing Miss Alexandra might have done; she was the most generous soul that ever lived. You didn't even have to ask, my Nana used to say. Miss Shannon told me not to tell anyone but I assumed the money must have come—I mean ... ," she floundered, then stopped.

"No, I assure you, it was her project, entirely. But if she swore you to secrecy, then you mustn't say a word to anyone," replied Michael. He led her to the edge of the dance floor and went to reclaim his wife.

"I hear you're doing good deeds again," he said, reaching for her hand.

"The best deed I ever did was the one we did together," she responded, "but right now I'd better sit down. Between pasta and pregnancy, this dress is a lot tighter on me than it used to be. If I keep this up, I may pass out right here in front of everybody. And wouldn't *that* cause a stir."

"I think we can find a remedy for you," he said, leading her to a chair where they could admire the dancing crowd, still swirling around them in a kaleidoscope of color. From one corner, Nick McAllister gave him a benign nod. The minister's face was still aglow from the wedding ceremony he had just conducted, as he returned to an animated conversation with Henry. The words uniting them had been short and simple and entirely personal, at Shannon's insistence. A few feet in front of him, her colleague from the network—Janie, was it?—was burning up the floor with Stu Siegel. Janie's hoop earrings swayed against her cheek as the two of them swooped theatrically through the hall.

Shannon smiled, too, as she watched her old friends, remembering her favorite producer's exuberant face as she stepped off the plane at Heathrow. Never again, Shannon promised herself, would she take her friendships for granted, or allow herself to lose touch with people she cared about. Surely, strong and enduring friendships were another part of the happiness that so abundantly filled her days. In fact, it occurred to her, as the twosome invented new dance moves every minute, Janie would make a wonderful godmother. And Stu certainly seemed to be enjoying himself...

Shannon hadn't been sure Stu would even come. He was shooting a story in Rome when she had called the bureau in London with the invitation and directions, so she was thrilled when his brown Rover 200 had pulled into the driveway just in time for the ceremony.

Stu had barely had time to get out of the car, his head swiveling to take in the view, when Shannon was out the door with a delighted squeal, racing across the gravel to give him an ecstatic hug.

"So this is where you've been hiding," he said, stepping back for a long look at her radiant face. "When you set out to disappear, lady, you sure know how to pull it off."

Shannon winced. She knew she deserved the criticism, but she was too happy to see him to let it bother her for long.

"I'm sorry. I know I should have called," she said. "Please forgive me. I can't tell you how glad I am to see you."

"Hmnf," he said. Stu's expression remained a little grumpy, but he allowed her to link her arm through his as she steered him toward the cottage.

"I have to admit, disappearing seems to have agreed with you," he conceded as she beamed up at him. "So you think this guy is the one you've been looking for, do you?"

"I don't think so, I know so," she replied. Seeing the flicker of disappointment in his eyes, she affectionately squeezed his arm with her own. "And you have one, too, out there somewhere. Remember? I told you that once before, but now I'm confident of it."

"Your mouth to God's ear," he sighed. "Problem is, how will I know?"

"You'll know," she promised, her voice ringing with confidence. "Believe me, you'll know."

"I guess I'll have to take your word for it, then. You're the most skeptical person I've ever seen, so if you believe it's true, it must be."

"Well, I have to admit I'm not such a skeptic anymore."

He gave her a long speculative look. She smiled back at him, until finally...

"What?" she demanded.

"You seem so different," he said. "Not just happy. Peaceful. Calm. You always looked like you were afraid somebody was going to take the plate away before you had finished eating. Kind of frantic and uptight, like you had to gobble it up before it vanished. You don't have that look any more."

"Maybe because I don't feel like that anymore," replied Shannon. "I'll have to tell you about it sometime."

"I'd like to hear it. Must be something to make you all starry-eyed like that," he couldn't help but tease.

"Oh, Stu, you have no idea. I just—I feel so blessed to have you and all my friends in my life. Not just Michael and the baby."

"The baby?" He blinked. Shannon had always seemed so conventional, and here she was pregnant before the wedding?

"Yeah, well, we kind of got things out of order," she smiled.

"Obviously," he noted with a wry grin. "Oh, before I forget. Remember the arms story?"

Shannon couldn't resist. She stared into the sky and frowned, as if she were trying to recall something so insignificant it couldn't possibly have remained in her memory.

"Hmm, arms story, arms story...," she mused, then gave Stu a withering look. "Don't be silly, Stu, of course I remember the arms story. That's why I quit the network, remember? What about it?"

"Well... after my little jaunt to New York, we did the interview and then the network decided the whole thing was just too hot for them to handle. Figures. I always knew Reardon didn't have any guts. I'm so glad he's gone. Anyway, I passed along my notes and the tapes to a friend at the Washington Post. He called last week and said they're almost ready to break it. You know these newspaper guys—even with a head start it takes them forever to get a story together."

Shannon's smile was philosophical. "Oh, well. Sorry it couldn't have been us," she said, "but so be it. At least the truth will get out, one way or the other."

"It does seem to, doesn't it?" he agreed.

Remembering their conversation as she watched Stu's energetic progress across the dance floor, Shannon smiled again. This time a year ago, it would have killed her for a competitor to break *her* story. There could be no more telling indication of how her priorities had changed than this: the relief that followed the brief stab of regret at Stu's announcement. It was an important story; finally, it would be told. What difference did it make, really, who would get the credit for telling it?

Across the crowded hall, Sol stood next to Aunt DeeCee, wondering what his favorite client could be thinking to make her look so nostalgic.

"Your niece is very talented, you know," he told her. "She could have had quite a career. The network really wanted her to come back."

"She is talented, and she'll always have work she enjoys," Aunt DeeCee said, her voice firm. "But she's also going to have a good life with her family. Balance, Mr. Hurwitz, balance. Perhaps you should consider it."

Sol, three times divorced and drowning in alimony payments, cocked his head and gave her an unwilling grin.

"Maybe I should at that," he replied.

From her perch across the room, Shannon jabbed Michael lightly in the ribs as she murmured, "What in the world do you think Sol and my aunt could be talking about?"

"I don't know, but they seem to be enjoying themselves," he observed. Michael nodded as he caught Sol's eye. He would probably never be Sol's biggest fan but he trusted his wife—splendid words, "his wife"—enough, now, to know that she would never abandon him or their baby.

Shannon surveyed the dance floor with satisfaction, chuckling as she caught a glimpse of Lily. The little girl had been eyeing a silver tray filled with custard and fruit tarts for the past several minutes. Finally, temptation got the better of her. Her basket of flower petals, now emptied of all but a few fragrant reminders of her important job this morning, was still attached to one arm, the white satin ribbon around its handle increasingly bedraggled by the day's adventure. As Shannon and Michael's eyes met in amusement, Lily stuck a cautious pinky finger in one tart, scooped up a taste of creamy custard and gravely licked it, leaving behind what they imagined was a small, perfectly round hole. The tart next to it suffered a similar fate, and the next. The newlyweds began to shake with laughter as Lily's horrified mother swooped down to entice her away.

"Oh well," Shannon observed. "I would have probably done the same thing when I was six. Besides, I'm sure Henry has plenty more in the kitchen."

"She is a little character, isn't she?" Michael said, then bent to whisper, "I hope ours won't be quite such a handful."

"I wouldn't count on it, if I were you. Especially given the gene pool."

"Oh dear," replied Michael, although he didn't sound at all alarmed.

Shannon rose to twine an affectionate arm around his waist.

"You know," she confided in a low voice, "I was just thinking. Maybe, after I finish this project for PBS, I should see if there's anything I can do for them about the environment, before I get too big to waddle."

Michael drew back in surprise. "The environment? I didn't know that was one of your interests."

"Well, it wasn't, before. But now there's another generation to think about, isn't there? Also, it occurred to me that if we were here a hundred years ago, it stands to reason that we—or someone—will be coming back again. I'd like it if there were still plenty of trees and fresh air and open countryside on the next round, too. Maybe I should try to do something about that now."

Her face was thoughtful as she looked around the room. "There's something else I'm supposed to do, too. I just haven't quite figured it out yet. But," she added, "I'm sure it'll come to me. Eventually."

Michael laughed as he tightened his arm around her. "Life is never going to be boring with you, is it?"

"Probably not," she conceded, with an impish grin. "Sure you want to stick around?"

He squeezed her close, wondering what he had done to deserve this amazing woman—in this life or any other. "With you? Forever," he murmured, planting a kiss on the top of her head.

"Oh, good," she smiled. "I was hoping that's what you would say."

# Epilogue

Jonathan Willoughby-Jones was focused on his feet as he took the narrow steps three at a time from the front of the grand limestone mansion onto a side patio facing the gardens. Hands jammed into his pockets, whistling a tuneless melody beneath his breath, he was almost on top of a weathered iron chair containing the still figure of his mother before he saw her and froze in mid-whistle. Jonathan knew better than to disturb her when she was meditating.

In less than a minute his patience was rewarded when she took a final deep breath and her eyelids flickered open. She sat quietly for a moment to refocus as she came back into the present, then turned her head to her son.

"Sorry for the noise—," he began to apologize, but she waved him off with a rueful smile.

"I've been running late this entire morning. Is it time for class?"

He nodded. "Everything's set up and ready for you. Looks like a big turnout today."

"Excellent." Shannon rose, her back straight, her figure as slim in her fifties as in her girlhood, and offered a smooth cheek to her son.

Grateful for the reprieve, Jonathan bent down for a quick peck. He had only been back from Oxford for a few weeks and knew how happy she was to see him. A rigorous class schedule had limited his visits home during his university years, as he read for high honors in PPE—politics, philosophy and economics. Jonathan knew it had been hard for his mother having him away. He was relieved that she seldom complained or made him feel bad about his prolonged absences.

They fell into step for the short walk to the Lady's Cottage, where a hand-lettered sign in Victorian script now proclaimed it as "The Benjamin Taylor Centre for Health and Healing." Shannon's spiritual journey had accelerated over the decades, and much to her surprise she had made quite a name for herself as a teacher and healer. The problem was, as she came to realize, she couldn't personally help everyone who came to her, and she was exhausting herself by refusing to turn anyone away. After she decided her time was best spent passing along her knowledge to as many others as possible, two best-selling books on her work had followed. The first, "Recognizing Your Life's Purpose," had led to public speaking engagements, workshops and seminars around the world that kept her on the road for weeks at a time. But the Lady's Cottage that she loved so much remained her favorite refuge, as well as the perfect place to hold classes and continue whatever individual healing work she could still manage comfortably.

Who could have imagined, she mused to herself more than once, *the big life I once wanted so desperately on television would show up in such a completely different way.*

"Any sign of your sister this morning?" Shannon asked, noting with interest the sudden rush of color to her son's tanned face.

"She's at the cottage," he growled. "Following Lily around like a little puppy dog."

*Ah. Well, you certainly know what that's like.* Shannon's lips twitched at the thought but she decided to keep it to herself.

Lily was a few years older than Jonathan, but the two had been inseparable growing up. When Jonathan failed to bring home any young ladies from university, heading straight for Lily's door as soon as he reasonably could after arriving home, Shannon suspected more than the ties of childhood were propelling him there.

With his winning personality, lanky build, and his father's piercing blue eyes, Jonathan had been attracting feminine attention since he was a baby. In early adolescence, he had decided to accept the gifts of his heritage and thought no more about it. The face he saw in the mirror every morning, framed by his mother's chestnut hair, was simply that—a face. He was always surprised when girls just past puberty to women of a certain age were occasionally reduced to stuttering as they looked into that face. His genuine indifference to them as romantic partners only seemed to increase the mystery, and the attraction.

The two strolled along in companionable silence, drinking in the warm summer air. The Lady's Cottage came into view as they rounded the bend.

"Mother," Jonathan blurted, "would you mind if I stayed for the class today?"

Startled, Shannon tried to appear as if it were an everyday request. Jonathan had always been respectful of her work but had steered a wide path around it, occasionally teasing that he was the only person he knew with a mother who—horrors!—was not only from America but presently resided in woo-woo land. He had heard the stories and seen the framed photos of his mother interviewing famous people, but only dimly remembered the days when she was known for being on television. More recently in the spotlight as someone who could heal people just by putting her hands on them, Shannon's latest role had more than once made him squirm.

"Of course. You know you're always welcome," she replied, biting her tongue to keep from asking what had prompted this sudden interest.

As if in response to her unspoken thought, Jonathan continued,

"It's just that I keep wondering what to do with my life. You know? Like, am I supposed to make a boatload of money to help keep Braeburn House going, or should I be trying to do some good in the world. Feed starving children in Africa. That sort of thing. Or take the public policy route, like Father, for the government. Or perhaps heal people, like you do. Only, I don't know anything about it or where to start."

"Well, sweetheart, those are all lovely thoughts," Shannon said carefully, "and the wonderful thing about being your age—actually, any age—is that *you* get to choose what's best for you. Nobody else. Not me, not your father, *you*. And you have plenty of time to make that choice. You already know, deep inside, what your life's purpose is."

"But that's where I keep getting stuck," he replied, a note of desperation edging into his voice. "I keep turning it over and over in my head and I don't seem to be getting anywhere. I keep thinking I must be here for a reason ... "

"I know, sweetie," his mother said, her eyes soft with compassion. "I know exactly what you're talking about. I wrestled with it for years. Good for you for even thinking about all this now! But it took me well past my thirtieth birthday before I was willing to slow down long enough to even frame the question."

"You? I thought you had all the answers," he said lightly, adding a smile to take the sting from the words. "You always seem to."

Shannon laughed. "Well, I'm flattered that you think I'm so smart, but believe me, I'm just like you and everyone else. Still trying to figure it out as I go along. The best advice I can give you is what a very wise man told me, back before you were born, and that is: forget what your head says. Your heart knows far more than your head does, anyway. Do you remember the antique sampler that hangs upstairs in the Cottage? The one that says, 'Be Still?' That's a good place to start. Spend some time alone. Get quiet. Visualize yourself doing each of those options in turn. See which of them feels right. And take your time. You don't have to decide right this minute."

*Hey.* A voice in her head suddenly interrupted. Grammie Lib's voice. *The boy's asking for a few sips of wisdom. You don't have to blast him with a water cannon.*

Shannon stifled a grin. Trust Grammie Lib to give good advice, as she had been doing for decades, now. Frequently in her healing work, Shannon could sense her beloved grandmother standing by her side, guiding, directing and encouraging her forward.

"This is your journey, Jonathan," she continued after a moment. "I can't take it for you. You'll have to find your own way, and I'm confident you will."

"Easy for you to say."

"Yes, I suppose it does sound that way. But you've already taken the first step, asking the question. Keep asking. The answers will come."

"Right. But what do I do in the meantime?"

"You live."

"Not much choice about that," he grumbled. "But it's not much fun if you don't know where you're going."

"Sure it is. The whole point of living isn't thinking that when you have the perfect job, *then* you'll be happy. Or when you've found the perfect partner, *then* everything will be great. The secret of life is to enjoy every moment along the way. Because if you can't be happy now, what makes you think you can be happy then? If all you're living for is the high points of life, infrequent as they are, what are you going to do the rest of the time?"

Jonathan looked up from the pebbles crunching beneath his feet and stopped short at the cottage steps.

"Well. What I'm going to do right now is let you go teach your class," he said, his voice firm. "You have about fifty people in there, waiting for you."

Shannon took a deep breath as she started up the wide white steps. "So I do," she smiled as she turned, her hand outstretched in welcome. "Ready?"

*The End*

# Reader's Guide

- At the beginning of the story, Shannon has a successful professional life in the seemingly glamorous world of network news. Still, she isn't happy. She feels buffeted by forces she can't control and at the mercy of what other people at the network and in the audience think of her. Have you felt required to live up to the expectations of others in your life instead of charting your own course to happiness? What did you have to give up or change in order to get there?

- Shannon had the advantage of a wise and loving grandmother who helped raise her until she was 11. How much can the presence of one caring grownup make a difference in a child's life, even at that early age? Did you have a Grammie Lib in your life? What did you learn from her?

- In part because she lost her mother at birth, Shannon has a real fear of death, even though in her job as a journalist she is frequently required to see and report on tragic events like the plane crash in Chapter Two. How do her later discoveries about who she really is, and was, change her perception of death and dying? What do you think happens to us when we die? Does it seem far-fetched or completely logical that we might have many lifetimes on earth?

- Shannon's loyal friend Stu would like to have more than a professional relationship with her, but she turns him down. Have you ever gone along with a romantic relationship that you knew wasn't right for you, just to keep from disappointing someone else? What was the result?

- From the moment Shannon arrives at the Lady's Cottage, she feels a powerful connection to it. Have you experienced a connection to a seemingly unrelated place? How did you account for it?

- Michael, too, seems to have it all: a title, a beautiful historic home and an absorbing career, but he's not happy either. Was he secretly looking for love or did he just fall into it somewhat unwillingly when Shannon came into his life? If he had known all along about her high-powered career in the States, might he have turned away before getting to know her?

- More than once, Michael seems to come to Shannon's rescue, first with a ride to the airport and then getting her to safety from a snowstorm. But in fact it's she who rescues him from a barren emotional life. When she dreams about him, she sees "a man encased in ice." Is it more difficult for men to open up emotionally? Or do they welcome the realization that a richer life can be available to them, even if sometimes they have to be pushed into it?

- As a child, Shannon never got along very well with the strict and stern aunt who stepped in to raise her after Grammie Lib died. When Ben's illness forces them to spend more time together, their relationship changes dramatically. Does understanding someone make forgiving them easier?

- Once Shannon realizes that she can have a happy life by claiming her power to create one, she begins writing down the steps that she thinks might get her there. Have you ever analyzed what makes you happy and how to have more of it? Are you happy now? What else do you need to feel true happiness and fulfillment? How might you achieve it?

- At Nick's urging, Shannon begins to send silent blessings to the people she meets. How does that alter her encounter with James the groom, when they meet outside Lily's schoolyard? Have you ever tried something similar? What was the result?

# *Acknowledgements*

This is a book that took 3 ½ months to write, then 18 years to edit and refine and prune and expand into what you see today. During all that time, characters sprang into life only to vanish; plot lines came and went; whole chapters whose every sentence I had sweated over had to be tossed aside.

To all those who read rough drafts, offered feedback, shared their own experiences in this realm, or just listened sympathetically as I tried to explain why I was doing this and why it was taking so long: thank you. I am terrified that if I tried to list each and every one of your names, I would inevitably leave someone out. So please accept this as my fervent, albeit anonymous, thanks. This is your book, too.

To all the spiritual teachers over the decades whose thought-provoking ideas, born of their own questions and struggles, helped launch my journey: many, many thanks for lighting the way.

My profound wish in telling Shannon's story is that *you* might find the distillation of these ideas empowering, inspiring, or entertaining. The trifecta is all three, of course; I will happily settle for any one of them.

# *Gail Harris*

Gail Harris began her career in journalism in high school as a teen correspondent for *The Atlanta Journal-Constitution* and *The Marietta Daily Journal*. She became one of the first anchorwomen in the USA in 1971, at WCTV in Tallahassee, FL. Her career as a political reporter took her to the statehouses of Georgia, Florida, North Carolina, and Massachusetts, and ultimately led to a Master of Public Administration degree at Harvard University's Kennedy School of Government.

Gail went on to work as a correspondent for ABC News, *Nightline*, and for many years was a correspondent/host for PBS and NPR. Her work on the PBS special *Hiroshima Remembered*, which she hosted and co-produced, was recognized with a National Emmy Award in 1986. Creator, executive producer, and host for the *Body & Soul* series on PBS, Gail also wrote the companion book, *"Body & Soul: Your Guide to Health, Happiness, and Total Well-being."*

Along the way, she discovered the power of a meditation practice in lowering stress, which led to a deep dive into many other practical methods of using spirituality to empower and improve life. Today, Gail continues her work as a teacher, lecturer, and executive coach, offering private sessions as well as Webinars. Her articles, blog, *Body & Soul* video segments and information about her Empowerment Webinars can be found at *www.gailharrisonline.com*.